T0374315

A SMUGGLER'S STORY

GYPSIES
in Paradise

JOHN LEVERONI

A SMUGGLER'S STORY
GYPSIES IN PARADISE

iUniverse books may be ordered through booksellers or by contacting:

iUniverse
1663 Liberty Drive
Bloomington, IN 47403
www.iuniverse.com
844-349-9409

ISBN: 978-1-6632-5731-4 (sc)
ISBN: 978-1-6632-5732-1 (e)

Library of Congress Control Number: 2023920911

Print information available on the last page.

iUniverse rev. date: 09/11/2024

'Life,
Liberty,
and the Pursuit of Happiness'

—◆—

Camerado, I give you my hand!
I give you my love more precious than money,
I give you myself before preaching or law;
Will you give me yourself? Will you come travel with me?
Shall we stick by each other as long as we live?

Walt Whitman, from the 'Song of the Open Road'

—◆—

Author's contact information:
Email... johnmarkleveroni@gmail.com

A SMUGGLER'S STORY
GYPSIES IN PARADISE
CONTENTS

PREFACE

Where were you in 1972?

Who were you, when you were twenty two?
If you're not yet twenty two, these stories aren't for you.

The United States is at a historical apex in 1972 with military bases on every continent and astronauts walking the moon. The U. S. Navy rules the world's oceans and America's nuclear weapons can be launched against enemies anywhere on earth at any moment.

'Baby Boomers' become adults in the era of 'Sex, Drugs and Rock n'Roll' during the 70's and 80's. The political chaos of the 60's changed theAmerican people forever when many of the country's 'Best and Brightest'were murdered while the United States continued its 'Manifest Destiny'becoming a world empire in the 'American Century'.Anything is possible, utopian democracy or radioactive hell as the U.S.A.'s 'Cold War'with the Soviet Union transforms into President Nixon's 'War on Drugs'.

"...The long 1960's ending around 1973 was not at all the frivolous decade it is so often painted...it was the most important post war period, the most pivotal, when man's condition- the nature of his very freedom- came under threat and under scrutiny, for the reason that his psychology, his self-awareness was changing. The shift from class base sociology to individual psychology, the rise of new groups to identify with (race, gender, students)..."

'The Modern Mind: An Intellectual History of the 20th Century' by Peter Watson

GANJA MAN IN NEGRIL

Children and the innocent be forewarned...These aren't Disney fairy tales.

January 1972

Our adventure begins in Jamaica as a bright orange sun sets into the turquoise blue Caribbean Sea. Palm trees sway in flower scented ocean breezes, while fishermen return to port with their daily catch. Three men stand on volcanic rocks overlooking 'Seven-Mile Beach' in Negril.

I'm Jack Collins, the guy with the 'G. I.' buzz haircut standing between Mike and Tony. The big sandy-redheaded bear of a man on my right is my Army buddy, Michael Casey. He's a six foot-two, two hundred twenty pound Irish-Seminole from Florida.

On my left is Anthony Ascot a.k.a. 'Jamaican Tony'. His Rastafarian dreadlocks blow in the wind, making him appear to be Mike's height. Tony's mahogany skin and jet black hair contrast with Mike's lobster red sunburn and long ginger ponytail. Luckily, I'm Boston 'Black Irish' and easily tan brown in the tropical sun.

I'm supposed to be in college, but like a Jack Kerouac character I seek action and adventure on the road. Mike is setting up a 'pot' deal in Jamaica and he paid for my ticket to escape New England's cold winter. The way I figure it, I get a tropical vacation and a chance to make some easy cash.

A year ago, Sergeant Michael Casey and I met in Fort Leonard Wood, Missouri.

I ran the 2d Brigade gym as a recreation specialist. Mike was the Brigade Colonel's driver and could fly home to Florida on weekend passes. He always had the best 'grass' on the base, real exotic stuff from the Caribbean and South America. Now, I'm getting a January suntan while searching for Jamaican 'ganja'.

Tony invited Mike and me to the Negril Yacht Club New Year's Eve party last night. Everyone from the Governor to the Police Commissioner came to the club. Anthony Ascot is a true Jamaican with the blood of a British plantation owner intermingled with Caribbean Arawak islanders and African slaves.

Tony kept his British grandfather's name and attended Eton College in England.

He returned to Jamaica to make his fortune when the island obtained independence ten years ago. All I can say is, I hope Tony isn't bull shitting Mike about his contacts.

Bright pink and magenta sunset pastels fade into twilight shadows as powerful waves surge against the rocks below. Mike looks at me with a contented smile.

"Jack, aren't you glad I brought you to Jamaica?"

I laugh. "Hell yeah. Last year we were freezing in the Missouri Ozarks making two hundred bucks a month and now we're gypsies in paradise."

Mike turns to Tony. "Man, I want to score beaucoup ganja."

Tony's lean seventy kilo body shakes, with a hearty laugh. He removes a huge cone shaped cigarette from his pocket and lights a silver-plated Zippo lighter. The wily Jamaican draws heavily on the oversized joint before releasing plumes of smoke into the air.

Anthony Ascot speaks slowly adding emphasis to his words. "Man, smoke this 'spliff' and enjoy my ganja. Maybe we can do some business. People tell me you can make big profits in America selling ganja."

Tony hands the spliff to Mike. "Bring a big boat to my beach on a new moon night and my men will fill it with Jamaica's finest 'Lambs Bread'."

Mike nods his head in agreement. He inhales the spliff and passes it to me. I fill my lungs with sweet cannabis smoke. A surge of euphoric warmth rushes through my body when I inhale the burning ganja cone a second time and my random thoughts float like a butterfly in a garden of colorful flowers. Damn, this weed is wicked good. I'm already stoned and my dry mouth needs a cold beer.

I watch a huge cream white orb rise from the sea and illuminate the night sky. "Wow, look at the full moon. I feel like I can touch it."

Tony looks up with a smile. "Enjoy this sunset. You will see rainbows in the moonlight tonight. Tomorrow, you leave my paradise and return home."

Mike bursts into laughter. "I see color trails already. I want to take a package back to Miami and set up a deal. How much does a pound of this ganja cost?"

Tony leans close to Mike and lowers his voice. "I have one pound you can purchase for eighty American dollars tonight. Bring me a twenty five thousand dollar deposit to Ocho Rios on a full moon and I'll have one thousand kilos of ganja delivered to Mammee Bay on the next new moon. Each kilo costs one hundred dollars. You'll pay another twenty five thousand when your boat picks up the shipment and the remaining fifty thousand dollar balance is due after my product is sold in America."

A broad smile comes to Mike's face. "Sounds very good."

I do the math in my head and can't believe the numbers. Forty dollars worth of Jamaican ganja could turn into five hundred in Boston. All I can say is. Where's Mike going to get a big boat and that kind of cash?

The cunning Jamaican continues. "Here's the Arawak Hotel telephone number in Ocho Rios. Call me collect, person to person. I won't accept charges, but I'll expect you to arrive with my deposit the following week. We'll work out the final logistics then."

Mike winks at me and extends his right hand to Tony. "You got a deal. I'll get the cash and boat together in Florida."

Tony gazes at the rising full moon. "I must go to Montego Bay tonight. Let's settle our business and I hope you will bring me a large deposit in the near future."

He walks into a nearby stand of Sea grape trees and returns with a tightly wrapped bundle of newspaper and hands it to Mike. "Here's one pound of Jamaica's finest 'Lamb's Bread' grown in the Blue Mountains by Rastafarians."

My Army buddy hurriedly rips open the newspaper wrapping and buries his face in the package. "This stuff smells real fresh. Jack, you have to smell this."

The ganja bundle is passed to me. The pungent aroma of fresh 'herb' overwhelms my senses as I think to myself... 'Man, this reefer has a powerful smell. How will we get a pound of stinking weed past the U.S. Customs?'

Mike hands Tony eight, ten dollar bills with a brotherly handshake. Their beaming smiles shine in the moonlight. "Tony, I hope you make me very rich. Let's share a bottle of Appleton rum to celebrate our success."

Tony shakes his head and raises his voice. "I don't drink rum. I only drink Veuve Clicquot Ponsardin, the finest champagne from Reims, France."

I'm surprised and impressed with Tony's choice of sparkling wine. My dad always said the best champagne came from Reims, France.

I ask Tony. "Did you travel in Europe? What did you think of the British people?"

A strident voice and fierce look betray Tony's bitter emotions. "I did not travel to the European continent. The English weather and people were cold and I was a second-class citizen in England. I truly missed my tropical paradise and now that Jamaica is free, I'll never leave my island home again."

Tony turns to walk away, then he looks back and issues a foreboding warning.

"Tonight is your last night at my aunt's cottages. Don't let Auntie Claire find your package. She is very religious and will destroy your ganja."

A smile returns to Tony's face. "My friends, I hope to hear from you soon."

Without another word, the shrewd Jamaican silently disappears into the surrounding jungle shadows.

Mike grins ear to ear, seeming to float in a cannabis smoke cloud. He chortles, "Man, this pot is kick ass and a big time score."

I shake my head in doubt. "How are you going to smuggle a pound of ganja into Florida?"

Mike slaps my back. "Man, don't worry. I've got everything covered. The Customs dogs won't smell a thing."

I hope Mike knows what he's doing. I don't want to end up in prison. Unexpectedly, the Sea grape branches open on the beach below. Instantly, Mike stashes the pound of ganja in his backpack.

My eyes focus on a beautiful girl climbing up from the beach. Jill Jensen is silhouetted in the full moon with her golden hair shining in the silver light. Mike Casey's slender raven-haired girlfriend, Debbie Boon follows Jill walking towards us.

Mike's elementary school sidekick, Jerry Siegel follows the two college roommates. His bell bottoms and high heeled shoes make his climb more difficult. Breathing hard, he finally reaches the summit and lights a Kool menthol cigarette.

Brushing aside his shag haircut, Jerry sniffs the air and tries to focus his eyes. "I smell 'reefer'. Pass the joint."

Debbie pulls herself into Mike's arms. He laughs while holding the burning ganja cone under his friend's nose. "Jerry, you're so nearsighted, you can't find the spliff."

Jerry suddenly snatches the huge Jamaican joint and fills his lungs with cannabis smoke until he violently coughs.

I'm getting good vibes from Jill. Beauty and brains in the same package, she's an English Literature major who has read most of the world's great authors. I'm glad Mike invited the girls, but why Jerry?

Mike loudly exclaims. "Jerry, don't 'Bogart' the joint." He grabs the burning spliff from his childhood friend and hands it to Jill.

She takes a long deep toke and passes it to her timid college companion.

"Debbie, now I understand why you're not returning to Ann Arbor next semester. I want to live in the tropics some day."

Mike's girlfriend draws lightly on the joint and returns it to Jill with an innocent look. "Come live with me at my parent's house in Florida."

The girls laugh together. Jill inhales another toke and passes the spliff to me with an alluring smile as I think to myself… 'How can I get close to this pretty girl?'

Debbie's wide, chestnut brown eyes are focused on Mike. He returns her gaze and reaches into his pack, with a sly grin. "Do you girls want to party tonight?"

Jill and Debbie reply. "Yeah man, it's our last night. Let's party."

Mike pulls out a bottle of Appleton rum. "A sunset toast to our new friends in Jamaica."

Jerry interrupts. "Man, can you get more of this weed?"

Mike chortles. "I have made a satisfactory financial arrangement with a local ganja merchant from Ocho Rios."

The bottle of rum circles the group, releasing demonic spirits to dance in the full moon light. A cloud of silvery blue smoke fills the air, when Mike bursts into laughter.

"The Casey clan has run moonshine for two hundred years. Now, we'll smuggle Jamaican ganja into America."

Mike reopens the bottle. "More shots for everyone."

He passes the half empty bottle to me. I take a swig and pass the bottle to Jill. She swallows her second rum shot and hands it to Debbie.

Jill seductively smiles at me. "Jack, let's take a walk."

A surge of magnetic energy passes through my body. "Sure, we can go skinny dipping under the full moon."

Jill chuckles. "I bet the water is warm."

Like a flash, Jill turns towards the surging sea and runs ahead of me in the moonlight with her golden hair blowing in the wind. She charges up the rock cliff edge and strips away her bikini.

I watch her statuesque silhouette dive into the undulating waves twenty feet below and resurface with a loud shout. "Jack, the water is perfect."

Silver moon rays sparkle on the dark cobalt blue Caribbean as I strip away my clothes and plunge into the sea. The warm salt water surges around me, massaging my naked body.

We swim together like Dolphins as I proclaim "Heaven can't be better than this."

Jill's sparkling blue eyes captivate me when we press our lips together in a passionate kiss. Time stands still floating together in the Caribbean Sea.

———◆———

The next morning, bright sunlight wakes me. My eyes slowly open to a blurred vision of a tall heavy-set Jamaican lady standing in our cottage entrance. Her mahogany-brown skin glows in a sunlit aurora.

Miss Claire Robinson inherited three small cottages overlooking the Caribbean Sea in Negril when her mother passed away after a long battle with cancer. Auntie Claire cared for her invalid parents during the last years of their lives and now she worries her nephew is doing the Devil's work.

Our innkeeper frowns with her large hands gripping her apron clad hips. Auntie Claire's loud passionate voice adds to my painful headache. "What are all of you doing together in the lady's cottage? I'm a proprietor of an honest establishment and this sinful behavior is not allowed. You are scheduled to check out today and your breakfast is prepared."

Jerry lays curled up on the living room sofa. He moans and turns away from the light. Mike Casey lies with Debbie in her bed. He shields his eyes from the sunshine with his hand. "Auntie, this reminds me of Army wake up calls. You've been so wonderful to us this past week. Can we sleep in this morning?"

Our landlady's powerful voice issues a forbidding response that awakens everyone. "Absolutely not. All of you must come to breakfast now."

Debbie sighs and buries her head in a pillow. I'm lying in bed with Jill as she raises her head from under white linen sheets covering our naked bodies.

Auntie Claire's glare expresses her disapproval. "I'm a baptized member of the Church of England. It is a sin for a man and a woman to sleep together outside of marriage."

Our Jamaican hostess exits the cottage and walks towards the kitchen. "All of you get up and come to breakfast."

Thirty minutes later, all five of us sit at the kitchen table drinking Blue Mountain coffee attempting to cure our rum hangovers. Breakfast aromas fill the air. Fresh banana bread and sweet rolls bake in the oven. Beans, tomatoes and plantains simmer in skillets on the stove as our hostess pan fries bacon and sausage with eggs cooked to order for her guests.

Auntie Claire's Jamaican style 'English' breakfast is served with sliced pineapple and papaya, along with homemade mango jam and fresh squeezed orange juice. Words of wisdom usually accompany her delicious meals.

Our hostess focuses her nut brown eyes on Mike Casey this morning. Her deep resonant voice expresses the truth. "The Almighty Creator has given mankind free will. Each of you will travel a road with many choices. Remember, the road to Hell is paved with good intentions. The Devil will seduce you through earthly desire and God knows my nephew, Anthony is on Satan's path. He'll do anything for money."

Hot coffee clears the alcoholic fog in my head as I think to myself... 'Did Auntie Claire find Mike's ganja and call the police? Should we make a run for the airport?'

She points her finger at Mike and looks up into the sky. "I know what you and my nephew are planning. I pray that you feel our Almighty Creator's love and stop what you are doing. Lord, protect your children from evil."

A second mug of Blue Mountain coffee completes my morning feast. This could be our last meal before we end up in Spanish Town prison. Man, I just want to get back home.

Auntie Claire surveys her contented guests and smiles with satisfaction.

"I'll clean up while you pack for your journey to America. Please consider our island tradition. Leave a pair of shoes and you'll return to our tropical paradise."

I'm relieved our hostess didn't find Mike's ganja and we're not going to prison today. "Cool. I'll leave my Celtics Converse sneakers behind."

Jill enthusiastically joins in with a smile towards Debbie. "We'll leave our slippers, so we can come back to Negril."

Mike gets up from the table and heads for the exit. "Let's get going. Jerry, you have to return the motorcycle you rented. We're leaving in fifteen minutes, so we can stop for gas."

I hastily pack my carry on bag and join Jill and Debbie standing next to the miniature Japanese rental car.

Jill asks her friend. "Where's Mike and Jerry?"

Debbie meekly smiles. "Mike's packing our luggage in the room and Jerry is returning the motorcycle."

A groaning Jerry reappears, carrying his bag. "I'm ready to go."

Jill inquires. "Did you return the motorcycle?"

Jerry shrugs his shoulders. "Yeah, I dropped it off with the owner."

Our inn keeper overhears the conversation and strides from the kitchen with a disconcerted look. "It is customary for the motorcycle owner to inform me that you returned his property. As proprietor of this hotel, I have a responsibility to call the owner."

Jerry flinches and tries to avoid her steady gaze. "I don't know their phone number."

Auntie Claire's broad shoulders straighten up. "Young man, you will be accountable for your actions."

Jerry slinks away and retreats into the nearby shadows as our hostess shakes her head with disappointment. Mike returns carrying his and Debbie's luggage. Ignoring the commotion, he opens the car trunk and fills it with everyone's baggage.

Auntie Claire smiles when she receives a colorful scarf and a tender hug from Debbie. "Thank you so much. You'll always be my auntie."

Our hostess warmly embraces Debbie. "All of you are God's children, therefore my children. May the Almighty Creator's grace always be with you."

Jerry reappears and attempts to bypass the intimidating inn keeper. He fearfully slips past her and hurriedly ducks into the back seat. Auntie Claire notices him and points her finger. "Son, you must do the right thing."

Auntie Claire pulls Jill and me into a powerful three way embrace. Her compassionate brown eyes focus on me while she holds my face to her ample bosom. "You must marry when you return to America. Remember to care for all God's children."

Jill gives our hostess a kiss on her cheek, with a gentle hug. "Don't worry Auntie, I've got birth control pills. Thanks so much for a wonderful holiday. You made it special."

Jill sits beside Jerry as I give our 'auntie' a farewell hug. "I'll try to come back soon."

I squeeze into the back seat next to my new girlfriend.

Debbie enthusiastically waves goodbye when Mike shifts the Toyota Corolla into first gear. Auntie Claire waves to her extended family.

"Please come visit again soon. Be good, my children and God will bless you."

The compact Toyota looks like an overloaded gypsy wagon as it slowly gains speed. Avoiding wandering animals and people along the single lane roads to Montego Bay will be a daunting challenge. Sunlight penetrating the palm tree canopy illuminates multi-colored flowers as dark shadows dance with jungle spirits in the afternoon sunshine.

Jerry is nervous and agitated. "Damn, this Jap car is built for midgets."

Mike looks at the gauges and shifts into fourth gear. "We have to get gas at the next station."

Our driver looks in the rear view mirror and unexpectedly shouts. "There's a car chasing us with a passenger waving a machete. Jerry, what did you do with the motorcycle?"

Mike's childhood friend squirms and turns his head. He and I look out the back window to see a large steel machete waving wildly in the air. The men chasing us look very pissed off.

Jerry moans. "Shit! That bitch called the owner."

Mike yells again. "What did you do with the bike? Don't lie to me!"

Jerry rolls his blinking eyes, whispering. "I didn't want to pay the bill and left it behind our cottage."

Mike and Debbie simultaneously howl. "You idiot!"

Jerry could get thrown in jail. I pull Jill closer. The Toyota 1.2 liter four cylinder engine strains to gain speed. Mike shouts in panic while maneuvering around potholes, dogs, goats, chickens and strolling Jamaicans. "I'm 'pedal to the metal' and 'running on empty'."

Debbie turns around and gives Jerry a fierce look as he cowers in his seat. "You know Johnny will feed you to the sharks, if anything happens to me."

The overburdened Toyota hurtles towards a roundabout and Mike instinctively turns right entering the circle. Suddenly, the grill of an oncoming truck ominously looms in front of us. The truck horn loudly blares a warning of impending death.

Screeching brakes and metal crunching metal surround us as we circle the rotary in the wrong direction avoiding oncoming traffic. Sweat dripping from his forehead, Mike wheels right then left. Luckily, we escape the chaos and continue on our way to Montego Bay.

"I forgot that Jamaicans drive on the wrong side of the road."

Mike's face is pale and his voice panic stricken as we approach the last chance gas station. "They're still right behind us and I can't stop."

Jerry gripes. "If I had my gun, I'd shoot those damn niggers."

Mike yells. "Shut up. You've already fucked up!"

I look back and to my surprise and relief. "The other car is slowing down. They need gas too. Maybe we have a chance to beat them to the airport."

The Toyota stutters as we enter the airport parking lot. Jerry jumps from the still moving car and runs towards the airport terminal entrance. Mike barks orders. "We don't have time to drop the car at the rental office. Debbie, you and Jill go to the ticket counter and check us in. Jack and I'll grab the bags."

Jill and Debbie dash into the terminal. Mike and I quickly pull the luggage from the car trunk. Without warning, I hear screeching tires pull up next to us and see a deadly machete shining in the sunlight. Three irate men jump from the pursuing car, loudly screaming. "Bloodclaat! Thief! Where is my property?"

Gasping for breath, I race into the terminal behind Mike. We quickly rush past security into the immigration line. I look back to see the three angry Jamaicans violently arguing with the airport police as Mike and I carry our bags onto the Miami bound Jamaica Airlines jet. The stewardess locks the airplane door as I thank God we made it.

Mike sits in the front row alongside Debbie and I join Jill in the back of the plane. Luckily, Jerry is nowhere in sight. Why does Mike hang around him?

I gently kiss Jill's cheek and take hold of her hand when the Boeing 727 pulls away from the gate. We both smile as the aircraft leaves the tarmac and roars into the air.

Jill pulls a hard bound copy of Ernest Hemingway's, 'For Whom the Bell Tolls' from her bag. "That was close. I like reading adventure stories, but I don't want to get hurt in one. Jerry nearly spoiled a great holiday."

I have to ask. "Who's Johnny? Debbie really scared Jerry, when she said his name."

Jill smirks. "Johnny Lionetti is Debbie's step dad. He's one of the most powerful men in Florida. If Jerry hurt Debbie, Johnny would feed him to the sharks."

The thought of sharks swimming in human blood, ripping flesh from a living human being sends a cold chill through my body. I want to get back to Jill's reading topics and our romance.

"What do you think of Hemingway? I liked 'Farewell to Arms' and 'The Old man and the Sea', but I'm more into Jack London's 'White Fang' and 'The Sea-Wolf'."

Jill chuckles. "I'm reading Hemingway for my English Lit class. D. H. Lawrence romances or W. B. Yeats' poetry are more my interest. I've read everything from Proust to Hermann Hesse and Joyce Carol Oates. What do you like to read?"

15

I have different literary interests and can't deny the truth. "CliffsNotes got me through English Literature, but I enjoyed reading Steinbeck and Twain. Hermann Hesse's 'Siddhartha' is on my list. National Geographic Magazine is my favorite. I've circled the globe many times in my imagination while reading it."

Jill smiles. "Me too. I want to go to Albania and Lithuania and see where my grandparents were born. I'd also like to visit the lands of poets and artists, Dublin to Venice."

An attractive Caribbean stewardess politely interrupts our conversatio. "Excuse me. Would either of you like something to drink?"

I point to Jill. "I'll have whatever the lady is having."

Without any hesitation, Jill orders our beverages. "We'll have two Red Stripe beers with two shots of Appleton rum on ice, please."

The stewardess laughs. "Right on, sister."

I pull the last of my last Jamaican currency from my pocket to pay the tab and ask Jill. "What movies do you like?"

She pours the drinks and raises her plastic glass. "First, let's toast our escape from near disaster in paradise."

Jill swallows a shot of rum and quickly follows it with a swig of Jamaican beer.

"I'm into movies with powerful female role models like Vivien Leigh as Scarlett O'Hara and Katherine Hepburn in 'African Queen'. Jane Fonda deserves the Oscar for 'Klute'. How about you? I bet you're into Clint Eastwood and Steve McQueen."

I laugh. "Of course, I'm into 'Dirty Harry' and 'Bullitt', but Humphrey Bogart in 'Casablanca' and Clark Gable as Rhett Butler are my all time favorites."

Later, I'm feeling a real good buzz when the stewardess opens the plane door in Miami. Mike and Debbie charge forward and quickly hurry off the jet. Jerry suddenly appears and follows closely behind, pushing past anyone in his way. Jill and I are in the back of the plane behind passengers and baggage filling the aisle ahead of us.

Finally, we get to the U. S. Immigration and Customs line. I don't see Mike or Debbie waiting at passport control. Jill approaches the U. S. Customs desk. A heavy set, Hispanic female agent brusquely asks. "Miss, where are you coming from?"

Jill proudly answers. "Jamaica."

The agent gives Jill an order with a stern voice. "Miss, I have to search your travel bag and purse."

Jill innocently smiles, handing over her bags. "Sure, I have nothing to hide."

The agent spills the contents onto the counter. A frown emerges on her face when she looks inside Jill's purse and turns her attention to me. "Are you traveling together?"

I hesitate, wondering why she wants to know. My mind races ahead in panic... 'Did Customs catch Mike with his pound of ganja? Are we 'busted'?

The agent becomes hostile and raises her voice, when I don't answer in a timely manner. "Your girlfriend has marijuana in her purse. You both must be strip searched. Do you know the penalties for smuggling illegal narcotics into the United States?"

Tears well up in Jill's eyes. "We smoked some pot in Jamaica and I didn't intend to bring any back. I don't know where it came from."

The female Customs agent ignores Jill's plea and signals another agent. A uniformed black man, the size of a refrigerator puts his giant hand on my shoulder and picks up my carry-on bag. Sweat pours from my glands, my knees shake and I want to piss when the agent commands. "Come with me."

Jill is escorted away as I'm led into a brightly lit, mirrored room with a steel table and chairs in the middle. An unseen second agent closes the door behind us. The massive black agent empties my bag on a table in the center of the room. I stand silent, observing him pick through my possessions hoping there isn't any weed in my bag.

My stomach feels queasy while the agent's bulky fingers open every zipper and pocket, intensely searching for contraband as I wonder if they caught Mike. The rules of the 'street' are: keep my mouth shut, admit nothing and ask for a lawyer.

The agent cuts into the interior lining with a pocket knife as a last resort. Finally, he lifts his head with a disappointed look and growls. "Strip off your clothes."

I pull off my t-shirt and slowly drop my shorts, exposing where the sun never shines to his prying eyes. I hope Mike knows some lawyers.

Finally, I hear. "He's clean. Get dressed."

Relief surges through me. I quickly pull up my shorts as my mind races ahead with worry... 'I hope Jill is alright. Did she get busted for the pot in her purse?'

The door suddenly opens, the imposing female agent reappears with Jill. "Young lady, we'll accept your excuse this time. Your personal information has been entered into our new narcotics smuggling computer database. You're lucky we're not charging you. Next time, you'll get jail time in a Federal Prison. Do you understand?"

Jill and I simultaneously say, "Yes, I'll never smuggle drugs."

The agent returns our bags and opens the door into the 'Land of freedom'. We hurriedly escape the Miami Airport like Cary Grant's airport dash in Alfred Hitchcock's movie 'North by Northwest'.

We collapse outside on the concrete sidewalk curb gasping humid air filled with diesel bus fumes. Jill tearfully whimpers. "We nearly went to prison. I was so humiliated when they strip searched my whole body. Do you think Debbie and Mike are alright?"

I hold Jill closely and attempt to reassure her. "Don't worry. Everything will be OK."

Out of nowhere, a big black '64' Lincoln Continental pulls up in front of us. Jerry Siegel is at the wheel with Jimi Hendrix singing 'Are You Experienced' on the car radio. Mike and Debbie sit next to Jerry in the wide front seat. I'm elated to see these guys, even Jerry.

I open the rear suicide door and grab our bags, quickly following Jill into the luxurious back seat. Mike has a wide grin. "I scored a pound of Jamaican ganja."

Debbie smiles. "Jill, can you believe Mike put the pot in my luggage and the Customs agent didn't open my bag?"

She gently nudges Mike. "I'm mad at you for not telling me."

The big Floridian chuckles.

"I learned a trick or two in Vietnam. Seal the pot in a Ziploc bag, then wrap the bag in more bags filled with coffee and dried hot pepper."

I smile, with a sigh of relief.

"I'm glad you guys didn't go through Customs with us. We were stopped for some weed in Jill's bag. Thank God, they let us go. We could have been arrested."

Mike lets out a hearty laugh and passes a burning joint to me with two pills.

"Here's some Quaaludes to steady your nerves."

Jill and I quickly swallow the pills, without asking questions. Our anxiety and fears dissipate into cosmic space as the joint is passed around, filling the car with ganja smoke.

Debbie smiles cheerfully. "Jill, you guys are invited to dinner at my step dad's restaurant in Ft. Lauderdale. Mom is preparing special Italian dishes for us."

Blue gray smoke floats from Jill's mouth with her answer. "I love your mother's cooking. My mother can't boil an egg."

Debbie's voice becomes passionate. "Jill, I'm so excited. Mike is going to meet my folks for the first time. Oh, I wish you weren't flying back to Detroit tomorrow. We've had so much fun and who knows, you could be my bridesmaid."

The big Lincoln Continental drifts towards the center of the road. Car horns explode all around us.

Mike hollers. "God damn it, Jerry. Watch where you're going."

We continue to roll north on Interstate 95 into Broward County. WSHE, 'She's Only Rock & Roll' plays Bob Dylan singing 'The Times They Are a Changin' on the car radio."

The black Lincoln comes to a halt in front of a huge neon sign 'Faraway Joe's Crab House'. Parking attendants open the car doors as Mike turns to his driver and hands him a twenty dollar bill. "Jerry, pop the trunk. Fill the tank and get dinner. I'll call you tomorrow."

Mike recovers our luggage and tips the attendants. Jerry puts the Lincoln V8 in gear. Screeching tires and a cloud of acrid smoke make his displeasure known. Jill and I follow Debbie as she pulls her man towards the restaurant. A good looking casually dressed couple greets us at the door.

Debbie introduces everyone. "Mom and Dad, you know Jill. This is my boyfriend Mike Casey and his Army buddy, Jack Collins. Guys, these are my parents, John and Mary Lionetti."

Mr. and Mrs. Lionetti look like any middle aged South Florida couple living the good life. Mary could be Debbie's older sister with amber hazel eyes and raven 'big hair'. At forty years old, Mary Lionetti's seductive beauty rivals Sophia Loren or Raquel Welch.

At five foot ten John Lionetti is about my height, but he's a lot heavier. His thinning silver gray hair makes him appear much older than his pretty wife. Chestnut brown skin betrays a Sicilian heritage and his dark ebony eyes are sharply focused on Mike.

A gold Rolex watch and diamond pinky ring shine brightly on Debbie's stepfather's wrist and hand, with an unlit cigar protruding from his mouth. "Nice to meet you kids."

Mary leads her daughter and Jill towards the dining room. "Girls, I want to show you what I'm making in the kitchen."

John Lionetti grabs Mike's arm and aggressively pulls him into a private bar room. "Kid, let's have a drink. I've got something to say before dinner."

Debbie's stepfather stares at Mike. "I know what you did in Jamaica and don't ever use my Debbie for business again. I'll cut your balls off and feed them to you, if you hurt my little girl. Understand?"

Mike looks startled and his voice becomes hesitant as his face turns pale. "Yes sir. I'll never do that again. Debbie's my girl. I wouldn't do anything to hurt her."

I see blood in the water and sharks feasting on my flesh when a bartender appears. Suddenly, our host's face changes from a deadly glare to a friendly smile. "Great. Now that we've had our little chat, let's have a drink. I'll have Chivas Regal rocks. What would you boys like?"

Mike looks relieved. "I'll have the same."

I hesitate. "Scotch isn't my drink. I'll have a Miller High Life."

The bartender delivers our order and leaves the room. John Lionetti's face turns businesslike. "Kid, call me Johnny. Debbie says you want me to open a new enterprise in Jamaica. We'll talk business after a police detective on my payroll checks you out. Let's have some drinks and enjoy Mary's homemade lasagna and manicotti tonight."

Our host walks us back into the restaurant filled with families enjoying seafood and pasta dinners. Pictures of the extended Lionetti New Jersey 'Family' with Frank Sinatra and the 'Rat Pack' hang on the walls throughout the restaurant along with autographed photos of celebrities like Joe DiMaggio, Jackie Gleason and Bob Hope. Debbie's stepfather opens a side door and leads us into a private dining room.

The meal begins with Italian Pinot Grigio wine accompanied by chilled stone crab claws and grilled shrimp skewers. More wine and a crisp Caesar salad follow the appetizers. Mary's delicious homemade pasta dishes complement the baked Florida snapper in garlic butter and wine main course.

Mary proposes dessert and coffee as we finish the main course. "Would everyone like to try my homemade Key Lime pie and espresso?"

My 'sweet tooth' always craves sugar. "I'll have some pie and coffee, thank you."

Johnny Lionetti hands out Montecristo cigars. "I import these from Cuba."

Mike sniffs the powerful tobacco aroma. "I thought you couldn't buy Cuban cigars after Castro and the communists took over."

A shrewd smile appears on 'Don' Lionetti's face. "Meyer Lansky and the 'Family' ran Havana under Batista during the 50's. Jack Kennedy let the communists turn Cuba into a prison camp. Today, JFK's dead, Nixon's in the White House and I'm still importing Cuban Montecristos."

The waiters bring Sambuca and Cognac with another round of coffee. Mary rises from the table. "Girls, join me in the kitchen. I want to show you my recipes."

Mike boasts. "I'm betting on Miami winning the Super Bowl this year. The Dolphins' defense intercepted Johnny Unitas three times in their last game. It's the first time the Colts have been shut out in a hundred games."

I have to ask. "Do you really think Shula's 'no name' defense can stop Tom Landry's high powered offense?"

My Army buddy is adamant. "I'm taking Miami and giving up three points."

Johnny shakes his head with a smile. "I don't gamble on games. I take bets and don't care who wins because I always get paid my 'vig' on both sides of the bet."

The cigars have burned down and our glasses are empty. I'm returning from the toilet and walking past the kitchen where Jill and Debbie are smoking Marlboro lights and drinking coffee with Mary. I pause and hear their conversation. Debbie tells her mother. "I've found the man I want to marry and love for the rest of my life."

Mary's voice betrays her fears. "Debbie, please don't get pregnant. Remember your father. We're lucky Johnny saved us from him."

My entry into the kitchen interrupts their fervent discussion. "Mrs. Lionetti, thank you so much for the delicious meal."

Mike Casey and Johnny Lionetti follow me into the room, smiling and laughing together. Johnny enthusiastically shakes Mike's hand. "Nice to meet you and remember what I said about taking care of our daughter."

Debbie grabs her purse and gives her mother a hug. "I'll drive Mike and Jack over to Mike's apartment."

Mary tenderly kisses her daughter's cheek. "Be careful."

Johnny receives a hug and a kiss from his step daughter. "Young lady, don't stay out late."

Debbie giggles as she walks towards the door. "Don't wait up."

Mike and I grab the bags and follow Debbie out the door. She unlocks a red Mustang convertible and we manage to pack the luggage into the small trunk. Debbie starts the Ford V8 engine and lowers the white rooftop.

Jill and I sit in the back seat while we drive past palm trees decorated with Christmas lights shining in the full moon light. Cool night air blows through my hair as we roll south towards Miami on I-95. The food, liquor and drugs have had their effect and my experience with the United States Customs Agency is a distant memory for now.

Bobby Keys' saxophone solo leads The Rolling Stones in 'Can't You Hear Me Knocking' on the car radio. Jill whispers. "I get so hot when I hear a saxophone."

Minutes later, we charge up the stairs into Mike's studio apartment with its tiny outdated kitchen and Murphy bed. Thick green shag carpet surrounds a couple of plastic chairs and an old sofa couch facing a portable Zenith black and white TV on a card table. Mike opens a bottle of rum and hands me a bag of pot. "Jack, roll a joint. Let's party."

Debbie looks at her watch and turns on the television. "I want to watch Johnny Carson. He has some great guests tonight: Natalie Wood, Jane Fonda and Woody Allen."

Jill agrees. "Jane Fonda is a hero of mine and I love Woody Allen's movies."

I recall my pre-teenage fantasies. "Natalie Wood was the first movie star I fell in love with when I saw her in 'Rebel Without a Cause'."

Jill responds. "She and Rita Moreno were great in 'West Side Story'."

Mike pulls a plastic baggie from his backpack. "I've got some more Quaaludes. Who wants to get happy?"

We consume the 'ludes' with rum shots and a fat ganja joint. I'm stoned with Jill in my arms when Ed McMahon announces. "Here's Johnny."

Later, Jane Fonda tells Johnny Carson. "I'm no suburban housewife in 'Leave It to Beaver' or 'Donna Reed'. As a liberated woman, I can do what a man can do and do it better."

Debbie pulls herself closer to her man. "I want to be Donna Reed and have a family."

Mike changes the topic. "Right now, I want enough money to move out of this dump."

Jill gently caresses my erection through my blue jeans. "I have everything I need as a liberated woman, but sometimes I want what a man has."

At orgasm my eyes close and I slowly drift to sleep.

The next morning, I hear a telephone ringing and reach for Jill, but she isn't next to me.

"Ring." "Ring."

Where's Jill? My mouth tastes like I ate aluminum for dinner. How did I end up sleeping on Mike's couch? Why doesn't someone answer the phone?

"Ring." "Ring."

I guess I'll have to answer the phone. I pick up the telephone receiver. "Hello."

Jill's voice is on the line. "Jack. Debbie and I are going to drive back to Mike's place."

My head throbs and I'm confused. "What happened last night? Where are you?"

Jill laughs. "Buddy, I'll tell you all about it when I get there. See you in an hour."

I put the phone down. Damn, I need a cup of Joe and a joint to fight this hangover. Mike staggers from the kitchen into the living room with a pot of coffee and a fat 'doobie'.

He pours me a cup of hot Joe and passes the smoking joint with a chuckle. "Man, that second Quaalude really knocked you out. We put you on the sofa and the girls drove back to Debbie's parent's place."

My headache slowly subsides. "That was a great dinner last night, but I hope you know what you're doing getting involved with Johnny Lionetti. He's a real gangster."

Mike sits down at the kitchen table and relights the joint. "The day I met Debbie, I knew her stepfather had the keys to my dreams."

The big Floridian opens a kitchen cabinet and removes a triple beam scale, the pound of Jamaican ganja and a brown leather handgun holster. He pulls out a nickel plated Colt .45. "I carried this in 'Nam'. It saved my life more than once."

Mike locks and loads a round into the semi-automatic pistol. "No one is going to fuck up my plans."

I look at the weapon and think…'The 'Law of the Jungle' is 'Kill or be Killed'.' "Mike, be cool with the artillery. You don't want more firefights in this lifetime."

A deadly look appears in Mike's brown Seminole eyes. "You need firepower to cover your ass. It's do or die on the streets, just like 'Nam'."

I swallow more hot coffee. "Why do you keep Jerry around? He's going to mess up your plans one of these days."

A cunning smile appears on Mike's face. "I keep Jerry around because we grew up together and I can trust him. He sells my weed on the street to tourists. I front him forty dollar ounces and make over six hundred per pound retail. You can see why a boatload of ganja could make me rich."

The pain in my head has subsided, but I have other concerns. "Can you trust Tony? People get killed for a lot less money?"

The big Floridian shrugs his shoulders. "I'll have to take my chances. My rust bucket Chevy van is going to turn into a new Corvette. Don't worry, I've got it under control."

Mike deliberately packs a Ziploc bag with ganja, placing it on the scale and then tossing it to me. "Here's an ounce. See what your friends in Boston will pay for Jamaica's finest 'Lamb's Bread'. Don't put this bag in your luggage. Stash it between your balls and your ass when you're on the plane."

A car horn sounds outside. Mike jumps up and puts everything back in the closet. I look down from the apartment window to see a brand new Ford Mustang parked next to Mike's van, surrounded by other rusting vehicles.

Jill and Debbie sit in her new convertible, listening to Eric Clapton's 'Layla' playing on the car radio. They wave. "We're here."

The girls charge up the steps into the apartment like a whirlwind. Jill gives me a big hug and a warm morning kiss. "Last night, you passed out during Bill Cosby's comedy routine. Debbie and I put you on the couch."

I'm bummed and don't remember anything. "That last Quaalude kicked my ass."

Jill gives me a tender look.

"Buddy, I wish we didn't have to go back to school. I'm going to miss you."

She pulls me closer. "Come to Ann Arbor in the spring. In fact, why don't you come to the 'Hash Bash' on April Fool's Day?"

I smile and hand her a note. "Sure, sounds like a plan. Here's my phone number."

Jill takes the piece of paper with a smile. "I'm moving into a new apartment. I'll call you, when I get a telephone installed. Maybe, I can hitch a ride to Boston this winter."

I gaze into Jill's fascinating eyes. "You can stay with me anytime you come to Boston."

We embrace and a passionate kiss seals our commitment.

Later, warm tropical breezes flow through swaying palm trees surrounding Miami's pastel colored 'Art Deco' buildings. Jimi Hendrix's 'Purple Haze' plays on the radio as Debbie's red convertible races towards Miami International Airport with the Goodyear blimp floating above us.

The Ford Mustang stops at the airport terminal entrance. Mike turns to me. "Jack, you should sell half ounce lids for forty bucks in Boston."

I give him a firm handshake. "Thanks, I'll let you know."

Debbie gives me a friendly hug. "Come back and see us."

I enthusiastically return her hug with a smile. "I hope to be back here again soon. Please thank your mother and father again for last night's wonderful dinner."

The two girlfriends wholeheartedly embrace and Jill smiles. "Debbie, come to Michigan this summer when it's warm enough for you."

Debbie tearfully responds. "Jill, you're my sister. My folks said you can stay with me anytime."

The girls hug again. Jill turns to Mike. "You and Debbie should visit Ann Arbor this summer. Maybe, you guys can come to the 'Hash Bash' too."

Mike has a cryptic smile. "If there's a decent business opportunity."

I pull Jill into a tight hug. We passionately kiss, until an announcement comes over the airport public address system.

"Eastern Airlines, flight 711 to Boston is boarding at gate 9."

I want to kiss Jill again, but I have to catch a plane. "You have my telephone number. Call me."

Jill smiles. "Buddy, I'll call when I get a new phone. Please come visit me in April."

"I'll be there."

Neil Young sings 'Heart of Gold' on a nearby transistor radio when I turn and run to the boarding gate."

NEW ENGLAND WINTER

Damn, it's cold outside. I should be in Jamaica swimming with Jill Jensen in the warm Caribbean Sea. Instead, I'm studying American History at UMass/Boston and living with friends on the Atlantic Ocean where freezing winds blow gray clouds onshore this time of year. Most homes are closed for the winter in the Massachusetts' coastal town of Hull.

A wood fire warms the living room where I'm reading Playboy magazine and listening to 'Sergeant Pepper's Lonely Hearts Club Band'.

"Happy Valentine's Day."

I look up from my magazine to see a radiant smile with stunning blue eyes surrounded by golden curls. Louise Peabody, a member of the renowned Beacon Hill family is wearing a Julia Child apron when she enters the room. She hands me a scarlet rose and gently kisses my cheek while whispering in my ear. "I'm glad we're spending Valentine's Day together."

My beautiful elegant lover focuses in on the magazine I'm reading. "I suppose you read Playboy for the well written articles."

I chuckle. "As a matter of fact, I'm reading an article about how the Manson family's gruesome murder of Roman Polanski's wife and unborn child created the fatalistic theme for his movie of Shakespeare's 'Macbeth', where all his characters are victimized by the corrupt world around them."

Louise listens patiently, then gives me an affectionate hug with a sweet smile. She whirls around and strides towards the kitchen. "It sounds like interesting reading and I'm sure you checked out the centerfold. Hugh Hefner may be your role model, but I want my man tonight and every night. I hope 'Shu' and Wendy show up with the turkey soon. We need to get it in the oven. The dinner rolls and pies are nearly done."

This Valentine's Day will be celebrated at 'Hull House', a shining beacon of light this cold dreary winter night. A rust covered Volkswagen Beetle comes to a stop with a horn blast. "Honk."

Neal Shuster's sandy brown ponytail blows in the wind as his lanky six foot frame leans forward and helps his girlfriend walk through the snow. Wendy Smith's long chestnut hair is hidden in her hooded winter coat. She clings to her boyfriend and tries to stay upright as they struggle up the ice-covered steps.

'Shu' has been my best friend since seventh grade at Pierce Junior High School. His family lives next to his father's clothing manufacturing company near the Mattapan Jewish Synagogue.

Neal turned me 'on' for the first time in the spring of '67'. We smoked some Mexican weed that kicked my ass. Shu is a traveling man during the summer selling weed and bootleg t-shirts at rock concerts around the country. We'll make money together, if Mike delivers the Jamaican ganja.

The front door opens and a blast of frigid air invades the living room with the new arrivals. Louise greets our guests with friendly hugs. She leads them towards the warm fireplace as they remove their winter coats and gloves.

Shu grins enthusiastically while handing a large paper shopping bag to Louise. "We got a bargain on a thirty pound fresh turkey. If we put this bird in the oven now, it will be cooked before midnight."

Louise takes the grocery bag with a smile. "You guys got here just in time. Wendy, let's prepare the turkey. I made chestnut stuffing."

This festive evening's bartender fills the ice chest with adult beverages in the next room. My TKE fraternity brother, Jan Kmiec is impeccably dressed in a Ralph Lauren black silk tuxedo with a well groomed mustache and goatee. He's an aspiring Shakespearean actor who enjoys the role of bartender at our parties. "My good man and lady, what would you like to drink tonight?"

Neal Shuster finishes helping Wendy remove her heavy wool winter coat and loudly orders. "A glass of Vouvray wine for my lady and a cold mug of your finest beer for me."

The bartender looks into the ice chest and finds the preferred Loire Valley Chenin Blanc. He fills a glass for Wendy and she joins Louise in the kitchen.

Jan pours a Miller High Life into a frozen mug. Shu admires his frosted pint of beer. "Merci beaucoup mon ami. Did you see Roman Polanski's 'Macbeth? I heard it was financed by Hugh Hefner and Playboy."

My fraternity brother smirks. "I'm a purist when it comes to Shakespeare's works. Polanski's character adaptations weren't what I expected, but I did enjoy Lady Macbeth's nude sleepwalking soliloquy. As far as I'm concerned Polanski is a film genius, but I'm prejudiced because he's Polish."

The CBS Evening News with Walter Cronkite comes on television in the living room.

"The White House announced President Nixon's visit to China this month in hopes of ending America's longest war. Secretary of State Henry Kissinger will join the President during this historic meeting with Zhou Enlai and Mao Zedong. This will be the first diplomatic activity between the United States and China since 1949.

The Nixon White House also announced plans to combine Federal drug enforcement agencies into one anti-narcotics department to win the 'War on Drugs'.

Finally, the United States' Treasury Department estimates America's National Debt exceeded four hundred billion dollars for the first time in history. And that's the way it is Monday, February 14, 1972."

Jan shrugs his shoulders. "As Shakespeare wrote over three hundred years ago, 'All the world's a stage where every man plays a part.'... Who knows what our future will be?"

I hear footsteps coming down the stairs as my thoughts drift... 'Could Nixon's 'War on Drugs' stop Mike's Jamaica smuggling plans?'

Roommates Chuck and Marsha enter the room. Shu boisterously yells out. "Let's ask Coast Guard Seaman Lievi about protecting the American homeland from Soviet subs and South American drugs."

The day of Charles Lievi's high school graduation, General Hershey and the Draft Board sent him an induction notice. Chuck's father pulled political strings to get him into the Coast Guard and stationed in Boston.

Seaman Lievi sarcastically chuckles. "The Coast Guard can't stop all of the drugs coming to America."

Marsha Hubbard is the pretty blond entering the room with Chuck. Marsha's father and my dad are partners in Hubbard, Collins & Associates Attorneys at Law. Our families live on

Brush Hill Rd. in Milton and we've known each other since kindergarten. We spent our summers together on Cape Cod, swimming and boating in Nantucket Sound.

I especially enjoyed boat trips to Baxter's Fish and Chips in Hyannis for fried clams and fries. Our daily summer breakfast included fresh blueberry or strawberry pancakes with Ma Getchel's eggs and farmer Murray's milk. Family sunset cookouts featured grilled lobster, quahog clams, Hansen's corn and tomatoes. Fresh churned strawberry or blueberry ice cream were my favorite desserts. I never wanted Cape Cod summers to end.

Marsha was my first 'puppy love'. Her chestnut eyes and long golden hair captivated me throughout elementary school. Our relationship changed when I went to Xaverian Brothers High School. Chuck and Marsha have been a couple since their sophomore year at Milton High. Sometimes I wonder what would have happened, if I hadn't gone to an all boys prep school.

Chuck is goalie and coach of our street hockey team, 'Beantown Boys'. He shares the third floor with team members Jim Quatromoni (Bait) and Richard Mason (Bone). Chuck plans to sell Frisbees at the Munich Olympics, after his June discharge from the Coast Guard.

Jan pours Marsha a glass of Merlot wine before she joins the other girls in the kitchen. Coast Guard Seaman Lievi puts on a heavy wool winter coat and looks at me. "It was great to see Robbie Ftorek and Team USA win the Olympic silver medal. I hope Bobby Orr leads the Bruins to another Stanley Cup this year."

Shu isn't into sports and changes the subject. "You guys should have seen Ike and Tina Turner do 'Proud Mary' on 'Soul Train'. Aretha Franklin might be the 'Queen of Soul', but Tina is the 'Queen of Rock n' Roll'."

Chuck laces up his Sorel Caribou winter boots. "They're both great, but Mick Jagger and The Rolling Stones are the greatest rock n' roll band of all time."

Shu smiles. "I got a deal selling 'knock off' t-shirts on the next Stones tour with Stevie Wonder."

Chuck walks towards the front door. "I'm going on a beer run. Anyone need anything?"

Shu shakes his head as I answer. "We're cool, man. I'm glad your Cadillac is the beer wagon in this weather."

Chuck gives me a thumbs up and exits into the freezing cold and quickly closes the door behind him.

Jan hands me a frosted mug of Miller High Life. "A toast to Jack and Louise. May the romantic rogue and the elegant lady become a couple for all time."

I smile and raise my beer. "Jan, you know what the Peabody family and my folks expect me to do. I don't see myself as a Beacon Hill lawyer or a State Street banker. Business and law bore me. My motto will always be: 'Freedom in pursuit of happiness'."

Shu puts an album on his Sony stereo turntable. Steve Winwood and the Spencer Davis Group's hit song 'Gimme Some Lovin' echoes throughout the house.

Shu yells into the kitchen. "Are Rudy and Mo on their way with lobsters? I hope they buy the cheaper one claw 'culls'."

Louise answers. "Rudy said he's buying Maine lobster 'culls' at the Yankee Lobster Company."

Reginald 'Rudy' Losordo went to Pierce Junior High School with Shu and me. He's a wild man on the drums, playing for our house band 'The Demon Deacons'. Keith Moon is his hero with the motto, 'The party doesn't end until the drummer passes out.'

Rudy was the first of my friends to get wheels. Some of my favorite high school memories are Shu and me cruising the Blue Hills in Rudy's Ford Torino, smoking weed and listening to Steppenwolf's 'Magic Carpet Ride'.

The front door opens and Maureen Fitzpatrick's fiery red hair bursts into the living room. Powerful union boss, Joe 'Tip' Fitzpatrick's youngest daughter is the princess of 'Southie'. Even Whitey Bulger and the notorious 'Winter Hill Gang' won't mess with her.

Maureen yells. "Jack, did you hear what the British did in Northern Ireland? The Army murdered unarmed Irish citizens in cold blood. We've got to free all of Ireland."

A distinct whiskey aroma permeates the room. "Mo, you smell like a liquor still."

Rudy laughs and closes the front door behind him. He carries two large paper grocery bags and follows his girlfriend into the kitchen. "We've been drinking Jameson shots and planning the next 'Irish Rebellion' while shopping for lobsters."

I can't relate to the Anglo-Irish 'troubles' across the Atlantic. My father is forever reminding me, the Collins family was lucky to escape Ireland during the 1848 'Potato Famine'. I was taught religion and politics don't mix. Mother was raised Presbyterian and had to join my father's religion as a condition of their marriage. Dad's parents were Roman Catholic and they required the Holy Roman Church to bless the nuptials. I'm thankful to be free from Europe's troubled history.

Joey and Teresa Palermo can be heard arguing on the porch as they approach the front door. Joey's father is a known associate of the Angiulo brothers, 'Godfathers' of Boston's Italian American community. I'm hoping Joey can move Mike's Jamaican ganja.

Teresa Marino was an eighteen year old virgin when she married Joseph Angelo Palermo at St. Leonard's Catholic Church in Boston's North End last year. Her elegant aristocratic demeanor was in sharp contrast to Joey's stout physique and awkward appearance. She's a Sicilian beauty with a fiery personality that doesn't take crap from anyone.

The front door opens with a burst of frozen air as the quarreling couple enters the living room. Maureen rushes out of the kitchen when Teresa screams. "Joey, you're full of it. You don't have to be a gangster. Why can't you be normal and get a real job?"

Joey Palermo vehemently answers. "Woman, someday I'll run Boston. I'm making a thousand a week 'under the table' at the Nantasket Beach parking lot."

Teresa shakes her head and pulls Maureen into the kitchen. "Mo, I need a cigarette."

Joey hands our bartender two bottles of Chianti Classico. "Jan, I need a double Jack Daniel's with Coke and ice? Thanks."

Jan chuckles. "Coming right up."

I break the seal on my baggie of ganja. A pungent tropical aroma surges into the stale winter air, bringing back memories of Jamaica. Joey Palermo is the only person I know who sells pounds of grass and Mike's ganja deal could be my ticket to travel the world. "Joey, my Army buddy is importing hundreds of pounds of Jamaican weed into Florida."

I pass Joey a freshly rolled joint. He fires up his Zippo lighter and inhales the sweet smoke. A blue gray smoke cloud billows into the air, followed by a loud cough. "Jack, Boston is flush with weed at Christmas, but things dry up in the summer and prices go up."

Joey inhales the joint again and a contented smile appears on his swarthy face following the release of another cloud of smoke. "This is wicked good shit. I'll pay five hundred a pound for everything you can deliver."

I smile. "Those numbers are cool. I'll call my partner. He plans to get his boat in the water soon."

Shu draws heavily on the joint. "Jack, count me in for a couple of pounds. I can sell lids on the summer rock n' roll tour."

My mind races ahead thinking of future wealth as I toke the joint… 'There could be big money selling ganja in New England. I hope Mike gets the stinking weed past the Coast Guard and Customs.'

Shu tries to pass the burning joint to my fraternity brother. Jan dismissively waves it away and raises his beer mug. "No thanks. I have enough trouble with the drink."

More beer, wine and another fat joint leads the 'Beantown Boys' to become 'The Demon Deacons' playing Led Zeppelin's 'Rock & Roll'. Richard Mason with his goatee and thick 'Elvis' sideburns looks cool on lead guitar. He and Jim Quatromoni exchange guitar licks as Rudy Losordo's blond curls bounce to his drum beat.

The Hull House midnight banquet begins with lobster appetizers and tossed green salad, followed by roast turkey, mashed potatoes and gravy. Louise made apple pie and Wendy bought Brigham's vanilla ice cream. My sweet tooth can't resist dessert. I gently kiss Louise's cheek. "Great Valentine's Day dinner."

The feast ends when Rudy tumbles onto the floor too drunk to stand as The Rolling Stones' 'You Can't Always Get What You Want' plays on the stereo. Maureen swallows another shot of

Jameson and doesn't miss a beat. She joins Louise and Wendy helping Rudy into the first floor guest room.

Joey Palermo announces. "I'll make sure Tip Fitzpatrick's daughter gets home safe."

Louise gives Shu and Wendy a worried look. "You guys look too tired to drive. Why don't you crash in the second floor guest room? The kitchen is clean and the leftovers are in the refrigerator for sandwiches tomorrow."

My lover turns to me with a sweet smile and whispers in my ear. "I need my playboy to warm me tonight."

She takes my hand and leads me upstairs into my bedroom. We escape the winter cold under heavy quilts and succumb to carnal desire. Exhausted at climax Louise falls asleep in my arms as I fade into a dream…

…A bright full moon illuminates a golden haired maiden astride a porcelain white mare galloping across the countryside with a riderless black stallion following in the darkness…

The next day, morning sun lights my bedroom as I awaken to beautiful innocence sleeping with me. Louise's soft physique lies next to me in my cozy bed. Damn, it's cold and I have to piss. The house is freezing and the living room fire has to be relit. Unexpectedly, I hear the telephone in the kitchen. "Ring." "Ring."

I reluctantly pull myself from my warm bed and rush down stairs to answer the phone. "Hello, Hull House."

A voice from my Jamaica travels surprises me. "Jack, this is Jill Jensen. I'm in Boston with my buddy, Bill White. We're driving to Vermont. Do you want to come with us?"

My heart skips a beat. "Sure, I'm up for a 'road show'. I'll take the Hull ferry into Boston. Can you find the harbor ferry dock near Quincy Market?"

Jill chuckles. "No problem, Bill and I are parked in a psychedelic VW van near there and we can see the dock. How soon can you get here?"

The ferry schedule comes to mind. "If I catch the twelve o'clock ferry I can meet you in an hour and half."

Jill exuberantly answers. "Great, we'll see you then."

I think to myself...'Louise isn't awake, so I'll leave her a note. She's wonderful, but I'm drawn to Jill.'

'Dear Louise, I've gone to Vermont with friends. I'll call when I return. Love, Jack xo'

I decide to wear my green Army jacket over a wool sweater and flannel shirt. My ganja baggie is in my jeans pocket as I grit my teeth while walking out the door into the freezing north wind. I check my Timex watch and put on leather gloves. "Damn, the Boston ferry is a mile away and it leaves in ten minutes. I better get running."

I'm gasping for air upon arrival at the ferry port and see the gangplank still attached to the dock. As the last passenger to board, I hastily pay my fare and take a seat inside the heated cabin. The small ship pulls away from land and surges through white capped waves dancing in the harbor's steel gray water.

A cold chill surges through me when the dreary colors of this dark winter day cause my mind to drift... 'Who's Bill White? Is Jill sleeping with him?'

The ferry boat horn announces our arrival at the Boston dock. I join passengers dressed in heavy winter clothing hurriedly exiting the ship into a frigid polar wind. A bright rainbow colored VW van comes to my attention in the parking lot.

Jill stands next to a bearded long haired dude, stretching and exercising near the van. Bright rays of sunlight peek through the dark gray clouds as I repeatedly wave and shout. "Jill." "Jill."

She finally notices me and waves back. "Hey buddy."

We rush together and embrace, melting into a passionate kiss.

I think to myself... 'This girl makes me feel special.'

Jill looks at her exercising companion. "Bill, this is my Jamaican 'joy boy', Jack Collins. Jack, this is Bill White. He's been my cosmic buddy since kindergarten."

A broad smile appears and Bill's inquisitive hazel eyes sparkle when he extends his right hand. "Howdy, William Randolph White. Great to meet you. Any friend of Jill is a friend of mine. Let's get rolling, the sun sets early this time of year in Vermont."

I'm getting good vibes from Jill's cosmic brother as we embark on a road trip into the Green Mountains. Crystal snowflakes swirl in the cold winter wind as the warm VW van leaves Beantown.

Jill looks concerned, when she pulls me close. "We're driving to Vermont to see a friend from elementary school. Susie Fishman and I met in first grade and we talked on the phone nearly every day, until Susie started college at Michigan State."

She pauses and shakes her head. "Susie was depressed about school and thinking of suicide two months ago. I suggested she get counseling and take a break from classes. The next week I got a postcard saying she moved to Vermont with a woman she met singing in a Chicago coffee house."

My buddy pulls an envelope from her coat pocket. "I got this letter two days ago. Susie's new friend is named Jane Monroe. Jane's father is a 'Nation of Islam' member and her mother is Israeli. Jane was panhandling in Haight Ashbury, until she became a Hindu and started singing in coffee shops. I hope Susie didn't join a crazy California cult."

Our driver listens patiently while navigating his van through swirling pearl snowflakes over ice covered roads as we enter New Hampshire's White Mountains. Cat Stevens sings 'Peace Train' on Boston's premier FM radio station, WBCN.

Bill smiles looking out at the snow covered road in front of us. "Jack, I hear you scored some righteous Jamaican ganja recently. Do you have any with you?"

I smile and reach into my coat pocket. "Yeah Man! I have some excellent 'Lamb's Bread'. I'll roll a joint."

Jill chuckles. "Bill has been importing Moroccan hashish from Canada for years. He wants in on Mike's Jamaican boat."

The van radio interrupts our conversation. "This is CBS News with Douglas Edwards. Secretary of State Henry Kissinger stated 'America will bomb North Vietnam until South Vietnam becomes a sovereign nation' on the eve of President Nixon's historic summit with Chinese communist leader, Mao Zedong.

In weather news, a freezing Arctic cold front from Canada will bring below zero temperatures to the Northeast, especially the New England mountains this week."

Bill smiles. "It might be cold here, at least no one is bombing us. Jack, how's that joint coming?"

I fire up the doobie. "The smoking lamp is lit."

Bill sniffs the air. "That smells great."

All of us take big tokes and fill the van with ganja smoke like in a 'Cheech & Chong' comedy skit as Steppenwolf plays 'Born to be Wild' on the radio.

Bill turns the radio volume up and smiles. "My favorite scene in 'Easy Rider' was when Peter Fonda and Dennis Hopper 'turn on' Jack Nicholson."

Jill interjects. "I didn't like the end of the movie, when they were murdered."

Our driver looks over at me with an impish grin. "Man, this is righteous weed. We can move a ton of this stuff at the Ann Arbor Hash Bash. Can your partner deliver by next month?"

I pass the joint back to Bill. "I hope so, but I haven't talked to him lately."

Jill looks at me quizzically. "What would you do, if you had ten thousand dollars to spend on anything you wanted. I'd like to travel Europe."

I smile. "I'll travel with you whenever I get that kind of money."

Bill joins in. "I'd buy land in the tropics to produce food and herbs year round. I plan to grow the best weed in the world someday."

A Dunkin Donuts' sign appears beside a road sign 'White River Junction Two Miles'. Jill smacks her lips. "I've got a serious case of the 'munchies'. Let's get coffee and donuts before we cross into Vermont."

The psychedelic van enters the restaurant parking lot. We exit the van and rush into the warm donut shop. The aroma of fresh baked pastries and brewed coffee excite my senses. A smiling freckled face clerk who reminds me of 'Howdy Doody' smiles and asks me. "How can I help you?"

I read the menu sign. "I'll have a Boston Cream and a Honey Glaze with a large black coffee."

Bill suggests. "Donuts are cheaper by the dozen."

Jill laughs. "Great idea. We'll buy a dozen and max out on sugar and caffeine."

Unexpectedly, I notice a New Hampshire State Trooper 'Smokey the Bear' hat circling our vehicle and I think to myself... 'Damn, I'm holding a bag of weed and I hope Bill doesn't have any hashish in his van.'

I pull on Jill's arm and look for the rest room to flush my ganja as I turn to Bill. "Check out the cop. I've got to get rid of my stash. Is there anything in the van?"

Bill shakes his head from side to side. "Don't worry, the van is cool. You don't have time to get to the toilet. Shove the ganja down your pants."

The door opens and a blue uniformed trooper wearing black leather boots enters in a cold mist and removes his Ray Ban aviator mirror sunglasses. My right hand pushes the baggie of weed between my legs, while my shaking left hand shoves a glazed donut into my mouth.

The State Trooper surveys the scene and announces. "I'm looking for the owner of the vehicle with Michigan license plates."

Bill politely answers with a broad smile. "Yes officer, I own the van. May I help you?"

The New Hampshire law man's steel blue eyes stare at us with contempt. "Son, we're on the lookout for communist agitators causing problems for our law-abiding citizens. You all look like trouble making pot smoking hippies. We don't want your kind around here."

I'm nervously sweating, trying not to scratch the itch between my legs and hoping the trooper doesn't search us. Jill's hands tremble as she drinks coffee sitting next to me.

Bill continues to smile and looks the trooper in the eye. "Officer, we're musicians traveling to Vermont."

The trooper turns his intense stare towards me. "What instrument do you play?"

I stammer. "I keep the beat."

Bill intercedes. "He's my drummer and she dances. I play the flute and hammer dulcimer. We're passing through your beautiful state on our way to Goddard College. Would you like to see our instruments in the van?"

The State Trooper looks out into the frozen wind swept parking lot. He shrugs his shoulders and gives us 'marching orders' as he exits the restaurant. "Get in your vehicle and drive out of my state. The next time you're passing through New Hampshire, keep going and don't stop."

As the law man retreats to his squad car, I'm relieved and thinking to myself… 'A strip search could have put me in prison.'

Bill turns to Jill and me with a satisfied smirk and without another word he leads us back to his van.

I'm hugging Jill when Bill turns the ignition key. The German 1200cc air cooled engine repeatedly sputters in the freezing Arctic air and won't start. Finally, the VW van sparks to life, dispelling my fear of imprisonment in the 'Granite State'.

Vermont winter sunsets begin in the early afternoon when the sky's muted steel gray colors fade into evening darkness. Bill steers his van onto the snow covered road and chuckles. "We were lucky back there. I have some hash in the van."

I smile. "Man, you were confident the cop wouldn't find your stash. I have to figure out a way to move pounds of ganja from Florida to Boston."

Bill nods his head. "I've smuggled hash and weed inside hidden compartments I built into cars and trucks for years."

Winter darkness surrounds us when we exit Route 2 near Goddard College and our van headlights illuminate a sign...

'National Organization for Women, Vermont Cooperative'.

Our driver stops the VW van as a short haired blond emerges from the house and signals us to come inside. Jill recognizes her childhood friend. "Susie looks great."

We exit the van and quickly enter a warm kitchen. The childhood friends rush together and hug each other as a tall copper tanned beauty with a mane of golden sienna hair appears in the kitchen doorway. Susie takes her hand. "I want to introduce the love of my life, Jane Monroe."

The two women couldn't look more different. Susie's short stature and boyish appearance contrasts with her lover's feminine elegance.

I'm enchanted by Jane's cat-like green eyes and exotic feline sexuality as Jill introduces us. "Susie and Jane, this is my buddy, Jack Collins."

Susie hugs Bill and me as Jane nods her recognition, while tightly hugging Jill. "Warm yourselves by the stove. We're having Indian curry for dinner and there's plenty for everyone. I'll open a bottle of Chianti."

An aroma of simmering Asian spices blended with Lavender scented candles and sandalwood incense fill the kitchen air. Jane raises her glass of wine. "May the Heavenly Goddess, Mother of the Universe bless this meal and those sitting around this table."

Jill smiles. "We're lucky to be here. A New Hampshire State Trooper hassled us, when we stopped at Dunkin Donuts."

Jane draws a large bread knife from a cupboard drawer and waves it in the air. "Damn pigs are always fucking poor people while rich crooks steal everything."

Susie looks at Jill. "Jane is still struggling with her Haight-Ashbury experience."

Jane slams the bread knife into the oak kitchen table and screams. "Fucking pigs! I was raped at fourteen and they said I had it coming, cause I was a runaway on the street."

Susie gently hugs her lover. "Babe, try to relax. You don't live on the street anymore and there aren't any 'Gestapo' pigs in Vermont."

Jill cautiously inquires. "Vermont seems so remote. What do you do for fun in the Green Mountains?"

Jane's mood changes instantly. She smiles and puts her arms around Susie. "We make love every chance we get and sometimes we go to a movie at Goddard College. Last night, we saw 'Fiddler on the Roof' at the college theater and Topol's rendition of 'Tradition' deserves an Oscar."

Jane kisses her lover's cheek. "Susie was deeply touched by the story of her people. Her parents are orthodox Jews and hoped she'd marry a good Jewish boy. Instead, we met and fell in love."

The two lovers look into each other's eyes and passionately kiss. Excitement surges throughout my body when their sensuous red lips press together.

After dinner, a dessert of fresh baked blintzes and homemade strawberry jam is served with Colombian coffee. Susie begins clearing the table, when Jane lights a Camel cigarette and removes a quart of Southern Comfort from a kitchen cabinet. "Does anyone want to join me in a shot of Janis Joplin's favorite whiskey? Let's drink a toast to women taking control of their lives."

I answer our hostess with a chuckle. "That sounds good. I used to 'walk a mile for a Camel' in the Army. Can I bum a cigarette?"

Jill joins me and Jane smoking cigarettes as Bill shakes his head and fires up his homemade lilac wood bong. "No thanks. I don't smoke tobacco, but I have Morrocan hash to share."

Jane swallows a shot of whiskey and begins to serenade us with a Janis Joplin verse. "Take another piece of my heart..."

Bill passes his smoking lilac bong to Jane and hands pieces of hashish to each of us. "Eat this before you go to sleep and you'll have colorful dreams."

Jane deeply inhales the hashish smoke and releases a cloud of blue gray smoke when she passes the bong to Jill. Susie calls out from the kitchen. "Carl Jung wrote dreams are the window to the Universe and his therapies helped Hermann Hesse finish 'Siddhartha'."

Jill passes me the bong. "Jack, I brought you my copy of 'Siddhartha'."

I inhale the sweet hashish. "Thanks. I'll start reading it while I'm here."

Time stands still as a second shot of Southern Comfort eases my piece of hash down my throat. Jane's mood suddenly changes when she chugs another shot of whiskey. "California will be a mecca of freedom when pigs like Nixon and Reagan are dead.

They're the enemies of the people, not Angela Davis. She's the future leader of America's second revolution."

Susie interrupts her lover's diatribe with a hug and a gentle caress. "Babe, things are getting better all the time. The National Organization for Women recognized sexual choice as a civil right and we can love anyone we choose."

Jill nods her head. "Congress should pass the Equal Right Amendment, so women can get paid the same as men."

Bill White quietly sets up his instruments as I slip into a stoned euphoria and give him a wink when I interject myself into the conversation. "Hugh Hefner's philosophy encourages women to express their First Amendment right by stripping for money."

Jane angrily yells. "Hugh Hefner is a pig and Playboy treats women like sexual objects. All women should support feminists like Gertrude Stein and Virginia Woolf."

Susie nods in agreement. "Add Betty Friedan and Gloria Steinem to the list."

Jill adds. "Include Anais Nin too."

Jane raises her glass. Women are no longer chained to a man and a birthing cycle."

Bill plays his hammer dulcimer and sings…"With a little help from my friends…"

Susie's partner swallows another whiskey shot and joins Bill in song as Susie tells Jill. "Jane is a generous and patient lover, she gave me my first orgasm the night we met."

My consciousness slowly fades into a dream…

... A tall State Trooper's Ray-Ban Aviator sunglasses reflect a black stallion running in the full moonlight. I chase after the stallion into the darkness...

———◆———

Late the next morning, I wake up wrapped inside a warm sleeping bag with Jill on the living room floor. I don't remember anything after eating the hash with the whiskey shot.

"Ring." "Ring."

The front doorbell breaks the morning silence. I look through an ice coated window to see a guy dressed in a green Army jacket and a girl wearing a pink winter parka standing on the snow covered front porch.

Susie rushes into the living room and opens the front door. She greets her guests with affectionate hugs. "Jimmy, come in out of the cold. We didn't expect you until next week. This must be Judy."

The new arrivals walk into the living room with a blast of frigid winter air that wakes my sleeping partner. Jill yelps. "Jimmy, what are you doing here.?"

Jill turns to me in the sleeping bag. "This is my ex-boyfriend. We dated in high school, until I went to college. Now, we're just friends."

The newcomers stand over us. The tall blond Nordic looking man extends his hand. "Howdy, Jim Sayjack here. This is Judy Ross. We're traveling to Canada to study at McGill University."

Judy shyly turns away, silently nodding in agreement. Jill unzips the sleeping bag and escapes our warm cocoon. Her naked body glistens in the morning sun as she embraces Judy on her way to the bathroom. "Nice to meet you, sister."

William White walks into the kitchen through the backdoor in a blast of frozen air. "Jimmy, how are you doing? The last time I saw you was at the Chicago anti-war protest, when you burnt your draft card."

The two men hug with friendly back slaps. Jimmy shakes his head and frowns. "I was drafted a month later."

Jimmy changes the subject. "Did I see you doing Tai Chi on the back porch?"

Bill White's face lights up. "For sure. Tai Chi clears my head every morning."

Jimmy smiles. "Judy is into Reflexology and gives a great foot massage. You'll have to try one."

A delicious aroma of walnut raisin muffins baking in the oven permeates the house. Susie calls out from the kitchen. "I'm making Celestial Seasonings Morning Thunder yerba mate tea. Does anyone want coffee?"

I need a cup of Joe, but I can't piss until my 'Morning Wood' relaxes.

Jane unexpectedly prances into the living room. An open red silk kimono robe reveals her firm copper toned breasts with chestnut nipples hardened by the cool morning air.

She calls to her lover. "Susie, please make coffee. I had too much Southern Comfort last night."

Minutes later, I join the crowd in the kitchen drinking coffee and tea attempting to cure the previous night's indulgences. Susie puts Jefferson Airplane's 'Surrealistic Pillow' on the stereo turntable and Jane joins Grace Slick singing 'White Rabbit'.

I roll a ganja 'doobie' and pass it to Jill. She takes a toke and passes it to Jane. Jane inverts the joint and fills Jill's lungs with Jamaican cannabis smoke until she closes her eyes and falls back on the couch.

Jane chortles. "What do you think of my shotgun?"

A contented smile appears on my buddy's face. "Wow. I'm seeing multi-colored trails. I heard you have multi-colored hallucinations when you take Acid. I've always wanted to try LSD. Jane, do you have psychedelic contacts from your days in San Francisco?"

Jane smiles. "Yeah, I knew 'Bear' Owsley when he made 'acid' for Jerry Garcia and the Grateful Dead. I still know people who make it."

I think to myself...'I enjoyed 'tripping' on 'Purple Owsley' and 'White Lightning' acid in the Army, but some fellow soldiers had bad trips.'

Jill serenely smiles at Judy when she enters the room. "Jimmy said you're a Reflexologist. Would you give me a foot massage? I'm sure Jane and Susie will let us use their bedroom."

Jane chuckles. "Of course. You girls have fun and I want the next massage."

Judy takes Jill's hand and they stroll into the bedroom as I enter the back living room and open Hermann Hesse's novel, Siddhartha...

'Atman, the Creator dwells within the heart of every living being on earth...'

I hear Bill White consoling Jim Sayjack inside the back bedroom. "Jimmy, it sucks you got drafted. Lucky for me, a kidney disorder deferred me. War is government murder and no one should be forced to do it."

Jimmy shakes his head. "Damn straight. I did everything to avoid the draft, even a conscientious objector petition. Now, I'm moving to Canada. My folks are upset, especially my father. He's a WWII Army veteran and pissed that I won't fight the communists."

Bill nods. "The Canadians are good people and hopefully Nixon can't keep the war going much longer."

Richie Havens plays 'Freedom' on the radio as the bedroom door opens and Jill leads Judy into the kitchen. "Thanks for the great massage. Let's have a cup of tea."

They join Jane and Susie drinking camomile tea while sitting around the kitchen wood stove. Jill wraps her arms around Judy. "We need to help our sister."

Judy tearfully sobs. "Promise not to tell anyone, especially my family and Jimmy. My date raped me three months ago and I haven't had my period since. He took me to a fraternity party and I drank too much. I'm terrified about having this baby and abortion is illegal in America, so I'm going to Canada to find a doctor who'll stop this pregnancy."

Jane joins Jill embracing Judy. "We're here for you. Thank God, I didn't get pregnant when I was raped."

The four girls cling together as Susie wipes away Judy's tears. "Abortion should be a woman's choice. Old men on the Supreme Court shouldn't decide a woman's right to control her body."

A blazing fire warms the farmhouse later that afternoon. I'm reading Hermann Hesse's story of Buddha's search for the meaning of life and heavenly bliss, while Jimmy reads Kurt Vonnegut's 'Slaughterhouse-Five'.

Bill looks up from tuning his hammer dulcimer. "Jack, you should read Thaddeus Golas' 'Lazy Man's Guide to Enlightenment'. It taught me to follow the path of least resistance."

I put my book down. "Bill, speaking of paths of least resistance. How would you smuggle a hundred pounds of ganja from Miami to Boston?"

Bill smiles. "I'd recommend a half ton truck or van. My family owned the first General Motors car dealership in Kalamazoo and I've worked on cars and trucks since I was a kid. I'm a woodworker and I'd build a hidden storage compartment."

The girls reappear from inside the kitchen. Susie announces "The raisin wheat bread is nearly done. I made a pickled cucumber salad and Jill is cooking potato pancakes for dinner. Does anyone want a hot bath? The temperature will be perfect in five minutes."

Jill suggests. "Judy, you go ahead. You've earned it."

Judy hesitates and shakes her head. "Susie should be first. She's been cooking all day. I'll get the bread out of the oven."

Jane takes Judy's hand. "We'll take care of dinner. Let your magic hands rest and enjoy a good soak."

I watch Judy disappear into the steamy bathroom and think to myself...'I want to get in the hot bath with Jill. No hash or whiskey for me tonight, I want to get laid.'

Jane offers everyone Southern Comfort following another wonderful vegetarian dinner and an impromptu music jam. I decline the offer with hopes of stimulating Caribbean passion with Jill in our sleeping cocoon.

Two hours later, Jill and I strip away our clothes and slide into the goose down sleeping bag. I press my lips to my lover's soft breasts and gently caress her thigh.

Jill's body tenses. "Buddy, I'm not in the mood to make love tonight."

I'm confused. "Did I do something wrong? Are you having your period?"

My buddy kisses on my cheek. "No, I'm not having my period and you didn't do anything wrong. It's been a long day and I just want to sleep. Tomorrow will be a better day."

<hr />

The following morning, I wake to a sapphire blue sky with outdoor temperatures far below zero Fahrenheit. Today's wintry scene reminds me of Jack London's life and death stories in the frozen Yukon wilderness.

Jill's warm supple body entices me as she peacefully sleeps next to me. I can't resist kissing her ear gently and whispering. "I want to make love with you all day or would you rather play with your girlfriends?"

My buddy suddenly scowls and unzips the sleeping bag. She pulls herself out of our sleeping cocoon and walks into the toilet. "We're sisters, not lovers. Men don't understand the difference between love and sex."

I'm surprised my joke upset Jill. A short time later, I join Bill and Jimmy drinking coffee and eating fresh baked cinnamon buns in the kitchen. I look into my stash bag. "Man, I'm down to my last couple of joints."

Bill shrugs his shoulders. "I'm low too. I only have a few grams of hash left. Let's hope your friend in Florida gets the Jamaican ganja across the border."

Jimmy shakes his head in disagreement. "Man, I wouldn't take the risk of getting busted. No amount of money is worth going to jail for."

William White smirks. "I'm like a magician. I can build a disguise to conceal anything."

The girls return to the kitchen and sit with the boys around the warm wood burning stove. Susie opens the Barre Montpelier Times Argus newspaper. "We should check our astrology charts before making definite plans for this year. I'm a Virgo and Jane is an Aries."

A smile comes to Bill's face. "I'm an Aries too."

Judy timidly asks. "My birthday is January 24th. What's my sign?"

Jane quickly replies. "You're an Aquarius, like the song 'Age of Aquarius' in the musical 'Hair'. Jill, what's your sign?"

Jill smiles while looking at me. "Jack and I are Scorpios. I hope the stars line up for us to travel to California this summer. I want to check out San Francisco and drive the Pacific Coast Highway to Hollywood."

Jimmy shakes his head. "Astrology is outdated nonsense. You can't base your life on pseudo science and myth."

My lover retorts and turns to me. "Jimmy and I aren't together and I'll make my decisions anyway I want to. Jack, what do you think about going out to California?"

I'm excited by the thought of crossing the country with Jill, but what happened last night? She didn't want to have anything to do with me. "I've always wanted to swim in the Pacific Ocean, but I don't have a car and I'm strapped for cash these days."

Jill smiles. "Buddy, we don't need a car or lot's of money. We can hitchhike and work anywhere in the country. All we need are thumbs."

The Mamas and Papas sing 'California Dreaming' on the kitchen radio, when Bill unexpectedly taps his hammer dulcimer and announces. "We should start back to Boston. Jill and I have a nine hundred mile trip to Michigan. We'll have to drive slow because the roads are covered with snow."

Judy and Jimmy put on their winter coats. Jimmy and Bill handshake. "We're taking off for Quebec. I'll send a postcard to your Kalamazoo, PO Box."

Jimmy turns to me and shakes my hand, then hugs Jill. "Hope to see you guys again soon."

I hug Judy and respond. "Nice to meet you guys. Good luck in Canada."

Jill puts on her ski jacket and joins Susie and Jane embracing Judy. "You know where we live and you have a home here. Call us, collect and let us know you're OK."

I give Jane and Susie a hug with a piece of paper. "Thanks, you guys were great. Here's my phone number, if you come to Boston."

Jane embraces Jill affectionately. "Please come back and visit us in the summer."

Jill smiles. "I have your phone number and I'll call when I get a telephone in my new apartment."

Jane turns to Bill. "Let's make music again soon."

The bearded musician twirls around in a Scottish jig. "I'll be back for sure this summer."

Bill starts the VW and warms it up for travel as the girls affectionately embrace one more time. We all wave as Bill steers his van on to Route 2 and heads south. Everywhere we look the

Vermont hills and forests are covered with snow and stripped bare of summer green.

The sun nears the western horizon as I pass a ganja joint. "This is my last doobie. I hope Mike does his Jamaica deal soon."

Jill smiles. "Yeah, you could sell pounds at the Ann Arbor Hash Bash."

Bill nods his head in agreement. "That would be great."

An hour later, Otis Redding sings 'Try a Little Tenderness' on the radio when Jill's blue eyes look into mine. She pulls me close and gives me a soft kiss. "Buddy, I'm sorry about last night. I had a lot on my mind and needed to sleep. Come visit me in Ann Arbor and we'll study the Kama Sutra together."

The van stops at the Boston Ferry dock as a crowd of commuters board the ship in the winter twilight. Bill shakes my hand. "Jack, it was great to meet you. Jill knows how to get in touch with me. Let me know if your friend scores."

Jill and I embrace in a passionate kiss as I step out of the vehicle. "Call me when you get a telephone installed in your apartment."

Bill puts his colorful VW into gear and honks the horn. Jill enthusiastically waves as the psychedelic van heads west. A nearby transistor radio plays the Temptations singing Smokey Robinson's 'My Girl' as I walk towards the ferry dock in the freezing rain, thinking to myself... 'Jill and I can travel the world, if Mike's ganja boat comes in.'

TROPICAL HEAT

Back in Florida on Valentine's Day, Mike Casey rides 'shotgun' in Jerry Siegel's Lincoln Continental driving towards Faraway Joe's Crab House. The big Floridian worries that his ganja deal is disintegrating. "I've got to convince Johnny to put up the cash for this Jamaican deal."

Mike joined the Army to escape Florida's Dixie Highway poverty where his widowed mother, 'Ma Casey' worked long minimum wage hours in nearby hospitals to care for her family. He knows Debbie Boon's stepfather controls the Southeast Florida criminal 'underworld' and believes Johnny Lionetti will help him make millions.

Tires squealing, the ten year old Lincoln roars into the restaurant parking lot hurtling towards a brand new red Cadillac Eldorado convertible parked at the restaurant entrance.

Mike screams. "Watch out! That's Johnny's Caddie!"

The driver slams both feet on the brake pedal, stopping the black Lincoln sedan inches from the Cadillac.

Mike moans. "This deal would be ruined if you hit that car."

Jerry shrugs his shoulders. "No big thing, we didn't crash."

Mike's face reddens with anger as he shouts. "I'm busting my ass trying to put this together and all you do is fuck things up. I don't know why I keep you on my payroll."

Jerry glares at his childhood friend. "You owe me cause I saved your ass from your cousin Corby. You'd be in jail for murder with him and Murph the Surf, if it wasn't for me."

The big Floridian shakes his head. "Yeah. Yeah. I've heard this shit before. All I can say is I'll cut you out of my action, if you screw this deal up."

Mike opens the car door and steps out of the Lincoln. He pulls a cash roll from his Levi's jeans pocket. "Here's twenty bucks. Fill the tank and get some lunch."

Jerry lights a Kool cigarette. "The Lincoln is nearly empty and premium costs forty cents a gallon. I need two quarts of oil, two cartons of smokes and a quart of Bacardi rum."

The big Floridian casually tosses a second twenty dollar bill onto the car seat. "Here's another Jackson. Come back in an hour."

Jerry puts his car in gear and accelerates towards the parking lot exit as Mike enters the restaurant.

Debbie Boon sees her lover and rushes into his arms. She embraces him with an affectionate kiss while her stepfather stands next to the cash register counting bills into his wife's hand. "Mary, here's five hundred. You ladies enjoy your Valentine's shopping."

Mother and daughter exit the restaurant as Johnny hands Mike a Montecristo cigar and leads him into a private bar room. "Let's have a smoke and drink with Ray."

A chill surges through Mike as he follows Johnny into the room and sees a small ashen white man dressed in black sitting at the bar. The little man's gray eyes stare coldly from his disfigured face as Johnny leads Mike to a seat next to him.

Frank Sinatra sings 'My Way' on a Rock-Ola Jukebox when 'Don' Lionetti steps behind the bar and pours himself a Glenlivet single malt Scotch. "Boys, I gave the bartender the day off. Ray, what are you having?"

The little man's baritone voice answers. 'I'll have a Jack Daniel's on the rocks."

Johnny turns to Mike. "What about you, Kid?"

Mike nervously answers. "Appleton rum on the rocks if you have it."

Johnny laughs. "I have everything from champagne to whiskey. I'll be a bartender again, if the baseball strike hurts my sports book. Right now, I'm getting a lot of action on Hank Aaron breaking Babe Ruth's home run record."

Unexpectedly, the ugly little man's demonic face flushes red. His eyes bulge and his voice chokes with anger. "Someone should shoot that nigger."

'Don' Lionetti dismissively waves his hand. "Ray, let's get down to business. This is Pat Casey's nephew. Pat ran my booze in the Panhandle before becoming a Navy 'lifer'. Kid, meet Ray Jackson."

Johnny pours another round of drinks and turns to Mike. "Kid, I'm betting you'll be a good earner. Are you ready to go big time?"

Michael Casey smiles while extending his right hand to 'Don' Lionetti. "I'm hundred percent in with you."

Ray Jackson ignores Mike's attempt to shake his hand and growls. "Johnny, who is this punk? What do you know about him? I've been with you for over thirty years."

The Miami 'Don' puts his arm on the little man's shoulder. "Ray, I've taken care of you since you were orphaned at fourteen. Haven't I been good to you? My Lauderdale vice squad rat checked out the 'Kid' and he's clean."

Johnny turns his intimidating chestnut eyes towards Mike. "Don't underestimate Ray. He's my 'ramrod' for collections and security."

Ray Jackson intensely focuses on his patron. "Boss, what's in this for me?"

'Don' Lionetti pours a third round of drinks. "This is a private deal and I'm financing the 'Kid' with my retirement money. You're in charge of security at the New River boathouse. Jimmy the 'Jockey' will run my Hatteras to pick up a ton of marijuana. The 'Kid' will sell the weed and I'll cut you in on the profits."

Johnny opens a safe behind the bar and puts a stack of cash in a paper lunch bag. He hands the paper bag to Mike with a powerful handshake. "Here's five thousand until we get this thing started. We'll work out the details later. I'll contact you through Debbie. I'm treating you like family, so don't fuck this up. I wouldn't like that."

Ray pulls open his leather jacket and reveals an ivory handle Colt Python .357 pistol in a shoulder holster. The gangster's fierce reptilian stare gives Mike a cold chill as he shakes his patron's hand. "Johnny, I know what to do."

Mike quickly exits the restaurant without another word. He dashes across the parking lot and jumps into the parked Lincoln Continental. Jerry is startled when Mike lets out a rebel yell. "Yee Ha! I have to call Uncle Pat and my cousins. They'll help move the ganja and I'll use Ma's farm on the Georgia border for storage. Now, we can pay off her mortgage."

Jerry shakes his head. "Can you trust your cousins?"

A broad smile comes to Mike's face. "They aren't like Corby. He's Uncle Pat's bastard son. Scott and Shaun are Georgia cousins. Ma had two brothers, Pat and Tim. Pat joined the Navy and Tim the Marines in 1941 when the Japs bombed Pearl Harbor. Lance Corporal Tim Casey survived Iwo Jima and Petty Officer Patrick Casey did thirty years at sea."

Mike pauses for a second. "Ma married Mike Clancy after the war. He died in the Korean War the same month I was born and Ma kept her maiden name. My cousins Scott and Shaun were orphaned two years later when Uncle Tim and his wife were killed in a car crash. Uncle Pat has been a father to all of us since then."

Jerry turns the ignition key and the Lincoln V8 roars to life as Mike waves the bag of cash. "The 'Casey Clan' is back in business. We're going to make millions selling Jamaican ganja."

———— ◆ ————

Six weeks later at his Miami studio apartment, Mike lies with Debbie in a loving afterglow while listening to CBS morning news report on a transistor radio. "North Vietnamese troops and tanks crossed the DMZ in a massive offensive against South Vietnam. Former Air Force General Curtis LeMay says, 'American B-52s should carpet bomb the communists until they surrender.' In other news, NASA announced Apollo 16 astronauts will drive a second Lunar Rover on the moon."

Debbie gently caresses her man's powerful chest. "Honey, let's get a new place together."

Mike shrugs shoulders. "I can't afford anything right now. I'm paying 'vig' on Miami's Super Bowl loss and I haven't heard anything from Johnny."

An impish smile comes to Debbie's face. "Baby, I forgot to tell you he wanted to see you this morning."

Mike tenses up. "What time?"

Debbie chuckles. "Honey, don't worry. I've taken care of it. We're having dinner at their house tonight. I'll pick up my mother's favorite flowers and chocolates as gifts from you. Dinner is at six and Johnny said to come early so he can talk with you."

The big Floridian frowns. "I hope Johnny isn't pissed off at me."

Debbie takes his hand. "Baby, everything's OK."

<hr />

Later, the sun sets in a pale blue sky as a rented Lincoln Town Car races north on Federal Highway. Debbie Boon lights a Virginia Slims cigarette when they enter Lighthouse Point.

Mike coughs and hands his girl a joint. "Babe, give up the butts and try some ganja."

Debbie puts her cigarette out and takes the joint. Mike turns the silver Lincoln east over a small canal bridge onto Lake Placid island's palm tree lined streets. Million dollar yachts fill ocean access canals surrounding the island's two and three story stucco mansions.

The big Floridian smiles. "Someday I'll live here."

Bob Dylan sings 'If Not for You' on the car radio as Debbie sighs. "Baby, all I need is you."

Mike finishes the joint and tosses the ganja 'roach' out the window. "I've lived on the wrong side of town all my life. Money is the name of the game and I'm going to get mine."

The silver sedan pulls into the Lionetti homestead. Johnny's red Cadillac is parked on a circular driveway with a white marble Virgin Mary and Christ Child statue at its center.

A seventy foot Hatteras Sportfish 'American Dreams' is docked behind a two story Mediterranean style mansion. Debbie leads

Mike through a manicured tropical flower garden to the front entrance. Johnny unlocks and opens a steel door with a sarcastic comment for his adopted daughter. "Debbie, nice of you to visit your mother."

Mike hands his host two dozen pink roses and a pound of Venchi chocolates. "These are for Mary."

Johnny smiles and pulls his stepdaughter into a warm embrace.

"Debbie, you and your mother are the loves of my life. I only want the very best for you. Please don't upset her, she worries too much."

'Don' Lionetti turns to Mike. "Kid, I covered your past due Super Bowl markers. You can pay me back when the boat comes in."

An appreciative smile comes to the big Floridian's face. "Thanks."

Debbie gives her stepfather a warm hug and a kiss on the cheek. Johnny's smile widens. "Help your mother in the kitchen. Mike and I are going to Cap's Place for a couple of drinks. We'll be back at six for dinner."

Johnny leads Mike out the front door to his Cadillac Eldorado shining in the setting sun. He starts the 8.2 liter V8 engine and lowers the convertible top. "Kid, what do you think of my custom built Hargrave Hatteras? It's one of a kind special order with a hidden compartment and a double hull."

Mike can barely contain his excitement. "She's a beauty. I want to own a boat like that someday."

'Don' Lionetti lowers his voice. I've smuggled everything you can think of through the Hillsboro Inlet. Remember you're family because of Debbie. My girls are my world and don't hurt my daughter. Understood?"

Mike nods his head in agreement. "I understand."

Johnny pulls a brown paper bag from under his seat. "This is the deal. I'll finance the upfront costs, including use of my boat. I expect a half million profit. Here's fifty large for the deposit and ten more for your expenses."

The Miami 'Don' hands Mike the paper bag with a keychain and a business card. "These are the New River house keys. Ray is the gatekeeper and lives in the houseboat tied to the dock. Call Joe Varon in Hollywood, if you need a lawyer. He takes care of legal issues. Everyone has to keep a low profile while this deal goes down."

Johnny looks up at the setting sun. "Kid, did you know Roman Emperor Julius Caesar was stabbed to death by his friend Brutus on the 'Ides of March'? Watch out for a Judas in your crew who'll knife you."

The red convertible comes to a stop at the end of the road on the Intracoastal Waterway. Johnny parks his Cadillac alongside a cluster of pinewood shacks hidden among swaying ironwood trees. "Kid, I own a piece of this establishment. It's been called Cap's Place since 'Prohibition' when Joe Kennedy's Scotch was smuggled from the Bahamas. Back in those days a lot of money was made selling illegal booze. Now, it's gambling. Next, it'll be drugs. My 'Family' will supply whatever people want for a large profit."

'Don' Lionetti leads Mike towards a rustic one story wood building on stilts in the sand. The structure's weathered exterior disguises its history. "Winston Churchill drank whiskey in this bar during the 'Big War'. Back then, the 'Family' worked with the F.B.I. to keep fascists and communists off the docks. Now, the bastards wiretap my phones."

Johnny opens the door and Mike lowers his head entering the bar room filled with historic photos covering the pine wood walls. A bartender with thick 'Elvis' sideburns and a black mustache pulls a bottle of Glenlivet 18 from the top shelf. He pours the premier single malt Scotch into a glass.

'Don' Lionetti takes the drink and puts a twenty dollar bill on the bar. "Thanks Joe, this is for you. My friend drinks Appleton rum. Leave the bottles and take a cigarette break."

The bartender pulls down a bottle of the preferred rum and picks up the Andrew Jackson. He exits the room as Johnny pours Mike a drink. "Kid, I wasn't born a 'made man'. I was a nobody from Newark when I joined a 'crew'."

Mike sips his drink as his mentor continues. "I earned and fought my way up from 'Soldier' to 'Capo'. Lucky for me, Santo Trafficante put me in Miami. My mother always said I was the chosen one. God rest her soul."

The Miami 'Don' makes the sign of the cross and nods skyward. "I cracked heads in my day like in 'The Godfather'."

Johnny raises his drink. "Here's to the women in our lives. I remember the first time I saw Mary outside Joe's Stone Crab on Miami Beach. She was so beautiful I had to ask her out. She turned me down because she was married. I found out she worked at Wolfie's deli and became a regular customer."

'Don' Lionetti swallows his drink and looks Mike in the eye while pouring another round. "I love Debbie like she's my own flesh and blood. What I'm about to tell you is a family secret. Don't talk with anyone about this."

Johnny thoughtfully pauses. "Mary can't have more children. Debbie's father forced her to have an abortion when she got pregnant a second time. I found out when Mary came to work one morning wearing dark sunglasses to hide her black eyes. I put a stop to that shit, then she divorced him and married me. No one hurts my girls while I'm alive."

The elderly patriarch's eyes moisten. "I hope Debbie gives me grandchildren someday. Whatever you do, don't hurt my little girl. Remember, what you did with her luggage in Jamaica will never happen again. Understood?"

Mike nods his head and raises his glass. "You have my word. Here's to you and your family."

Johnny laughs. "Yeah, that's everybody who owes me money, including you."

A small handsome well dressed man wearing a blue blazer and white chinos enters the bar. Johnny shakes the dapper dandy's hand and turns to Mike. "Kid, meet 'Jimmy the Jockey'. He rode trotters at Pompano Park for me in the 50's and 60's, now he's captain of my Hatteras. Jimmy, this is Mike Casey."

The diminutive jockey firmly shakes the big Flordian's hand. "Nice to meet you, Mike."

The stylishly dressed bantam barely stands five feet tall in his Stefano Ricci leather shoes. A Courvoisier XO Cognac on the rocks is handed to the newcomer. He swallows the drink in one gulp. "Johnny, we've been friends for nearly forty years. Ray is getting too violent and I don't need to take risks at this stage of my life. You know my granddaughter has cancer and the Jackson Memorial doctors don't give us much hope."

Johnny puts his arm around the jockey's shoulders and pours him another drink. "Jimmy, I've always had your back and you know I'll take care of your family. I want you to go fishing in the Bahamas and take a side trip to Jamaica."

The jockey sips his second drink and listens intently while 'Don' Lionetti continues. "The Hatteras has the latest Loran-C navigation equipment and we'll add disposable fuel bladders to extend the travel range for a nonstop round trip from the Turks and Caicos to Jamaica. Stay offshore near Ocho Rios and the Jamaicans will fill the hidden storage compartment with bales of marijuana. You'll fiberglass the compartment entry and return to the Bahamas without any record you were in Jamaican waters."

'Don' Lionetti turns to Mike. "The Kid will fill you in on the details."

The big Floridian leans close to the jockey. "The package will be on Dunn's River Beach at 18.4 degrees north and 77.2 degrees west on the new moon. Navigate to one mile offshore after sunset. Call 'Wild Jack' on C.B. channel 19 using 'Golden King' as your 'handle'. Look towards shore for flashlight signals, two short followed by one long. Keep calling on the radio every five minutes, until you see the flashlight. Return the same signal and lead them to you."

The Miami 'Don' slaps his friend's back. "Jimmy, I guarantee you twenty five thousand."

The jockey grins as he raises his glass. "I'm in."

Johnny hands Jimmy a brown lunch bag. "Here's ten large for expenses and remember to stay out of Cuban waters, they'll confiscate 'American Dreams' if they get a chance. There's a full moon tonight and if you head out in the next forty eight hours, you can be off the Jamaican coast by the next new moon."

John Lionetti thoughtfully pauses and turns to Mike Casey. "Don't visit Faraway Joe's or talk business on telephones. If you need to speak with me, have Debbie visit Mary to set up a meet. I've got a lot at risk and I expect a big pay day."

Mike hesitantly asks. "Can I call my uncle Pat to tell him to meet me at the New River compound?"

Johnny nods approval and raises his glass. "OK, one phone call from the payphone out back. Here's to a profitable voyage."

The trio exits the bar after the phone call. A metallic blue 1960 Corvette convertible is parked next to Johnny's red Cadillac. Jimmy shakes 'Don' Lionetti's hand. "Thanks, I'll have the boat ready to go in twenty four hours."

The jockey starts the Corvette 283 cubic inch V8 engine and heads west as a cream white full moon rises above the palm trees in the east. Johnny opens the car door. "Kid, fly to Jamaica tomorrow and get this deal going. Now, let's go home for dinner. Mary worries if I'm too late. Remember, no more phone calls."

Minutes later, Johnny leads Mike into his home filled with delicious Italian culinary aromas. Mary calls out from the kitchen. "John, I'm glad you're not late. Please open a bottle of Chianti. We're having garlic veal with sweet peppers and onions in marinara sauce. The antipasto and Caesar salad are on the table. Garlic bread just came out of the oven and I made your favorite dessert, almond cannolis."

Mother and daughter move effortlessly from kitchen to dining room finishing the evening meal preparations. Debbie adds Tiffany sterling silverware to a linen covered mahogany table set with fine Lenox China as Johnny pours Barone Ricasoli Chianti Classico into Waterford Crystal wine glasses.

Mary is a congenial hostess. "Michael, I'm so glad you and Debbie could join us for dinner. I don't get much time with my only child these days. I have to take her shopping on Worth Avenue to see her."

Debbie squirms in her seat. "Mom, don't play passive/aggressive games with me. It's not that I don't want to see you, I just want to be with Mike."

Johnny sighs. "I guess I paid for this college psychology lecture."

Mike interjects. "Mrs. L., this is the best homemade Italian meal I've ever eaten."

Debbie's mother smiles broadly. "Thank you Michael. Please call me Mary. You have to try my cannolis."

Johnny smiles. "Kid, have a Sambuca and espresso with a cannoli. I want to show you my Samurai sword collection."

Mike winks at his host with a smile. "I'd like to, but I'm meeting my uncle in a half hour.

The family patriarch nods his head. "OK, remember our agreement."

Mary hugs her daughter, while looking at Mike. "Michael, promise me you'll protect my little girl."

Debbie kisses her mother's cheek. "Don't worry, I love you."

The young couple quickly escapes out the front door into the Lincoln Town Car. Paul Simon sings 'Mother and Child Reunion' on the radio as they drive away.

———————◆———————

The New River boathouse is a thirty minute drive from Lighthouse Point. The compound is surrounded by a ten foot high wooden fence topped with razor wire and security cameras.

A gangly bearded 'Popeye' character wearing a sailor's cap, Levi's and a Navy t-shirt leans against the fence. He waves at the oncoming headlights as the steel entry gates open to allow the silver Lincoln into the compound.

Patrick Michael Casey doesn't have his nephew's height, but his fair skin and sandy reddish hair show they share similar genes. Mike stops the car and jumps out, embracing his uncle in a friendly bear hug. "The wandering Casey has returned to homeport. What do you think of this place?"

Uncle Pat laughs. "Johnny's sports book must be paying off big to set you up like this."

Mike unlocks the main house front door. "Uncle Pat, this is Johnny's daughter Debbie. Let's have a drink before we walk the compound. I brought tequila to make Margaritas."

The old sailor shakes Debbie's hand with a smile. "So, you're Johnny's daughter. Nice to meet you."

Mike interrupts. "My uncle taught me most of my bad habits. Watch out, he'll charm you out of your clothes."

Uncle Pat winks at Debbie with a sly smile. "My nephew exaggerates my persuasion powers. I'm just a sea dog looking for his next ship."

A short time later, the old sailor serves Jose Cuervo Margaritas while gulping tequila from the bottle. He turns to his nephew. "Mike, what's your plan for me?"

The big Floridian takes a swallow of his uncle's tequila concoction. "This deal is bigger than anything we've ever pulled off before. Jamaican ganja will be delivered here during the next month. You'll guard this compound '24/7'. No betting the ponies and watching the flamingos at Hialeah Park. You make a hundred a week expense money and three thousand when the boat comes in. All you do is keep an eye on things while banking your pension."

Mike turns to Debbie. "My uncle smokes and drinks from sunrise to sunset like every day is Saint Patrick's Day."

The weathered sailor laughs and coughs. "Thirty years in the Navy gives me the right to do what I want. No more officers giving me orders. Now, I drink breakfast Bloody Marys, Budweiser lunches and sunset Margaritas."

Mike gives his uncle a troubled look. "Do you still have those war nightmares?"

The old sailor's face becomes ashen as he swallows a large gulp of tequila. "I still see my 'Bunker Hill' shipmates burning in that Okinawa Kamikaze attack."

Uncle Pat puts the tequila bottle to his lips and then looks disappointedly into an empty bottle. "Mike, do you have more tequila?"

Mike reaches into the grocery bag, removes another fifth of Jose Cuervo Gold and hands the bottle to his uncle. "This is the last one for tonight."

Retired Petty Officer Casey quickly opens the liquor bottle and chugs a gulp.

"I've spent most of my life at sea trying to stay one step ahead of the Devil. I'll never settle down, until I'm in my grave."

The big Floridian chuckles. "I hope to pay off Ma's farm mortgage before the Devil gets you. She's earned it after cleaning bedpans for thirty years."

Debbie leaves the room and goes to the bathroom. Mike pulls his uncle close. "I've got a thousand kilos on the boat."

Uncle Pat gives his nephew a skeptical look.

"Don't overload. Too much weight will cause it to ride lower in the water and reduce range."

Mike shrugs his shoulders. "Don't worry, I've got everything under control."

Debbie returns and pulls her man towards the back door. "Baby. I want to check out the guest cottage."

The big Floridian laughs and picks up his girl. She squeals with delight as he carries her out the door. Uncle Pat grabs the Jose Cuervo Gold and quickly follows the loving couple.

The Casey patriarch hands Mike the half empty tequila bottle inside the guest cottage. "Nephew, you've done real good for yourself. Where does an old sea dog bunk?"

Mike smirks. "You sleep in the main house's first bedroom, where you can see the boathouse from the window. Remember to put a water bucket next to the bed. I don't want you to burn the place down."

Debbie opens the bedroom closet. "Baby, I'll put sheets on the bed and we can sleep here tonight."

Her lover shakes his head. "Not tonight, Babe. I'm flying to Jamaica tomorrow. You'll have to stay with your folks while I'm gone."

Debbie frowns. "Why can't I go with you?"

Mike smiles. "Johnny said so and he's the boss."

He kisses his lover's cheek and turns to his uncle. "Let's recon the compound."

The two men walk outside into the boatyard. Mike points at a cluster of iron wood and sea grape trees on the river. "Ray Jackson lives in a houseboat behind those trees and he has surveillance cameras everywhere. He's our guard dog."

The old sailor burps and draws heavily on a Lucky Strike cigarette. "I remember 'Little Ray' Jackson from the old days. He's always been a paranoid hombre. I'm glad Scott and Shaun are meeting you at the Miami Airport tomorrow."

Uncle Pat discards his cigarette. "I pray Saint Patrick protects us from Little Ray."

Mike pauses and stares at the razor wire topped fence surrounding them. "I'm counting on Johnny to keep that psychopath on a short leash, not Saint Patrick."

———◆———

The following day, Mike Casey and Jerry Siegel sit in a Miami International Airport bar drinking Bloody Marys and watching the WTVJ television news at noon. "Henry Kissinger's efforts to negotiate a ceasefire have failed and North Vietnamese troops continue to advance throughout South Vietnam. In sports news, the Major League Players Association has called a strike closing spring training camps on Saturday, April 1st."

Mike signals the bartender for another Bloody Mary. Jerry quickly swallows his drink and stands up. "Order a double for me. I have to piss."

The big Floridian adds pepper to his early afternoon breakfast drink, while talking to himself. "I wonder if Jack is going to the Ann Arbor 'Hash Bash' this weekend?"

An announcement comes over the airport address system. "Air Jamaica Flight 69 to Montego Bay begins boarding in forty five minutes."

Jerry returns as Mike finishes his drink. "My cousins should already be here."

Suddenly, two burly bearded men wearing plaid shirts and Levi's walk into the terminal, with a pair of blond ponytailed pixies following the striding giants.

Mike yells out. "Shaun." "Scott."

Jerry yelps. "Man, your cousins brought 'chicks'."

Mike growls. "No screwing around, You've got a job to do in Jamaica."

Jerry's shifty eyes turn away from his childhood friend's glaring stare as the approaching bearded giants yell. "Yee Ha! Cousin Mike is here."

The three burly cousins shake hands. "I'm glad you guys made it in time. We fly to Montego Bay in a half hour."

One of the blond pixies speaks up. "Scott promised us a first class trip to Jamaica."

Scott sheepishly shrugs his shoulders. "I met Kim last night at the Jacksonville Beach 'Foxy Lady' and asked her to come with me. She said we had to bring her twin sister. So here we are. Kim and Karol Terry meet my cousin Mike and his friend Jerry."

Mike studies the stunning twins and grins. "Scott, these beautiful ladies deserve a first class party in Jamaica."

———◦———

A pretty Air Jamaica stewardess opens the jet door to tropical paradise. "Welcome to Montego Bay. Please watch your step on the stairway down to the tarmac. Airport employees will direct you into the terminal."

The Casey clan charges into the steamy humid air, joining a slow shuffling line of visitors passing through Jamaican immigration and customs. Jerry wipes the sweat from his forehead and moans. "Damn, it's hot."

Mike is the first through customs and puts on Ray-Ban Aviator sunglasses as he walks over to a taxi stand under a blooming mango tree. He approaches a group of card playing drivers seeking relief from the late afternoon sun. "Man, I need taxis to Ocho Rios."

The drivers look up from their card game to see the Casey entourage and smile. "No problem. Three taxis, one way to Ocho Rios fifty U.S. dollars each."

The big Floridian frowns and reaches into his blue jeans. "Give me two taxis to Mammee Bay for thirty U.S. dollars each."

Two taxi drivers reluctantly shrug their shoulders. "Yeah, man."

Mike pays the first driver and turns to his entourage. "I rented one taxi for you guys. Squeeze together and go to the Jamaican Hilton at Mammee Bay. I'll meet you at the hotel bar for sunset cocktails and dinner after I take care of business."

He peels six fifty dollar bills from his cash roll and winks at the Terry twins.

"Scott, here's three hundred. Get a couple of first class rooms for these pretty ladies."

Jerry gets in the second taxi backseat and lights a Kool cigarette. "Let's get some beers for the road."

Mike frowns when he smells the tobacco smoke. "No smoking butts in my taxi."

He turns to the driver. "Man, take us to the Arawak Hotel and along the way pick up some cold Red Stripes."

Beads of sweat on the taxi driver's mahogany skin shine in the afternoon sun when he puts the taxi in gear and begins driving east towards Ocho Rios.

"No problem, man. Daniel, give you good service."

Late afternoon sunlight filters through swaying palm trees as colorful hibiscus flowers dance in gentle Caribbean breezes. Anthony Ascot dreams of the money he'll make selling Jamaican ganja to America while he relaxes in front of his Arawak Hotel apartment.

Tony's hearty laugh echoes throughout the hotel courtyard when he sees Mike Casey's huge frame exit a taxi in front of him. "My friend has returned with a deposit for me."

Mike opens his shirt, pulls an elastic money belt from his waist and hands it to Tony. "Yes, I did and my boat arrives on the next new moon."

Tony smiles and retreats into his hotel bedroom. "Come inside and meet Joy Brown. She'll serve you champagne while I do my accounting."

Jerry follows Mike into Tony's well appointed apartment decorated with Caribbean masks and mahogany furniture. A pretty teenage girl with coffee cream skin and golden sienna hair pours Clicquot champagne into crystal glasses. Jerry takes a glass of the sparkling wine and quickly swallows it.

Mike smiles at the attractive hostess as he lifts his glass of champagne. "Joy, how did you get your beautiful green eyes?"

The pretty Jamaican shyly smiles. "My father was a British Naval officer and my mother is Jamaican."

Tony returns to the living room with a wide smile. "Michael, we're now business partners. My men will press one thousand kilos into fifty five, forty pound bales. The ganja will be at Dunn's River beach on the new moon. My cousin's glass bottom boat will deliver the package to your boat offshore. What are the C.B. 'handles' and flashlight signals?"

Mike nods his head. "My boat captain will be a mile from the beach at sunset. He'll call on C.B. channel 19 every five minutes, 'Golden King calling Wild Jack'. When your cousin hears the call, launch the package due north. The flashlight signal is two short flashes, followed by a long one. My captain will use the same signal to lead him."

Tony raises his champagne glass. "To our enterprise."

The wiry Jamaican pulls a plastic baggie from his pocket and hands it to Mike. "Try some of my 'gum'. It will give you good dreams tonight."

Mike hands the baggie to Jerry. He breaks off a large piece of hashish and swallows it with another glass of sparkling wine. "I'll need a lot more of this stuff."

Tony winks at Mike and nods toward Joy. "Jerry, enjoy my champagne and let my lady dance for you in the bedroom, while I speak with Michael."

Jerry swallows another piece of hashish and follows Joy into the next room. Tony turns to Mike with a serious look and lowers his voice. "I only have a Winchester shotgun and a Smith & Wesson .38 revolver. I need automatic weapons to guard our business. Jamaica will change when the ganja money flows and our police will no longer be unarmed marionettes blowing whistles in the wind."

Mike nods his head. "I'll send automatic pistols and rifles on the next run."

Joy returns to the living room and smiles at Mike. "Your friend fell asleep. Would you like some more champagne?"

Mike grins as Joy refills his glass. "Thanks, I love that fragrance you're wearing."

The pretty Jamaican teenager smiles. "Tony bought Chanel #5 for my birthday."

Jerry suddenly staggers into the room and struggles to stand. Mike steadies his intoxicated friend and leads him towards the exit. "The ganja hash and champagne kicked your ass. Let's hook up with my cousins at the Hilton."

Mike turns to his host as Jerry stumbles out the door. "Tony, we're going to make a lot of money together. I'll see you tomorrow."

The big Floridian follows his friend staggering down a jungle path towards the Jamaican Hilton. Jerry mumbles to Mike. "I'll need some women to play with if I'm going to be stuck on this island."

Mike shakes his head. "Keep your shit together. We've got to get all fifty five bales on Johnny's boat in two weeks. You'll have time to play with the ladies later."

Mike leads Jerry into the Hilton Hotel bar, just as his cousins and the Terry twins enter the mirrored mahogany room filled with vases of colorful tropical flowers and ceiling fans lazily circulating the humid air. A tall ebony bartender with a pearl white smile stands ready to take their orders.

The big Floridian calls out. "Bartender, Appleton rum punch and menus for everyone. Let's start with some 'jerk' chicken and conch salads."

Mike pulls himself close to his younger cousins after the bartender delivers drinks and the twins go to the ladies toilet. "We're a 'go' for delivery on the next full moon in Florida."

Scott chugs his rum punch and yells. "Yee Ha."

Shaun raises his glass. "I can't wait to make some real money, but I don't understand why you wanted me and Scott to come here."

Mike shrewdly smiles. "I want you to know how to get back to Ocho Rios, if necessary."

Jerry finishes his drink and removes the Jamaican hashish from his pocket. Scott notices him tearing apart the gummy treasure and snatches it, quickly swallowing a large piece.

Mike jokes with his cousin as the Terry twins return. "Scott, you're going to sleep well tonight. Tony's 'gum' is one hundred percent ganja resin."

Jerry and Scott are semi-conscious with 'Cheshire Cat' grins a short time later as Kim and Karol study the jukebox music choices.

Mike smiles at the pretty twins. "Ladies, play something you like."

Kim downs her drink and winks at Mike. "Here's looking at you big guy. Give me a buck for the jukebox and I'll dance for you."

The Rolling Stones' hit 'Let's Spend the Night Together' explodes from the rock & roll music machine. Kim's hips gyrate to the rhythm while she pulls Mike onto the moonlit dance floor and whispers. "I want you tonight."

At the other side of the bar, Shaun stands up and points to a corner booth. "They both passed out. Karol and I are going to my room. I'll see you tomorrow."

The jukebox plays Elvis Presley's 'Burning Love' when Kim gently massages Mike's thigh and says. "I'm glad we're alone, now we can make love under the full moon."

The big Floridian stands up and lifts the pony tailed pixie high in the air. "Babe, you're a fox."

Mike turns to the bartender. "Me and the little lady will have another rum punch for the road and give me the check."

Kim kisses Mike's ear and whispers. "I want you now."

Mike pulls cash from his Levi's and looks over at Scott and Jerry. "Hold on, beautiful. I have to cover the tab. Bartender, here's an extra twenty for you to help my two friends into their hotel room."

'One Way Out' plays on the jukebox when Mike carries Kim out of the bar into the moonlit gardenia scented night.

———◆———

Late the next morning, Mike wakes to the sound of water running in the bathroom. Kim's taut naked physique glistens in the morning sunlight when she exits the shower. She hears her lover wake while drying herself. "Good morning. Did you enjoy yourself last night? You were a wild man."

The big Floridian moans and buries his face in a pillow. "What have I done?"

Kim confidently strides out of the bathroom to the edge of the bed. "Don't worry baby. No one will ever know about last night. I'm not telling anyone and I want you to come back to me whenever you want."

A sudden knock on the door and Tony's voice interrupts their conversation. "Michael, we need to talk."

Kim quickly grabs her clothes and retreats to the bathroom, while Mike pulls on his Levi's and opens the door. Blinding sunlight and Tony's smiling face greet the big Floridian's burning eyes. He falls back on the bed and curls into a fetal position. "Come in. Please excuse my condition. Last night's rum punch knocked me out."

Minutes later, Kim struts out of the bathroom wearing a tight pink t-shirt and short shorts. She cheerfully smiles at Tony. "Good morning."

Tony returns her smile. "Good morning, sister. You made the women very jealous last night when your passionate pleasure awakened them from their dreams."

Kim winks at Mike and passes him a slip of paper. "This stud wouldn't stop. Here's my phone number. Call me and I'll cook you dinner anytime."

The pretty pixie jumps up and walks past Tony into the sunlight. "See you later, alligators."

Mike looks at the note and puts his head back on the pillow with a moan. "She gave me a Miami phone number. I thought she was from Jacksonville."

Tony laughs. "You were thinking with your little head last night. She's a hot chick, but you better focus on our business. What should I do with your friend, Jerry?"

Mike nods his head. "Give him a room and food at the Arawak with a couple ounces of ganja. That should keep him out of trouble until he closes the hold and flies back to Miami with the timetable. I'll cover all his expenses when I come back."

Unexpectedly, Auntie Claire's voice is heard with a loud knock on the hotel room door. "Anthony, your mother is in the hospital with lung cancer and you don't visit her. My dear sister worked on her hands and knees to feed you. Now, she desperately needs five hundred dollars for her treatment. God will punish you, if you don't help your sick mother."

Mike stays in the shadows when Tony opens the door as Auntie Claire continues her tirade. "Why are you living with that girl? You should be home with your wife and children. Anthony, give up these wicked ways and return to your family."

Tony grimaces and pulls cash from his pants pocket. "Here's a thousand dollars. Pay the hospital bill and keep the rest for yourself. My mother never saw that much money in her miserable life."

Auntie Claire squares her broad shoulders and accepts the handful of cash. She counts out five hundred dollars and pushes the remaining money into her nephew's hands. "Anthony, I won't accept your blood money. I've taken what is needed to pay your poor mother's medical bills. May God save your soul."

Tony closes the door when his aunt turns and walks away.

Mike rolls over and thinks to himself...'Johnny will have Little Ray feed me to the sharks alive, if he finds out about Kim.'

———◆———

At the same time in Florida, an unmarked police car is on stakeout parked in the shade of a banyan tree near the New River. Ft. Lauderdale vice squad Lieutenant Dan Brady sweats through his seer sucker suit as he gulps black coffee while eating Krispy Kreme donut.

He gives his partner, Sergeant Richard Guerrette a concerned look. "Dick, I heard Pat Casey got out of the Navy and is back in town. He's been a smuggler all his life and I've got a hunch the Caseys are up to something."

HASH BASH HITCHHIKING

Van Morrison sings 'Into the Mystic' on an eight track stereo as I look out the car window at gusting winds and spring showers shaking budding tree limbs. Louise and I are no longer lovers, but we're still friends. I haven't heard from Jill, except for a cryptic postcard about her moving again and calling me when she got a telephone in her new apartment.

Mike Casey hasn't called me either. I phoned his Miami number and the operator told me it was disconnected. Mike's involved with serious people and Johnny Lionetti isn't a man to mess with. I hope his Jamaican ganja deal is still on. Boston is 'bone dry' and I haven't smoked a joint in two weeks.

Yesterday, I cashed my G.I. Bill check and decided to hitchhike to Michigan. I'm hoping to see Jill, even though I don't know where she lives. My search will begin at her old Ann Arbor address. I must be crazy to hitchhike this time of year in pouring rain and near freezing temperatures.

It's Easter break and class is out for two weeks. I'm rolling through Ohio in an orange Plymouth Barracuda driven by a blue eyed beauty with golden curls. She rescued me from the cold roadside earlier this morning.

My driver turns to me and impishly smiles. "Jack, do you want to smoke some super 'Thai Stick'? My boyfriend sends me weed from Thailand."

I'm amazed that this pretty girl has Asian pot. "Molly, I love to smoke a joint. How does your boyfriend smuggle Thai 'herb' into the states?"

My driver's bright blue eyes sparkle with delight. "He flies B-52's from Thailand to Guam and sends me stereo equipment from Andersen Air Base. I'm expecting another stereo next month. You'll have to visit me at Michigan State when it comes in."

Molly smiles at me and ejects the eight track tape and turns on the radio. "Let's see if we can pick up Cleveland FM stations."

Crosby, Stills and Nash play 'Marrakesh Express' on the radio when Molly lights a joint and passes it to me. A couple of deep tokes of Thai smoke sends me into space as the roadside landscape accelerates into a colorful blur.

I haven't been 'stoned' since I was in Vermont months ago. Euphoric energy surges through me as blue gray smoke escapes my mouth. "This reefer is wicked outrageous. Do you have any for sale?"

A wide grin appears on Molly's freckled face. "Jack, I get fifty bucks for half ounce lids at college. I like you, so I'll sell you a full ounce for fifty. Open the glove compartment. There's four ounces in a cigar box. Pick one and put the cash in the box."

Unable to resist a golden opportunity, I pull my hundred and fifty two dollar life savings from my jeans pocket while thinking... 'A fifty dollar investment can turn a profit and leave plenty of stash for me.'

I count five ten dollar bills. "Ten, twenty, thirty, forty and fifty. Molly, you're a sweetheart."

Later, cold wind gusts and rain showers scatter students in every direction when the orange Barracuda arrives at the University of Michigan Student Union.

Molly turns the car radio volume down. "Jack, do you want to start looking for your girlfriend here?"

I shrug my shoulders, recognizing the difficult task facing me. "Yeah, Jill said her old apartment is near the Student Union. She could be anywhere, but this is the place to start. Molly, you're an angel. Thanks for the reefer and ride. Can I give you some gas money?"

The beautiful 'Little Orphan Annie' smiles and passes me a slip of paper, with a gentle kiss on my cheek. "No way on the gas money. My dad's a Getty Oil vice-president and I have a company credit card. Here's my phone number in case you don't find your girlfriend."

I grab my backpack and jump out of the car. "Molly, thanks again."

"Be good, Jack."

The Chrysler drives away and disappears from sight as I think to myself...

'Tomorrow is April Fool's Day and I'm eight hundred miles from home without a clue of where I'm going.'

Rays of sunlight suddenly burst through dissipating storm clouds creating a rainbow that lifts my spirits. Without warning, a fox terrier's incisors bite into my Levi's. The dog's owner cries out. "Lucille, come here!"

I shake my leg free from the fierce little canine and see Jill's golden hair shining in the late afternoon sun. She doesn't recognize me with a beard and ponytail, until her distressed look becomes a wide smile. "Jack, is that you? It is you."

We embrace and passionately kiss. The terrier charges forward again, viciously growling. Jill quickly intercedes and picks up the wild eyed animal. "Lucille, this is Jack."

My buddy smiles at me. "Lucille will trust you, after she gets to know you better. I can't believe my little dog found you."

Jill gives me a sheepish look. "I'm sorry for not calling, but I had to move and lost your number. I'm staying with friends and no one's supposed to know where I'm living."

I'm confused. "Buddy, are you OK?"

Jill shrugs her shoulders, with a tentative smile. "Don't worry, I'll figure out my problems. I'm glad you're here in time for dinner. Laurie is making pasta and I have salad fixings in the fridge. By the way, Debbie sent me a letter. She and Mike moved to Ft. Lauderdale."

I nod. "I hope Mike is still doing the Jamaican ganja deal. Did she give you a phone number?"

Jill shakes head. "No and when I called her parent's telephone, the operator said the number had been changed to an unlisted number."

Jim Morrison and the Doors sing 'Light My Fire' on a nearby stereo as we stroll towards Jill's place along streets lined with budding azalea and dogwood trees. Multi-colored daffodils and tulips burst from the thawing earth along our path as cannabis smoke intermingles with pizza aromas in cool spring air. Lucille spies a pack of dogs and squirms from her master's arms and joins the hunt.

Night shadows overtake twilight pastels in the western sky. Noses to the ground, Lucille leads the dog pack in search of squirrels. Jill apprehensively looks over her shoulder and surveys our surroundings when the pack of mutts run up a flight of stairs into a two story house. My buddy takes my hand. "This is where I live now. Come meet the 'tribe'."

A radio plays Marvin Gaye singing 'What's Going On?' when we enter a kitchen filled with the distinct aroma of garlic and onions simmering in tomato sauce. Ordered chaos prevails under the direction of a tiny raven haired female choreographer. She lowers large shaded eye glasses to allow her violet eyes to scrutinize me.

Jill makes introductions. "Laurie Sugar, meet Jack Collins. I hope he'll spend the night with me."

The little woman in charge of the kitchen gives me a command. "Jack, call me Sugar. Our community rules are simple. Work and expenses are shared equally, that includes housework. We've got cooks, so you're a dishwasher tonight."

A smiling handsome face with a charcoal pony tail appears from the kitchen. He firmly shakes my hand and hands me five dollars. "Howdy, Gray Tucker. Nice to meet you. Would you mind going to the store for Chianti?"

I smile. "No problem. I detect a Boston accent."

Gray laughs. "Guilty as charged. Born in Wellesley and still a Red Sox fan."

Sugar quickly intercedes. "Gray, get back in the kitchen and cook the pasta already. Jill, you know where the liquor store is. Get the beer and wine while I make the salad."

Jill pulls me out the door with Lucille and the other hounds. Minutes later we enter the liquor store while the pack of dogs run through the neighborhood in search of trash dumpsters. "Jack, I'll get two bottles of Banfi Chianti. You choose the beer and get a couple packs of Kools for me."

I grab two six packs of Miller High Life and order the cigarettes. The clerk takes two five dollar bills and fills paper grocery bags with the beverages. Jill hands me a dollar and quickly snags the cigarettes as I pick up the loose change with the bags of beer and wine. She hurriedly opens a pack of Kools and lights a menthol cigarette, inhaling the mentholated tobacco smoke into her lungs.

I give my buddy a concerned look. "Didn't you stop smoking butts in Jamaica?"

She shrugs her shoulders. "I started again to calm my nerves."

Lucille suddenly jumps into Jill's arms attempting to avoid a Doberman pinscher's fangs. My buddy kicks the larger animal on its way. "Bad dog! Get out of here!"

Fifteen minutes later, Lucille leads the dog pack up the stairs into 'Ann Arbor House'. Jill and I follow the stray mutts into a busy kitchen when Gray opens the oven door. "Hot stuff, sourdough garlic bread is done. Jill, did you study for our English Lit test?"

Jill nods her head. "I don't have to study. I've been ready for this test since Junior High. Back then, I was reading Yeats and T. S. Eliot. Now, it's Camus and Sarte."

Gray continues. "You have to read Hunter Thompson's latest 'Fear and Loathing' article in Rolling Stone."

Sugar interrupts. "Let's stay focused on dinner. All of us have to study tonight. Jill, please finish making the salad. I'm cooking more sauce for Jack. Gray, how long before the garlic bread cools?"

The breadmaker looks at his Timex watch "About five minutes. How about the pasta sauce?"

Sugar stirs the bubbling red marinara sauce. "Nearly ready."

I open a bottle of 'High Life' and hand it to Gray. "It's Miller time."

Lucille barks at footsteps coming up the stairs. Jill commands. "Quiet Lucille. It's Marc and Gwen coming back from school."

Two large ebony Afro's blow in the wind as they enter the kitchen. Maise and Blue scarves show school colors as the newcomers remove their parka coats. Smiling mahogany faces, with bright chestnut eyes emerge from cold weather clothing.

Jill takes my arm. "Jack, meet my friends, Marc Humphries and Gwen Stevens."

Marc shakes my hand firmly and winks. "Nice to meet you. Call me 'Hump'."

Gwen gives me a hug. "Jack, don't pay attention to him."

Gray looks up from the pasta. "Marc, how did you do on your Asian history exam?"

Hump shrugs. "I only missed two questions on Indian Sikhs and Central Asian Turks."

Sugar announces "Dinner is ready."

We all sit at a large oak dining table set for six. I open the wine as Gray cuts the bread, releasing a fresh baked sourdough aroma. "Let's eat."

Gwen reaches into her backpack and removes a small plastic electronic device. "Gray, check this out. My dad bought me a Hewlett Packard HP-35 scientific calculator. Now, I won't need a slide rule to do my math calculations."

Gray admires the machine. "Wow. Where did your father get it and what does it cost? I want one."

Gwen smiles with pride. "Dad's a Ford design engineer. He paid the company four hundred dollars. He says American homes will have personal computers like the one on Apollo 16 in the next twenty years."

Marc laughs. "Four hundred bucks buys a good used car these days."

After dinner, Jill takes charge of the cleanup as the other roommates hit the books. "Jack, let's clear the table. I'll wash dishes, you and Marc can dry. I wish we had some smoke for the Hash Bash tomorrow."

I smile. "Good news, I scored an ounce of Thai weed on the way here."

Jill looks at me with disbelief. "How does Thai pot get to America?"

I chuckle. "My ride said her boyfriend ships it from Thailand on B-52's bombing Vietnam."

Hump shakes his head. "The word around Detroit is Asian heroin comes in on military planes. A Yale professor named Alfred McCoy published evidence of CIA trading weapons for drugs with Chiang Kai-Shek's renegade army in Thailand."

Gwen returns to the kitchen and interjects. "Marc, enough conspiracy politics. If you want me to type your Economics thesis this weekend, we have to start soon. I can only make two mistakes per page and I have a calculus exam Monday. So, finish up."

Jill turns to me. "I was told to watch out for undercover 'narcs' at the Hash Bash tomorrow. They'll 'bust' you for dealing."

Suddenly, loud dog howls are heard in the kitchen pantry. Jill rushes towards the noise and finds her feisty terrier aggressively winning dinner scraps. Lucille sinks her teeth into the neck of the biggest mutt as I think to myself... 'It's not the size of the dog in a fight, it's the size of the fight in the dog.'

The canine combatants are quickly separated and Lucille leads the pack out the back door. Jill turns to Hump and me. "I'll clean up after the dogs. Marc, go study with Gwen. Buddy, you can take a shower in the second floor bathroom. I lit candles and put fresh towels on the bed in my room at the top of the stairs."

I'm excited by Jill's instructions as I enter her inner sanctum with Kama Sutra love on my mind. Lavender scented candles flicker in the moonlight shining through her bedroom window. 'Stairway to Heaven' plays on a nearby radio when I toss my travel bag on the bedroom floor and pull off my shirt.

A large deadbolt lock on Jill's bedroom door intrigues me as I remove my blue jeans and cover my naked ass with a towel. I then walk across the hall into the bathroom shower where hot water and soap cleanse my body and revitalize my spirit.

I step from the shower and dry myself in front of a steamed mirror, then return through the hallway into the candle lit bedroom. Jill rests on a Futon mattress dressed in a red silk Kimono with her eyes closed listening to 'Let It Be' on her stereo.

My buddy's eyes open when my bath towel drops to the floor and exposes my naked physique. A terrified look appears on her face. She buries her head in a pillow and pulls herself into a fetal position. "No." "No."

I sit on the Futon. "Jill, what's wrong?"

Tear filled bloodshot eyes stare back at me. "Buddy, I took a Valium for a terrible headache. Let's sleep tonight and talk tomorrow?"

Jill pulls me closer and shuts her eyes. "Tomorrow will be a better day."

I think to myself… 'Maybe I made a mistake coming to Ann Arbor. Jill isn't the same person I met in Jamaica. She's so depressed.'

"Some 'Thai Stick' will help you relax and sleep."

I light a joint and hand it to Jill. She takes a long deep 'toke' and gradually relaxes in my arms. I gently caress her as she drifts to sleep while The Rolling Stones play 'Paint it Black' on the radio.

Early the next morning, a gentle kiss and soft caress wakes me. My half open eyes attempt to focus on Jill dressed in running clothes standing over the bed. "Jack, thanks for spending the night. I'll be back in an hour or two. There's oatmeal with raisins and honey for breakfast in the kitchen."

Jill leaves the room as I drift into a dream...

...Storm clouds encompass a full moon. Three naked girls wildly whirl around a blazing fire with their faces flickering in the flames. Jane and Susie are hand in hand with Jill dancing like Sufi Dervishes. Shadows and flames fade into darkness as a hot coffee aroma carries me into daylight...

I wake up and go to the bathroom. The books beside Jill's bed catch my eye as I put on my blue jeans. 'One Flew Over the Cuckoo's Nest' and 'The Feminine Mystique' make me wonder if I should go back to Boston.

The aroma of bread baking in the oven draws me towards the kitchen. I walk down the steps into the mid morning sunlight and pour myself a cup of black coffee. Unexpectedly, Lucille leads the dog pack into the room, followed by Jill. "Jack, did you have breakfast?"

I shake my head. "Got up late. I'm having coffee and toast. How was your walk?"

Jill sits next to me. "OK. I feel trapped in my room at night and I have to get outside when the sun comes up. Thank God for Sugar and her friends in this house."

Laurie enters the room while reading the Detroit Free Press. "M.C. Escher died this week. His three dimensional drawings, especially 'Drawing Hands' were inspirational."

Gray Tucker joins us in the kitchen.

"That's my favorite too. Art creates itself, with mathematical precision."

Jill smiles thoughtfully. "Escher's 'Ascending and Descending' captures the limitations of human visual perception."

Gray looks at the kitchen clock with concern. "Sugar, we don't want to be late for our biology study group."

The studious couple hurriedly pack their books and head out the door. "See you guys later."

Marc Humphries joins us in the kitchen and picks up the Detroit newspaper. "Can you believe astronauts driving a car on the moon again? What next? A golf course."

I smile. "American astronauts flying to the moon on Wernher von Braun's rockets is better than destroying the world with hydrogen bombs."

I chuckle. "Remember Slim Pickens riding the H bomb in 'Dr. Strangelove'?"

Hump laughs. "Yeah, Peter Sellers and George Scott were brilliant in that movie. Kubrick's latest movie 'A Clockwork Orange' is playing in town tonight."

Gwen appears. "Marc, we have to study at the library. Let's get going."

Unexpectedly the front door opens as Marc follows Gwen out of the room. Bill White springs 'cat like' into the kitchen. "April Fool's, let's party."

Jill looks stunned. "Bill, how did you find me?"

The longhaired bearded gnome pulls his childhood friend into a dance.

"I know people in the Registrar's office who gave me your new address. I couldn't go to Ann Arbor's first Hash Bash without you."

Bill prances into the living room and carefully places a vinyl disc on the stereo turntable. T-Bone Walker's 'Stormy Monday' comes to life. "Check out the latest Allman Brothers' album 'At Fillmore East'. It was recorded live before Duane crashed his Harley."

Bill turns to me. "Jack, is there any good news about your friend's ganja boat?"

I shrug my shoulders. "I haven't heard anything in months."

A bright twinkle comes to Bill's eyes as he pulls a Ziplock baggie from his backpack. "Don't worry kids, the doctor has a cure for the blues. I brought 'Orange Sunshine' from 'The Brotherhood of Eternal Love'. Bear Owsley taught them how to make primo LSD."

Jill gives me a hesitant look. "I wanted to try 'acid' in Vermont, but I'm not sure about doing any now. I've heard stories about bad 'trips'."

Bill attempts to reassure his childhood friend. "LSD clears your mind of negative thoughts. The C.I.A. used it as a truth drug and Timothy Leary says, you can't lie when you're 'tripping'."

I remember my Army LSD experiences and think to myself... 'I enjoyed 'tripping', even though some of my friends 'freaked out'. Maybe, a psychedelic adventure could help Jill return to being the woman she was in Jamaica.' "Bill, I'm in with you and Timothy Leary."

The bearded musician's smile becomes a wide grin as he turns his attention to his childhood friend. "Jill, let's drink 'electric' Kool-Aid and go to the Hash Bash."

Jill manages a timid smile. "OK, I'm in. But, I have to put a collar on Lucille. The cops tried to bust her as a stray the last time we were in the park."

Bill goes into the kitchen. He mixes three LSD tabs into a pitcher of grape Kool-Aid and then empties the remaining Ziplock baggie contents into the pitcher. "I added a couple broken pieces. It'll make our 'trips' more intense."

Jill retrieves the offending neck wear, with a tiny bell attached to it. Her dog rolls on the ground struggling for freedom. "Lucille, you have to wear a collar."

She finally attaches the neck band and lets her pet run off ringing the bell.

Bill fills Dixie cups with psychedelic Kool-Aid. "A toast to our adventure. I'm your guiding 'Wizard' into the psychedelic world of 'OZ'. Go with the flow and don't get uptight. You'll sense energy in everything around you when you're 'peaking'. Normally, LSD wears off within eight hours."

Jill looks over at me with a timid smile. "I'm counting on you guys to take care of me."

She drinks her cup of psychedelic liquid, while I hold her hand firmly and gulp down my electric grape drink. "You're safe with Bill and me."

The front door opens. Gray and Sugar enter the room in animated conversation. "Gray, I know you'll be a nuclear engineer, but you should read John Hersey's book 'Hiroshima'. Nuclear power isn't a solution to the world energy shortage. Radioactive waste is toxic for hundreds of years and a nuclear reactor meltdown is too great a risk."

Gray answers. "Humans have engineered solutions from the beginning of civilization."

Bill interrupts and raises the pitcher. "Want some 'electric' Kool-Aid?"

Sugar shakes her head. "No time, I've got to study for exams."

Gray smiles. "Me too. You guys have a good 'trip'."

Powerful energy pulsates throughout my body and I can't stop smiling fifteen minutes after we finish the last of the 'electric' Kool-Aid. My surroundings continuously change color and form as I digest my psychedelic drink.

Rose magenta rainbows tint the afternoon sunlight when time stands still and the universe pulsates within me. Perceptions repeatedly transform in the changing light and shadows. Rainbow color trails follow Bill White as he prances and dances to The Moody Blues' 'Legend of a Mind'.

Jill's smile looks like the Cheshire Cat in 'Alice in Wonderland' when she joins Bill White whirling around the room. They take my hand and pull me into their 'Dervish' dance.

Our psychedelic wizard's face and head transforms into a multi-colored Jello bust, expanding and contracting with his every word. "Let's walk to the 'Hash Bash' on the 'Yellow Brick Road'."

Bill leads us outside into the bright afternoon sunshine filled with lilac scented breezes. 'Lucy in the Sky with Diamonds' plays on a nearby transistor radio as we hop, skip and jump past budding apple trees along a tulip bordered path to the Hash Bash.

The park entrance is guarded by huge oak and elm tree sentinels. Clouds of cannabis smoke drift above a crowd of people playing drums and guitars surrounded by uniformed police circling like blue uniformed wolves in a grotesque Fellini movie.

Later as the sun disappears and shadows darken the evening sky, Bill leads us into a liquor store. Two bottles of Korbel sparkling wine and a pack of Kools will do fine. Lucille rolls on the ground attempting to dislodge her collar as we exit the store.

Nearby, a movie theater neon light illuminates a sign headline... 'A Clockwork Orange', 6 p.m. and 9 p.m. shows tonight.

Bill stares at the movie billboard. "That Malcolm McDowell poster blows my mind. I saw '2001: A Space Odyssey' on 'blotter acid' and the trip was far out."

Jill releases her dog and smiles. "The photography in '2001' was fantastic. Let's go to the movies. Lucille knows her way home."

I hold Jill's hand when we enter the darkened theater. The show begins when Moog synthesizers fill the room with Beethoven overtures. On screen, lead characterAlex Delarge is in the mood for violence. His 'Droogs' want to hurt someone and a night of mayhem is planned when he gives the audience a menacing look.

"You can't have a society, with everybody behaving in my manner of the night."

Jill gasps and hides her face when the 'Droogs' bludgeon a homeless man unconscious and attack a helpless family in their home. The mistress of the house valiantly defends herself, before succumbing to a savage gang rape.

My buddy suddenly jumps up and runs for the exit. "Oh my God! I can't watch this."

I follow her out of the theater and quickly catch up. "Are you alright?"

Jill shakes her head. "That movie is too violent for me. I want to go home."

My buddy shrivers in the cool night breeze as we quickly walk towards Ann Arbor House. She charges up the stairs into her room and joins her sleeping pet dog on the bed. "My Lucille came home."

The little terrier licks her master's face as I join them on the bed. "Jill, please tell me what's going on."

Her blood shot eyes survey me closely. "I'm afraid to tell you what happened. Even my family doesn't know. I feel defenseless knowing the bastard could come back."

I shake my head. "I don't understand. Who could come back?"

Jill trembles in my arms as she tells her story. "I moved into a new apartment last month and didn't change the locks. Two weeks ago, I studied late for my midterms at the library and walked home alone. Someone knocked me out when I opened the front door. I woke up naked with my arms tied behind my back and a rag in my mouth."

She pauses trying to hold back tears. "I tried to pull free, but couldn't move as his sweaty body crawled on top of me. I'll never forget his words, when he pressed a knife to my neck. 'Bitch, I'm going to fuck you like they fucked me in jail.'."

I'm stunned beyond words while Jill sobs and quivers between words as she continues. "He was a white kid, who used to live in the apartment with his girlfriend. She got him busted for pot and he was raped in jail. The bastard shoved a knife in my mouth and threatened to kill me, if I called the cops."

I angrily howl. "I'll kill the son of a bitch!"

My buddy groans and shakes her head. "Killing him won't help me. Thank God the school health clinic gave me penicillin and valium. The doctor said I was lucky to be taking birth control pills."

Jill leans on my shoulder. "I was fortunate to meet Sugar at the clinic and she took me in."

Flickering candles light the room as the LSD slowly fades from our bodies. "Jill, let's open a bottle of Korbel and smoke a joint to mellow out. Why don't you put on some music and I'll give you a foot massage."

My buddy reluctantly nods her head. "I don't think I can ever listen to Beethoven again. 'A Clockwork Orange' brought back vivid memories of my rape. I'm still afraid to tell my family and friends. Dad might have another heart attack and mother would drink more."

Emotionally overwhelmed and exhausted, Jill and I huddle together. She swallows a blue Valium tablet with a sip of wine as I pass her the joint and begin the foot massage.

I think to myself... 'Jill needs my help, but I'm supposed to go back to college and finish the semester.'

The Valium and pot slowly take effect on my buddy. "Jack, please stay with me tonight."

I give Jill a firm hug. "Don't worry. I'm here for you."

James Taylor sings 'You've got a Friend' on the radio as Jill falls asleep and I drift into a dream...

...Blue uniformed wolves circle me in the night shadows with their yellow eyes and blood stained teeth shining in the moonlight...

The following morning, Lucille barks from under the blanket covers. I wake with Jill in my arms. Our bloodshot eyes open to see the unlocked bedroom door swing open. Sugar leads Gray and Bill into the room.

Laurie sits on the bed and tenderly embraces my buddy. "Bill told us about last night. Lonny Higgins is an OB/GYN friend of mine. She opened a women's health clinic and commune in Denver last month. I sent her a letter about you and she wrote back, saying you should visit as soon as possible."

Jill gives me a desperate look. "Jack, will you go with me? We can take 'incompletes' in our classes and I've got a hundred dollars. We'll hitchhike to Denver and get jobs."

I think to myself... 'Hitchhiking to the Rocky Mountains with Jill sounds like fun.'

"OK, I can take my exams in September. Let's hitch to California after we make money in Colorado."

A tentative look appears on Bill White's bearded face. "I wish I could drive you guys to Denver, but I'm contracted to sell instruments on the 'Bluegrass Circuit' this week."

Bill takes Jill's hand. "Khalil Gibran wrote 'The strongest souls are seared with scars of suffering...' I know you'll find happiness and let's hook up in Vermont this summer."

A short time later, my buddy and I pack up for our cross country journey while listening to Douglas Edwards report the CBS Morning News on the radio...

"On Easter Sunday, North Vietnamese troops overran South Vietnamese provincial capital Quang Tri. President Nixon authorized B-52s to carpet bomb the advancing army as over a million refugees flee the communist juggernaut. Alabama Governor George Wallace leads the 'Old South' Democratic

Presidential primaries and his 'states rights' campaign is gaining support with Midwest white middle class voters."

Later, the afternoon sun warms the entrance of Interstate Highway 94 as I stand on the side of the road holding a 'Denver' cardboard sign. I have eighty bucks in my pocket after covering last night's wine and movie tickets. Luckily, Rudy rented my Hull House room for the summer and my G.I. Bill checks continue through next semester.

My buddy looks like an angel dressed in a pale blue Parka jacket sitting on a backpack with Lucille at her feet, writing postcards announcing her 'drop out' plans to family and friends. "Jack, I'm sending your Hull address on a postcard to Debbie at her parent's house."

A canary yellow Corvette C3 convertible stops in front of us. The driver looks like James Dean reincarnated, when he smiles and rolls down the window. "Get in. I'm driving to Gary Indiana. I'll take you to I-80 and you can head to Colorado from there."

We eagerly pack our bags behind the passenger seat and Jill sits on my lap with Lucille quivering in her arms. The Beatles' 'Long and Winding Road' plays on the car radio as the Corvette 454 V8 roars west into the setting sun.

COLORADO
COMMUNE HIGH

The morning sun tints the Rocky Mountains rust red. A Kenworth tractor trailer belches black exhaust smoke skyward while discharging passengers on Pearl Street at a road sign, 'Denver the Mile High City'.

Jill Jensen releases her pet dog for a run. She reaches into her pocket book and anxiously unzips various compartments. Suddenly, her voice reverberates throughout the derelict neighborhood. "Damn it! I need a smoke and my money is in Ann Arbor. Jack, do you have any cash?"

It's been a difficult trip. A skunk sprayed Jill's pet in Iowa and I had to rent a motel room for two nights. We attempted to rid the putrid odor by repeatedly washing the little dog with tomato juice. Luckily, a kind truck driver gave us a ride in spite of the lingering smell.

This hitchhiking journey cost more than expected and the truck driver's breakfast drained the last of my cash. Jill's hundred dollars was supposed to carry us until we found jobs in Denver. I shake my head in frustration. "I'm down to a 'Buck' and some coins."

Jill gives me an exasperated look. "I need a cigarette bad. There's a 7-11 on the corner. I can get a pack of Kools there."

I hand over my last 'George Washington'. "OK, get me a black coffee."

Lucille rummages around dumpsters as Jill runs into the store. Dr. Higgins' health clinic is supposed to be nearby, but their telephone hasn't been installed. Pawn shops and liquor stores line the streets of this run down neighborhood where sturdy brown men stand in the shadows waiting for pickup trucks to take them to nearby farms.

Jill returns from the store, with a cigarette hanging from her mouth. "One dollar only buys two cups of coffee and a pack of smokes. Here's the eighteen cents change. We need jobs."

She notices her pet dog digging in a pile of rotting garbage at the side of the store. "Lucille, you'll get worms. Come!"

The terrier reluctantly returns to her master's side. Jill sips hot coffee and hurriedly lights a second cigarette. She gives me an apprehensive smile. "I hope the clinic is around here."

I give Jill a quizzical look. "You said you knew the address."

She hesitates. "Sugar said Pearl and Elk near the South Platte River. I can't remember if she said street or avenue. I wish their telephone was connected."

I shake my head. "Shit, we're broke, homeless and no idea of where we're going."

Tears well up in Jill's eyes. "I'm sorry. I'm not good with directions."

Sensing her vulnerability, I pull my buddy close. "Don't worry, we'll find the clinic."

Buffalo Springfield's 'For What It's Worth' plays on a nearby radio: "Stop children. What's that sound?..."

Latino workers scatter in every direction when a 'Black and White' police car appears out of the shadows and comes to a stop in front of us.

Guns drawn, two beefy crew-cut blond Denver police officers jump from their cruiser. "What are you hippies doing in this neighborhood? I bet you got dope in your backpack."

Lucille growls menacingly from Jill's arms. Both officers point their Smith & Wesson .38 caliber service revolvers at the small terrier. "Keep that dog under control."

The baggie of pot in my backpack worries me when the policemen turn their weapons towards me. "Hands against the wall and spread your legs."

I take the position and hear one officer say. "Partner, what do you think about a hippie wearing an Army jacket? We ought to take this punk into the desert and shave his head."

The other policeman responds.

"Yeah, this punk is disrespecting our boys in Vietnam wearing that jacket."

Jill cries out while clutching her growling terrier. "Why hassle us? We didn't do anything wrong. We're lost. You should help us."

I turn around and face the police. "The last time my head was shaved, I was in Army basic training wearing this jacket."

Both policemen give me disbelieving looks. "Bullshit!"

I stare back. "I've got a DD 214 in my backpack."

The bigger policeman nods at me. "Go ahead, show us your paperwork."

I cautiously remove the military record from my backpack and hand it to the officer. He unfolds the typed document and slowly reads it. "Son of a bitch, he got an Honorable Discharge with an official government seal to prove it. I guess you're a veteran."

They shrug their shoulders as my Army discharge paperwork is returned to me. "OK, what are you doing in this neighborhood?"

Jill hurriedly responds. "We're looking for Dr. Higgins' women's health clinic."

The policemen holster their service revolvers and retreat to their cruiser. The short officer points north on Pearl St. "Dr. Higgins opened a clinic at Elk Place last month. You're lucky the sun is up. I wouldn't go out in this neighborhood at night."

I smile with relief when the police cruiser drives away. "Maybe, my two years in the 'Green Machine' finally paid dividends. The cops could have busted us, if they searched my backpack."

We walk around the corner to Elk Place to see a pothole filled street, lined with rusting old cars and decaying buildings.

Jill turns to me with a confused look. "I'll go crazy, if we don't find the clinic soon."

Unexpectedly, Lucille barks and charges up the stairs of a run down two story Spanish stucco building. The little dog runs to the entrance. Jill quickly follows. "Lucille. Come!"

A voice from inside the house. "Welcome little friend. You must be Lucille."

A tall handsome, square jawed man with a cheerful smile appears at the front door. His blue eyes twinkle with an impish grin as Lucille runs up to him. "Dave Higgins here and you must be Jill and Jack. I've heard good things about you both from Gray and Sugar. We've been expecting you guys."

Lucille continues barking at the kitchen door. It abruptly opens. Sugar jumps out. "Surprise! I found your money after you left, so Gray and I drove here for Easter break."

Handshakes and hugs all around. Wow our luck turned 180 degrees, from broke and homeless to a clean bed and dinner with friends.

Suddenly, two small giggling children appear and run circles around us. Dave chuckles and points at the kids. "That's Jessica and David, my wild offspring. Lonny's out buying groceries and you arrived in time for lunch."

Fifteen minutes later, a Checker Marathon station wagon pulls up in front of the house. A whirlwind of energy explodes from the bright yellow car. Dr. Higgins' long brown hair blows in the wind as she takes command.

"David, please carry groceries to the kitchen."

Sparkling hazel eyes and an engaging smile dominate the doctor's attractive face. She embraces Jill, with a nod towards me. "Call me Lonny. I'm here to help you."

Lonny leads us through the half century old house into the kitchen. Paint and plaster peel from walls as ceiling fans circulate the building's stale musty air. David Higgins pours cold lemonade into ice filled glasses while the groceries are being stored and Lucille's dog bowl is filled. Laurie hands Jill her missing hundred dollars and the two girlfriends embrace. "Sugar, thanks so much. You're an angel."

Dr. Higgins gives Jill a welcoming smile. "Dave will show you where to sleep. We made up a bedroom on the second floor. I hope you like waterbeds, there's a queen size in the room. Also, you have a private bath with clean towels in the closet."

Our hostess pauses with a serious look. "The commune rules are simple. All chores are shared. You can work on the house or at the women's shelter to pay your share of expenses. We have a zero tolerance for violence, including verbal abuse. Hard drugs and liquor are prohibited. Smoking is only allowed on the roof deck."

Lonny smiles. "Now, clean up and we'll eat a midday meal together."

Dave leads us to our second floor bedroom. Lonny's voice can be heard in the kitchen. "I'll stir fry sesame tofu with vegetables and spices. Gray, please put the apple walnut muffins in the oven and I'll take out the bread to cool in ten minutes. Sugar, could you make a pitcher of iced mint tea?"

Fresh baked bread and muffin aromas permeate the house as Jill and I walk through a living room filled with photos on our way back to the kitchen. A photo of Dave, with Pope John XXIII and Muhammad Ali catches my eye. "Were you in the Rome Olympics?"

Our host chuckles. "Yes, Gray's brother and I rowed in the '60' Olympics. We trained on Lake Albano near the Pope's summer residence 'Castel Gandolfo'. Ali, then known as Cassius Clay, had just won the light heavyweight Gold medal. He and I had an audience with Pope John on the same day."

Dr. Higgins removes fresh baked bread from the oven and passes it to Jill. "I'm fond of Pope John because he rescued Jews from the Nazis during World War II when he was a parish priest. Most of my European family were murdered during the Holocaust. Fortunately my father accepted a Tufts University professorship in 1939 and moved to Boston where I was born."

Lonny gives her husband a tender look. "My life changed when I met Dave."

Dave wistfully smiles. "We met at a Charles River 4th of July Boston Pops concert and we've been together ever since."

Jill nods her head. "What brought you guys to Denver?"

Dr. Higgins hands Jill a large paperback book. "Good friends of mine wrote, 'Our Bodies, Ourselves'. It's a comprehensive health journal, written by women for women. I decided to open a women's health clinic when I finished my 'OB/GYN Residency at Tufts University."

Lonny takes Dave's hand. "Last year, we got a Colorado state grant to start a low-income health clinic and Dave created a 501 c 3 charity for abused women. We're helping women take control of their lives. After lunch, Dave will orient you while I work at the clinic this afternoon. I'll show you our operation tomorrow morning."

I ask. "We want to pay our share of house expenses. Do you know where the state employment office is? Is there a public bus service?"

Dave nods his head. "Sure, the Colorado employment office is nearby and you can help paint the house while you wait for paychecks. We have a second car you can use to get to work. It's a Plymouth Valiant push button automatic."

Jill hugs Lonny. "Thanks so much for treating us like family."

———◆———

Later that night, the smokers gather on the rooftop deck under a star filled sky. Jill fires up a Kool cigarette and hands the pack to Sugar. I light a joint and pass it to Gray. He takes a quick toke and stares into distant galaxies while passing Jill the joint. "Wow, we're looking back to the beginning of time. The light you see has traveled millions of years."

Sugar inhales the joint and looks up into the night sky. "I'm reading Carlos Castaneda's 'Teachings of Don Juan: A Yaqui Way of Knowledge'. Castaneda lived with a Shaman who claimed his spirit traveled the Universe on peyote."

Gray smiles. "Aldous Huxley said mescaline enhanced his appreciation of Mozart's music and Botticelli's paintings."

Jill turns to Gray. "Tell me about Dave Higgins. Sugar said you went to high school together and your families came to America with the Pilgrims."

Gray smiles. "It's true the Tucker and Higgins families came to Boston in the 1600's. I met Dave at Milton Academy while I was a freshman and he was a senior with my brother. Dave Higgins is a true 'Renaissance Man'. He's an attorney, Olympic athlete and he once sailed across the Atlantic using only a compass and the stars for navigation."

Sugar takes Jill's hand. "You're in good hands with Dave and Lonny. They live every day to the fullest. They even plan to run in the Honolulu Marathon.

Early the next morning at the Denver Women's Health Clinic, we approach a crowd of weary mothers forlornly staring into space while patiently waiting for entry into the clinic. Their children's cries echo in the cool morning air as the clinic doors open.

Dr. Higgins frowns when Jill lights a cigarette. "My father died of lung cancer at sixty. He smoked two packs of Chesterfields every day. Cigarettes will kill you."

Sugar observes the huddled families. "These women look hopelessly destitute. My life in New York is so different. How can they survive such poverty?"

Lonny nods her head. "Day to day. Most of my patients are Mexican agricultural worker families. They're shadow workers without 'Green Cards'. Cesar Chavez and the United Farm Workers haven't organized Colorado's migrant laborers yet."

Sugar turns to Jill. "Gray and I have to start back to Ann Arbor to finish the semester."

Jill hugs Laurie. "Sugar, you're a wonderful friend. Jack and I plan to stay in Denver, until we make enough money to go to California."

———— ◆ ————

The following day, Jill and I sit in the Colorado State Employment Office lobby. Jill's number is finally called after waiting nearly two hours in the cigarette smoke filled room. My number is called minutes later.

A disheveled crew cut employment counselor seems disinterested in me, until he sees my Army DD 214. "Son, I can get you a great paying job at Hughes Industries if you cut your hair and shave your beard. They pay the highest wages in Colorado and veterans have priority for jobs. You get ten bucks an hour and double for overtime. The plant runs three shifts seven days a week. You can start tomorrow and make six hundred a week."

We shake hands. "Sign me up. I'll cut my hair and shave. My highest monthly pay in the Army wasn't half that."

I exit the office with the job address and see Jill walking ahead of me towards our blue Plymouth in the parking lot. She lights a cigarette when we get in the car. "Jack, the only job for me was sewing clothes 'piece work'. The other jobs for women were typists, housekeeping or waitressing for tips. Did you get a job?"

A smile comes to my face. "I did. I have to cut my hair and borrow Dave's Gillette razor to shave my beard. Starting tomorrow, I'm building bombs for the Air Force."

The local news comes on the radio when I start the car. "Denver Police advise residents to lock their homes, due to recent rapes. Citizens are asked to report suspicious activities to local police."

Jill looks over at me. "I'm glad we're living with Dave and Lonny. I feel safe with them."

Later that evening, Jill and Lonny prepare green chili rellenos tortillas for dinner as Dave places 'Jamming with Edward' on the stereo turntable. "I heard Stevie Wonder is opening for 'The Rolling Stones' at the Denver Coliseum in June."

Jill has a wistful faraway look. "I remember seeing 'Little Stevie Wonder' in Detroit."

A telephone rings unexpectedly. Dave walks into the living room. "Some good news, 'Ma Bell' finally installed the telephone. I'll answer our first call."

Dave picks up the telephone. "Hello. Dr. Higgins is here. An emergency! She's on her way."

———◆———

Three days later, Jill and I arrive home from work to a warm greeting from Lucille and a hot water shower while Dave prepares homemade pizza for dinner in the kitchen. "Lonny will be late. She delivered another baby today after twenty hours of labor."

David Higgins chuckles to himself. "The greatest experience in my life was being in the delivery room when my kids were born. You guys get cleaned up. Supper is nearly ready."

The CBS Evening News with Walter Cronkite is on television. "China is sending the American people two Giant Pandas as gifts. 1971's Time magazine 'Man of the Year', Richard Nixon is being considered for this year's award. Jack Nicklaus won his fourth Masters Tournament yesterday. The 44th Academy Awards will be held at the Dorothy Chandler Pavilion in Los Angeles tonight. And that's the way it is, Monday April 10, 1972."

Jill and I finish showering and return to a kitchen filled with fresh baked pizza aromas. Dave is setting the table with his children running around the room.

I pull two cold Coors beer bottles from the refrigerator and hand one to Jill. "Dave, do you want a 'cold one'?"

He shakes his head. "Maybe later."

I respond, "I've got some Thai smoke too."

Dave smiles. "No thanks. A true athlete never smokes. How's work going? Jill, is your boss still harassing you?"

Jill sips her beer. "The bastard keeps trying to get me alone and when I resist he rejects my work. I'd quit if we didn't need the money."

Our host frowns. " I wish I could help, but subcontractors aren't employees under current labor law. Jack, what about you? How's working double shifts for the 'Military-Industrial Complex' going?"

I shrug my shoulders with a gulp of beer. "I'm bored working sixty hours a week putting washers and nuts on screws, but my weekly pay should be six hundred bucks after taxes. That's the most money I've ever made."

Tonight's chef pulls the homemade pizza pie from the oven. "Kids, watch out. The hot cheese will burn your mouth."

Dave looks at me. "The Bruins should win the Stanley Cup this year, if Bobby Orr stays healthy."

I raise my beer glass. "I'll drink to that."

Dave turns to Jill. "Do you want to watch the Oscars? 'The French Connection' is favored to win Best Picture."

Jill smiles. "Sure, I hope Jane Fonda wins best actress for 'Klute'."

Later, the Academy Awards show begins when host Jack Lemmon introduces John Gavin and Ann Margret to present the evening's first award for 'best cinematography'.

Dave smirks. "Ann Margret is nominated for best supporting actress in Mike Nichols' 'Carnal Knowledge'. Georgia recently declared the R rated movie obscene even though X-rated 'Midnight Cowboy' won Best Picture, three years ago."

Jill frowns. "Dustin Hoffman's 'Ratso' in 'Midnight Cowboy' was so tragic and completely different from his role in 'The Graduate'."

I smile. "Ben and Elaine's church escape scene at the end of 'The Graduate' was wicked good. I went to the 'Drive-In' a dozen times to see that movie when I was in high school. My friends were hot for Mrs. Robinson, but I fell for Katherine Ross."

Jill rests in my arms with Lucille on her lap when Isaac Hayes' 'Theme from Shaft' wins Best Original Song. A short time later, Dr. Higgins returns from the clinic and enters the room when Jack Nicholson announces this year's best picture award. "The winner is 'The French Connection'."

Dave smiles. "Gene Hackman deserved Best Actor as Popeye Doyle, the relentless cop hunting drug smugglers."

Jill and I sit together on the rooftop deck the following weekend. A crescent moon accentuates the star filled 'mile high' Colorado sky. American astronauts are fulfilling Jules Verne's dream of traveling to the moon tonight. I cashed my inaugural paycheck this week and purchased a small brass hash pipe to conserve my Thai weed.

Jill counts our cash and smiles. "We've saved over five hundred dollars and we'll easily save another thousand in the next two weeks."

My buddy frowns. "I want to quit my job. The boss is molesting migrant girls without green cards. Dave suggested the workers form a union and I'm hoping my friend, Sarah White Dove will do it. She doesn't need a green card because she's a Navajo native born in America."

Jill gives me a pensive look. "Sarah says peyote can purge the negative energy from my soul. Her family and tribe are going to a secret spiritual gathering in the Grand Canyon on the next full moon. She'll prepare peyote buttons for us to take at her house trailer while she's in Arizona. Will you do mescaline with me?"

I embrace my buddy. "Sure, I want to make love with you again."

———◦———

Twelve days later, I'm sleeping soundly with Lucille at my feet while B.B. King plays 'The Thrill is Gone' on the radio.

Nearby in the bathroom, Jill stares out the window at a nearly full moon and whispers to her reflection in the mirror...

"My mother drowned her dreams in a gin bottle. Lonny says, 'Life is like a game of chess. A queen moves in any direction across the board and a pawn is confined to one space. Queen or pawn, it's my choice to fear and hate.' I hope taking peyote will free me to love again."

Later the sun is setting late Friday afternoon when we return from work. Lucille dances about and jumps into Jill's arms as we enter our bedroom to see a large L.L. Bean box on our bed. I open the attached note.

'Jill & Jack,

Thanks for painting the house. The pastel colors are fantastic. Please do us a favor. Pick up the kids at the clinic daycare and take them to Dave's office. I have a breech birth to deal with and it could take all night. Enjoy your new travel gear.

Love & Hugs, Lonny & Dave'

Jill quickly opens the box. "Dave and Lonny gave us a tent, two backpacks and sleeping bags. They're so generous, they've helped us save over fifteen hundred dollars."

On our drive to Dave's Legal Aid office, we take the Higgins children to Baskin Robbins where Lucille entertains them, dancing for ice cream treats.

A short time later Jill enters the Legal Aid office and gives Dave a big hug. "Thanks for the gifts. You guys have been wonderful to us."

The attorney graciously smiles. "You're very welcome. We love the house paint job. I hear you're visiting friends this weekend."

Jill turns for the door. "Yes, see you on Sunday."

———— ◆ ————

My excitement rises in anticipation of our peyote adventure as we drive into the prairie towards a setting gold red sun. Lightning filled clouds appear on the distant horizon when Willie Nelson sings 'Help Me Make It Through the Night' on the radio.

Jill fills the brass pipe with a tiny pinch of pot and fires it up. I steer the Plymouth Valiant into a golden sunset as she holds the pipe to my lips. "Sarah joined the American Indian Movement. She believes Native Americans have the right to live on their ancestral land. Her tribe took over a trailer park, next to an abandoned World War II Army base and set up a commune."

I exhale the Thai smoke. "That's cool, maybe they can rebuild the communal society the European colonists destroyed."

My attention shifts as I watch the sun set behind the mountains. "We should have enough cash to hitchhike to California soon."

Jill suddenly points at a side road exit. "There's the trailer park."

Lucille shakes with excitement as we drive down a dirt trail towards a collection of run down mobile homes. An eerie silence greets us when we exit our car in the empty trailer village. Jill points towards a white and brown single wide mobile home on blocks. "That's Sarah's place. The key is under the mat."

Ceremonial Navajo bird masks adorn the walls with portraits of family and tribe inside the modest home. I'm drawn to a photo of Apache chief Geronimo standing with a Springfield rifle as my Buddy picks up a welcome note from the kitchen table.

'Jill,

Drink the peyote herbal tea from the Thermos. You and Jack will feel queasy and vomit before the peyote kicks in. Enjoy your experience. Eat any food in the refrigerator. Peace & Hugs, Sarah'

A half hour later, Jill and I sit on the trailer steps while the peyote concoction gurgles in our stomachs. Without warning, vomit spews from Jill's mouth. Minutes later, I groan with displeasure when I convulse a similar sour bile explosion. Unexpectedly, rainbow colors sparkle in the moonlight as energy waves surge through my body.

Lightning flashes explode in the night sky. A powerful thunder clap follows seconds later. Lucille fearfully retreats into the trailer when heavy rain starts to fall from the sky.

Jill jumps up and pulls off her t-shirt in one motion. She drops her jeans and runs naked into the darkness. I take off my clothes and follow after her shadowy silhouette dancing among fiery electric flashes.

Finally, I catch her. We passionately kiss and come together on the rain soaked prairie.

Later, our mutual carnal bliss overwhelms me as Jill rests in my arms in a loving afterglow while my thoughts become hallucinations...

...Multi-colored Navajo masks dance around a raging fire. A chanting Shaman rises in the flames. 'All who seek the spirit world come join me.' Steel swords and silver crosses appear in the moonlight as robed clergy and blood stained Spanish Conquistadors lead women and children on a trail of tears in search of gold. The fire fades to hot ash and smoke as the Shaman reappears with a foreboding warning. 'Prepare to meet the demon within everyone.'...

———————•———————

The full moon shines brightly on this clear April night over Ft. Lauderdale, Florida. Michael Casey's mind is filled with anxiety as he leads Uncle Pat towards the New River boathouse. Tonight could be the first step towards Mike's lifelong dream to become a millionaire.

Uncle Pat pulls a pint of Jack Daniel's from his jacket and takes a long gulp. He then passes the bottle to his nephew, with an apprehensive look. "I hope the Jockey doesn't run out of fuel."

Mike takes two gulps of whiskey and opens the boat house door. Little Ray sits in the corner with his back to the wall, cleaning and loading a MAC-10 machine gun. He scowls. "Where the fuck is the jockey? The inlet is only a half hour away and he should have been here two hours ago. I'll kill the son of a bitch, if he loses the package!"

Uncle Pat's ears perk up when he recognizes an approaching outboard motor and looks out the window. He sees a dinghy towing a Hatteras Sportfish up the canal. "Jimmy's here. I'll get Shaun and Scott."

———◆———

Back in Colorado early Saturday morning, a large raven pecks at Sarah's mobile home trailer window. "Tap. Tap."

Inside the mobile home, my eyes open to the black bird knocking on the window as I smell fried bacon and hear my buddy humming Beethoven in the kitchen. A contented feeling of bliss surges through me. "Jill, the bacon smells great. How did you sleep?"

A blissfull chortle comes from the kitchen. "I slept great. How do you like your eggs?"

My quick response. "Anyway you cook them with lots of bacon."

Jill's naked breasts glisten in the morning light as she carries a breakfast tray into the bedroom. Lucille follows the food as my lover joins me on the bed. "I made cheese spinach scrambled eggs, bacon and toast. I used vegetables and herbs from Sarah's organic garden. Maybe, we can start a herb garden in Vermont."

The Temptations sing Smokey Robinson's 'My Girl', while Lucille pirouettes on her hind legs for bacon. Jill smiles. "I'm looking forward to Sarah's Cinco de Mayo party."

———◆———

A week later, Lucille leads Jill and me into the kitchen as Dave stirs sizzling beef with vegetables and herbs in a wok on the stove. "Dinner is nearly ready."

Lonny puts fresh bread on the table. "Jill, did your friend unionize the clothing workers?"

Jill frowns. "The boss threatened to fire anyone who talks about starting a union."

An urgent bulletin interrupts the local radio program. "The 'Night Rapist' struck again in downtown Denver last night. Citizens are advised to keep their homes locked at all times."

Dave looks over at me. "Remember when the 'Boston Strangler' hysteria was really crazy until Albert DeSalvo was captured."

The telephone rings and interrupts Dave. Lonny answers. "Hello, Dr. Higgins."

The color drains from the doctor's face. "I'm on my way."

Lonny puts down the phone. "Dave, watch the kids. There's an emergency at the clinic. Jill, please come with me. I might need your help tonight."

Fear comes over Jill's face as she takes my hand. Lonny reaches for her other hand. "Don't worry, you're strong enough to help me now."

———●———

Later at the clinic, volunteer medical staff circle a bandaged woman lying on a blood stained bed. Her severely bruised face surrounds swollen 'black and blue' eyes. The victim moans in pain as skilled medical professionals hurriedly attempt to save her life.

Dr. Higgins sizes up the critical situation. "The patient has multiple rib and facial fractures, including a broken jaw. Once she's stabilized, we'll transfer her to the hospital for emergency treatment and x-rays. Collect tissue samples from her fingernails and swab her vagina for seamen. We'll store it for testing and someday, DNA will identify the rapist. Move quickly and get her to the hospital ASAP."

Just before midnight, a waning full moon is high in the sky over the Higgins' residence.

Jill shakes my shoulder to wake me and whispers in my ear. "Jack! There's someone hiding in the bushes near the front porch."

My heart 'double-times' when I raise my head to look out the window and see a shadowy form moving in the shrubbery below.

I whisper. "It could be the 'Night Rapist'. We should call the police."

Dave's voice startles us from the next bedroom. "I called. They should've been here by now."

Suddenly, a police car spotlight illuminates the front of the house. Red and blue lights flash, with a loud siren wail. The shadowy form in the bushes escapes into the darkness when two crew cut policemen exit the patrol car and charge into the shrubbery. The frustrated officers ring the doorbell, after failing to capture their quarry.

Dave unlocks and opens the front door. A visibly upset police man asks. "Did you call about a prowler on your property?"

Dave nods his head. "Yes officer, someone was lurking in the bushes."

The young policeman shakes his head in disgust. "He's not there now. Why didn't you guys grab him and kick the shit out of him?"

Lonny intercedes as the policemen bitterly frown and withdraw to their squad car. "Officer, we're not vigilantes. This neighborhood needs police protection."

———◆———

Lucille joins Jill and me on the roof an hour later. My buddy's eyes betray her inner panic. "I don't feel safe here anymore and I can't stay another night. Let's donate our last paychecks to the clinic and hitchhike to California. I'll write a note to Lonny and Dave."

I nod my head. "Yeah, Dave's a lawyer and he'll know how to cash the checks. Let's pack up and hit the road at sunrise."

———◆———

The morning sun slowly rises over the horizon at day break. Jill and I stand at the side of the road facing west-bound traffic holding a cardboard sign 'California'. Lucille jumps up when a lime green Ford Econoline van comes to a halt in front of us. The side door opens and the little dog jumps in. Jill quickly follows her pet.

The smiling driver wearing a Stetson cowboy hat and his petite raven haired companion warmly greet us. "We saw your dog and had to stop. I'm Jeannie and this is Rich. We're the Armstrongs"

Jill smiles as her pet climbs on Jeannie's lap. "Thanks. That's Lucille. I'm Jill Jensen and this is Jack Collins."

I close the van side door as Paul Harvey concludes his radio broadcast. "America lost a great leader in the war against communism, when F.B.I. Director J. Edgar Hoover died."

The van driver shifts the Ford into gear and changes the radio channel. Crosby, Stills, Nash and Young sing Joni Mitchell's 'Woodstock' as we drive towards the Rocky Mountains.

CALIFORNIA DREAMERS DANCING IN THE DESERT

A 'peace medallion' hangs from the rearview mirror in a Ford van driving us into the Rocky Mountains. Lucille sits on the raven haired copilot's lap riding shotgun. I take hold of Jill Jensen's hand in appreciation of our good luck as the little dog stretches her nose out the window to sniff fresh mountain air.

The driver's braided sandy brown ponytail extends from under a Stetson hat decorated with eagle feathers. "Howdy Jack and Jill, Rich and Jeannie Armstrong here. We're taking Route 40 through Berthoud Pass to spend the night at Steamboat Springs, then we'll drive west to California. You're welcome to join us. Can you guys chip in for gas?"

Jill smiles and nods her head. "Sure, we'll keep the tank filled."

I'm enthusiastic about soaking in a hot spring on our way to San Francisco. Berthoud Pass is one of the highest mountain passes in North America and freezing temperatures are possible in the glacier covered Rocky Mountains this time of year.

Rich Armstrong steers his van through switchback turns as we rise two miles above sea level at our apex, then Rich's overloaded vehicle rapidly descends in another series of harrowing turns.

Colorado's beautiful scenery overwhelms me while I watch Rich desperately struggle to maintain control of his van. He drives in second gear and repeatedly presses the brake pedal as we hurtle down the mountain.

A bright orange sun sets in a cloudless blue sky when we arrive at a Steamboat Springs 'hippie' campground. Jill and I hurriedly unpack the L.L. Bean tent and erect our transient home while Rich and Jeannie gather firewood.

Rich pulls a cooler from the van. "We caught trout yesterday and kept it on dry ice. We'll fry it with brown rice and veggies for dinner. Let's get cooking. I want to soak in the hot springs after dinner."

The evening meal is prepared and promptly consumed around the fireplace as a myriad of star constellations appear in the twilight. Jill and I clean the dishes before stripping away our clothes and jumping into the steaming mineral water pools.

Lucille hunts rodents in the nearby woods as the fire fades to glowing ash. Jeannie and Rich are setting up their van for sleeping, when Rich asks. "Jack, do you hunt or fish?"

I shake my head. "I'm more city than country. I went pig hunting in Arkansas when I was in the Army. I didn't shoot anything, but my partner killed a boar with a Mossberg 500 twelve gauge. Rich, what do you hunt with?"

Rich Armstrong reaches into his van and removes a long barrel shotgun. "I've got a twelve gauge Remington 870. It's great for hunting and personal defense. Even a little woman like Jeannie can fire it. I'd live off the land, if the government would let me. Jack, have you ever eaten bear or rattlesnake?"

I chuckle "No, but I did try alligator when I was in Florida."

Jeannie's brown eyes twinkle as she laughs. "I hear gator tastes like chicken. Rich makes a rabbit pie that tastes like a chicken pot pie. Where are you guys from?"

Jill grins contentedly in the steaming mineral water. "Jack's from Boston and I'm from Kalamazoo. We're taking a break from college and hitchhiking to San Francisco for the summer. How about you guys, what's your story?"

Jeannie smiles. "We're both from California. Rich makes and sells silver turquoise jewelry on the art show circuit from Santa Fe to San Francisco. We met at the Sausalito Art Festival last year."

Rich puts a piece of 'Red Man' chewing tobacco in his mouth and gives Jeannie a hug. "The first time I saw this little woman, I knew she was the only one for me. I took her out for a steak dinner and we've been together ever since."

Jeannie smiles. "I grew up bouncing around foster homes and was lucky to meet my 'knight in shining armor'. Rich made me feel safe for the first time in my life."

Richard Armstrong smiles at his wife. "I never would have met Jeannie, if my family hadn't lost the ranch. My family came to California during the 1848 'Gold Rush' and took up ranching north of San Diego. Ten years ago, Dad died of lung cancer and my mother got Multiple Sclerosis. I quit high school and took care of her by making jewelry. After she passed away, I had to sell the ranch to pay off the mortgages for the medical bills."

Jeannie points into the darkness. "Don't you love the night sky high in the mountains. There's so many stars to see. Over there, the Big Dipper points to the North Star."

Rich reaches into the van and removes a leather satchel. He pulls out a Bugler tobacco can. "I've got some rolling tobacco and papers."

Jeannie laughs. "Richard, I'm sure our guests want a 'Rocky Mountain High'. Breakout our Michoacan and let's smoke a joint."

Rich chuckles and quickly rolls a joint. He and Jeannie strip off their clothes and join us in the warm mineral water. Jill notices a tattoo on Jeannie's thigh. "Who did your 'Woodstock Peace Dove' ink?"

Jeannie smiles. "Lyle Tuttle in San Francisco."

I reach into my backpack and pull out the brass pipe with my weed. "I've got some Thai smoke to share with you guys."

Rich's eyes sparkle with delight when I hand him the pipe. "Wow, 'reefer' from the other side of the world. Cannabis has been cultivated for thousands of years in Asia and it was a primary herbal medicine in America until the 1930's. George Washington and many of the 'Founding Fathers' cultivated hemp and smoked 'Indica Flowers'."

The big Californian takes a deep 'toke' and resumes his historical monologue. "Congress made cannabis illegal when it passed the 'Marihuana Tax Act' in 1937. The Supreme Court declared the tax unconstitutional in '69' and Nixon classified 'marijuana' as a 'Schedule 1 Drug' with heroin to bust anti-war protesters."

I shake my head. "Weed shouldn't be illegal. Alcohol 'Prohibition' failed during the '20's' and hopefully pot will be legal someday like booze is."

Rich exhales a cloud of blue gray smoke and smiles. "Man, this is righteous herb."

I laugh. "Dude, you're the first real cowboy I've ever met."

Rich's large body heaves with laughter. "My family is part of the 'Wild West' story. George Armstrong Custer is a distant cousin of mine."

Jill lights the Michoacan joint. "All I know about Custer is he died at 'Little Bighorn' when 'Sitting Bull' and the Sioux defeated the Seventh Cavalry."

Rich nods his head. "My distant cousin wasn't anything like me. I'm more like the Lakota Sioux. I'd rather roam the wild countryside than live in a city. You have to be self reliant to survive in God's country. Cities are filled with dependent people, desperate for government solutions to their problems."

Lucille barks in the distance. Jill cries out. "Come Lucille!"

Jeannie takes a toke and passes the joint to Jill. "Why did you name your dog Lucille?"

Jill smiles. "She was a stray and adopted me at my last house. One night, I was listening to B.B King and she started howling, so I named her after his guitar."

Rich reaches into his leather satchel. "I've got my 'Blues Harp'. I'll play Sonny Boy Williamson blues anytime you want."

Jill nods. "Lucille will sing or I should say 'howl', if you play your harmonica. Are you guys going into San Francisco? We're hoping to score some weed in Haight Ashbury."

Jeannie frowns and shakes her head. "The San Francisco psychedelic 60's ended at Altamont. It was supposed to be 'Woodstock West' with The Grateful Dead, Jefferson Airplane and The Rolling Stones on stage together. Instead, the Hells Angels killed a guy."

I nod my head. "Yeah, the movie 'Gimme Shelter' showed the murder."

Jeannie smiles at her husband. "I moved to Haight Ashbury after my foster parent raped me. I was addicted to heroin when I met Rich. He introduced me to Lao Tzu. Now, I'm off dope and traveling the 'path of least resistance'."

Tears form in Jill's eyes as she reaches over to Jeannie and tenderly hugs her. "I'm recovering from a rape, too. I'm glad we met, even if we don't go to San Francisco. Either way, I've always wanted to ride the Pacific Coast Highway."

Jeannie takes Jill's hand. "Be patient, you'll find peace within yourself. We're heading to San Diego and you can hang with us."

Without warning, Lucille painfully howls and runs into the campground. Five sharp porcupine quills protrude from her bloody nose and mouth.

Instantly, Rich jumps out of the hot springs and picks up the howling fox terrier. "Jeannie, get the first aid kit from the van. Jack, hold Lucille down, while I pull the quills. Jill, boil some water to clean the wounds. These quills are barbed and this is going to hurt."

I grab Lucille tightly around the chest with both my hands. Rich holds her head with his left hand while his right quickly pulls one barb then another, until all five are removed.

Jill and Jeannie rush in with clean towels to stop the bleeding and sanitize the wounds. Lucille's painful cries ring in our ears until she calms down in Jill's arms.

Rich walks to the van and pulls out a bottle of Jose Cuervo Especial Gold. He takes a gulp, then passes it to me. "My Cinco de Mayo tequila will help us sleep tonight. Tomorrow, we'll camp on the Colorado Utah border. I bet Lucille will be running around first thing in the morning."

Jill carries her whimpering pet towards the tent. "Thanks, you guys are good people." The adrenaline wears off and our exhausted bodies collapse inside our canvas home.

My buddy cuddles her little dog. "I hope Lucille is OK tomorrow. Rich really saved her. We're lucky they're taking us to California."

I tenderly kiss Jill. "Let's get some sleep."

We spend the next morning soaking in the hot springs while Lucille recovered from her prickly porcupine encounter and resumed hunting. Later, our afternoon drive from Steamboat Springs took us through spectacular mountain vistas filled with glacier fed streams. Jeannie and Jill shared childhood experiences while Rich Armstrong's homespun humor and wit entertained me.

A red orange sunset turns into magenta twilight when we arrive at Dinosaur National Monument Park where million year old dinosaur fossils are buried in layers of rock and sand.

The exhilarating mountain air stimulated our appetites. Tonight's Cinco de Mayo dinner is true cowboy fare: homemade black beans, bacon with salsa on cornmeal tortillas and Jose Cuervo tequila with Mexican 'herb'.

Rich passes me the tequila bottle and lights a joint. "I've talked it over with Jeannie about you guys buying weed with us. We've saved a couple thousand bucks and plan to buy some Mexican Michoacan to sell in Idaho. We'll get a better price if we pool our money."

I look over at Jill and swallow a tequila shot. "That sounds good. Can we score 'weight' this time of year?"

The big Californian proudly smiles. "My dealer sells pounds year round."

Jill stirs the beans and bacon. "The beans are ready."

Jeannie lifts the bottle of tequila. "To new friendships."

Cool north winds chill the mountain air after dinner as the cooking fire turns into glowing red embers. I fill the brass pipe with the last of my Thai weed and pass it to Rich. He hands it to

Jeannie and pulls out his blues harp. "Fire it up. I'll play some John Lee Hooker."

Lucille howls to the music when Jeannie turns to Jill. "It looks like the sky is going to be clear tonight. We should sleep under the stars. Rich and I plan to buy farmland in the Idaho mountains. You'd love the night sky there."

Later, we all set up our sleeping bags outside near the dimming cooking fire. Jill gazes into space and smiles. "Maybe, we'll see meteorites."

Lucille curls up between Jill and me while I stare into the infinite cosmos thinking of Prophet Muhammad's words 'Man cannot fathom the Almighty Creator's image'...

I slowly drift into a dream...

...Hundreds of thundering hooves pound prairie sod around me. The Seventh Cavalry charges into a Cheyenne village with guns blazing while screaming women and children attempt to escape into the wilderness. The dogs bark louder as the ground under me violently shakes...

Lucille frantically growls a warning. Rich suddenly jumps up, waving his arms and shouting in panic. "Ugh!" "Ugh!"

The large Buck deer leading the stampede bounds to one side. I jump up and scream as dozens more deer rush past our campsite.

Rich looks at me with a wide smile after the last of the wild herd disappears into the night. "Thank God for Lucille. Those deer would have crushed us."

Jill reaches into her backpack and retrieves a Milkbone. The little terrier pirouettes. "Lucille deserves a treat. We nearly got killed."

Rich pets Jill's dog. "Thanks, Lucille. You saved us tonight."

Shivering in the cold night air, we all retreat into our warm sleeping bags. I hug Jill with her pet at our feet. "It's a miracle we weren't hurt."

I fall asleep dreaming...

...Lucille whimpers in pain while rolling on the ground with porcupine quills jutting from her face. The little dog fades into my childhood. I'm gasping for air inside an 'Iron Lung' surrounded by family. A black raven cries out. 'All is but a dream within a dream.'...

———◆———

My eyes open to a serene mountain wilderness under a clear blue sky. Jill is drinking coffee by the breakfast fire with Jeannie and Rich. I pull myself from the sleeping bag and join Jill for morning 'Java' with my nightmare still on my mind.

"I was in an Iron Lung last night and heard 'I'm a dream within a dream'."

Jill's eyes light up. "Edgar Allan Poe wrote 'All that we see or seem is but a dream within a dream.' I bet last night's death experience triggered memories of the 50's polio epidemic."

Jeannie smiles. "Jim Morrison wrote 'The future's uncertain and the end is always near'. We have to live each day like it's our last."

Rich pulls out a Rand McNally map. "Our route takes us through the Bonneville Salt Flats past the Great Salt Lake into Reno Nevada, near Lake Tahoe. We'll take I-80 across the Sierra Nevada mountains to San Francisco and then cruise the Pacific Coast Highway through L.A. into San Diego."

———◆———

Two weeks later, I'm sitting on Hotel del Coronado beach enjoying the late afternoon sun. This is the same hotel where Marilyn Monroe and Jack Lemmon filmed 'Some Like It Hot' in 1959.

Jill and Jeannie are swimming in the ocean while Lucille chases seagulls near bikini-clad teenage girls dancing to The Beach Boys' hit 'Good Vibrations'. Rich is hooking up with his pot dealer and we're supposed to meet him at Farrell's Ice Cream Parlor after sunset.

Our travels took us from the Donner Pass to Randolph Hearst's San Simeon Castle and James Dean's fatal crash site. Rich and Jeannie caught fish at every stop on our road trip through Mormon territory to California. Unlike Tony Bennett we didn't leave our hearts in San Francisco, but we did enjoy Chinatown lobster dinners.

Horace Greeley was right to say 'Go West Young Man' one hundred years ago and California 'The Golden State' is exceptionally beautiful with its sundrenched beaches and gardenia scented ocean breezes. The Pacific Coast Highway ocean views were spectacular. Camping like a 'Hobbit' in a Big Sur redwood forest was surreal and like a Hollywood movie, the Los Angeles Lakers celebrated their first NBA championship when we drove through 'Tinseltown'.

I'm reading a San Diego Union Tribune newspaper this morning...

'The attempted assassination of George Wallace overshadows the upcoming Presidential conventions. Secretary of State Henry Kissinger announced the United States and Soviet Union will sign a Strategic Arms Limitation Treaty, while anti-war protests continue on college campuses throughout America.'

The next article in the local section of the newspaper is about the upcoming holiday...

'The Gypsy Joker Motorcycle Club plans to ride in the San Diego Memorial Day parade.'

I think to myself...

'I hung out with a Gypsy Joker biker named Pete Logan when we were stationed at Ft. Leonard Wood. He and I took acid one night at Lake of the Ozarks and he confessed to nearly committing suicide when he couldn't attend his mother's funeral while serving in Vietnam.

Pete was very close to his mother. She was a Mexican Apache beauty who fell in love with a Nebraska sailor named Peter Logan. They had a honeymoon without a marriage ceremony and Seaman Logan was killed in a Japanese kamikaze attack during the battle of Okinawa. Pete never recovered from his mother's family rejection that led to her early death from alcoholism. I wonder if Pete is in San Diego for the parade?'

Lucille follows Jill and Jeannie running towards me on the beach. The girls grab towels to dry off when Lucille showers me with salt water. Rich Armstrong unexpectedly appears at the beach park entrance. He looks disappointed and his confident stride has disappeared.

I ask. "How did it go? Did you get a sample?"

Rich shrugs his shoulders as Jeannie hugs him. He turns to Jill and me with a sigh. "My guy was supposed to have ten pounds for us. Instead, he drove me to a West Hollywood dealer, who demanded we bring large bills to the desert tonight."

Jeannie pulls Rich close. "That sounds dangerous."

I nod my head in agreement. "No way we go into the desert at night."

Jill frowns. "What are we going to do now? I thought we would score for sure."

Jeannie manages a smile. "All we need is another contact."

The newspaper article comes to my mind. "Maybe I know someone who can score for us. When I was in the Army, Pete Logan always had good Mexican grass. He's a Gypsy Joker and his club is riding in the San Diego Memorial Day parade. The paper said they own the 'Wild Joker Bar' outside of town."

Rich nods his head. "Yeah, I know where that bar is. We can drive there after I tune up the van."

Jill looks at me. "Jack, should we take a chance?"

I embrace Jill. "Don't worry. We'll visit the bar during the day. I'll go in and ask for Pete. What's the worst thing that can happen?"

———————⬤———————

The next weekend, hot Santa Ana 'Devil Winds' gust across the Anza-Borrego desert. Rich's Ford van struggles through waves of sand on the road. 'Bad Moon Rising' plays on the radio when Rich turns to me. "Jack, I hope we can trust this guy. Jeannie and I don't want to lose our savings."

I look Rich and Jeannie in the eye while holding Jill's hand. "Pete and I are 'back to back' and I trust him with my life."

Rich drives east through the hills and steers his green van into the 'Wild Joker Bar' parking lot. A dozen 'buffed' Harley Davidsons are neatly parked in front of a replica Hollywood cowboy saloon.

Jeannie hands me a rubber band wrapped roll of twenties. "Here's a thousand."

I hand it to Jill. "Bring the cash, if I signal OK."

I walk to the bar front door and look inside to see black leather jackets dancing to The Grateful Dead's 'Friend of the Devil' in a smoke filled room. The music and boisterous conversation goes silent when all eyes focus on me in the entryway.

Pete Logan is standing at the bar surrounded by bikers dressed in club regalia. His lean angular face and pencil thin mustache looks the same, but his long braided jet black hair is no longer the GI crew cut I remember. A raven haired beauty standing at his side swallows a tequila shot while I face the deadly end of a shotgun and call out. "Specialist Logan report for duty."

Pete squints through the thick smoke and laughs. "Jack Collins. I didn't recognize you with hair. Man, you nearly got your head blown off. We're at war with the Hells Angels."

I shake Pete's hand. He turns around and looks at his crew. "Jack's cool. We were in the Army together. We have to talk."

I'm led into a side room where Pete's piercing ebony eyes focus intensely on me. "Jack, I can't believe you walked in here. The 'Angels' kicked us out of Oakland and we're hanging in San Diego until we move 'Down Under'. I did 'R & R' in Australia' during my tour in 'Nam' and the 'Outback' is filled with open roads to ride in."

Pete slaps my back. "Man, I thought you were in college."

I laugh. "That's a long story that I'll tell another time. My old lady and I are hitchhiking cross country and we're looking to buy weed. I'm holding sixteen hundred cash."

Pete smiles. "Jack, you've come at the most opportune time. We've got primo crystal meth and weed action you can get in on."

I walk to the front door and give an 'OK' signal. The van doors open and Lucille jumps out. Jill enters first carrying Lucille. She hands me her little dog and the cash. Rich and Jeannie follow as

I make introductions. "Pete, this is Jill, her dog Lucille and our friends, Jeannie and Rich."

Pete shakes Rich's hand, then kisses Jill and Jeannie on their cheeks. He pets Lucille and gestures towards his crew. "Meet my old lady, Maria and the Gypsy Jokers."

Maria's alluring chestnut eyes have a cat-like beauty. I order drinks for everyone and Jill loads quarters into a Seeburg jukebox. Otis Redding is singing 'The Dock of the Bay' when Pete pulls me into a side room. "Jack, you've got to try this 'speed'. It's 'better living through chemistry'. College kids make methamphetamine for us to trade for weed. We're riding into Mexico tonight to exchange 'crystal meth' for Michoacan and set up our exit to Australia."

Pete removes a dinner plate from a side cabinet and empties a plastic baggie filled with white crystals on it. He pulls out an eight inch Bowie knife and chops the glass like crystals into powder lines. "This shit is rocket fuel. You'll love it. There's big money in 'meth' and it's easier to travel with. Snort a couple of lines and you'll party for hours."

I give my Army buddy a friendly pat on the back. "I'll try it, but dealing meth isn't my thing. We want to score some righteous 'herb'."

The Gypsy Joker leader rolls a fifty dollar bill into a straw and quickly inhales two lines. He passes me the plate with a devilish smile. "No worries. Try this shit and give me your cash. We'll cut you in on the Michoacan deal. You can party with Maria and girls, until we get back tomorrow."

I hand Pete sixteen hundred dollars and snort two lines of 'crystal meth'. Razor sharp glass shards rip into my nasal passages. Euphoric electricity surges throughout my body moments later. A smile comes to my face. "Wow. This is wicked powerful."

My host smiles as he picks up the plate and walks towards the back door. "Fucking A! Let's party in the clubhouse next door."

We walk through the back door past two brand new Ford 150 pickup campers parked next to a multi-story building behind the bar. Pete explains. "The bar is a 'front' for our crystal meth action. The chemicals are stored in the warehouse basement, the first floor is the clubhouse and our cribs are upstairs. We use the pickup trucks to haul weed and chemicals from the border."

I follow Pete into the second building where we enter a room filled with bubbling lava lamps and black lights illuminating 'Day-Glo' posters. Cannabis and tobacco smoke fills the air as serpentine shadows gyrate to Wilson Pickett's 'In the Midnight Hour'.

The crowd cheers and raises their tequila bottles when they see the plate piled with white powder. Pete puts the crystal meth on the table in front of Rich and Jeannie as I slide next to Jill. Smiling ear to ear, Pete hands Jill a rolled fifty dollar bill. "Pretty lady, try some rocket fuel."

Darkness envelops the nearby sand dunes when a blood red sun sets and the Gypsy Jokers ride 'locked and loaded' to their night rendezvous in the Mexican desert.

The Joker 'old ladies' dance to 'Honky Tonk Women' swallowing pills and tequila, while Lucille becomes the clubhouse mascot pirouetting for meat in Maria's hand.

The last methamphetamine crystals are long gone when Maria places a tequila bottle on the table. She pulls a baggie filled with multicolored capsules from her black leather jacket. "Take these F.D.A. approved pharmaceuticals to crash. The red devils are Seconal, the yellows are Nembutal and the rainbow blues, Tuinal. They'll get you where you want to go tonight. Me and the ladies are crashing upstairs. There's mattresses in the side room for you guys."

Maria leaves the bag of pills and the tequila bottle on the table. She turns and struts out of the room. My jaw is sore from a perpetual methamphetamine smile. I swallow two yellow capsules with a double shot of Jose Cuervo. Jill quickly follows suit.

Rich and Jeannie, each cautiously take a capsule with a tequila shot. Jeannie gives Jill a hug. "We'll sleep in our van. See you guys tomorrow."

I gulp another tequila shot as Rich and Jeannie return to their van. Jill takes my hand. "Let's find those beds."

———◆———

The same day in the 'Sunshine State', a silver full moon rises from the Atlantic Ocean as Jerry Siegel's Lincoln Continental slowly approaches Cap's Place. Johnny Lionetti's red convertible is parked next to a black Cadillac Fleetwood sedan.

Mike Casey squirms in the passenger seat wondering why Johnny called an urgent meeting this night. Could his mentor know about Kim? Mike's worst fears come to mind at the sight of the black Cadillac. "Damn, why is Little Ray here?"

Mike stares at his driver. "Keep your mouth shut about Jamaica or we'll both be shark chum. Drop me off and wait by the dock. I've got to settle this, one way or another."

The big Floridian bends his frame through the Cap's Place swinging doors and enters the historic pine wood paneled room. He sees two patrons sitting alone at the bar without a bartender.

Little Ray growls. "He's here."

Johnny turns and smiles. "Kid, what are you drinking tonight? We're celebrating the half million I made from your boat load."

141

Mike nods his head and smiles. "That's great. I'll have Appleton rum on the rocks."

'Don' Lionetti hands Mike a drink and pulls him into a seat at the bar. "Things are looking good. The Vegas casinos are rolling in cash and 'Deep Throat' is making millions. Best of all, Carmine Persico 'whacked' 'Crazy Joe' Gallo and took control of the Colombo Family. Now, the New York 'Families' can get back to business."

Johnny gulps his Scotch. "Some things still worry me. Hoffa refused to take his Teamster retirement package and the new Federal R.I.C.O. Law could cost me everything. I can't have any loose ends."

Mike notices Johnny's dark Sicilian eyes focus on him. "Kid, ask yourself one question. Why have I called this 'meet'?"

'Don' Lionetti pauses. "Remember, I own this town. The girl you were with in Jamaica dances in my clubs and escorts special guests for me."

Johnny arches his eyebrows and refills Mike's glass. "I was young once and remember the need for strange pussy. But, I don't want fuckups in my outfit. Do you understand?"

Mike's hands tremble as he gulps his drink and answers. "I understand."

Johnny pats Mike on the back. "Good. All my girls are 'STD' tested and I'll let you work with them as long as it doesn't interfere with family. Debbie and Mary can never know about this."

Little Ray eyeballs Mike with a sadistic grin as he pulls open his coat, exposing his ivory handled .357. "Your drunk uncle and Jew friend better not fuck up."

Earlier in California, I wake to Lucille licking my face. Jill moans and covers her head with a pillow. I have a headache and my stomach is queasy. The barbiturates and booze must have knocked us out. Lucille shakes her tail, when I jump up and open the warehouse door to the desert.

I empty my bladder with pleasure, while I watch a red orange sun set into a rust colored dust cloud on the western horizon and think to myself... 'How can it be sunset? We must have slept 24 hours. Where's Pete and the Gypsy Jokers?'

The van door opens, Rich and Jeannie emerge. Rich stretches and moans with a shy smile. "I heard bikes last night, but they were gone when we got out of bed this morning. The bar is locked and the clubhouse is stripped bare, except for the upstairs kitchen."

Jeannie points to the stairs. "Let's make some coffee."

I nod my head and follow them inside. "Man, I need a joint too."

Jill pulls on her jeans and joins us walking upstairs into the kitchen. Empty cans and bottles are strewn everywhere. We attempt to clear our heads drinking strong coffee, when my buddy's bloodshot eyes look at me with a frustrated frown. "Shit! They ripped us off. We worked hard for that money. What will we do now?"

I shake my head. "Pete wouldn't rip us off. He must have been ambushed."

Jeannie sighs and shakes her head. "I don't know. They nearly took everything."

Rich stands up and thoughtfully pauses. "We took a chance and our horse didn't come in. We'll ride another one in the future. For now, we'll go to work and start over."

I continue to shake my head in disbelief. "Only a bullet would stop Pete."

<hr />

Three days later, Jill and I stand beside Interstate Highway 8 while Lucille hunts rodents nearby. What a difference a day makes. All of us thought we were ripped off, until I remembered Pete always kept his weed frozen. I found five kilos of Michoacan in the kitchen freezer with a note.

'Jack, See you down under mate. Pete'

Jill and I wrapped our two kilos in dirty laundry and put them at the bottom of our backpacks. We paid Rich and Jeannie a Ben Franklin to balance accounts. They dropped us outside El Centro and headed north to Idaho with three kilos. We gave them my Hull address and promised to stay in touch through the Post Office.

Rich gave us specific travel instructions. "In Arizona head north from Phoenix to Flagstaff, then take I-40 through the high country to Albuquerque, New Mexico. Don't go south on I-10 to Tucson. This time of year, the desert heat is deadly."

The afternoon sun is high in the sky and temperatures are near one hundred degrees Fahrenheit. Lucille crawls into Jill's shadow with her tongue hanging from her mouth. My mouth feels like sandpaper as the blazing sun melts the asphalt under our feet.

I'm thinking of 'Mad Dogs & Englishmen' when a weathered white '56' Chevy pickup stops in front of us. National Public Radio plays Beethoven on the radio as the driver yells. "Throw your packs in the back and get in up front."

Lucille jumps on the driver's lap and licks his tanned wrinkled face as Jill sits in the middle. The pickup driver exposes his long white hair when he tips his hat. "Howdy. Adolph Hess, Deputy

Sheriff and Justice of the Peace. Lock the door. I don't want you falling out of my truck."

The elderly lawman gives Jill a curious look. "What are your name's and if you don't mind me asking, why are you hitchhiking across the desert?"

I reluctantly close and lock the truck door as Jill smiles at our driver. "That's my dog, Lucille. I'm Jill and this is Jack. We're on our way to visit friends in Vermont before we go back to college in September."

Mr. Hess gives Jill a patronizing smile while he puts his pickup in gear and returns to the highway. My German grandparents rode the Santa Fe Trail to settle on the Gila River a hundred years ago. Mother was a Kumeyaay native and her tribe has lived in these hills thousands of years before the Spanish sailed to America. I remember General 'Black Jack' Pershing chasing Pancho Villa through these parts. This is dangerous territory and you should take a Greyhound bus for your safety."

The elderly Andy Griffith look alike with his white mustache and mutton chop sideburns chuckles when I respond. "My grandfather served on General Pershing's staff during World War I. 'Pop' loved the Paris nightlife, especially the Moulin Rouge 'Can Can'."

Suddenly without warning the Chevy pickup steers south from I-8 onto state road 111. Our driver turns to us with a smile. "I have to deliver food to a Lutheran mission school across the border in Mexicali. It'll only take an hour. Afterwards, I'll drive you to a safe campground where you can catch the bus."

I'm panicking and thinking to myself... 'We'll end up in prison if the border guards find our weed.'

Jill gives me a terrified look and squeezes my hand as the old pickup races towards the border crossing. I'm sweating and wondering what to do... 'We can't jump out and leave our packs in the back of the truck.'

I speak up. "Mr. Hess, we don't have passports."

Our driver chortles while driving full speed towards Mexico. "Don't worry my children. I cross this border nearly every day doing God's work. I am a devout Lutheran Christian and it would be a sin for me to leave you in the desert."

The American border guards smile and wave at the Chevy pickup racing past their checkpoint. If the Mexican guards don't bust us, I'm sure we'll get strip searched by the Americans on our return.

The Mexican border guards look like 'The Treasure of the Sierra Madre' bandits, wearing 'badges'.

My knees shake, when Mr. Hess slows his truck to a stop at the crossing. I look through the windshield at the approaching guards and try to control my facial reaction.

The sheriff sees my distress. "Don't worry, you're with me."

True to the sheriff's word, the Mexican guards let us cross the border after Mr. Hess gave them two bottles of tequila. The old lawman delivered food and medicine to the mission school and we returned to America within an hour without stopping. He seems to have spiritual powers that transcend ordinary boundaries. His parting words to us were...

"Water is more valuable than gold or oil in the desert. Water is essential for all living things on Earth to survive. Christ's teachings are like water, they will lead you through the valley of death to eternal life. Bless you both."

Later that night, Jill and I feel lucky to be back in the USA and not rotting in a Mexican jail. Mr. Hess drove us to a bus stop desert oasis on the Arizona border. Our campsite costs two bucks a night, including hot showers. Night blooming jasmine flowers scent the air as Jill falls asleep in my arms and I slip into a dream...

...I'm wandering in a barren desert surrounded by coiled rattlesnakes. Bloodshot eyes stare at me from dark shadows. "I want your woman."...

The next morning, I'm stirring raisins and brown sugar into a pot of oatmeal cooking on the campfire. I haven't told Jill about my bizarre nightmare, because I don't want to worry her. All I know is, we should get back to Vermont as soon as possible.

A radio in a nearby campsite plays The Rolling Stones' 'Sweet Black Angel', when the 'D.J.' breaks in after the song. "An all white jury will begin deliberations today in the Angela Davis murder trial. Attorney General John Mitchell says Daniel Ellsberg's release of the 'Pentagon Papers' is the worst case of treason since the American revolution. Arizona desert temperatures could exceed one hundred degrees today."

Jill emerges from the shower, wraps her long golden hair in the towel and dries herself. She pulls a thin pale blue t-shirt over her tan breasts and puts on bright red shorts.

I notice four pairs of eyes staring from the nearby bushes watching Jill feed raisins to Lucille. All at once, tiny emaciated children jump from the shrubbery. Their wide eyes stare at the dried fruit in Jill's hand as they quickly join Lucille begging for treats.

Jill gives me a concerned look. "I think these kids live in that old station wagon on the other side of the campground. They're hungry and we've got food to share."

I add more powdered milk and brown sugar to the cereal pot. Two bowls of oatmeal become six. The children's brown eyes sparkle along with appreciative smiles as they hastily consume their unexpected meal like Charles Dickens' characters.

After breakfast, we gather some of our food supplies and follow the children. They cheerfully lead Lucille towards a rusting 1960 Ford Galaxie station wagon, with an Army surplus tent attached to the rear door. John Steinbeck's 'Grapes of Wrath' migrant families come to mind as we approach a gaunt couple next to a campfire.

A thin unshaven man standing over six feet tall with stooped shoulders, translucent skin and thinning gray hair looks at us with dark fearful eyes. A tiny white haired woman tends a coffee pot on the fire. The children circle around her as she looks up through her thick eyeglasses. "I hope my children are being good. Would you like some coffee?"

The children yell excitedly. "Mommy and Daddy, we have friends."

Jill approaches the campsite with a smile. "Coffee sounds great. I'm Jill and this is Jack. Your kids have been very good."

The father's hands shake as he pours two cups of thin watery coffee. He attempts to hide a facial tic, while passing the hot beverage. "My name is Joseph Thompson and this is my wife Mary. We're sorry we don't have much to offer you. I'm unemployed, because of a nervous condition."

Mary reaches over to her husband and takes his hand. "Don't worry, Joseph. The Lord watches over us. Our family is together and that's what matters. I don't want the welfare people taking you away from me and our children."

Jill shakes her head. "That's not right for the government to break up poor families. How do you survive without money?"

The bespectacled mother smiles tenderly at Jill. "Christ the Lord provides for us in mysterious ways. The camp groundskeeper doesn't charge us and he gives us water for our vegetable garden. Occasionally, the Lord sends good people to help us."

I hand Jill the sacks of food I'm carrying. She turns to Mary and smiles. "We have some supplies for your family. Whole wheat flour, brown sugar, powdered milk, beans and rice. Also, here's the last of our raisins, peanut butter and honey. We wish we had more to give."

Our gifts are humbly accepted as Joseph leads his family in prayer. "Praise be to God for he watches over his flock. In the name of Christ, we're thankful for our new friend's charity. May our Lord watch over them in the valley of darkness."

———◆———

Later that afternoon, the sun is high in the sky and there's no escape from the searing heat. The bus driver wouldn't let Lucille ride with us, so we're holding our cardboard Vermont sign at the entrance to I-8 near the Colorado River. Jill looks at me sheepishly. "I gave Mary fifty dollars. I had to help them, they were so desperate."

I hug Jill. "I gave Joseph fifty bucks. I felt sorry for a father unable to feed his family."

Jill's bronze skin glistens with perspiration when she pours water from a canteen into her hand for Lucille to drink. My Buddy takes a gulp, then splashes water on her head and neck as road traffic takes an afternoon siesta.

Jimi Hendrix's 'Foxy Lady' plays in my head when I notice Jill's breasts protruding through her wet t-shirt.

Unexpectedly, a black Oldsmobile 88 sedan with three men inside comes to an abrupt stop in front of us. A smiling Latino driver steps out and opens the car trunk. "We're driving to Phoenix. Put your packs in here and take the back seat."

The desire to escape the sun's unrelenting heat makes the air conditioned automobile irresistible. I jump in the back seat, next to a short ferret faced man. Jill carries Lucille into the vehicle and sits by the window with her pet. 'Midnight Rambler' plays on the radio as the driver puts the General Motors V8 in gear.

The black sedan quickly accelerates to one hundred miles an hour. All three car occupants are tan with thin jet black mustaches and long ponytails. The biggest man rides shotgun and gives me an indifferent look. I turn to the ferret faced man sitting next to me and notice a coiled snake tattoo on his left arm. He devilishly smiles when the driver speaks. "Your woman is very beautiful. Every man should have a pretty lady like her."

These guys make me feel uneasy. Our backpacks are in the trunk and we can't jump out of a car traveling at high speed. Jill looks frightened as I try to develop a strategy when a road sign appears... 'I-10 north Phoenix 20 miles'. I blurt out. "Thanks for the ride. You can drop us off at the Phoenix exit."

Lucille squirms in Jill's lap as the driver's bloodshot eyes coldly stare at me in the rear view mirror. Chills run through my body when he lustfully leers at Jill and produces a pint bottle of liquor. "Have some tequila. I like your woman."

Jill trembles and tightly grips my left hand while I push the bottle away with my right. "No thanks. We have relatives expecting us in Phoenix this afternoon."

The Oldsmobile 88 approaches the I-10 exits. One exit goes north to Phoenix and Albuquerque and the other south to Tucson and Las Cruces. The driver coldly stares at me in the rear view mirror and steers the black sedan south.

He angrily raises his voice. "Man, I want your woman. Give me your woman!"

Jill gasps and lets go of my hand when the 'Ferret' pulls a four inch switchblade knife from his pocket. He gives me a crooked smile and sticks the steel blade against my chest while the third man riding shotgun timidly turns away.

Lucille escapes from Jill's lap and drops to the car floor when the driver screams. "Man, give me your woman!"

Suddenly, I feel the steel knife penetrate my chest skin into a rib bone. Debilitating pain causes me to react instinctively. My right elbow smashes the 'Ferret's' nose while my left hand knocks the dagger to the car floor. My bloodied adversary withdraws and cowers in the corner.

The car abruptly stops and the driver pulls out a Smith & Wesson .44. I look into the driver's blood shot ebony eyes as he points the deadly weapon at me, when I answer. "It's a woman's choice. She decides who she goes with."

Jill's eyes fill with tears when her voice cracks. "Would you want someone to rape your mother or sister?"

The shotgun passenger shrugs his shoulders and frowns at the driver. "Mi madre? Mi hermana? No!"

The driver shakes his head and puts the pistol away. Jill quickly opens the rear door. Lucille emerges from under the front seat and escapes into the blazing heat. I quickly join my buddy and her little dog in the hot desert.

The Oldsmobile begins to drive away and Jill yells. "They have our backpacks and water!"

Unexpectedly, the black sedan stops in a cloud of dust. The driver jumps out and opens the trunk. He retrieves our packs and throws them on the side of the road. Jill clings to me as we watch the Oldsmobile 88 disappear over the horizon.

Jill treats my flesh wound and affectionately kisses me as the sun sets. We gently caress each other while succumbing to uncontrolled passion under a crimson red sky.

The following morning, a pepper laden pickup truck rescues us from the blazing hot desert. The driver calls himself 'Cuco', even though his Christian name is Juan Martinez Garcia. He is descended from Spanish Conquistadors who came to America in search of gold.

Cuco's family have been proud Americans since the 1848 Mexican-American War and they own property on both sides of the border. Cuco took us to his Las Cruces vegetable farm and then drove us on I-25 north through New Mexico to Denver.

Later at a Denver I-76 truck stop. A black Peterbilt eighteen wheeler stops in front of us as we thank Cuco for our rescue. The 'big rig' driver opens his door. "Howdy, my name is Fred Briscoe. I saw your sign and little dog. Hop in, I'm running beef to Vermont."

Lucille instantly jumps into the truck cab and two hours later, we're rolling east on I-80 towards Nebraska, listening to Steve Winwood's 'Feelin Alright'.

Fred Briscoe looks like football legend Jim Brown. His full 'Afro' blows in the wind as his Ray Ban shades reflect the road ahead.

The CB radio comes to life. "Breaker. Breaker 19. 'Dirty Bandit' calling the black 'Pete 359' heading east. What's your 'handle' and' '99', good buddy?"

The big rig driver grabs the CB microphone. "Dirty Bandit. This is 'Big Stick' in 'Midnight Lady', hauling 'prime cut Angus beef' to 'The Green Mountain State'."

VERMONT SUMMER

A gilded gold sunset fades to twilight as the Peterbilt tractor-trailer I'm in races past Nebraska corn fields towards Iowa. Jill's and my hitchhiking journey across America has been a roller coaster ride. One day we're dead in the desert, the next we're cruising the 'Great Plains' in an eighteen wheel 'big rig'.

Fred Briscoe is at the helm. Handsome and square jawed, Fred's ebony skin shines in the twilight as we run full throttle towards the Mississippi River listening to Charley Pride sing 'Kiss an Angel Good Mornin'.

Jill and Lucille are asleep in the truck's soundproof sleeper cab while I ride shotgun high on Benzedrine watching the passing countryside as powerful Cummins diesel engine vibrations surge through me.

Fred's big rig 'Midnight Lady' is a tripped out Peterbilt 359 EXHD with chrome moon wheel hubcaps and neon lights silhouetting the jet black cab. The interior is red and black leather, with walnut wood panels. A Motorola CB radio and RCA quadraphonic eight track stereo enhance our travel experience.

The FM radio announces the evening news. "An all white jury acquitted Angela Davis of murder charges today in Santa Clara, California. President Nixon authorized the Air Force to use precision guided bombs against North Vietnam in 'Operation Linebacker'."

I'm listening to Fred talk 'a mile a minute' while 'wired' on the 'speed' he gave me.

"Jack, the 'bennies' will keep us up until we get to Chicago. I only do this when I'm on the road. I don't smoke anything or drink alcohol. Working hard and living a clean life got me this rig free and clear. My folks were Mississippi sharecroppers in debt to the 'company' all their lives. 'Jim Crow' killed my daddy at fifty. That's not going to happen to me."

Fred checks the truck gauges and shakes his head. "I'm surprised a white jury found Angela Davis not guilty. I don't believe in white man's justice. In '58' the 'Klan' murdered a neighbor and my mother sent me to live with her sister in Chicago. White folks were still lynching 'negros' in 60's when Martin Luther King Jr. was murdered in Memphis."

Muddy Waters and Bo Diddley sing 'I'm a Man' on the radio when Fred gives me an intense look. "The F.B.I. murdered Fred Hampton because he threatened the white power structure. Muhammad Ali was nearly sent to prison when he wouldn't fight in Vietnam."

I nod in agreement. "Doing the right thing cost Ali his title. Frazier's left hook would never have landed, if Ali hadn't been banned from boxing."

A 1st Infantry Division hat hanging from the window visor comes to my attention. "Fred, were you in the Army? I just got out of the 'Green Machine' and it's good to be free again."

The driver's baritone voice has a solemn tone. "I did six years active duty with two tours in 'Nam'. The Army was supposed to be my escape from the ghetto, instead I ended up fighting a racist war in Vietnam."

Fred shakes his head and continues his righteous diatribe. "At the end of the Civil War African slaves believed Lincoln freed them, but white Americans didn't want them free and a hundred years later we still ain't free. Thanks be to Allah. Nation of Islam leaders

Elijah Muhammad and Malcolm X taught me self-reliance. I'm my own man and no one's slave."

Benzedrine 'speed rushes' surge through me. "Man, your world is so different from mine. The only black kid in my high school was one of my closest friends. Nat Butler's father was Haitian and his mother French Canadian. We played on the baseball team and Nat endured racial slurs at every game."

Sammy Davis Jr. sings 'Candy Man' on the radio when Fred nods his head and turns to me. "I bet your friend's parents got hassled from both sides. Sammy married a white woman and Southern Democrats prevented him from performing at JFK's inaugaration. Most of my family are against mixed race couples, but my thinking changed in Vietnam. Now, I don't care what race a pretty lady is."

Fred smiles at me. "Have you dated any 'Soul Sisters'?"

Diana Ross and Mary Wilson come to mind as we listen to 'Brown Sugar' on the radio. "I haven't had the opportunity, but my uncle partied with 'Sisters' in Boston's 'colored' jazz clubs during the 50's, when Redd Foxx and Malcolm X were 'Chicago Red' and 'Detroit Red'."

The muscular truck driver shakes his head. "Redd Foxx made millions as a comedian and Malcolm X was murdered for speaking the truth."

Creedence Clearwater Revival's 'Fortunate Son' plays on the radio. Fred's voice has a stern tone. "My time in 'Nam' taught me that skin color doesn't tell you about a person's character. I don't care what a person looks like as long as they have my back."

Fred thoughtfully pauses. "My auntie had my back and kept me out of trouble when I was a teenager. Most kids from my neighborhood got into dope and ended up dead or in jail. Life in 'Chi Town' is 'dog eat dog', just like 'Nam'."

The big rig driver continues 'rapping' while 'Midnight Lady' rolls east on highway I-80. "The rules are different for rich white people. They own everything and can buy anyone. The white media talks about the Kent State massacre, but doesn't mention the black students murdered at Jackson State. Worst of all, black Americans will suffer the most in Dick Nixon's 'War on Drugs'. It will turn America's poor black ghettos into 'war zones'."

Fred looks at me grimly. "Jack, did you go to 'Nam'?"

Billy Preston and The Beatles play 'Get Back' on the radio as I remember my time in the Army. "No, I was lucky in Basic Training. My 'D. I.' Sergeant Lester Goff talked me out of going to war. He's a Louisiana Cajun from New Orleans who earned a Bronze Star and Purple Heart in two combat tours as a '1st Air Cav' Airborne Ranger. Goff said he had to be tough on our all white platoon, because his mission was to save our miserable lives."

A melancholy feeling comes over me. "I did 'Basic' at Ft. Polk in December '69' and our company got a two week Christmas 'leave'. I took a bus to Boston through the deep South past poor sharecropper families living in wood shacks."

Another memory changes my mood and makes me chuckle. "I scored an ounce of good weed while I was on leave. The day I returned to the base, Goff warned me the First Sergeant was inspecting the barracks and anyone with contraband goes to the stockade."

Fred grins. "Sounds like you're between a rock and a hard place. What happened next?"

I laugh. "I gave up my stash and the next weekend Goff took me to the mess hall after lights out. The cooks were smoking my pot and listening to Motown inside the kitchen. Goff and I joined in and later that night we satisfied our 'munchies' by eating ice cream from five gallon containers."

I pause and carefully recollect my thoughts. "Goff told me about his Vietnam experience. He was on a long-range recon patrol guarding a watering hole when a Viet Cong walked out of the jungle. The 'V.C.' looked up at him just as Goff fired his M16. They were 'eye to eye' when 'Charlie's' head exploded. Goff relives this moment nightly and he convinced me to change my MOS. I did two years active duty stateside, running gyms and driving trucks. Fred, did you drive a 'deuce and a half' in Vietnam?"

The big rig driver focuses on a road sign and turns to me as 'Run Through the Jungle' plays on the radio. "The 'deuce and half' was my primary ride in 'Nam'. I have to top off my tanks at the Iowa 80 Truck Stop. Get me a large coffee while I fuel up. I like my 'Joe' hot and black, just like my women."

I slowly open the sleeper cab, knowing Jill needs her rest. Lucille rises from her slumber, stretches and wags her tail. "Buddy, are you awake? We're pulling into a truck stop. Do you want to use the restroom? I can walk Lucille."

Jill rolls over and covers her head with a pillow. "I'm good. Thanks."

Lucille jumps from the truck and I quickly follow. The little dog runs into a nearby corn field, while I rush into the restaurant. After a quick piss, I buy two large black coffees and a local newspaper... 'The Des Moines Register' headline is 'Senator George McGovern is the frontrunner to win the Democratic nomination for President.'

Jill's pet Terrier follows me across the truck stop parking lot filled with eighteen wheelers. Diesel fuel vapors permeate the air as storm clouds fill the night sky. 'Midnight Lady' is refueled and Lucille rejoins her master in the sleeper cab.

The radio plays The Band's 'The Shape I'm In' when Fred Briscoe puts his big rig in gear. He sips his hot coffee and cautiously smiles. "A hail storm is following us from Nebraska. We'll have to outrun it. Speed limits slow down after we cross the Mississippi and I get a twenty percent bonus if I deliver the beef to Vermont in the next forty eight hours."

'Theme from Shaft' comes on the radio while Fred maneuvers past trucks adorned with Nixon/Agnew stickers decorating their bumpers. He hands me another orange Benzedrine pill when we exit the parking lot. "Nixon let 'Mafia' gangsters take over big unions. I had a run in with the Teamsters when they tried to muscle Cesar Chavez out of the union business in California."

The eighteen wheeler rolls down I-80 at nearly eighty miles an hour, when Fred turns to me. "The 'Pentagon Papers' prove the American government lied about Vietnam. America got involved after World War II supporting the French rejection of Ho Chi Minh's home rule proposal. Vietnam became America's war, when the communists defeated the French Army at Dien Bien Phu. Now, over fifty thousand Americans are dead for nothing."

Fred's face appears pensive as the radio plays Bob Dylan's 'Knocking on Heaven's Door'. "I never talk about my time in 'Nam', but tonight I'll tell you my story. I did two tours humping supplies from Saigon to Da Nang. I was with the Big Red 1 in 'Operation Cedar Falls' during my first tour in '67'. It was a search and destroy mission, using Agent Orange to drive peasants from their villages into concentration camps."

Suddenly, the CB radio comes to life. "Breaker. Breaker. Smokey in the bush. Smokey in the bush at the Joliet city limit."

Fred takes his foot off the gas and grabs the CB microphone. "That's a big 10-4. Powerful wind coming east 'Lincoln Bound'."

The CB radio crackles with electricity. "10-4, good buddy."

The Grateful Dead plays 'Truckin' as Fred glances at his watch and gives me a thoughtful look. "Speed trap in five miles. We'll have to run 'double nickel', then I'll get back up to seventy five."

Later, gale force winds buffet 'Midnight Lady' when we approach Gary, Indiana. Fred steers his eighteen wheeler through the gusting crosswinds while listening to Michael Jackson's first solo hit 'Got to be There'.

The radio news comes on the air. "U.P.I. correspondent Helen Thomas questioned President Nixon about his secret plan to get out of Vietnam and the President declined to answer. Senator George McGovern is expected to win the California Democratic primary later this week. Locally, thunderstorms and tornadoes are moving east across Illinois."

Fred's voice has a somber tone. "I lost close friends in the 1968 Tet Offensive. Bill Gorham and Tony Arias were my best friends. Bill and I did 88M training together and flew to 'Nam' on the same plane. He was from West Virginia, happy to get a monthly paycheck. We met Tony humping supplies from Da Nang. Tony escaped Castro's Cuba and wanted to repay America for his freedom."

A distant stare comes to Fred's eyes. "We were hauling jet fuel and ammo to the fly boys at Tan Son Nhut, when all hell broke loose and a 'VC' landmine vaporized Tony in the lead gun truck."

Fred pauses. "Bill and I were driving tanker trucks filled with high octane jet fuel.

A 'RPG' turned Bill's tanker into a red orange mushroom cloud. I saw him jump from the truck in flames and burn to death on the side of the road. I couldn't do anything to save him. In seconds, both of my closest friends in the world were dead."

———◦———

A bright orange sun sets in the cobalt blue western sky as 'Midnight Lady' rolls towards the New York state line on Interstate 90. We've traveled nearly fifteen hundred miles in twenty four hours by running nonstop except for quick 'pit stops'. Fred's eight track tapes of Muddy Waters and Howlin'Wolf playing Willie Dixon 'Chicago Blues' tunes carried us through Ohio and Pennsylvania.

I'm still high on 'trucker's speed' and in need of a hot shower. Joe Cocker and Steve Winwood sing 'With a Little Help from My Friends' when the sleeper cab slider opens and Jill's smiling face appears. "It seems like I've been asleep for most of this trip. Where are we?"

I chuckle. "New York State, home of the Rockefellers and Roosevelts. We're approaching Niagara Falls where Nikola Tesla made Buffalo the world's first electric city."

A road sign appears… 'Attica Correctional Facility, Batavia exit on Rt. 98 south'.

Fred's powerful muscles flex. "Nelson Rockefeller murdered those Attica prisoners."

I frown and nod my head. "His grandfather killed striking Colorado miners and their families, sixty years ago."

Fred shakes his head with disgust. "The world's empires are built by serfs and slaves. Every human being deserves liberty and happiness."

'Midnight Lady' rolls east in the darkness on I-90. The radio plays Chuck Berry's 'Johnny B. Goode' and 'Maybellene' as Fred's eighteen wheeler passes over the Hudson River.

Out of nowhere, a red Jaguar convertible races past us. Fred puts his 'pedal to the metal' and turns to me with an excited glint in his dark eyes. "Did you see that gorgeous soul sister driving that 'Jag'? I'm hauling ten tons of beef, but 'Midnight Lady' can catch her."

Excited by the chase, Lucille sits up. Jill chuckles. "You guys are like dogs in the hunt."

Fred laughs and puts a Jimi Hendrix tape in the eight track player. "Everyone searches for a soulmate and maybe this sister is meant for me."

The stereo plays 'Foxy Lady' as the Peterbilt 359 picks up speed and closes on the red convertible. The Nubian lady's 'Afro' blows in the wind as we nearly pull alongside her. The pretty lady smiles and waves as the Jaguar V8 takes off.

Fred lets out a hearty laugh. "The chase is on."

We stay tantalizingly close, but the 'Jag' keeps the lead as we race into 'The Bay State'. Fred unexpectedly takes his foot off the gas and signals his exit north towards Vermont on I-91 with a blast of his air horn. The Jaguar head lights blink and continue east on the 'Mass Pike' towards 'Beantown'. Fred downshifts under a waning crescent moon rising in the eastern sky. "Beautiful lady, I hope we meet again."

Our driver pets Lucille when she climbs on his lap to stick her head out the window. Fred smiles at Jill and me. "We're making good time on this run. I'll drop you guys in Plainfield on my way to St. Johnsbury. I'm sure you want to get out of those clothes and take a shower."

Stevie Wonder sings, 'Signed, Sealed, Delivered, I'm Yours' when 'Midnight Lady' stops in front of a roadside sign... 'Green Mountain Women's Co-Op Inc.'.

Jill gives our driver a hug. "Thanks for the door to door service."

I shake Fred's hand. "Here's my Boston address and phone number. Anytime you're passing through, you've got a place to stay. 'Happy Trails' my brother."

Fred puts 'Midnight Lady' in gear with a blast from the air horn. "Thanks for the invite. I might take you up on the offer. Great rapping with you. Be good."

As the sun rises, light rain showers create a multi-colored rainbow over Vermont's green countryside. Sweet lilacs scent the moist morning air as birds chirp their summer delight. Our desert travels are a distant memory and I can't believe we made it to Vermont with two kilos of Mexican weed in the summer 'dry season'. I've got to get in touch with Joey and Shu.

Without warning, Lucille picks up a scent and charges across a nearby stream. Jill calls out. "Lucille. Come Lucille!"

I laugh. "We probably smell worse than Lucille. Let's go skinny dipping and clean up before we visit Susie and Jane."

———◦———

The Florida sky is pitch black on this moonless night in June. Mike Casey and his Uncle Pat join Johnny Lionetti and Little Ray Jackson in the New River boathouse. Little Ray loads a 9mm Mac-10, while Uncle Pat swigs Jack Daniel's whiskey from a pint bottle as Mike puts his loaded Colt .45 in his belt.

'Don' Lionetti looks at his watch. "Ray, this Colombian has got some balls not showing up on time. I thought he was a businessman. I'll give him another fifteen minutes and that's all."

Little Ray shrugs his shoulders. "He's flying into Lauderdale Executive Airport with his bodyguards. Don't worry, this deal is bigger than anything you've done before."

Minutes later, a car horn sounds. Little Ray looks at the security camera monitor and opens the gate. Two Cadillac Fleetwood sedans enter the compound. Four men in long black leather trench coats, carrying Uzi submachine guns emerge from the first car.

The driver of the second Cadillac opens the rear car door. A tall elegantly dressed man in a charcoal tuxedo steps out. He carries a four foot long, ribbon wrapped cardboard box.

The boathouse door opens, two submachine gun toting bodyguards enter without a word. Ray puts his weapon down and greets the new arrival. "Francisco, this is my boss, John Lionetti. Johnny, this is Francisco Diego Valencia, the man who can make you millions."

Uncle Pat reaches for the pint of whiskey in his pocket. The bodyguards quickly lock and load their weapons. The old sailor hesitates and shows his bottle.

'Don' Lionetti calmly steps forward. "Bienvenido mi amigo. We're all amigos here."

Francisco smiles and presents the ribbon wrapped box to Johnny.

"Don Lionetti, this gift is a token of appreciation for your consideration of my business proposal. I was told you collect Japanese Samurai swords. Please add this sixteenth century 'Muramasa Katana' to your collection."

Johnny opens the box and admires the four hundred year old ivory handled masterpiece. He accepts his gift with a wide smile. "Gracias mi amigo. It will be at the center of my collection. Let's get down to business."

A bodyguard hands his patron a black leather briefcase. The debonaire Colombian removes a Ziploc bag filled with pearl white crystals and puts the package on the table.

Francisco's ebony eyes focus on 'Don' Lionetti. "The guaranteed purity of my product is eighty eight percent cocaine. Kilos sell for ten thousand dollars in Colombia and Raymond suggested a possibility of delivering one thousand kilos of my product to Florida through your Jamaican connection. You can retail this product for ten times the cost."

Johnny looks over at Little Ray and Mike. "Is this stuff worth the trouble? My sportsbook is booming. I'm even getting action on Bobby Fischer beating the Russian in chess. I made a nice profit on the Jamaican weed and 'Deep Throat' is doing a million dollar box office. Ray, what's my risk reward on this deal?"

Little Ray looks at Francisco with a crooked grin and turns to Johnny. "Cocaine profits are huge, ten to twenty million a boatload."

Johnny smiles while looking at Mike. "That's some serious cash. Can you get your Jamaican on board?"

Mike considers the proposal as all eyes are on him. "I'll get Tony on board, but we can't run another boat until hurricane season ends in November."

'Don' Lionetti nods agreement as Francisco stands up. "I will visit Montego Bay in August and meet your Jamaican contact. If he is acceptable and you deposit five hundred thousand dollars in my Vatican Bank account, I'll arrange to put one hundred kilos on your boat."

Francisco's piercing ebony eyes focus on Johnny while handing him a business card. "Here is my banker's information. If you are satisfied with the first hundred kilos at ten thousand apiece, pay the half million balance and deposit one million for your thousand kilo boat load. We'll settle the balance in ninety days at no interest."

Johnny nods his head. "No 'vig' sounds reasonable."

'Don' Lionetti extends his hand to his new Colombian partner with a broad smile. "We've got a deal. How does the Kid arrange your Jamaica meet?"

Francisco turns to Mike. "I'll be attending a coffee growers conference at Rose Hall during the last week in August. Contact me there and we'll discuss logistics. Buenas noches."

Without another word, Francisco Diego Valencia confidently strides out the door into the darkness followed by his bodyguards as Uncle Pat sucks the last drop from his whiskey bottle.

Johnny turns to Mike when the Cadillac sedans drive away. "Kid, you know what to do. Fly to Jamaica tomorrow and set up this deal. Let me know when you get back through Debbie. Remember, no telephones."

'Don' Lionetti smiles at his lieutenant. "Ray, this is bigger than anything I've ever done before. I'll parlay the half million I made in the Jamaican deal and my 'Family' doesn't need to know about this action."

———————◆———————

The following day, a taxi comes to a stop in front of the Arawak Hotel reception entrance. Mike Casey has an exciting financial proposition for his Jamaican partner. He exits the back seat and pays the smiling taxi driver. Anthony Ascot calls out from his apartment. "Michael, I hope you've come to retrieve Jerry. The 'bloodclaat' costs me money."

Joy Brown smiles when Mike enters the room and Tony gives his friend a brotherly hug. The big Floridian whispers. "I need to speak to you alone about a business opportunity."

Tony turns to Joy with a smile. "Put champagne on ice and go to the fish market and get the biggest lobster for our guest. I think we'll have something to celebrate this evening."

Joy dutifully follows instructions and leaves the room. Mike opens a Ziplock baggie, filled with white crystalline powder. "My boss is putting up a million cash to start this Colombian cocaine deal. We plan to ship one hundred kilos to Florida with the next ganja shipment. You get a thousand dollars for each kilo delivered. You and I will meet a Colombian at his Rose Hall villa in August."

Tony nods his head. "Ya Man. I'm in, but I'll need those automatic weapons you promised me."

Mike smiles. "I'm sure the guns won't be a problem. Keep this deal top secret. Only you and I should know about this. If Jerry finds out, he could cause problems."

Suddenly, the apartment door opens and Jerry appears. Tony quickly conceals the bag of cocaine under his jacket as Mike rises to greet his childhood friend. "I hear you're hassling the hotel staff."

Jerry walks into the room and shrugs his shoulders. "What can I do? I'm stuck here with no money. When do I get paid for the ganja shipment?"

Michael Casey reaches into his jeans pocket and slowly starts counting fifty dollar bills. Tony retrieves a baggie of Jamaican 'gum' when Joy returns with lobster and more champagne. She opens a bottle of Clicquot and pours glasses of bubbly for everyone.

Mike hands Jerry a handful of cash. "Here's the five thousand I owe you. We're flying to Florida tomorrow."

Jerry quickly stashes the money in his pocket and gulps a full glass of sparkling wine. "I can't wait to get back to Florida. I'm tired of being a broke white nigger in Jamaica."

Tony winks at Mike and hands him the baggie of hashish, while Joy refills Jerry's glass.

Mike takes a piece of 'gum' and passes the baggie to Jerry. "Have some hash and we'll crash early tonight."

———◆———

The week before, Jill and I wash ourselves with Ivory soap in a Vermont mountain stream. The crystal clear cold water cleanses our bodies and refreshes our spirits while Lucille hunts rodents nearby. My mind races with excitement... 'Jill and I can sell the Mexican weed for over a dollar a gram wholesale. We'll easily make a thousand dollar profit with plenty of stash for ourselves. I have to call Hull House.'

Without warning, a wave of water splashes over me. A bearded oversized elf springs up from the stream. Jill rushes into her friend's arms. "Bill, you're here."

William White laughs. "I heard Lucille barking, so I decided to surprise you."

Jill smiles. "We just got back from California and you won't believe our trip. I feel reborn after escaping 'Death Valley'."

I extend my hand to Bill. "Man, our last ride was a totally tripped out Peterbilt eighteen wheeler. The driver was a cool Vietnam 'Vet' and we rapped on Benzedrine from Denver to Plainfield."

Jill dries herself in the golden sunlight. "We're lucky to be here."

I step out of the stream. "Bill, we've got two kilos of good Mexican weed. We're hoping to buy a pickup truck to haul Jamaican ganja from Florida."

The bearded musician laughs. "Great. There's no smoke around here. I'll give you a hundred twenty for a quarter pound."

I counter his offer. "Throw in a lilac bong and you've got a deal."

Lucille jumps into Bill's arms, when Jill asks. "Did you hook up with a lady on your trip?"

An impish smirk appears on Bill's bearded face. "I met Panama Red in North Carolina and we partied in Key West. Red and I had a lot of fun, but she had to go back to work delivering Hatteras Yachts to the Caribbean."

Jill chuckles. "How's Susie and Jane doing?"

Bill surveys the pale blue sky and smiles. "Great. The cooperative has two new members. Sonya and Butch are a pair of opposites. Butch served as a combat nurse on a Navy hospital ship in Vietnam and she carries a Smith & Wesson .38 all the time. Sonya is a beautiful world traveler, who studied art and music at the University of Paris. You'll meet them at lunch."

An hour later, Lucille leads us up the path towards the Green Mountain Women's Co-Op building. Susie jumps for joy when Jill enters the kitchen. The two childhood friends rush together into a tight embrace. Jane quickly joins her lover hugging Jill as I notice the two other women in the room.

One is a stunning athletic beauty with long raven hair and cobalt blue eyes. The other is a handsome muscular crew cut blonde, with intense brown eyes. She's wearing a carpenter tool belt and has a Navy anchor tattoo emblazoned on her bulging right bicep.

Bill introduces me. "Jack, meet Butch."

The well-built woman firmly shakes my hand. "Nice to meet you, Jack."

The raven haired blue eyed girl smiles at me and embraces Jill. "My name is Sonya and I hope we'll become close friends. Join us for lunch and tell us about your travels."

The kitchen table is set with bowls of salad greens, hot split pea soup and fresh baked whole wheat bread. Janis Joplin sings 'Me and Bobby McGee' on the transistor radio while Butch slices bread and Susie pours mint ice tea.

Sonya smiles at Jill. "I'd like to add you to my 'Impressionist' painting with Jane and Susie in a rural pond setting."

Jane brings a second pitcher of tea to the table and smiles at Jill. "Sonya studied art all over Europe. Her work with oil on canvas is so professional."

Jill smiles. "Sure, I'd love to pose for you."

Susie excitedly joins the conversation. "We got a letter from Judy. She and Jimmy got married and moved to Vancouver Island, Canada. She's expecting a baby early next year and asked Jane and me to midwife the birth."

Jane takes her lover's hand. "Susie and I want to invite all of you to our marriage celebration on August 26th. Butch will officiate as co-op chaplain and Sonya will produce Shakespeare's play 'A Midsummer Night's Dream' for the wedding's entertainment."

I can see Jane's personality has dramatically changed since she moved to Vermont. Last winter, she was filled with negative energy and now she's so mellow.

The two new co-op members are an odd couple for sure. Sonya is a vivacious woman with high cheekbones and sensual red lips that add symmetry to her wide eyes and upturned nose. In sharp contrast, Butch's muscular masculine body reminds me of my days working out in an Army gym.

The former Navy nurse finishes her meal and lights a Pall Mall cigarette.

"We've got a lot of work to do. All play and no work means the chicken coop and bee hive boxes won't get built. Everybody can help."

James Taylor sings 'Fire and Rain' on the radio as Jane pulls Susie close to her side.

"The organic farm is Susie's idea. Her grandmother passed away and left enough money to buy this place. We're growing organic vegetables and fruit. Maple syrup from the nearby forest will be our first cash crop."

Susie chimes in. "We already make goat milk yogurt and cheese. Our free range chicken eggs get the highest price at the farmers market and we'll have honey bees soon."

<hr />

Two weeks later in Vermont, 'The CBS Midday News with Douglas Edwards' airs on the radio. "A recent Associated Press photo of a naked Vietnamese girl burned in a napalm attack reignited anti-war protests around the country. George McGovern's California primary win guarantees him the Democratic Party Presidential nomination. Five men were arrested for breaking into the Democratic National Committee Watergate headquarters last night."

Susie announces. "We should work on Bernie Sanders' Liberty Union campaign. Bernie supports ratification of the women's Equal Rights Amendment."

Jane begins to sing 'We Shall Overcome' when Sonya picks up a Martin guitar and Butch starts to beat bongo drums.

Bill pulls out his hammer dulcimer and lilac bong. "Jack, let's smoke some of your Mexican weed."

After dinner, Jill and I lie on our sleeping bags under a moonless star filled sky. Jill hasn't been this content, since we were in Jamaica. My calls to Boston didn't go as I expected. Everyone in Hull House is out of town and Joey Palermo is in Sicily.

Jill smiles. "Sonya agreed to give me piano lessons and Susie found an old Dodge pickup in the barn. Bill said he can fix it. Maybe we can buy it."

Lilac and honeysuckle scent early summer breezes flowing through nearby maple trees as Jill falls asleep in my arms and I slip into a dream…

…Standing in the moonlight I watch a towering Amazon warrior ignite a flaming bonfire. Fairies dressed in transparent silk appear and dance in the fiery shadows...

Cold night air wakes me when Lucille snuggles between Jill and me on top of our sleeping bag. I wake my lover with a gentle kiss. "Let's move inside. June nights in Vermont are still too cold to sleep outside."

———— ◆ ————

The Green Mountains come alive with flowers and birds during the summer in sharp contrast to the frozen winter months. Americans around the world celebrate Independence Day this week and I still haven't heard from anyone in Boston.

Bill helped build chicken coops and beehives before going to Maine to sell instruments and bongs. Jill and I paid two hundred dollars for the rusted Dodge pickup Susie found on the farm. Bill said the twenty year old truck needs a lot of 'TLC' and he'll help rebuild it when he returns.

Sonya and Butch coordinated building a series of defenses to protect the crops from rabbits and deer while Jane and Susie organized the crop planting.

Jill is happy we returned to Vermont. She applied for a college transfer to UMass/Boston and wrote Debbie with my Hull address again. We paid our college fees and hope Jill gets accepted in September. Susie and Jane told Jill to send wedding invitations to the 'sisters' who helped her recover from her rape. We mailed RSVP invitations to Ann Arbor and Denver.

Butch and I finished painting the chicken coops this morning. The Moody Blues' 'Nights in White Satin' plays on a nearby radio as I clean my brush. "Butch, I'd like to ask you a personal question and don't answer if it offends you. Why do you want to be a man?"

The Navy veteran lights a Pall Mall cigarette. "No offense taken and I often ask myself the same thing. I've always felt I was a boy. When I was a kid, playing with dolls wasn't my thing. I played baseball and football, built tree houses and worked on cars. My real troubles began when I was a teenager, when girls attracted me. I had to hide my sexual orientation from people around me, especially my family. I joined the Navy, hoping to disguise my sexuality with a uniform."

Butch shrugs her shoulders. "I had my first affair with an older officer and fell in love with her. When the Navy discovered our relationship, my lover was reassigned to a different command and I was given a General Discharge for conduct 'unbecoming'."

The former nurse lights another cigarette. "That shit is past history. Now, I have a different outlook on life, because Sonya taught me to follow my heart to inner happiness. She's like a beautiful butterfly and I hope we stay together, but I can't cage her."

Butch sighs. "I'm happy for Jane and Susie, they're true soul mates. Jack, how about you and Jill? Are you lifetime mates?"

I smile and shake my head. "Jill and I are more like butterflies flitting flower to flower."

Later, Van Morrison sings 'Moondance' on a nearby radio as I walk down the hill to the local pond and notice Jill lying naked on a rainbow colored quilt near the water's edge.

Jane and Susie float in a raft on the other side of the pond. Jill's tanned body gleams in the setting sunlight. Sonya busily brushes oil on canvas. She smiles at Jill.

Sonya puts her paintbrush down and suddenly pulls off her painting smock, exposing her nude physique. She quickly joins Jill on the quilt. The two girls passionately kiss and caress each other. Their erotic ecstasy excites my desire to share their pleasure.

It's been nearly two months since Jill and Sonya's 'passion by the pond'. I resisted the urge to join them that day and haven't discussed their relationship with anyone since. I can't complain, Jill is the self-confident girl I met in Jamaica and our time together in Vermont has been fantastic.

Chuck and Rudy drove up from Boston a month ago. I 'fronted' them a five hundred dollar pound, so they could sell 'lids' in Boston this summer. Joey is still in Italy and Shu is touring with the 'Stones'.

Bill White returned to Vermont last week, after selling instruments and bongs in Maine. He agreed to restore the rusted Dodge truck including parts for a pound of weed. We tuned and updated the 'flathead six' engine with new wires, plugs and a six volt battery.

Bill bought five new truck tires and built a camper top, with a secret compartment. Jill and I filled the rust spots with Bondo and sprayed the pickup cab canary yellow. We finished by painting the truck bed black and the plywood cabin white.

Our truck is ready to test drive today. Bill attaches the battery cable and gives a thumbs up. "Put the truck in neutral and turn the ignition key to the on position. Let the six volt electrical system warm the coil for ten seconds and then adjust the choke to a rich fuel mixture. Next, step on the foot starter until the engine turns over."

I follow instructions. The twenty year old truck comes to life, with a cloud of black smoke exploding from the exhaust pipe.

Bill yells. "Yee Haw! Jack, tamp down the choke as the engine warms up. Take her for a drive and test the brakes. Remember, you can't downshift into first gear."

Jill and Lucille join me on the seat in the truck cab. I adjust the choke, press my left foot on the heavy clutch pedal and shift into first gear. The Dodge 95 hp engine begins to pull the heavy 1/2 ton pickup forward. I double clutch into second gear and honk the horn in celebration. Lucille sits on Jill's lap and sticks her head out the open passenger window.

I turn onto Route 2 and shift into third gear. Gathering speed, the twenty year old truck powers up a nearby hill. Our downhill speed peaks at a mile a minute as we circle back to the Co-Op. Just as I turn into the driveway, I press the brake pedal to the floor.

"Shit! No brakes!"

I downshift into second gear, pull the handbrake and desperately try to stop the three thousand pound pickup truck by steering into the farm compost pile.

"CRASH!"

Lucille jumps through the truck window when the vehicle stops. Jill quickly opens the door and chases after her little dog.

Bill rushes over to the stalled pickup and inspects the undercarriage. "Jack, we'll need to replace the brake lines and wheel cylinders. That's not a problem, if I can find parts."

Later that night, a nearly full August moon shines brightly through the open bedroom window. Jill sleeps soundly next to me as unanswered questions race through my mind in a circle of worry...

'The truck needs brakes and Joey is still in Italy. I haven't heard anything from Chuck and Rudy. What if UMass/Boston doesn't accept Jill's transfer? Would she stay in Vermont with her friends?'

In the distance Foghat plays Willie Dixon's classic 'I Just Want to Make Love to You'. Slowly, I drift into a dream...

...Bill White plays hammer dulcimer while Jane sings Willie Cobbs' 'You Don't Love Me'. Jill and Sonya dance together in the moonlight. Their multi-colored gowns swirl about as they vanish into darkness...

The radio wakes me the next morning. "Today is Friday, August 25th. George McGovern's Presidential campaign continues to flounder in spite of his replacing Senator Eagleton with Sargent Shriver as his Vice Presidential running mate. The Twentieth

Olympiad begins in Munich, Germany tomorrow. Mark Spitz and America's swim team are our best hope for medals. Finally, 'American Top 40' host Casey Kasem is encouraging eighteen year old first time voters to vote for George McGovern."

I gently kiss Jill as Lucille pokes her head from under the sheets. Our Ann Arbor friends are expected to arrive today for the wedding. Lonny Higgins couldn't leave her practice, so she and Dave sent a gift of Waterford Crystal champagne flutes with a thank you note for our donations to her clinic.

Jill slowly opens her eyes with a smile. She hugs me and whispers. "Jack, I had a fantastic dream last night. We named our yellow truck 'Donna Dodge' and drove to Miami under a full moon. What do you think?"

I chuckle at the thought of driving a Dodge pickup named 'Donna'. "That sounds great. I hope Mike comes through with a boatload of ganja."

———◆———

An early afternoon sun warms the hillside when Lucille barks and excitedly wags her tail at the sound of an approaching car. A Volvo station wagon horn announces the arrival of our Michigan wedding guests.

Four car doors open simultaneously, Marc Humphries talks baseball as he emerges from the mud covered vehicle. "The Tigers will win the Pennant."

Gray Tucker gets out of the driver's seat and shakes his head, with a smile. "No way! Luis Tiant will take the Sox to the World Series."

Sugar and Gwen rise from the back seat. Everyone is admiring the vibrant green hills surrounding the farm, when Lucille charges and leaps into Sugar's arms. The little dog licks Laurie's face as Jane and Susie join Jill hugging the new arrivals.

Jane shows off the recent construction and fencing. "This summer we built another chicken coop and more honey bee hive boxes. Our latest project is better fencing to keep the deer and rabbits from eating our heirloom vegetables."

Hump nods and smiles. "Sounds great. We need more organic farms and less chemical pollution. I'm reading Rudolf Steiner's 'Biodynamic' theories on organic agriculture and he says chemical fertilizers, pesticides and herbicides poison the soil. The World population could double in our lifetime and the Earth can't support six billion people using chemicals to sustain food production."

In the distance, Butch calls out from the wedding stage. "As a minister in the Universal Life Church and master of ceremonies, I welcome Jane and Susie's wedding guests to participate in Sonya's adaptation of 'A Midsummer Night's Dream'. Come join us for a rehearsal lunch prepared in your honor."

The wedding party gathers for a sumptuous buffet: green salads, chilled tomato bisque, fresh baked wheat bread, Vermont cheeses, potato pancakes with applesauce and a fine German Riesling wine.

Sonya appears in costume as 'Puck'. Each table setting has a play script and costume; masquerade masks for all, flowered shirts and tights for men and rainbow colored gowns for ladies. Bill emerges from behind the stage dressed as the Greek god 'Pan', playing a flute as the girls pick up their costumes and excitedly dance about.

Butch taps the table. "Settle down. We have a lot to do before the wedding tomorrow."

Sonya stands up. "Welcome fellow fairies and courtiers to Jane and Susie's 'Midsummer Night's Dream'. Each of you will have a role in tomorrow's wedding play. We'll have a costume rehearsal after lunch. Now, let's toast Jane and Susie. May their love last forever."

<hr>

The next afternoon, Bill and I finish bleeding air from the Dodge truck brake lines, when a Cadillac horn sounds. I look down the driveway to see Chuck Lievi's '61' Cadillac DeVille driving towards me. Rudy's at the wheel, with Joey Palermo riding shotgun. The silver sedan stops and Joey opens the door. "Jack, I hope you got weed to sell."

I laugh and give Joey a handshake. "You're just in time, I've got a couple pounds left."

Rudy and I shake hands. "Where's Chuck? Did you guys sell the pound I fronted you?"

Rudy reaches into his jeans pocket, with a frown. "I have two fifty, but I need twenty for gas. The 'Caddy' only gets ten miles to a gallon. Chuck said he'll cover the rest of the bill, after he sells his Olympic Frisbees in Germany."

I shrug my shoulders when Rudy hands me the cash. "OK, Chuck owes me when he gets back from Munich."

I turn to Joey. "I hope you got cash."

Joey laughs and pulls a roll of bills from his pocket. "I've got two thousand dollars. Here's some Zig Zags, let's taste what you got."

I take the rolling papers and pull out the Mexican weed from the truck camper. "I have two pounds of Michoacan for five hundred each."

Joey hands me ten Ben Franklin's and smiles. "Who owns the truck?"

I chuckle and light a joint. "Me and the old lady bought it. We built a secret compartment under the camper to carry Jamaican ganja."

Joey smiles and nods his head when I hand him the joint and the two pound package. "Count me in."

He takes one look at the contents and inhales the fresh aroma. "This smells wicked good. We have to get this weed back to Boston tonight."

Rudy reaches into his shirt pocket. "Jack, I nearly forgot your mail from Hull. Jill got letters from UMass/Boston and Florida."

A surge of curiosity runs through my mind as Rudy hands me the envelopes... 'Did Mike send a message in the Florida letter? Did UMass/Boston accept Jill?'

———— • ————

Later a setting sun highlights pink and white rose arrangements adorning the dinner tables. Sonya added a 'Moonlight Delight' electric fruit punch from Amsterdam to the beverage list with German Riesling wine selections and Lowenbrau beer.

Sonya plays Beethoven 'Piano Concerto #5' as a cream white full moon rises in the sky. Handsomely dressed in a black and white tuxedo, Butch signals Jane and Susie to lead the entourage down the aisle when Sonya plays Felix Mendelssohn's 'Wedding March'.

Butch announces. "We gather here today to witness the loving union of Jane and Susie in a lifelong marriage bond."

The wedding couple gaze into each other's eyes as the master of ceremonies asks. "Do you agree to love and care for one another for as long as you live?"

The two lovers place gold rings on each other's fingers and simultaneously say, "I do." Butch raises her right hand over the wedding couple's heads when they passionately kiss. "As a Universal Life Church minister, may the Goddess of the Universe bless this union."

A sumptuous vegetarian feast featuring Cabot cheddar cheese souffles, homegrown organic salads and vegetables, with strawberry and blueberry cheesecake desserts is enjoyed by all. Beer and wine flow freely throughout the evening as the wedding guests dance and consume the last of the electric fruit punch in the silvery moon light.

The party concludes with Sonya reciting Puck's final words as the full moon sets at sunrise. "I am that merry wanderer of the night. If we shadows have offended, think but this and all is amended. You have slumbered here while these visions did appear. And this weak and idle theme, no more yielding than a dream."

———◆———

A bright full moon shines over Ft. Lauderdale the previous night. 'Don' Lionetti drinks Scotch whiskey with Little Ray in a Coral Ridge Country Club private bar room while watching Jim McKay and ABC cover the Munich Olympics.

Little Ray becomes agitated as he finishes his Jack Daniel's rocks and pours another. "Where the fuck is the Jockey?"

Johnny dismissively waves his hand. "I told Jimmy to show up later, because we have to talk. My lawyer checked out the Valencia family and they're highly respected throughout Colombia. I'm doing this deal without Santo and Carlos approval. I wired a half million into Francisco's bank yesterday. He'll meet the 'Kid' in Jamaica and set up the shipment."

Little Ray swallows a gulp of whiskey and grins. The bar room side door opens abruptly and Jimmy the 'Jockey' staggers in. "Johnny and Ray, I just won five grand at the track."

The gangster's eyes bulge with anger. "You better keep your shit together."

'Don' Lionetti steps between his lieutenants. "Jimmy, glad you made it. Have a drink. How's your granddaughter doing?"

Johnny hands the jockey the bottle of Courvoisier VSOP Cognac and a glass. Jimmy fills his glass. "Thanks for asking. The doctors hope chemotherapy and radiation treatments will save her. We're praying for the best. Why the urgent meeting?"

'Don' Lionetti pushes a brown envelope into the jockey's shirt pocket. "Here's twenty big ones to help pay the medical bills. I have a deal that's worth millions. I need you to go fishing in the Bahamas with a side trip to Jamaica after Thanksgiving."

———◆———

At the same time across town, Mike Casey and Uncle Pat are drinking Budweisers with Jose Cuervo tequila shots as Jerry Siegel's black Lincoln enters the New River boat compound followed by a brand new brown GMC pickup, towing a matching horse trailer.

Jerry and the pickup driver enter the main house kitchen. "Mike, this is my cousin's partner J.R. He wants to haul five hundred pounds of ganja to California in the horse trailer outside."

The Caseys put down their drinks and stand up to meet the ponytailed California newcomer dressed in denim, cowboy boots and a Stetson hat. Mike shakes J.R.'s hand. "Nice to meet you. I'm always looking for paying customers"

The big Floridian removes a cocaine filled baggie from his shirt pocket and pours the contents on the Formica kitchen table. "We're expecting a Christmas delivery and you'll want to get in on this Colombian snow too."

———•———

The full moon illuminates the Jamaican shore the following evening when a taxi carrying Mike Casey and Anthony Ascot stops at the Rose Hall Great House entrance. Tonight's meeting with the wealthy Colombian makes Mike and Tony anxious. They're both dreaming of becoming millionaires as a Rolls Royce 'Silver Shadow' pulls up beside them and two men dressed in black tuxedos open the passenger doors. "Gentlemen, please enjoy a short ride to your destination."

Tony and Mike grin at each other while sitting in plush leather seats. A bottle of Veuve Clicquot chills with crystal champagne glasses in the portable bar. The rear center console has a cocaine filled silver bowl inside. The two men sip champagne and inhale near pure cocaine on the short ride up to a hilltop estate overlooking the Caribbean Sea.

Armed guards lower their Uzi submachine guns when the Rolls Royce passes through the crimson bougainvillea shrouded entrance gate. The 'Silver Shadow' parks in front of a two story white stucco villa as four more guards carrying Uzi's surround the limousine.

Two women wearing gold silk gowns walk down a long staircase to greet the arriving guests. The beautiful ladies open both passenger doors. A blue eyed blond greets Tony as a copper toned raven haired beauty takes Mike's hand. The girls gently caress and massage their escorts as they lead them up the stairs.

Francisco Diego Valencia appears at the top of the staircase dressed in a custom tailored cream white Italian silk dinner jacket.

The Uzi carrying guards fade into the shadows when Francisco greets his guests.

"I hope you enjoyed the necessary weapons search. We can never be too careful these days. Come join me on the balcony. I have a champagne and lobster buffet prepared for you."

The elegant Colombian turns to Tony. "Anthony, I am told that you can deliver my product to Michael's boat. You will be handsomely rewarded if this is true."

———◆———

The same day at the Ft. Lauderdale police station cafeteria, Lieutenant Dan Brady drinks black coffee while Sergeant Dick Guerrette sips Lipton tea. Brady leans close to his partner. "Dick, a Justice Department drug task force is coming to town before Christmas. The unit will include a U.S. Attorney, with interstate jurisdiction and authority to prosecute drug dealers anywhere in the country."

———◆———

Earlier in Vermont the day after Susie and Jane's wedding, hot water flows in the shower while I rub Dr. Bronner's Castile Soap over my exhausted body and think to myself...

'Wow, that wedding was one hell of a party. Jill and I danced until sunrise drinking Sonya's 'MDMA' laced electric punch. We celebrated Jill's transfer to UMass/Boston and Debbie Boon's December wedding invitation. Donna Dodge is ready to travel and we'll have fifteen hundred dollars when Chuck pays us.'

The shower door unexpectedly opens exposing Sonya's naked athletic physique. I'm focused on a red and black scorpion tattoo adorning her thigh when she enters the shower.

She seductively smiles. "Jack, I've noticed the way you look at me. Now, show me what you've got."

Later that day, 'Let It Be' plays on a transistor radio in Donna Dodge while our friends wave goodbye to Jill and me. Our pickup truck is loaded with fresh organic vegetables bound for the Boston Food Co-Op as I honk the horn and put the yellow Dodge in gear. "Beantown here we come."

MOON OVER MIAMI

Jill and I finished our fall semester final exams this week and we're looking forward to Mike and Debbie's Christmas wedding in Florida. Last month's Presidential election was a disaster for the Democrats. George McGovern lost forty nine states, with Massachusetts being the lone exception. Nixon's landslide victory strengthened his demand for South Vietnam to be an independent nation.

Tragedy struck the Munich Olympics earlier in September when P.L.O. terrorists murdered Israeli athletes. That same month, White House advisors G. Gordon Liddy and E. Howard Hunt were indicted for the Watergate burglary rumored to have been authorized by former U.S. Attorney General John Mitchell.

Christmas lights shine in the winter twilight as Chuck Lievi's silver Cadillac stops in front of Hull House. The 'Beantown Boys' street hockey team steps into the freezing chill. Chuck yells. "World Street Hockey Champions!"

I open the front door and 'high five' the team as they walk past me into the warm house. "The fire's hot and the beers are cold."

Our canary yellow Dodge pickup is parked next to the silver Cadillac and ready to travel south to Florida. Tonight's foreboding darkening gray sky forecasts a possible winter blizzard. The logistics of a twelve hundred mile journey in a twenty year old truck require snow tires, a gallon of 10-30 motor oil, two gallons of radiator antifreeze and five twenty pound bags of sand with rock salt.

Chuck enters the living room, removes his heavy wool overcoat and gives me an envelope. "Jack, here's the two seventy I owe for the Mexican pot. I would've paid sooner, but the Olympic frisbee deal was a bust. When are you taking off for Florida?"

I nod my head. "Thanks for the cash. We should leave soon because a 'Nor'easter' is coming tonight. It will take three days to make Ft. Lauderdale running at fifty-five."

Ten minutes later, Lucille dashes from the warm house and jumps into the heated Dodge truck cab. The little dog's master quickly follows her pet into the pickup.

I'm thinking to myself and hoping Mike has ganja for sale when Jill's departing comments become poetry to my ears. "We say so long to ice, snow and cold north winds on our journey south to the land of parrots, palm trees and tropical breezes."

I put the 'flat head 6' in first gear as Wayne Cochran sings 'Going Back to Miami' on my transistor radio. We'll run 'Double Nickel' down I-95, using 'Donna Dodge' as our 'handle' on our new Motorola CB radio. The weather and traffic will set the pace.

Marvin Gaye is singing 'I heard it through the Grapevine' when a radio news bulletin interrupts the music. "A severe winter storm is expected throughout New England tonight. Snow accumulation could exceed twelve inches along the coast, with two feet possible in the New Hampshire and Vermont mountains."

Jill looks at me with trepidation in her eyes. "Should we turn back?"

I answer, without hesitation. "Hell no. Florida here we come. Let's smoke a joint."

We roll through Rhode Island and Connecticut in a cannabis induced haze as frozen sleet collects on the windshield and highway. Thick gray clouds fill the sky threatening to unleash an avalanche of snow on us.

WABC disc jockey 'Cousin Brucie' announces. "Let's hear two #1 hits from the 'King'. Elvis Presley's first #1 hit 'Heartbreak Hotel' and his last 'Suspicious Minds'."

Jill stares at the somber winter landscape passing before us. "Sonya called me this morning. Butch moved to Provincetown with her Navy lover. I hope Sonya comes to the Hull House New Year's Eve party with Susie and Jane."

My buddy turns and looks at me. "Did you know Sonya is a Scorpio like us?"

I'm afraid to acknowledge Sonya's scorpion tattoo or our recent sex in the shower. Jill and I haven't discussed her passion on the pond either. My eyes remain focused on the snow covered road. "I got to know Butch better than Sonya. We didn't talk about astrology, but she did say she fell in love with a Naval Officer."

Cousin Brucie announces, "Next up, Leon Russell's 'This Masquerade'." Jill wistfully gazes into the night. "I want to play piano like Leon Russell someday. My 'Nanny' taught me the basics on a 'Speakeasy' piano when I was a kid. Sonya was teaching me to play Mozart this summer."

The World Trade Center dominates the New York City night skyline when we enter the 'Big Apple' on the Cross Bronx Expressway. Bright city lights illuminate sparkling snowflakes accumulating on the roadway. I turn to Jill. "We'll stop for gas after we cross the George Washington Bridge. Can you drive in this snow?"

Jill pulls a small rhinestone jewelry box from her purse and opens it. "Yeah, I'll drive and we have two Dexedrine tabs each to keep us awake."

The Vince Lombardi travel plaza is the first stop on the New Jersey Turnpike. A cold north wind blows freezing sleet across nearby wetlands. I fill the gas tank and check the engine oil while Jill walks Lucille and buys coffee. I look out over the bleak landscape and question the New York Giants decision to build a football stadium at the Meadowlands.

My buddy returns with Howard Johnson's hot 'Java' to boost our Dexedrine high. She puts on a pair of eyeglasses and takes the driver's seat with Lucille on her lap, then shifts Donna Dodge into gear.

Junior Walker plays saxophone in 'What Does It Take (To Win Your Love)' when I light a joint and pass it to Jill. She gives me a concerned look through a cloud of hazy blue smoke. "I wish Debbie's wedding invitation had a phone number. I hope her wedding is as wonderful as Susie and Jane's. Debbie has very high hopes for her marriage to Mike, but I'm not so sure he's the marrying type."

A smirk betrays my thoughts. "Most men want sex, not marriage. I'm a one woman man, one at a time."

Jill's face contorts with feigned distress. "You men are alike, your hard-on dominates your thinking. Women are different. We want lifelong commitments."

I chuckle. "My father says 'Women are like flowers, nourish them and they blossom'."

Jill shakes her head. "That's so old school. Women don't need men to nourish them."

Red lights and flares along the roadside suddenly slow traffic to a crawl. Jill downshifts from third to second gear as I stash the weed in the toolbox under the seat. New Jersey State Troopers appear to be everywhere in the shadows. Bright emergency lights spotlight a huge eighteen wheel tractor trailer lying on its side.

We sigh with relief when a gray uniformed State Trooper waves us through the debris strewn highway. Jill struggles to keep the old pickup on the frozen snow covered pavement. She squints into her eyeglasses peering through the ice covered windshield and shifts into third gear. "I'm glad Lonny got me these new prescription lenses. I couldn't see the road without them."

Cousin Brucie and WABC fade from the airwaves when Frank Sinatra sings 'Let It Snow'. The song reminds me of my father driving to my mother's Virginia family for Christmas in year's past.

I check a Rand McNally Road Atlas as we approach the end of the New Jersey Turnpike. "We've been driving for nearly eight hours and still haven't crossed the Delaware Bridge. The snow storm has slowed our average speed to under thirty miles an hour. We won't make the wedding, if we don't pick up the pace."

I adjust the transistor radio dial to a Baltimore station and Stevie Wonder comes to life singing his latest hit 'Superstition'.

Earlier in Florida on the December new moon. 'Don' Lionetti drinks single malt Scotch with his lieutenants at Cap's Place. "Ray, I don't like being out gunned by anyone."

Little Ray shakes his head. "I can't do much about Francisco. He's a Colombian diplomat and travels with armed bodyguards everywhere he goes."

Johnny waves his hand dismissively. "I've got a lot of money tied up in this deal and I'm worried about Jimmy in Jamaica. I'm not sending automatic weapons to the Jamaicans."

The Jockey nods his head. "All I have on board is a twelve gauge Remington."

Little Ray growls. "Don't give the 'nigger' nothing."

'Don' Lionetti shakes his head. "I'll send some .38's and shotguns."

Johnny pauses and swallows his single malt. "Another thing, I just got word from my snitch. There's a Federal drug task force coming to town with a special U.S. Attorney and my lawyer said I won't be able to cut deals with local prosecutors and judges."

<hr />

The same dark night at the New River compound main house, Mike Casey meets with Jerry Siegel. His childhood friend waves his arms wildly and raises his voice.

"Mike, my cousin's fifty large deposit should cover his five hundred pounds and a hundred for me. I'm paying you an extra fifty bucks a pound."

Mike shakes his head. "Little Ray will kill us both, if I lose that kind of cash. I'll need Johnny's OK to do the 'front'."

Uncle Pat hands his nephew a beer. "Mike, how are you going to collect from California?"

Jerry glares at the old sailor, then shifts his eyes back to Mike. "You owe me. I need this."

Mike nods his head with a slight grin. "Alright, I'll talk with Johnny."

<hr />

Twelve days later, Mike and Uncle Pat stand on the New River boat dock drinking margaritas. Mike looks up into the night sky at a nearly full moon and smiles. "This Colombian coke deal could make me a millionaire."

The old sailor nods his head. "Cocaine can take control of you. I smoked opium in Hong Kong when I was in the Navy. 'Riding the Dragon' was a wild blast, but I had to 'hole up' in a hotel room for a week with 'Old No. 7' to get off that shit."

A truck horn blares at the entrance. Flood lights illuminate the compound when J.R.s' brown GMC pickup and trailer enters. The vehicle headlights spotlight Uncle Pat's black Labrador 'Moonshine' coming forward to greet the new arrivals.

Mike notices a stunning curly haired blonde riding shotgun when J.R. turns off the V8 engine and dims the lights. The California cowboy gets out of the truck and pulls a Stetson hat over his ponytail.

The big Floridian greets his guests. "J.R., introduce me to your lady friend."

The pretty blonde teenager exits the pickup and Moonshine buries her nose between the newcomer's legs. The California Cowboy smiles. "Mike, meet Michelle. We hooked up in Hawaii this summer. Man, our drive from L.A. on 'bennies' drained me. I need a shower really bad."

Mike chuckles. "The second guesthouse is set up for you."

Michelle smiles while she pets the nuzzling canine. "Nice to meet you and your dog."

Uncle Pat steps out of the shadows. "Pat Casey here, I'm Mike's uncle and this is my dog, Moonshine. Nice to have a pretty woman in the house. I'll get the blender going."

------◆------

Earlier the same day the five o'clock shift ends at the Ft. Lauderdale Police Chief's office. Chief Bill Evans introduces Federal Bureau of Narcotics officers to his men. "Agent Dobbs and Thorsen, this is Lieutenant Brady and Sergeant Guerrette. They're my best men on the Vice Squad. I've assigned them to work with the interagency task force."

Dan Brady extends his hand to the taller of the two crew cut Federal officers. "Good to be on the same team."

Agent Dobbs' steel gray eyes stare straight ahead as he shakes Lieutenant Brady's hand firmly. "Let's hope so. We hear you've got a 'rat' in your department."

Sergeant Guerrette nervously twitches as his hand goes limp in Agent Thorsen's iron grip when he hears Agent Dobbs' words. The police sergeant manages a slight smile. "What brings you guys into our quiet little city?"

A baritone voice answers from the back of the room. A tall man, dressed in a Brooks Brothers blue pinstripe suit stands up. Crew cut red hair and piercing blue eyes add intensity to his words. "I'm Thomas P. Stack, U.S. Attorney appointed to lead the Florida Federal Drug Interdiction Task Force. Your chief has chosen you to join us on the frontline in America's war on drugs. Our mission is to stop illegal narcotic shipments entering the country from the Caribbean and South America."

Born and bred in Michigan, U.S. Attorney Thomas Paul Stack earned his assignment after graduating from the University of Michigan Law School. Congressman Gerald Ford nominated him to lead the multi-level federal interdiction effort to apprehend and prosecute drug smugglers across America.

Tom Stack strides to the front of the room and takes command. He has a fervent belief in the righteousness of his mission. "Thank you Chief for your continued assistance. Lieutenant Brady, I've assigned Agents Dobbs and Thorsen to work with you and Sergeant Guerrette. The task force command center will be up and running next week and we start full time in January. So, don't let your holiday celebrations get out of hand."

The U.S. Attorney pauses and smiles. "On that note, where can a man get a pint of Guinness in this town? I'll buy the first round."

A nearly full moon illuminates the Caribbean Sea on this December night as a DC-3 cargo plane approaches a remote coastal landing strip near Ocho Rios, Jamaica. Four British Land Rover IIAs light up a short asphalt runway.

Sitting in his new Land Rover III, Anthony Ascot contemplates the exciting opportunity unfolding in the moonlight. His dream of becoming the richest man in Jamaica is within reach. Tony perks up at the sound of an approaching plane and yells out. "Load up and take different routes to the warehouse."

The DC-3 comes to a stop at the end of the runway. Tony's crew quickly rushes the cargo plane and begins unloading plastic wrapped bundles into the waiting vehicles.

Francisco Diego Valencia signals Tony to board the airplane. His host passes him a cocaine covered mirror. "Anthony, I brought AK-47 rifles and ammunition to guard my product."

The wily Jamaican inhales a large line of cocaine while the elegant Colombian removes a 24k gold necklace from a leather briefcase. Francisco slides the case towards his Jamaican associate. "Here's one hundred thousand dollars for delivering the hundred kilos to the Floridians. Now, let me present to you a gift worthy of a lion among men."

Anthony Ascot's eyes are riveted on the precious stones embedded in a gold medallion attached to the necklace. A diamond and ruby inscription spell 'Champion' within an emerald Jamaica silhouette.

Francisco Diego Valencia places the sparkling jewelry around his protege's neck. "Anthony, I brought you one hundred kilos in addition to the one thousand for the Americans. Guard my product and you'll be handsomely rewarded. I will personally load the American boat next month."

The debonair Colombian pulls a Pyrex glass pipe from a second leather briefcase and seductively grins. "Mi amigo, I have something special for you. Inside this case are the tools and recipes to enhance your enjoyment of my product."

<hr>

Back in in America, Jill and I continue driving south towards Florida on I-95 in Donna Dodge. The Grateful Dead plays 'Truckin' on the transistor radio as we cross the Potomac River into Virginia. Dry pavement allows us to pick up the pace and roll into North Carolina. 'America Love It or Leave It' bumper stickers can be seen everywhere as passing truckers honk their air horns and give us 'Smokey Bear' warnings over their C.B. radios.

My Virginia grandmother took me to Civil War battle sites throughout the 'South'. 'Nano' was a Daughter of the American Revolution and fiercely proud of her heritage. Colonial Williamsburg was always included in tours of her home state. She respected General Robert E. Lee, but she believed President Lincoln was right to free the slaves.

A Charlotte radio station plays Otis Redding singing Sam Cooke's hit 'You Send Me' when we approach South Carolina. We're halfway to Miami and could make it to the wedding on time, if we can keep up this pace.

Jill looks at the winter landscape and notices a road sign 'South of the Border'. "My family bought fireworks here on our trips to Florida when I was a kid. Let's stop and get gas."

The C.B. radio crackles to life. "This is 'Rock and Roll Redneck'. There's a 'Smokey Bear' convention at the Carolina border on I-95."

Donna Dodge's 95 hp straight six cylinder engine is maxed out, traveling a mile a minute. I laugh. "No need to worry about speed traps. Hopefully, we'll be cruising in the 'Sunshine State' tomorrow morning."

A pale orange sun is low in the gray winter sky when we approach South of the Border's mascot 'Pedro'. The radio announces entertainment news. "Diana Ross, Billy Dee Williams and Richard Pryor received rave reviews for their performances in 'Lady Sings the Blues'."

I steer the Dodge pickup into the parking lot as Jill turns to me. "Diana Ross should win an Oscar for her role as Billie Holiday and Richard Pryor's acting talent surprised me."

Twenty minutes later, our truck is refueled and Krispy Kreme donuts supplement hot coffee for the final run into Florida.

Jose Feliciano sings 'Feliz Navidad' when Jill takes the wheel, with Lucille in her lap. "I can't wait to swim in the ocean. Do we have time to stop at St. Augustine Beach."

I check the maps again. "We're six hundred miles from Ft. Lauderdale. We could make it there tomorrow afternoon. Let's keep trucking."

Jill smiles. "OK, let's go for it buddy."

An hour later, I finish the last donut and light a joint as Jill drives 'pedal to the metal' in the darkness, listening to Ray Charles sing 'Georgia on My Mind'.

"BOOM!!"

"Thump! Thump! Thump!"

The half ton pickup heaves wildly to the right. Jill strains to hang onto the wheel as she steers into the breakdown lane. Lucille licks her master's worried face when Donna Dodge comes to a stop. Lucky for us, the flat is the rear passenger tire and we have a spare.

I turn on our Eveready lantern flashlight. "Jill, you handled that like a pro. I'm glad Bill talked me into buying a five ton jack. Shut off the engine and turn on the emergency blinkers to warn traffic. I'll get the spare and raise the rear axle."

The cold night air chills my hands when I set the jack under the truck and attach the lug wrench. I use a pipe and fulcrum for leverage in my attempt to turn the lug nuts. Damn! They won't budge. The water and road salt must have rusted them tight. We're fifty miles from nowhere and the temperature is near freezing. What are we going to do now?

------◆------

The following day, the Goodyear Blimp floats in a pale blue sky as an orange sun sets. Lucille sits on Jill's lap smelling the fresh salt air outside the driver's window. A cream white full moon rises from the Atlantic Ocean as we approach Ft. Lauderdale.

Last night, we had a flat tire in South Carolina due to the metal debris we drove through in New Jersey. We were cold and nearly out of hope, when farmer Chris Brown drove up on a John Deere tractor.

WD-40 loosened the rusted tire lug nuts and his tractor recharged our run down battery. The polite elderly African American declined payment for his services with kind words. "Someday you'll do the same for someone in need. Merry Christmas."

WSHE plays The Eagles' 'Take It Easy' on the radio, when Jill drives Donna Dodge into the New River compound under a silver full moon. She brakes the pickup and parks next to the main house. The front door opens and a black Labrador charges out.

Lucille barks at a gray bearded man speaking from the doorway. "Moonshine, be a good dog. These are friends."

Jill's pet terrier jumps headlong from the truck. The two dogs quickly smell each other and mark territory together. Jill steps out of our mud covered pickup and takes a deep breath of tropical air. "The oleander and gardenia flowers smell wonderful."

Dressed in boxer shorts and a sailor cap, the bearded stranger introduces himself.

"I'm Mike's uncle, Pat. You must be Jack and Jill. Mike and Debbie are in the guest house. You're bunking with me in the main house. Come inside. I make the best Margarita in Florida. Do you want one?"

Jill and I answer in unison. "Sure, I'd love one."

Mike and Debbie come through the back door led by Lucille and Moonshine as we enter the kitchen. Debbie smiles when she sees Jill. "I was worried you weren't going to make it. I'm so glad you're here."

The two college girlfriends rush together and embrace as Mike smiles at me. "Jack, you look like a long haired hippie freak."

I chuckle as we shake hands. "Yeah, I hear you're 'tying the knot'."

Uncle Pat is handing out margaritas when Debbie pulls Jill into a side bedroom with a distressed look. "Come with me. I have so much to tell you."

Mike raises his cocktail glass as the girls leave the room.

"Congrats Jack. You're in time for the Jamaican shipment. Johnny doesn't allow any phone calls, so I had Debbie send the 'wedding invitation'. The boat is expected in the next twenty four hours."

I nod my head and smile. "Man, you've moved up in the world."

My Army buddy laughs. "Yeah, I live here with Debbie. This is where you pick up product from now on. Uncle Pat is our gatekeeper and stays here full time."

Mike Casey grins. "Jack, I've got a big surprise for you. There's a hundred kilos of coke on that boat worth millions."

Nearby in the side bedroom, Debbie lights a Virginia Slims cigarette. "Jill, there isn't going to be a wedding this week. Mike told me to send the invitation, because his Jamaican boat is coming in on the full moon."

Debbie takes hold of Jill's hand. "I want to marry Mike and have a baby."

Jill wraps her arms around her girlfriend. "Are you sure you want a baby?"

Debbie's brown eyes fill with tears.

"I want to be with Mike forever. Don't you feel the same way about Jack?"

A hesitant look crosses Jill's face. "It's different with Jack and me. I'm not ready to settle down and my life has changed a lot since I saw you last."

The door abruptly opens. Moonshine leads Lucille into the room. The little terrier jumps into Debbie's lap and gives her a dog kiss. Jill smiles. "Lucille really likes you."

Later that night, a distinctive car horn triggers the New River boat compound steel gates to open. Jerry Siegel's black Lincoln enters the compound with the Casey cousins in the back seat. Dressed in dark clothes, the car occupants quickly enter the main house. Mike greets his crew in the kitchen. "Let's get down to the dock. The boat is in."

Jerry follows Mike and his cousins, walking towards the dock. Uncle Pat and I make up the rear. My heart races with excitement as we approach the river boathouse.

Uncle Pat points at a houseboat hidden in the shadows. "Little Ray lives there. You'll meet him tonight."

The old sailor gulps a whiskey shot. "I hope Johnny keeps Little Ray on a short leash."

Inside the boathouse, flashlights shine on men working in the dark as electric saws quickly cut into the fiberglass fishing yacht. Little Ray opens the hidden hold and turns to his mentor. "Johnny, it looks good. You've got one hundred kilos of coke and a ton of weed."

'Don' Lionetti slaps Jimmy the Jockey on the back. "Great job."

A car horn sounds at the gate. Ray grabs his MAC-10 and checks the security camera monitor. "The Colombians are here. I'll open the gate."

Johnny smiles. "Kid, start unloading the packages and you know what to do with the grass. Ray, you're in charge of the cocaine. You and the Kid get a kilo each to start up sales. Lock the rest in the boat house storage locker and bring me the key."

Four Uzi toting bodyguards dressed in black leather trench coats enter the boathouse while we unload the ganja and cocaine.

A cold chill surges through me when I see an elegant Latin man dressed in a black tuxedo enter the room.

I think to myself… 'This is the 'Million Dollar Man' that Mike talks about.'

'Don' Lionetti steps forward with a smile and open hand. "Francisco, I'm happy your package has been successfully delivered."

Francisco Diego Valencia points to a coiled red fanged black viper design on the cocaine bales. "My logo guarantees product purity. In anticipation of your deposit, I've delivered one thousand kilos to Jamaica. The next shipment is ready to load as soon as your boat returns to Ocho Rios."

The tall Colombian grins. "I must forewarn you. My Russell's vipers will guard the shipment until I'll personally remove them upon delivery."

Francisco hands Johnny a small envelope. "I've established a new Vatican Bank account for your deposit and future payments. The account information is in the envelope. As I'm taking most of the risk, I expect payment of the nine millions balance within ninety days after delivery."

Johnny nods his head. "We're in agreement regarding the payments. I'm sending shotguns and pistols to Jamaica on my next boat and I don't want the Jamaicans to have automatic weapons. I'm sure you understand my concerns."

The elegant Colombian straightens up and turns for the door with a wave of his hand. "I understand your concerns and we're in agreement regarding our business venture. Remember, do not open the hold until I retrieve my pet vipers."

Francisco and his gun toting entourage silently exit into the darkness.

An hour later, the brown GMC pickup and trailer is parked next to the main house under the bright full moon. Mike Casey sits inside the kitchen with J.R. inhaling cocaine on the kitchen table.

The California cowboy smiles and puts some coke on his tongue. "Mike, this is high quality. I've got an upscale 'Hollywood' clientele. They'll pay top dollar for this 'snow' all over the country, from L.A. to New York."

J.R. grins with a twinkle in his eye. "I can pay fifty thousand a kilo. Front me a quarter pound to set the stage for future business."

Mike nods his head with a grin. "I'll put a package together."

Jerry enters the kitchen. His nearsighted eyes focus on the leftover crystalline powder on the mirror. He quickly snorts the last line and licks the mirror clean while staring at Mike and J.R. "Where's my piece of the action?"

Nearby in Debbie's guest house bedroom, she laughs with Jill and Michelle while passing a fashion mirror covered with neat cocaine lines. "Girls, try some Colombian 'snow'."

Jill toots a line and forwards the mirror to Michelle as Debbie caresses the newcomer's hair. "I've always wanted blonde curls."

Michelle inhales cocaine and chuckles. "I wanted hair like you and Joan Baez."

She rolls her eyes as the cocaine crystals melt into her brain. Her buxom body quivers and a wide grin appears on her face. "I hope J.R. brings some of this coke to Maui."

Jill inhales a second line of white powder.

"Michelle, what's Maui like? I dream of living in the tropics. Maybe I can visit the islands when I graduate college."

Michelle licks the mirror clean. "Hawaii is the best place in the world. The weather is nearly perfect most of the time. My mother and I sailed to Honolulu from San Diego last year. I moved to Maui with J.R. a month ago and now I'm a 'Maui Girl'."

Debbie nods her head. "Maybe Mike and I'll honeymoon in Hawaii this spring."

The full moon sets over the New River main house when Mike hands J.R. a Ziplock bag. "Here's your quarter pound starter package."

The California cowboy places the cocaine inside a hidden compartment under his pickup seat, while Mike Casey's younger cousins load plastic wrapped ganja bales into the horse trailer compartment covered with manure. J.R. closes the tailgate. "The horse shit will keep the cops from finding the stash. We'll hit the road at sunrise."

Mike hands cash envelopes to his younger cousins while they clean up a short time later. "Here's five thousand for unloading the boat and expenses. Rent a couple of Lincoln Town cars with big trunks and drive five hundred pounds each to the Jacksonville farm."

A perplexed look appears on Mike Casey's face. "Where's Jerry?"

Scott laughs. "He's probably looking for more coke in the guest house."

Mike nods his head. "Uncle Pat, tell Jerry to meet me in the main house's back bedroom."

Jerry stumbles into the bedroom. Mike pulls a cocaine filled plastic baggie from his shirt and pours sparkling crystalline powder on a small mirror as he hands his childhood friend two brown envelopes. "The fat envelope is twenty five large for Tony.

The small one is ten for you. Tell Tony, he'll get the rest of his money, when we sell the ganja."

Mike passes the mirror, with a rolled fifty dollar bill to Jerry. "Try some of my 'moon rock'. It's the best I've ever had."

Jerry grabs the envelopes and picks up the mirror. "What do I get for J.R.s' coke deal?"

Mike shrugs his shoulders. "You'll get five hundred a kilo after I get paid."

Jerry inhales the cocaine. "What about some powder for the road?"

Mike grins. "Yeah, keep this quarter ounce as part of your referral fee."

Jerry grabs the baggie and licks the cocaine mirror clean. Mike escorts his childhood friend towards the door. "It's nearly sunrise. Leave your car here and take a cab to the airport. Catch the first flight to Jamaica and pay Tony. Tell him, I'll see him in ten days."

A taxi horn honks at the front gate and Jerry exits into the shadows.

───────◆───────

The next day, Uncle Pat's Christmas party begins in the compound main house. Margaritas are flowing to the sounds of James Brown's 'I Feel Good' when 'Don' Lionetti walks into the kitchen through the back door. He pulls Mike aside and walks him outside. "Kid, come with me."

Johnny leads Mike into the compound courtyard. "I need you to stay focused on business. We have a lot of money to make."

Mike hands Johnny a small brown paper bag. "Don't worry. Here's a hundred thousand towards my bill and I have a top dollar coke buyer in L.A. who'll pay fifty thousand a kilo."

'Don' Lionetti smiles. "Kid, you sound like my future son in law. Now, let's settle accounts with Ray and Jimmy. They're 'dipping their pens in company ink' with my club girls."

Little Ray answers the door dressed in boxer shorts while holding a Colt .357 in his right hand. He recognizes his 'Don' and lowers his weapon as he opens the door.

Jimmy the Jockey deals cards to three ladies wearing silk lingerie in the living room listening to 'Foxy Lady' on the stereo. Bottles of Dom Perignon champagne chill in ice buckets surrounding a coffee table with a cocaine covered mirror on it. Little Ray leads Johnny and Mike into the living room. "Girls, take a break in the bedroom. The men have business to do."

The three exotic women excite Mike as they walk past him towards the bedroom. A tall platinum blonde rubs the big Floridian's swelling crotch when she passes. "Stick around for the party, big boy."

Mike blushes and smiles. "What's your names?"

The pretty blond shimmies her buxom breasts and purrs with a Texas twang. "I'm Donna. These are my Brazilian girlfriends, Sophia and Peaches. We're going to party all night."

The scantily clad ladies saunter into the bedroom and Donna winks at Mike when she closes the bedroom door. Little Ray turns up the Kenwood stereo volume. Jimi Hendrix sings Bob Dylan's 'All Along the Watchtower'.

Johnny opens Mike's brown bag, counts out fifty thousand dollars and divides it into two bundles, handing one to Little Ray and the other to Jimmy the Jockey. "Here's twenty five large for both of you. Jimmy, refit 'American Dreams' for the next fishing trip. I want you in Jamaica on the January 5th new moon."

'Don' Lionetti turns to Little Ray. "I covered Francisco's second deposit from my retirement cash. I want the cocaine to move fast, so I'm financing the Kid. He's got an upscale California market."

Little Ray's eyes bulge with rage as he takes the cash and shakes his head. "You said I was in charge of this deal."

'Don' Lionetti puts his hand on the little man's shoulder. "Don't worry, you're in charge. I want the Kid in on the action at twenty five thousand a unit. There's plenty of cash for everyone. You and Jimmy know what to do. Now, get to work"

Johnny smiles at Mike. "Mary expects us on time for Christmas Eve dinner and Debbie invited your Boston friends to join us."

Outside the houseboat, Johnny lights a cigar as he gets in his Cadillac and turns to Mike. "You have to go to Jamaica to set up the January shipment. Keep the Jamaicans under control and don't let them fuck this up. I have over a million dollars at stake in this deal."

———— ◆ ————

Warm sunshine makes the Christmas holidays in Florida different from New England. Bright multi-colored lights illuminated the Lionetti Lighthouse Point home stem to stern last night when Mary served Christmas Eve dinner.

Nat King Cole's 'The Christmas Song' added to the festive mood as we feasted on fresh Florida snapper and Mary's pasta dishes. Later, we enjoyed homemade cannolis while watching 'A Christmas Carol' and 'It's a Wonderful Life' on TV.

Everyone has hangovers this Christmas morning. Jill and I have to drive back to Boston in two days. She and Debbie are together in the New River guest house as I join Mike in the main house. Bing Crosby sings, 'I'm dreaming of a White Christmas' while Mike fills plastic baggies with cocaine and weighs them on his Ohaus triple beam scale.

He hands me a mirror covered with white powder and a rolled Ben Franklin. "Jack, have a line and let's talk business. I'll front you eighty pounds of ganja for twenty four thousand."

Mike holds up a plastic baggie. "Colombian cocaine sells for three thousand an ounce in L. A. and New York. You can easily 'step' on this stuff a couple of times."

I inhale a line of sparkling crystals and think to myself... 'Donna Dodge's hidden compartment can easily hold eighty pounds of ganja and at five hundred a pound, Jill and I could make a sixteen thousand dollar profit.'

My nose and forehead numb as a sense of euphoria takes hold of me. "Man, this coke is wicked good. This stuff sells for top dollar in Boston."

Mike gives me an envelope and two Ziploc baggies filled with crystalline powder. "Here's two thousand cash and a couple ounces of coke for unloading the boat. Find out if those college kids in Boston like Colombian cocaine. Your price is twenty five thousand a pound."

The big Floridian gives me a stern look. "Remember, no phone calls to me. Uncle Pat is here '24/7'. Fly to Miami when you get the money and take a cab to the New River Marina Bay Hotel. My cousin Corby parks cars there. He'll let me know you're at the hotel."

<hr />

I can still hear Moonshine and Lucille's farewell howls two days after our Christmas departure. We saw alligators, manatees and pelicans driving north through the Florida Everglades. Jill and I will miss the Sunshine State's warm ocean breezes and pastel sunsets.

There was no time to visit Disney World or eat Gainesville 'magic' mushrooms. We nearly lost Lucille during a gas stop in Ocala when a large barn owl attacked the little dog. Lucky for Jill's pet, holiday food scraps made her too heavy for the flying predator.

'Inca marching powder' kept Jill and me rolling through the 'Southland' in a cloud of ganja smoke. The weather and road conditions were perfect, until we crossed the Delaware Memorial Bridge two hours ago.

Dark winter clouds fill the sky as Arctic winds blow snow across the New Jersey Turnpike. Road traffic has slowed to thirty miles an hour while I struggle to stay on course in near 'white out' conditions.

I stare through the ice covered windshield at dim red tail lights ahead and think to myself... 'We've got eighty pounds of ganja, two ounces of coke and a couple thousand in cash. Not bad for one weeks work.'

'Moonlight Mile' plays on the radio as Jill finishes chopping cocaine lines on her pocket mirror. She rolls a dollar bill and toots a line of coke. "We only have three hundred miles to go. I hope we make it to the New Year's party."

My buddy hands me the mirror and bill, while taking the wheel. I quickly inhale my line. Seconds later, a numbing euphoria surges through me as I take the wheel back.

"We can make it, if the snow doesn't block the roads."

Jill gives me a pensive look. "Do you think this trip is worth the risk?"

I smile. "I think so. We have ganja worth a year's pay in the truck and who knows how much we can make on Mike's coke deal. I'll break out some lines at the New Year's Eve party and see if there are any coke buyers in Boston."

My buddy sighs. "I guess you're right. I hope Sonya comes to our party."

The evening news report comes on the radio. "Last week's Nicaraguan earthquake death toll surpassed five thousand with many more missing. The United States Department of Transportation authorized police officers to intercept drug smugglers on the Interstate Highway System. In sports news, George Steinbrenner purchased the New York Yankees for ten million dollars. Finally, twelve inches of snow is expected throughout the tri-state area tonight."

I turn to Jill as I steer Donna Dodge onto the Vince Lombardi exit. "It's midnight and we're near the George Washington Bridge. Let's fill the tank and check the oil before we cross into New York. We'll make a quick pit stop. You take Lucille for a piss while I gas up Donna."

Just as these fateful words come out of my mouth. The twenty year old truck headlights flicker and turn off. Donna Dodge's six cylinder engine sputters to a stall. I push in the clutch pedal and shift into neutral. "Damn, the engine shut down!"

The powerless pickup slowly coasts down the off ramp towards a distant unlit service plaza. Lucille shivers on Jill's lap. I shake my head. "The station doesn't look open."

A terrified expression appears on Jill's face. "What are we going to do? We'll freeze tonight."

Suddenly, bright red and blue lights illuminate the snow filled darkness around us. I yell. "It's the cops. Hide the stash!"

The disabled truck slowly rolls towards the darkened gas station garage. Donna Dodge comes to a stop as a trooper's 'Smokey the Bear' hat emerges from the police cruiser.

My bladder wants to let go as I desperately remove pot 'roaches' from the ashtray while Jill hastily pushes the bag of coke and mirror behind the seat. At the last second, I notice the rolled dollar bill on the floor when the trooper's flash light shines in the door window.

The policeman loudly commands.

"You're driving without lights. Roll down your window. Show me your license and truck registration."

BEANTOWN BOYS
AND GIRLS

A grim faced New Jersey State Trooper stares at me through my ice covered pickup truck door window. He sternly commands. "License and registration."

My mind races with worry. If the cop sees the rolled dollar bill on the floor, he'll search the truck and we'll go to prison for sure.

Lucille growls in the background when I step on George Washington's face and reach into the glove box for my vehicle paperwork. A gust of freezing air blows into the truck cabin when I open the window.

Without warning, the gas station neon lights illuminate the darkness. A large red haired man dressed in a mechanic's uniform opens the garage door. "Officer, can I help you?"

Before the State Trooper answers, I yell. "We lost power coming down the exit."

Accumulated snow falls from the trooper's hat as he nods and retreats to his cruiser. "OK, no ticket this time. Get your truck fixed before you get back on the road."

I look at Jill and we both sigh with relief. The garage attendant approaches the driver's side door with a Marlboro cigarette hanging from his mouth and snowflakes collecting on his Horn-rimmed eyeglasses.

Lucille abruptly springs through the open window into the stranger's burly arms. He catches the little dog and laughs. "I'm

Bob Davis, owner, mechanic and cleanup crew of this garage. I love your '52' Dodge. I've got a 'Power Wagon' in the back. Let's get you guys inside out of the cold."

He gently passes Lucille back through the window. I turn the steering wheel over to Jill and join the tall redhead pushing Donna Dodge into his repair shop. Lucille creates yellow snow, before joining us in the warm garage.

The big mechanic slides under our twenty year old pickup and checks the problem.

"It looks like an electrical system short. I'll work on it tomorrow. I've got to get home to my wife and kids in Queens. You'll stay warm in here tonight. The bathroom and shower are next to the kitchen. My refrigerator is full of Christmas leftovers and Budweiser."

Our host puts on a heavy wool winter overcoat and turns for the exit. "New York City may be bankrupt and snow removal is terrible, but my Dodge Ram will get me home tonight and back tomorrow morning. See you then."

A blast of arctic wind blows into the room as Bob Davis exits and closes the garage door. Jill stares at me and blurts out. "That trooper could have put us in jail."

I hug my buddy tightly. "The good news is we didn't get busted and we're in this warm garage tonight. Hopefully, we can fix Donna Dodge's electric system tomorrow."

Jill's pet groans for attention and springs onto her owner's lap. "Lucille, I bet you're hungry."

The little dog jumps to the floor and charges into the kitchen. Jill follows and opens the refrigerator. Lucille dances on her hind legs while Jill removes a loaf of Wonder bread with a platter of turkey and ham. "Jack, grab the mayo and salad stuff."

My buddy holds a piece of turkey over Lucille's head as the terrier pirouettes for meat while I remove sandwich fixings and two Budweisers. "Let's have a 'Bud' with dinner."

The sandwiches and beer go well together. After dinner, I light a joint and turn on the radio to Dick Clark's American Bandstand. We clean the kitchen listening to Roberta Flack sing 'The First Time I Saw Your Face'.

Jill fills Lucille's bowl with water and gives me a pensive look. "I've been thinking about Debbie. She wants to have a baby with Mike. Do you think he wants kids?"

The question catches me off guard as I take two more beers from the refrigerator.

"As far as I know, Mike's making money and doesn't want to get tied down with children."

My lover nods her head. "I'm not ready for kids. I want to finish college and travel."

I hand Jill a Quaalude. "Here's to getting Donna Dodge fixed tomorrow. Let's crash and get some 'Z's'."

We crawl into the truck camper bed exhausted from our cocaine fueled cross country journey. Lucille slumbers at our feet as we fall asleep listening to Simon and Garfunkel's 'Sounds of Silence' on the radio.

I drift into a dream...

...Jill lies naked on a scarlet red blanket under a silver full moon. Sonya suddenly appears in a transparent vermilion fairy costume, when a cold chill wakes me...

———◆———

"Bang." "Clank." "Bang."

The garage door opens and closes. Freezing winter air and coffee aroma surge into the garage. Jill and I look outside from our cozy bed onto a snow covered winter wonderland.

Bob Davis whistles while setting up Dunkin Donuts and coffee on the kitchen table. Lucille squirms out of bed and runs into the kitchen. She sniffs the air and stands on her hind legs.

The mechanic lights a Marlboro cigarette while Jill's pet terrier pirouettes in front of him. He removes a plastic baggie from his pocket. "I have a treat for the little dog."

I put on my jeans and jump out of the camper as Lucille dances for bacon. "Bob, thanks for the 'Joe' and donuts. We owe you for a couple of sandwiches and four Budweisers."

Jill joins us in the kitchen and opens her cup of coffee. "You saved us last night. Do you think we can fix our truck today?"

The tall mechanic smiles. "No problem, the sandwiches and beer are 'on the house'. Let me check your electrical system again."

Bob drops to his knees and surveys the pickup frame as Lucille joins him under the truck. He quickly announces his assessment. "Just like I thought last night. Rock salt corroded the old cloth wiring and the electrical system shorted out. We can rewire everything today, but you might need a new battery. I'll put this one on the charger."

I look at Jill and turn to Bob as he lights another cigarette. "How much do you think the repairs will cost?"

He laughs. "You pay for parts and I'll only charge you a couple of cases of 'Bud' for my labor as a Christmas present. Your bill shouldn't be much more than a hundred bucks."

Bob changes the kitchen clock radio station to Jimmy the Greek in Las Vegas. "Oddsmakers make the Miami Dolphins heavy favorites over the Pittsburgh Steelers on New Year's Eve. Don Shula's undefeated football team is picked to win Super Bowl VII in Los Angeles next year."

<hr />

Robert Davis is a man of his word. We didn't need a new battery and he only charged us ninety bucks for parts and beer. Frank Sinatra sang 'New York New York' when we hit the road yesterday afternoon. Snowplows cleared the way and our trip into Massachusetts was uneventful. We were exhausted and went straight to bed upon arrival at Hull House.

The Times Square 'Ball' drops tonight and Guy Lombardo's band will play 'Auld Lang Syne' at midnight. I'm sitting with Chuck and Shu drinking cocktails and smoking ganja by the living room fire.

Jill is in the kitchen with Marsha and Wendy. A twenty five pound turkey roasts in the oven and Veuve Clicquot champagne chills in the refrigerator. Joey and Teresa Palermo should arrive soon with Rudy Losordo and Maureen Fitzpatrick. I told Joey to bring his Ohaus scale.

The front door opens with a burst of freezing air. Teresa and Maureen rush into the warm house followed by Rudy and Joey carrying a large grocery bag. He closes the door. "Damn, it's cold outside. Jack, let's do some business."

Shu laughs. "Joey, this Jamaican ganja is wicked good."

Rudy heads for the bar and pours a Jack Daniel's and ginger ale. Teresa and Mo join the other girls in the kitchen as I lead Joey into a side pantry and pull a plastic wrapped bale of weed from the closet. "There's forty pounds of ganja in this package and I have another one with forty more. How much do you want?"

Joey removes a cash bundle from his overcoat and starts counting hundred dollar bills. "I'll take everything you got at five hundred a pound. Here's twenty thousand for this bale and I'll pick up the rest next week. Why did you want me to bring the scale?"

I stuff the cash into a brown paper lunch bag and pull two cocaine filled plastic baggies from my jacket. "I've got two ounces of South American 'snow' and I need a scale accurate to a tenth of a gram."

Joey's eyes focus on the cocaine filled baggies as he opens the grocery bag and hands me his Ohaus Triple Beam scale. "If that coke is as good as it looks, I'll buy all of it and give you the scale. I can get another one tomorrow."

I place each baggie on the scale. One weighs twenty eight grams and the other is missing the gram Jill and I did on our trip from Florida. I drop a crystalline rock on a small mirror and chop it into lines with a razor blade. "This is near pure cocaine. My Florida partner has kilos for sale and you'll get a great deal with cash."

Joey rolls and unrolls a Ben Franklin in anticipation as I pass him the mirror and he hurriedly inhales two lines. He grins and passes me the mirror with a roll of cash. "Here's five thousand for fifty grams. Keep the scale and I'll throw in a gram for tonight's party."

I take the five grand with a wide smile. "You've got a deal."

On the island of Jamaica, Anthony Ascot enters Francisco Diego Valencia's Rose Hall villa decorated for New Year's Eve. Tony owes his recent financial success to his host and hopes Francisco will continue assisting him in his quest to become the richest, most powerful man in Jamaica.

Both men are elegantly dressed in formal attire for tonight's occasion. Francisco raises his Waterford crystal champagne glass, when Tony enters the room. "Anthony, a toast to our profitable business enterprise."

The wily Jamaican grins ear to ear. "Yes, selling cocaine is much more profitable than ganja. Here's to the millions we'll make this year."

Crystal champagne glasses click together. Francisco gives his associate a cautious look. "Anthony, I'm concerned the Manley government could threaten our enterprise. We'll need to defend our property and my friends in the C.I.A. have offered us financial assistance to create a 'freedom militia'."

Tony nods with a cunning grin. "Manley is Castro's stooge. I can recruit a 'freedom militia', if the Americans supply weapons and ammunition."

———— ● ————

Back in Ft. Lauderdale, Mike Casey and Uncle Pat celebrate the Miami Dolphins'A.F.C. Championship 21-17 win over the Pittsburgh Steelers on New Year's Eve at the New River houseboat.

The big Floridian is disappointed. "The Dolphins didn't cover the spread."

John Lionetti smiles at Mike and pats Little Ray on the back. "Looks like '73' is going to be a great year. Francisco has his deposit and Jimmy's sailing to Jamaica as we speak."

'Don' Lionetti turns to his lieutenant. "Ray, Francisco gets ten thousand a kilo and I get the same. I expect you and the Kid to work together on this cocaine deal. I'm financing the Kid's cost at twenty five large because he's family. Everyone else pays your price."

Little Ray shrugs his shoulders and gives Uncle Pat a fierce look. "Your bastard kid is supposed park cars and not fuck the maids. He got parole, because Johnny got him the job. He better not fuck up our plans."

━━━━◆◆◆━━━━

U S Attorney Thomas P. Stack operates on 'Lombardi Time' and expects his agents to arrive fifteen minutes early for their meeting on January 2, 1973. Ft. Lauderdale Police Detectives Dan Brady and Dick Guerrette are the last to enter the room at task force headquarters.

A Coast Guard Captain in dress uniform briefs the agents. "Gentleman, I'm here to update you regarding the coordinated Navy and Coast Guard drug interdiction effort north of the Windward Passage between Cuba and the Bahamas."

Dan Brady leans close to Dick Guerrette and quietly whispers. "The word on the street says Corby Casey is out on parole parking cars at the Marina Bay Hotel. We better keep a close eye on the Caseys."

Tom Stack's baritone voice erupts from the back of the room. "Brady and Guerrette, are you on my team? Get with the program and listen to the Captain."

━━━━◆◆◆━━━━

This moonless January night, a thick fog covers the calm Caribbean Sea off the coast of Jamaica. Jimmy the Jockey sends flashlight signals into the night, until he hears multiple engines approaching him. Two boats appear out of the darkness.

One racing at high speed straight at 'American Dreams'. The other moves slowly and rides low in the water. Jimmy the Jockey takes the safety off his Remington 1100 shotgun and loads a 'Double 00' buckshot round into the chamber.

A powerful twin engine Riva Aquarama pulls alongside the seventy foot Hatteras Sportfisher. Jimmy recognizes two of the five men on board the powerful speedboat. Anthony Ascot and Francisco Diego Valencia stand on the deck of the approaching watercraft along with three AK-47 armed bodyguards. Jimmy waves the new arrivals on board.

Francisco's bodyguards follow him boarding 'American Dreams' as the second boat arrives. Tony barks orders to his men on the incoming boat. "Load the bales in the hold."

The cocaine is quickly stored below deck as Jimmy leads Francisco and a bodyguard carrying a small wire cage into the storage compartment. Two tan and brown Russell's vipers peer from inside the steel mesh.

Francisco releases the snakes into the cocaine filled hold and turns to the jockey. "Fiberglass the entrance and my pets will guard the shipment until I retrieve them in Florida on the full moon."

<hr />

Radio news wakes me in Hull. "The Washington Post reports John Mitchell and the Committee to Re-elect the President attempted to cover up the Watergate burglary. House Majority Whip, 'Tip' O'Neill recommends the UMass/Boston Dorchester campus as the site for the John F. Kennedy Memorial Library."

Chuck Lievi usually drives Jill and me to the Pemberton Point ferry dock on most mornings to join coffee cup commuters traveling across Boston Harbor. Our college, UMass/Boston is called the 'Working Man's Harvard' because of the school's many Ivy League educated professors and its factory-like red brick structure.

The Hull House New Year's Eve party was a fun filled champagne and cocaine party even though Sonya was a no show. Jill's and my Florida trip profit will be over twenty thousand dollars when Joey pays for all the ganja.

There hasn't been much time for class work this semester, so I've become creative trying to get credit for my classes. Professor Simmons likes Scotch, so I left him a bottle of Glenfiddich with my past due thesis on Barrington Moore Jr.s' 'Reflections on the Causes of Human Misery'.

I have two morning classes today, Tanda Dube's 'Twentieth Century African History' and Ivonne Buck's 'Spanish literature translated into English'. David Hunt's 'Vietnam Revolution' is my afternoon class, but first I have to pick up my financial aid package.

I walk into the neon lit wood paneled Registrar's office. A petite raven haired beauty greets me. "How can I help you? I'm the Registrar's secretary."

The pretty girl's dazzling smile stuns me. I stammer. "I'm here to pick up Jack Collins' financial aid package. I mean John Collins."

The vivacious secretary laughs and bends over in a tight red mini dress while reaching into a file cabinet. "My name is Charlene. Should I call you John or Jack?"

She hands me a sealed manilla folder as I gaze into her golden hazel eyes. "You can call me Jack. You're the prettiest girl on campus. Where are you from?"

Charlene's smile widens. "New Bedford and my family is from the Cape Verde Islands. Jack, are you hitting on me?"

We both smile and chuckle, when Charlene hands me a business card. "My apartment phone number is on the back. Call me, with any questions."

I gently kiss her cheek and take the card. "Thanks."

Professor Dube teaches my first class. He was born in Kenya, educated in South Africa and Oxford, England. Tall, pencil thin with a shaved mahogany head, Tanda Dube supports Nelson Mandela's African National Congress. Today's topic is 'African Nationalism and the Apartheid system.'

Jill promised to help me with Professor Buck's Spanish Literature class. Ivonne Buck is an elegant thirty year old lady from Argentina. She has me reading Pablo Neruda and Gabriel Garcia Marquez, without Cliff Notes.

My afternoon class professor, David Hunt lectures on 'European Imperialism suppressing indigenous nationalism in the Twentieth Century'. He theorizes the American Vietnam War originated when America supported French territorial claims and rejected Ho Chi Minh's independence petition at the end of World War II.

February's moon is nearly full on Valentine's Day. The night sky is crystal clear this cold winter evening as zero degree temperatures chill the air. Colorful begonia flower baskets hang in Jill's and my second floor bedroom bay window inside Hull House.

Gato Barbieri's saxophone plays 'Last Tango in Paris' while Jill sits with Maureen Fitzpatrick on a queen bed chopping the last of her cocaine stash on a small mirror.

Jill toots two long crystalline lines and quivers when she passes the mirror to Maureen. "Mo, 'Things go better with Coke', especially sex."

The pretty redhead inhales a line and bursts into a wide smile. "This shit is wicked good. Rudy and I know a lot of musicians seriously into 'nose candy'. Can Jack get anymore to sell?"

Marsha and Wendy join Teresa preparing tonight's feast downstairs in the kitchen while Chuck and Shu make a booze run in the silver Cadillac.

A blazing fire warms the Hull House living room. Jimmy Cliff's 'You Can Get It If You Really Want' plays on the stereo as I share the last of my cocaine with Joey and Rudy. "Do you guys want me to pick up some more coke in Florida?"

Joey inhales two lines and quickly passes the mirror to Rudy. "Jack, let's talk."

I lead Joey into the side pantry. He pulls two large Manilla envelopes from his coat pocket. "Here's what I owe plus a hundred thousand down on five kilos at three hundred large."

———— • ————

Two days later, my taxi exits I-95 and turns west into the sunset on Marina Mile Blvd as a cream white full moon rises in the east. The ride from the airport seemed to take forever in rush hour traffic. I plan to meet Mike at the Marina Bay Hotel.

Jill and I had our first fight last night. She wants to stop dealing drugs and finish school. My plan is to 'strike while the iron is hot'. Joey's offer is too good to pass up and Mike needs cash.

I hope to make a hundred thousand dollar profit on this trip and we plan to buy a Caribbean waterfront bar together, so she can play piano with our friends.

The taxi turns into a palm tree filled courtyard and stops at a red bougainvillea covered stucco hotel entrance in front of six double deck houseboats moored on the New River. I exit the taxi with my bag and hand the driver two Andy Jackson's. "Keep the change."

A square jawed man in the shadows nods at me as I walk towards the hotel reception desk. Tattoos cover his bare athletic arms and I see a resemblance to Uncle Pat. Inside the office, a pretty receptionist hands me keys to a room. "All of our units are two bedroom suites, with Jacuzzi hot tubs. Call the front desk, if you need anything."

Five minutes later, I'm in my room listening to Howard Cosell interview Joe Namath on the radio. "Howard, that little Dolphin kicker cost me big in the Super Bowl."

I turn the radio channel to WSHE playing Carlos Santana's 'Evil Ways' as I pull three Ziploc cash bundles from around my waist and put them in the toilet water bowl.

"Knock." "Knock." "Housekeeping."

I open the door to see the prettiest 'maid' I've ever seen holding a bottle of Veuve Clicquot champagne in an ice bucket. The shapely blonde pixie dressed in a tight pink t-shirt and short red shorts prances into the room. "You must be Jack. I'm Kim. Mike's on his way. He said you're my date tonight."

Kim's amber brown eyes check me out. "I didn't expect you to look like a cop."

I laugh. "Mike told me to clean up my act."

Three gorgeous ladies appear. A tall buxom blonde carrying more champagne followed by two copper tanned beauties enter the room. I hear Mike's familiar voice as he strolls into the suite. "Nice shave and haircut 'Troop'. You're ready for your next mission."

I shake Mike's hand. He gives me a 'lude' and smiles at the ladies. "Jack, you've met Kim. This is Donna and her two Brazilian friends, Peaches and Sofia. Let's party."

He turns to the pretty ladies. "Girls, get some glasses from the mini-bar and pop a bottle of 'bubbly'."

I'm drawn to Kim's alluring smile as she fills my champagne glass. Mike finishes chopping a long crescent shaped cocaine line on a glass living room table. He passes me a rolled Ben Franklin. "Jack, start things off. There's tons more where this came from."

I fill my nose with 'candy' and pass the rolled bill to Kim. She matches me and puts a taste on her tongue. The other girls join Mike snorting coke from the glass table top. Kim fills my champagne glass again as Mike passes me a fat joint, with another Quaalude. "Jack, you've got to catch up. We're all way ahead of you."

The following morning, I wake up in a drugged haze. Damn, a camel must have camped in my mouth while I slept. Last night's party was beyond awesome. The Brazilian girls made love together in the moonlight and I did things with Kim in the hot tub that I've never done before.

Kim opens her eyes with a gentle caress and smiles as her soft body slides on top of me. "Do you want to start where we left off last night?"

A half hour later, I gaze into her amber brown eyes. "Beautiful, when can I be with you again?"

Kim smiles. "Anytime Mike pays the bill. He calls the shots."

She smirks when I give her a stunned look.

"A girl has gotta do what she's got to do in a man's world."

In the next room, Mike yells out. "Fun's over troop, rise and shine."

Kim smiles and kisses my cheek. "Baby, I'm going to shower."

I hear the other girls packing up in the other room, when Mike enters my bedroom. "Jack, we've got work to do."

Later at the New River compound, I watch Mike weigh cocaine-filled baggies on his Ohaus triple beam scale in a bedroom littered with discarded baby formula containers.

He removes a large 'pearl' rock from a kilo package and gently places it on the scale. "This is nearly pure. Push the cocaine rock through a strainer into a bowl with an equal amount of Mannitol. You and your friends can easily turn one of these quality kilos into two. That's why we had to drive around town buying baby laxative powder."

Mike smiles. "I've turned five kilos into six for you. You're paid up on the ganja and the five kilos cost fifty thousand each. Two hundred fifty thousand minus your hundred thousand deposit leaves a balance of one hundred fifty large. Also I'm throwing in five hundred Quaaludes as a bonus."

I grin while rolling a joint. "Cool."

My Army buddy chuckles. "Isn't Kim something else? She and the other girls work for Johnny. He lets me hire them for business as long as they don't interfere with his family. Best of all, They're STD tested monthly."

Mike pauses. "Kim would be my girl, if I wasn't committed to Debbie."

I fire up the joint and pass it to Mike. "Kim is awesome in bed and I could get hooked on her too."

The big Floridian laughs heartily. "Yeah, she and her sister, Karol can make a thousand a night hustling 'Sugar Daddies' in Johnny's clubs."

Mike removes a suitcase from the closet. "I bought you some American Tourister luggage."

He puts six plastic wrapped kilos in a tan hard suitcase. "I'm sure you'll be back for more next month. Do you have enough cash for bail and travel expenses?"

I reach into my jeans pockets and touch my saved profits.

"I'm good. I've got a return Eastern Airline ticket and twenty large. I'll take a cab to the airport from the hotel."

"Knock." "Knock."

The bedroom door opens. Budweiser in hand, a visibly shaken Uncle Pat enters the room.

Mike finishes packing my suitcase and looks at his uncle. "What's up?"

The old sailor takes a gulp of beer. "Corby's drunk and wacked out on Quaaludes. He wants to settle his beef with Jerry."

Mike shakes his head and looks at me. "Shit, I knew this could happen. I did a jewelry burglary with Corby and Jerry as teenagers. Jerry was look-out and I was the driver. Instead of warning Corby when the cops showed up, Jerry ran and told me to take off. Corby did time and he figures Jerry owes him. I've got to square Corby away, before he fucks everything up."

The full moon is high in the sky above Montego Bay this same February night. Antony Ascot sits with Francisco Diego Valencia on his Rose Hall villa veranda. Waitresses dressed in colorful silk negligees serve the two men a late evening dinner at a well appointed mahogany table.

Tony is casually dressed in Calvin Klein slacks and a floral print silk shirt with 18K gold chains. He contemplates his future success while enjoying fresh snapper covered in garlic and spices... 'I'll be the richest Jamaican in the world soon.'

Francisco sips a glass of Christal champagne with a disingenuous smile. "Anthony, will your mother's passing interfere with our business enterprise?"

Tony shakes his head and raises his voice. "Nothing interferes with our business enterprise, but I am very upset that my bloodclaat aunt returned the ten thousand dollars I sent for my mother's funeral."

———•———

A month later, the March full moon sets over the New River boathouse when Francisco Diego Valencia recovers his pet vipers from the 'American Dreams' boat hold. He places a heavy canvas cover over the wire mesh cage and turns to Little Ray. "I expected to speak with John about the past due four millions on the January delivery."

Little Ray tries to stand taller. "Don't worry, I'm in charge now. I'll have your money wired to the Vatican Bank account within seventy two hours."

Francisco cunningly grins. "Raymond, I look forward to your payment. The remaining ten millions is due in ninety days and failure to make payments will have consequences."

The Colombian turns away and leads his entourage from the building into waiting black Cadillac sedans.

———————◆———————

My life in Beantown has been a whirlwind since I returned from Miami six weeks ago. Jill went to class without me this morning, because I was selling coke all night.

The radio plays the morning news. "Watergate burglar James W. McCord Jr. implicated Attorney General John Mitchell as the 'boss of the Watergate burglary'. U.S. District Judge John Sirica will hear testimony this week from President Nixon's staff, including White House Counsel John Dean."

I turn the radio dial to WBCN and Pink Floyd's 'Money' pulsates throughout the bedroom while I think about my last trip to Florida... 'Joey bought five kilos for three hundred thousand and I gave him a four hundred Quaalude bonus. Maureen and Rudy agreed to pay twenty five hundred an ounce on a 'front', so they can sell grams and 'eight balls' to the late night disco crowd.'

Chuck went sober and joined the Church of Scientology on St. Patrick's Day. Wendy got a postcard from Shu in Acapulco saying he's hiking in Mexico until May. Jill and I hope Sonya comes with Susie and Jane to our Saturday night April Fools' party.

My buddy continues to work hard trying to graduate, while I fall further behind in my classes. I should be enjoying springtime in Boston instead of dealing cocaine '24/7'.

Dogwood and lilac trees bloom in the Boston Common this time of year. Van Gogh and Gauguin paintings are on exhibit at the Museum of Fine Arts, while the Boston Symphony Orchestra plays Mozart and Beethoven at Symphony Hall.

Last week, Professor Buck announced that recent democratic elections in Argentina allows her to return to her home country.

She escaped 'La Noche de los Bastones Largos' six years ago when the military junta attacked the University of Buenos Aires.

This afternoon, 'Vietnam Veterans Against the War' activist John Kerry is on campus speaking about the 'Paris Peace Accords' and missing American P.O.W.s in Vietnam. UMass/Boston humanitarian award winner Stevie Wonder will visit next week. Tonight, Jill and I plan to watch the Academy Awards with Joey and Teresa.

A brand new black Porsche 911 Carrera RS arrives at Hull House as the sun sets. Joey and Teresa brought an Italian feast from the 'North End' for tonight's dinner. Teresa joins Jill in the kitchen as Joey leads me into the side pantry and gives me a leather briefcase. "Jack, here's the two hundred large I owe you, plus a hundred thousand deposit for another five kilos. Also, get some more Quaaludes. Everybody wants them."

Inside the kitchen, the girls warm Mama Maria veal parmigiana dinners. Teresa nervously lights a cigarette. "Jill, I'm pregnant and I'm afraid to tell Joey."

Later in the evening, we enjoy cannolis and espresso while watching the Oscars on TV. Roger Moore and Liv Ullman open the award envelope. "The winner for Best Actor in a leading role is Marlon Brando. Accepting the award for Mr. Brando is Sacheen Littlefeather, representing Native Americans."

The pretty Native American girl takes the microphone. "Marlon Brando regretfully cannot accept this generous award on moral grounds. I have come to this ceremony to bring attention to the world, the desperate Native American poverty in the United States. I speak of today's poverty, not one hundred years ago. At this moment, American troops surround the Pine Ridge Indian

Reservation at Wounded Knee. Many Native American lives are at stake. Please support the American Indian Movement."

———◆———

At the same time at the Lionetti home in Florida, the Academy Awards ceremony is in bright color on a new Zenith TV. Johnny puts down his espresso and looks over at Mike Casey with disgust as Sacheen Littlefeather walks from the stage without the Oscar statuette. "What the Hell is Brando thinking? Vito Corleone was his best role."

Mike smiles. "Brando's latest movie 'Last Tango in Paris' got an x-rating."

Mary and Debbie clean the kitchen together. Debbie lights a cigarette and looks over at her mother with a pensive smile. "Mom, I have something to tell you, but you have to promise not to tell anyone."

Debbie earnestly stares at her mother. "Promise you won't tell anyone. Especially Johnny."

Mrs. Lionetti stops wiping the countertop and turns to her daughter with a worried frown. "Sweetheart, what's wrong. You must tell me."

Debbie shakes her head. "No, not until you promise to keep a secret."

Mary pulls her only child into a tight embrace. "I promise not to tell anyone, even Johnny."

Debbie smiles and gives her mother a hug. "Mom, I missed my period."

———◆———

The Hull House April Fools' Party is tomorrow. I'm packing Mike's cash into a leather legal briefcase while listening to T-Rex's 'Get It On' when I hear guests arriving downstairs at sunset.

The front door opens and I hear Sonya speaking to Jill. "Jane and Susie couldn't make it. They have too much farm work this time of year. Bill and I drove down from Vermont this afternoon. He went to the store for champagne to celebrate our announcement. We've been living together since Christmas."

Jill embraces her friend. "Why didn't you tell me?"

Sonya smiles. "I wanted to be sure about our relationship before I told anyone."

Jill takes hold of Sonya's hand. "I'm so excited for you both."

I grab a quarter ounce of snow and hurry down the stairs as Bill White opens the front door, carrying grocery bags filled with beer and wine. A broad smile comes across his bearded face. "Sonya and I are moving to Belize."

Bill launches a champagne cork skyward while I chop cocaine into lines on the Formica kitchen counter. My bearded friend grins ear to ear.

"Sonya and I saved ten thousand for this move. We can grow 'herb' year round in Central America and the mahogany is great for carving."

Sonya smiles. "When you guys finish college, come down and visit us."

I chop eight neat lines of cocaine on a dinner plate and give Bill a rolled Ben Franklin. He quickly toots half a line and looks up at me with a smile. "Jack, did you finish reading Siddhartha?"

I laugh. "No, but I'm reading 'One Hundred Years of Solitude' on Colombian coke."

William White chuckles. "Damn, this stuff is too powerful. I'll stick to smoking weed."

Sonya toots a line and passes the rolled Ben Franklin to Jill. She finishes two lines and turns to Sonya. "I want to visit you guys when Jack and I cash out."

Bill pours more champagne while I light a ganja joint. "Jill and I want to open a waterfront bar in the tropics and Belize has the largest coral reef in the Caribbean. Maybe we'll move there too."

I hand the joint to Jill and she turns to Sonya. "I hope you're staying for our party tonight."

Bill White is pragmatic and shakes his head with a smile. "We should get rolling soon and drive at night. Traffic in Connecticut and New York is stop and go during the day."

———— ◆ ————

Early the next morning at sunrise, Jill and I lie naked on our bed in a loving afterglow. Sonya and Bill missed a wicked good party last night. Champagne flowed with cocaine throughout the night and the party peaked when the 'Demon Deacons' got everyone dancing to the Isley Brothers' 'Shout'.

'Can't You Hear Me Knocking' plays on the bedroom stereo as I take a gulp of champagne and pass the bottle to Jill with a Quaalude. "Buddy, Joey ordered another five kilos and Rudy has a guy who will pay five hundred thousand for five kilos. We could own a Caribbean hotel with the profits from another Florida run."

Jill swallows the 'lude' with a gulp of champagne. "It would be great to live with Sonya and Bill in the tropics, but do you think another trip is worth the risk?"

The April full moon rises above the New River compound. Mike Casey counts stacks of cash inside the main house kitchen as Uncle Pat opens a bottle of Jack Daniel's and pours a round of whiskey. The old sailor turns to Mike. "You can't trust Little Ray."

Mike shakes his head. "I don't trust Little Ray, but Johnny guaranteed me all the coke I can sell and this is the opportunity of my lifetime. There's millions of dollars to be made. We'll use Ma's farm for a storage area and I'll have to find a way to keep Corby away from Jerry."

Earlier the same day, US Attorney Tom Stack updates his taskforce in his Miami office. "Listen up, we're expecting another wave of South American narcotics through the Caribbean. Coast Guard and Navy assets will continue to intercept drug shipments offshore, while we coordinate with state and local law enforcement agencies. Cooperation between all government agencies is essential to win this drug war."

Tom Stack's blue eyes focus on police lieutenant Brady and sergeant Guerrette. "We especially need intel surveillance on local criminal gangs and operatives."

MIAMI MAD MONEY

Southeast Gulf Stream breezes warm Florida's weather this April morning. Mike Casey has a substantial cash payment for his patron in his new custom black Corvette C3 Coupe as he drives into the Mai-Kai restaurant parking lot.

Johnny Lionetti sits in his brand new red Eldorado convertible with the top down when the Corvette pulls alongside the parked Cadillac. Johnny lights a Cuban cigar and smiles. "Nice ride Kid. I hope you saved some cash for me."

Mike shuts down his Corvette '454'V8 and grabs a large duffle bag from the passenger seat. He locks up his ride and puts the bag on the Cadillac back seat. Johnny raises the convertible top while Mike takes the 'shotgun' seat. "Kid, that's enough sun for me today. My doctor says it causes skin cancer. If he's right, you Irish are dead."

The big Floridian chuckles. "Well, I better settle with you before the 'Grim Reaper' gets me. Here's a million towards my bill."

Johnny starts the Cadillac V8 and hands Mike a Montecristo cigar as Frank Sinatra sings, 'It Was a Very Good Year' on the eight track tape player. "Kid, that's what I like to hear. I have to see Ray at the houseboat. He's been taking care of my action and collecting 'vig' on the Super Bowl bets while I was out of town."

'Don' Lionetti puffs his cigar while driving towards the New River. "I just got back from New York City. You should see what we're hijacking these days. My cousin grabbed a truckload of Intel 4004 microchips. Those things are black market gold. Speaking of gold, my bankers say the dollar is losing value big time this year."

Johnny chuckles. "Things are changing fast. Can you believe I made a phone call from my limousine on the way to the airport today? I was talking on a phone in a moving car."

The Miami 'Don' gives Mike a wink of his eye. "I'm getting old and can't keep up with you 'Young Turks'. It's time for me to retire and raise grandchildren."

Mike glances at his future father in law. "Thanks for the mortgage your finance company gave Debbie and me. Now that we live next door, we'll never miss Mary's Sunday dinners."

Johnny smiles and exits I-95 towards the Marina Bay Hotel. He turns into the hotel lot and parks the Cadillac in the shade of a palm tree.

He relights his cigar and lowers the convertible top. "Kid, I've ordered another Hatteras Sportfish for you and it should be ready for sea trials in November. I want you and Ray to run my businesses soon."

'Don' Lionetti's chestnut eyes concentrate on Mike's facial reaction. "Jimmy told me about Ray's Bahamas Quaalude shipments. I have to tax Ray and I don't want trouble between the two of them. Jimmy is paying his granddaughter's cancer medical bills and doctors don't work for free."

Johnny pulls a Smith & Wesson snub nose revolver from his pants pocket. "Kid, how's your business doing? When I was young, my .38 settled disputes. Remember, it's better to be feared than loved."

Mike attempts a confident smile. "Everything is cool so far. My California connection says, Hollywood stars are paying top dollar for our product. I've opened up Chicago, Atlanta, Boston and New Orleans, besides L.A. and Vegas. I'll need eighty kilos this month."

Johnny starts the 8.2 liter Cadillac engine while raising the convertible top. "No problem. Let's go talk with Ray at the houseboat."

'Don' Lionetti drives towards the nearby New River compound. "I got some info on Francisco Diego Valencia. The Vatican and King Ferdinand of Spain granted his family land titles in the 1500's. They own banks, emerald mines, cattle ranches and coffee plantations. Francisco went to college in Switzerland and is known for a 'Monte Carlo lifestyle', while his Harvard educated brother successfully manages the family empire."

Johnny's red Cadillac enters the New River compound and parks in front of the houseboat dock. Mike grabs the cash filled duffle bag and follows his mentor.

The houseboat's front door opens and Little Ray lowers his .357 pistol when 'Don' Lionetti walks past him into the living room. Mike follows Johnny carrying his duffel bag.

The Miami 'Don' strides to the bar and pours himself a Johnnie Walker Black rocks. "Ray, did you transfer the cash to the Colombian's bank account?"

Little Ray shakes his head. "Cash flow is slow. I sent him two million last week and I'll pick up another two this week. Your banker charged ten percent and he says the Fed's are monitoring seven figure foreign bank transfers. We should move cash by boat through the Bahamas from now on. The Jockey can run to Nassau in twelve hours."

Little Ray pauses and pours himself Jack Daniel's rocks. "I told Francisco the product is on the street and he'll get his money when we get it. What's in the bag?"

Johnny signals Mike to drop the bag. "The Kid brought in a million."

The little man growls at Mike. "Did you count it all?"

A cold chill runs through Mike's chest, knowing he didn't open every cash package. "I figured we'd do it together."

'Don' Lionetti puts his hand on the little man's shoulder. "Ray, you owe twenty percent on the pills from the Bahamas. I'm getting out of the action, but I get paid on everything. Also, the 'Kid' needs another eighty kilos."

Johnny smiles and raises his glass. "Now, let's drink to our success."

Little Ray frowns and pours his boss another Scotch.

Johnny gestures to Mike. "Pick your poison."

Mike pours a Bacardi 151 rocks as Johnny jubilantly raises his drink again. "Our cocaine business will expand worldwide now that Bebe Rebozo vacations with President Nixon on Key Biscayne."

'Don' Lionetti turns to Little Ray with an intimidating look and taps his glass. "Remember, I always get paid first on everything."

———◆———

Later, the full moon rises at sunset when Johnny arrives home in Lighthouse Point to find Debbie and Mary sitting in the living room listening to Maria Callas sing 'Carmen' on the stereo.

Their conversation ends abruptly when he enters the room. Johnny hugs his wife and daughter. "What are my girls discussing so intensely?"

Mary kisses her husband's cheek and walks towards the kitchen. "I'm encouraging our daughter to take care of her health. Supper is nearly ready. Debbie, are you staying?"

Debbie shakes her head. "Mike is taking me to dinner and a show tonight."

Johnny hands her a Ben Franklin. "Have a good time. What are you going to see?"

Debbie takes the cash and kisses her step father's cheek with a hug.

"Thanks. Mike wants to see 'The Getaway' with Steve McQueen and I want to go to the Coconut Grove Woody Allen comedy festival."

Mother embraces her daughter. "Don't worry sweetheart, everything will be OK."

Mary returns to the kitchen when Debbie leaves. Her husband pours himself a Glenfiddich Scotch and joins her. Johnny listens to 'La traviata' as he affectionately hugs his wife and whispers in her ear. "Mi amore, this opera inspires me to make love with you. Onassis should never have left Maria Callas for Jackie Kennedy. If a man finds a good woman, he should hold onto her for the rest of his life."

The aroma of four cheese 'Alfredo' sauce permeates the air. Mary turns around and tenderly kisses her lover. "Sweet heart, I'll get dinner on the table. Please pour me a glass of Pinot Grigio. I want to make a toast."

Mary raises her wine glass. "May we be blessed with many healthy grandchildren."

———◆———

Meanwhile at the New River guest house, Mike Casey packs for a flight to Jamaica. He quickly closes the suitcase when he hears Debbie's Ford Mustang arrive.

Janis Joplin sings 'Piece of My Heart' on the radio as Debbie excitedly rushes into the guest house bedroom. "I hope we're still going to the movies tonight."

Mike doesn't hesitate. "For sure. You'll love 'The Getaway'. Ali MacGraw is in it and the ending is different from 'Bonnie and Clyde'."

Debbie frowns when she notices the luggage beside their bed. "I'm tired of being stuck at home, while you run around doing business."

Mike holds his girlfriend close, knowing her volatile nature. His burly arms lift her into a tight embrace. "Babe, Johnny says I have to go to Ocho Rios to stop Jerry from fucking up our Jamaica deal. I'll be back in a couple days. Let's stay in tonight. We'll get takeout and watch TV like we used to."

Debbie hugs her man with a smile. "I'll order pizza and we can watch 'All in the Family'."

Mike points at the refrigerator. "There's a bottle of Moet in the fridge."

Debbie picks up the telephone. "Champagne with pepperoni and mushroom pizza sounds good."

Thirty minutes later, Debbie hugs her man tightly in a loving 'afterglow' when the doorbell rings. Mike pulls on his blue jeans and opens the door. He trades two Andy Jacksons for a large pizza box and quickly closes the door. "Dinner is served."

Stevie Wonder sings 'You Are the Sunshine of My Life' as Debbie sips champagne and presses closer to her man. "Honey, would you want a kid someday?"

Michael Casey hesitates between mouthfuls of pizza. He's no longer a begging pauper and has recently tasted the sweet fruit of success. "We'll have kids after I take care of business with Johnny. Right now, I have work to do."

Debbie pensively sighs as Mike turns on the late evening WTVJ television news. "Henry Kissinger denies Fidel Castro's accusations of a pending American coup d'etat against Chile's President Allende. In national news, Senator Sam Ervin wants the Senate Watergate Hearings televised live. American Indian Movement activists continue to resist U.S. Marshals surrounding the Pine Ridge Indian Reservation in South Dakota."

Mike fills Debbie's wine glass and points at the last slice of pizza. "You have to eat, otherwise Mary will worry about your health."

Debbie smiles and gently caresses Mike's chest. "Let's have some coke for dessert. We can watch Johnny Carson tonight. Lily Tomlin is on with Bob Hope and his U.S.O. show."

Mike pulls out a television magazine and passes a mirror covered with cocaine to his lover. "Bob Hope's shows were the best when I was in Vietnam. The T.V. Guide says world bodybuilding champion 'Mr. Olympia' is on too. I can't pronounce this guy's last name, Arnold 'Schwarz-en-egger'."

Debbie finishes chopping cocaine lines and toots her share when Ed McMahon calls out. "Here's Johnny."

'Ernestine the Telephone Operator' follows Johnny Carson's monologue. Debbie laughs uncontrollably at Lily Tomlin's act.

"I loved her and Goldie Hawn in 'Laugh In'."

Mike picks out a half joint left in the ashtray. He lights the doobie and passes it to his girl. "We have Baskin Robbins ice cream in the freezer. Do you want some?"

Debbie inhales the joint and snuggles in her man's muscular arms. "I have everything I want, when I'm with you."

———————•———————

The next morning, Mike is late for his meeting at the Mai Kai restaurant. He parks his black Corvette next to Johnny's red Cadillac convertible and runs to the restaurant entrance. A sign on the door reads 'Closed'.

The door suddenly unlocks and Johnny's smiling face appears. "Come in. The owner is a friend and opens early for locals like me."

'Don' Lionetti leads Mike into the Polynesian bar. "Kid, get down to Jamaica and sort out your Jew friend. Jimmy said the Jamaicans want him off the island and I don't want my retirement plans screwed up."

Johnny goes behind the bar and pours drinks. Mike notices a stunning blond in a booth. "Wow, that lady is gorgeous."

Johnny smirks. "That's Vikki LaMotta, Jake's wife. She's a local too. Jake was middleweight champ in the late 40's until he lost to Sugar Ray Robinson. Pound for pound Sugar Ray is the best boxer I ever saw, but Jake LaMotta was the toughest."

'Don' Lionetti clicks Mike's glass with his drink. "Keep your shit together and stay focused on business. The Bahamas will be independent soon and the new government will help me set up offshore operations. Now that the dollar is no longer tied to gold, I'm buying bullion and South African Krugerrands."

Mike looks at his brand new 18k gold Rolex President watch. "Damn, my Jamaica flight takes off from MIA in two hours. I've got to go."

Earlier in April, Jill gave me a sobering look when we woke up at sunset two days after the Hull House April Fool's party. "Buddy, let's quit the 'business' and graduate college."

I reach for a cocaine covered mirror on the bed nightstand and quickly inhale a long pearl white crystal line. "Joey agreed to guarantee Rudy's five kilo deal for two thirds of the profit. I'll fly to Florida as soon as I get the deposit."

Jill rolls away from me and groans. "There's no future in dealing drugs. We've got enough money to join Sonya and Bill in Belize. Let's pay Mike off and finish school. I don't want to be an outlaw. Do you?"

I chuckle. "The pay has been good. We were down to our last 'buck' in Denver a year ago and now we have a hundred thousand with a chance to make a quarter million."

Jill frowns. "Teresa's pregnant and wants Joey to quit the business."

I shrug my shoulders. "Joey's making big money and he won't quit because Teresa is pregnant. I want to make as much cash as we can now. Money gives us power and I don't want to be like that poor California family. I'm withdrawing from my classes and doing this deal to buy our Caribbean hotel."

Jill stares at me with frustration. "I want the piano bar, but I don't want to end up in prison."

I give my buddy a reassuring hug. "Don't worry. The third time's the charm. We've made the run twice and one more gives us a lifetime of guarantees."

Jill shakes her head. "I hope so and by the way, yesterday was the last day to withdraw without penalty."

Later, I enter the UMass/Boston Registrar's office. Charlene looks gorgeous, dressed in a peach blouse and tight yellow miniskirt. She smiles when she sees me. "John, call me Jack Collins. How can I help you?"

I smile and whisper. "Beautiful. I'm hoping you could do me a favor."

———————◆———————

Caribbean sea breezes attempt to cool the air this mid-April afternoon as Mike Casey stands under a blooming red orange Royal Poinciana tree at the Montego Bay airport entrance on April 19th.

He recognizes Jerry Siegel sitting in the passenger seat of an approaching Toyota Corolla. Jerry quickly retreats to the back seat when the car stops. "Brocco, get the man's bag."

Mike ignores his childhood friend and tosses his bag on the back seat. He shakes the ebony driver's hand. "I'm Mike. Tony tells me, you're his right hand man."

The driver laughs heartily. "Yeah Man. Brocco is Tony's right hand."

Mike looks over his shoulder at his fellow passenger. "Tony says you've wasted all your money and you're abusing locals by not paying bills. I'll have to take you back to Miami."

Jerry Siegel raises his voice. "I guess I'm the white 'nigger' to be thrown out with the trash. Tony's making millions moving coke. He calls himself 'Sir Champion' and is buying real estate all over the island. He even bought the Arawak Hotel."

Jerry's discontented tirade continues on the uneventful drive from Montego Bay to Mammee Bay. Mike notices a tall elegant woman speaking with Tony in front of his Arawak Hotel apartment when Brocco steers the Toyota into the courtyard.

At the sight of the car, the beautiful Caribbean lady gracefully retreats to a nearby cottage. Brocco parks the car and Jerry quickly escapes into the shadows.

Anthony Ascot welcomes Mike Casey with a wide smile and handshake. "Michael, good to see you. I'm glad you're here. Come inside. Join me in a glass of champagne. We have a lot to discuss."

Mike enters the apartment, decorated with recently purchased antiques and art. "Who is that lovely lady you were talking with?"

Tony opens a bottle of his signature champagne and smiles. "That pretty lady is another future mother of my children."

Mike laughs. "Speaking of beautiful women. Where is Joy Brown these days?"

Tony points towards a bedroom door. "She's getting dressed in there."

The pretty island lady appears in the doorway attired in a rainbow colored thong bikini. Mike gazes at her shapely coppertone body. "Joy, you're as gorgeous as ever."

Tony hands his girlfriend the open Veuve Clicquot bottle and gives Mike a baggie filled with 'farmers pride' ganja.

Joy pours champagne into Waterford crystal glasses as Tony opens a mahogany cabinet. "Listen to Bob Marley sing 'Get Up, Stand Up' on my new Kenwood stereo."

Anthony Ascot removes an eighteen carat gold Rolex timepiece from his wrist and hands it to Mike. "I receive these watches from Switzerland at reasonable prices without taxes."

The wily Jamaican picks up a polished cherry wood box from his clothing closet and pulls out a huge gold medallion and chain wrapped in red velvet.

"Michael, I must thank you again for the classic John Browning shotgun. Let me show you a gift I recently received from our Colombian friend."

Mike observes the gem stone pattern on a large gold medallion. 'Sir Champion' is spelled with diamonds and rubies inside an emerald studded Jamaican outline. "Tony, you look like you're Jamaican royalty. But, I have a problem calling anyone 'Sir'. So, I'll call you 'Champs'."

Tony pauses for a second and then bursts into laughter. "I like it."

The big Floridian pulls out a cash roll. "I can see you don't need money, but I want to cover Jerry's screw ups. What's the damage?"

Anthony Ascot shakes his head violently from side to side. "The bloodclaat has been very troublesome. First, he got drunk on rum and crashed a rental car. I had to pay one thousand dollars to repair it."

Tony raises his voice. "Last week, he used ganja gum and cocaine to seduce a fifteen year old girl in her mother's home. Worst of all, the bloodclaat knocked over a candle and burned the house down. It cost me two thousand dollars to rebuild it."

A tall Jamaican man follows Brocco into the room. Mike hands Brocco a burning spliff. Tony nods towards the new arrival and turns to Mike. "This is my cousin, Bond. He ferries your packages in his glass bottom boat."

Mike shakes Bond's hand as Tony continues to complain. "The night we delivered your last package, Jerry put bad fuel in Bond's boat and it stalled past the reef, fully loaded with no power.

245

Luckily, my cousin revived the engine. Otherwise, we could have lost everything to the authorities."

The big Floridian counts out fifty, one hundred dollar bills and hands them to his host. "This should cover everything."

The wily Jamaican counts his money and walks into his bedroom while Jimmy Cliff sings 'The Harder They Come' on a nearby radio.

Minutes later Tony re-enters the living room dressed in a purple silk robe, with the gold medallion and chain around his neck. He cradles a bottle of 1945 Château Mouton Rothschild Bordeaux, Pauillac wine in his hands.

Mike grins. "You look like Hugh Hefner. Are we drinking Bordeaux tonight?"

Anthony Ascot returns his liquid treasure to the bedroom. "No, this bottle is a thousand dollar long term investment. I have an alternative gift for you today. Let me introduce you to 'freebase' cocaine."

Mike notices Jerry joining Brocco and Bond standing at attention in the back of the room. Their eyes follow Tony's movements as he brings out a Pyrex glass pipe and places a small crystalline cocaine rock on a wire screen in the pipe bowl.

Tony fires the Ronson butane lighter vaporizing the freebase stone and inhaling the sickening sweet smoke. He closes his eyes and holds the cocaine vapors deep in his lungs. Slowly, a feeling of omnificence overcomes him. Tony realizes Francisco Diego Valencia has given him the ability to control people with money and cocaine.

Everyone stares at 'Sir Champion' with envy when he gradually opens his mouth and releases a cloud of blue gray smoke.

The acetone scented cloud fills the room. Tony's eyes slowly open and he gestures to his guest. "Michael, I'll reload the pipe and send you to the moon."

The mesmerized onlookers intently watch their 'master' refill the pipe and pass it with the lighter to his guest. Mike Casey heats the freebase rock and fills his lungs with cocaine vapors until the powerful stimulant enters his bloodstream causing his body to pulsate in harmonic vibration with the universe.

The big Floridian releases an acetone smoke cloud and turns to his host with a wide grin. "This high is orgasmic."

Anthony Ascot passes the pipe with a crystalline rock to Joy. He signals the bystanders in the back of the room to come forward and hands each their free-base rations. They all vaporize their cocaine rocks as fast as the pipe cools.

Bond and Brocco thank their employer and exit the room. Mike's euphoria fades into an overwhelming urge for more cocaine as he watches Jerry desperately search the floor for free-base rocks.

There's a loud knock at the door and a stout muscular Jamaican, with long dreadlocks strides into the room. Tony passes the newcomer the pipe and lighter without a word. The stout ebony man quickly inhales the cocaine free-base and exits.

Tony observes Mike's curiosity. "Logs is my night watchman. He spends nights in the trees around the hotel. Cocaine will keep him awake until sunrise."

Mike desperately craves another freebase hit, but he doesn't want to beg or crawl on the carpet like his groveling childhood friend.

Tony fires up another cocaine rock and turns to Mike. "Immanuel Kant wrote 'Mankind created a supreme being' and Darwin theorized 'Man evolved through survival of the fittest.' I say man makes his own destiny. I'm 'Sir Champion, Lion of the Caribbean' and I'll rule Jamaica someday."

Mike smiles when his host hands him the refilled pipe and lighter. "Champs, I don't believe in God and I didn't study philosophy in England. All I know is, what the street taught me. Everyone makes their own way alone in this dog eat dog world."

The big Floridian fires up the pipe and closes his eyes as he inhales powerful cocaine vapors deep into his lungs. He opens his eyes to see Jerry sneak into Tony's bedroom and reappear holding the vintage Rothschild wine bottle. In the next second, the valuable vintage Bordeaux falls from Jerry's hands and the glass bottle shatters on the tiled floor.

He whines. "I just wanted to trade the wine for another hit."

Tony instinctively leaps to his feet. The sight of his vintage liquid treasure in a scarlet puddle on the floor sends him into a rage. He quickly draws a Buck knife from his belt. "I'll cut you into a 'pussyclaat'!"

Mike calmly stands and pulls out his cash roll and begins counting. "Tony, you paid a thousand for the bottle. Here's two 'big ones', that's a hundred percent profit."

Anthony Ascot's mood changes quickly at the sight of cash. "Jerry, you're lucky to have Michael as your friend. Leave now, before you fuck up again."

Joy cleans the mess as Jerry whimpers and walks out the door. "It wasn't my fault."

Tony gives Mike an earnest look when the door closes. "The Europeans are being driven from the Caribbean. Independent islands need investors and you should join me in these opportunities."

The shrewd Jamaican refills the pipe with the largest free base rock of the evening and hands it to his guest. Mike vaporizes the cocaine and fills his lungs again. His mind and body vibrate harmoniously as he releases another acetone scented cloud into the room.

Mike opens his eyes and grins at his host. "Let me think about investing in the Caribbean. But, I do have a gift for you. I'm taking Jerry back to Miami."

Anthony Ascot grins. "Good riddance to the bloodclaat."

Birds awaken in the jungle at sunrise when Mike walks into Jerry's bedroom and shakes his sleeping friend. "Wake up. We're taking a taxi to Mo Bay in a half hour."

Jerry staggers out of bed and pulls on his Levi jeans. He packs his meager belongings and follows Mike towards a taxi parked at the hotel entrance.

Unexpectedly, Tony's aunt steps from the cab. Jerry quickly ducks behind the hotel wall as Mike greets his former landlady. "Auntie Claire, I'm sorry to hear of your sister's passing."

The matronly Jamaican woman's face betrays her deep sadness. "Thank you for your condolences. May my poor sister's soul rest in peace. I'm here to see my nephew about his responsibility to his wife and children. He failed to care for his loving mother and I pray he'll abandon his sinful ways." Auntie Claire hugs Mike. "Be good my son and may God bless you."

Jerry returns from the shadows and joins Mike in the taxi when Auntie Claire walks towards Tony's apartment. The driver puts the Toyota Corolla in gear and steers towards Montego Bay as Jerry shouts. "I can't wait to get back to Miami."

Two weeks later, a waning full moon shines on the New River when Johnny Lionetti's Hatteras Sportfish 'American Dreams' returns to Florida. Jimmy the Jockey slowly maneuvers the seventy foot fishing boat into the darkened boat house. He successfully avoided a tropical storm while delivering two million in cash to the Bahamas and picking up another Quaalude shipment. Jimmy hands the boat keys to Little Ray. "Looks like hurricane season is early this year."

Little Ray grins as he finishes loading boxes of pills into his new concrete storage bunker. He secures the dead bolt locks. "Jimmy, let's get some girls and party tonight. I'll be the 'Boss' soon and you have a chance to get in on the ground floor of my operation."

Late the following night, Mike Casey and his cousins remove eight ten kilo cocaine bales from Little Ray's concrete bunker and load them into two new Ford 150 camper pickups. Uncle Pat watches his nephews make the transfer.

Little Ray growls as he locks the bunker. "Casey, this adds two million to your bill. You owe three million now and remember you owe me, not Johnny."

The ugly gangster's ominous grin chills Mike to the bone. Little Ray turns and walks to the houseboat as the Casey cousins drive towards the compound exit.

Uncle Pat lights a Lucky Strike cigarette as the steel gate closes and the pickups disappear into the darkness. "Mike, what about Corby's hassle with Jerry?"

Mike shrugs his shoulders. "Everything's under control. I have Jerry running twenty 'keys' to J.R. in L.A. and picking up a million dollars. Johnny says he'll pay off Corby's parole officer and arrange to move him to Jacksonville. Coby had weapons training in the Navy and he can guard Ma's farm. Let's have a drink before I meet Jack at Marina Bay in an hour."

———•———

Later at midnight in the Marina Bay Hotel, Pink Floyd's 'Money' plays on my room clock radio. A leather briefcase full of cash sits beside my bed as I hope Kim is my date tonight.

"Knock." "Knock."

"Who's there?"

"Mike"

I look through the peephole and open the door. "Man, am I glad to see you."

The big Floridian carries a large Samsonite metal suitcase into the hotel suite living room. "Jack, I hope you have cash, because I've got plenty of product."

I laugh and point at my briefcase. "There's three hundred fifty thousand dollars in the case. That's more money than most Americans make in a lifetime."

Mike picks up the briefcase and looks inside. "I'll count it later. Little Ray is running the show now and I've got another eighty kilos to move. You have ten untouched 'keys' in this suitcase. Your bill is now three hundred large after the deposit and you should easily clear a quarter million profit."

———•———

Outside the Marina Bay Hotel, occupants of a black Ford Galaxie stare through Bushnell binoculars at the parking lot. Lieutenant Brady grunts his frustration to Sergeant Guerrette.

"Can you believe the parole office allowed Corby Casey to move to Jacksonville?"

Just then, Dan Brady looks through his binoculars to see someone exit the hotel. "Dick, look at who's getting into the taxi. Isn't that the same guy who was down here last month with Mike Casey?"

Sergeant Guerrette nods his head. "Yeah, he looks like a Boy Scout."

Lieutenant Brady growls. "We'll have to find out who he is."

MAUI GIRL IN MOONLIGHT

Today is Cinco de Mayo and UMass/Boston classes ended yesterday. The Kent State and Jackson State student murders are remembered in prayers and protests around America as President Nixon dismisses his White House advisers, H.R. Haldeman and John Ehrlichman in response to impeachment rumors circulating Capitol Hill.

Kim Terry and I didn't hook up on my last Florida trip. Mike said she and her sister, Karol moved to Jacksonville Beach. Jill and I got postcards from friends around the country. Sugar and Gray are traveling in Europe. Marc and Gwen got married and moved to San Francisco when she got a job at Intel computer company.

Susie and Jane plan to live with us this month while they attempt to sell their organic honey and maple syrup in Boston. Everyone in Hull House is living large on cocaine money. Rudy Losordo got a tattoo and bought the 'Demon Deacons' new instruments. Joey Palermo is happy Teresa is pregnant and they both hope for a boy.

Lilac scented ocean breezes cool the air this Saturday afternoon. I'm pulling on my blue jeans, when I hear Susie greet Jill downstairs. "Congratulations on graduating."

Jill's reply surprises me. "Not quite yet. I have to finish my philosophy thesis."

I walk downstairs and hug the new arrivals. "I dropped my classes this semester."

A frown appears on my buddy's face as I explain. "A friend at the Registrar's office changed my withdrawal dates."

Neal Shuster appears from the kitchen. "I'm making Cinco de Mayo Margaritas."

Jane quickly responds. "I'll have the first pour."

———————•◆•———————

Later a red sun sets in a pale blue sky when I join Shu and Joey Palermo watching Secretariat run past the Kentucky Derby field in record breaking time.

Shu exclaims. "Wow, that horse could win the Triple Crown."

Joey nods his head. "No one has won it since 1948. We'll know more when they run the Preakness in two weeks."

The kitchen buzzes with conversation as the girls prepare today's celebration meal.

Maureen Fitzpatrick asks Teresa Palermo. "Have you seen 'The Streets of San Francisco'? Michael Douglas is such a 'hunk'."

Teresa smiles. "Just like his dad, Kirk."

Susie holds Jane's hand while she gives Jill a wistful look. "Judy is expecting a second child and Sonya's last postcard said she's pregnant. Jane and I want a family too, but child services won't let us adopt."

Later, everyone enjoys Veuve Clicquot champagne as Rudy sets up his new Gretsch drums at midnight. 'Bone' Mason joins him plugging his Fender Telecaster into a 100 watt Marshall Amp, while 'Bait' Quatromoni adjusts a new Fender P-Bass.

Rudy taps his drums as Jane joins the 'Demon Deacons' playing Dave Mason's 'Feelin'Alright'. The band plays until Rudy joins Mo searching for cocaine sales in Boston's 'after hour' clubs.

The May full moon rises over the New River compound eleven days later. Mike Casey is worried his plans for wealth and power are falling apart.

Uncle Pat pours one of his tequila concoctions for his nephew in the main house kitchen. "I put a bet with Johnny on Secretariat winning the Preakness. He said the cops have Marina Bay under surveillance and he wants you to move the action to Pier 66."

The big Floridian gulps half his drink. "That's all I need now! First, Jerry goes missing with J.R.s' million, then Debbie tells me she's pregnant. What's next?"

Mike finishes his Margarita. "The only good news is Corby's parole paperwork was approved and he's on his way to Jacksonville. All I can say, Jerry better show with my cash or he's shark bait."

On the other side of the compound, 'Don' Lionetti converses with his lieutenants in the houseboat. "Ray, gold cost thirty five dollars an ounce two years ago and now, it's over a hundred. I'm buying everything I can get and moving it offshore. I need you and Jimmy to run a shipment to the Bahamas soon."

Earlier at the Ft. Lauderdale Police H.Q. cafeteria. Lieutenant Dan Brady's face is flushed red with anger as he drinks coffee. "I can't believe the Chief locked us out of the meeting because of 'National Security' concerns. Damn! I've been on the force for twenty years and I fought the 'commies' in Korea."

Sergeant Guerrette lights a cigarette and sips a warm cup of Lipton tea. "The Fed's will leave Florida sooner or later and we've got to protect our pensions."

Upstairs in the main conference room, Federal narcotics agents Dobbs and Thorsen sit alongside Ft. Lauderdale Chief of Police Bill Evans. Lawyers, accountants and field agents fill the remaining chairs. A tall strawberry haired beauty stands in the front of the room.

Officially, Mary Ellen O'Connell is the State Department Caribbean and Central American liaison officer. In reality, she's a C.I.A. agent attached to the Florida and Caribbean drug interdiction task force. U.S. Attorney Thomas P. Stack stands next to the stunning agent.

U.S. Attorney Stack addresses the expanding Florida drug interdiction task force. "Thank you Miss O'Connell for explaining the intricate relationship between the State Department and our task force. Are there any questions for Miss O'Connell, other than will she have a drink with you?"

Everyone in the room smiles, including Mary Ellen. A hand is extended in the back row and a crew cut field agent stands.

"Sir, what's our primary mission? Stopping drugs or communism? It seems like we have to dance around these Caribbean and South American governments."

The U.S. Attorney gives the young agent a stern look. "Don't let international diplomatic issues or politics interfere with our mission. Miss O'Connell and her staff will resolve any interagency conflicts."

The same day in Jamaica, a vermilion full moon rises from the Caribbean Sea at sunset. Jasmine flowers scent the air when Anthony Ascot joins Francisco Diego Valencia on his Rose Hall villa veranda.

The debonair Colombian turns to his Jamaican partner. "Anthony, have a glass of champagne. Reliable diplomatic sources say Cuban

256

communists infiltrated Kingston slums intending to take over the government. Eventually, They may interfere with our business enterprise."

Tony jumps from his seat with fire in his eyes. "The bloodclaat communists won't destroy my paradise!"

Francisco attempts to reassure his Jamaican partner. "Anthony, the C.I.A. has agreed to assist us. A coastal freighter from my shipping company will deliver American weapons to arm five hundred men."

A cunning smile comes to the Colombian's face. "It is time to recruit our freedom militia. I intend to increase cocaine production and we'll export my product around the world through your island."

Tony grins and nods his head. The thought of becoming the richest, most powerful man in Jamaica nearly excites him to orgasm.

———◆———

Massachusetts flower blossoms bloom in warm Gulf Stream breezes during the month of May. Jill and Jane prepare bread rolls while listening to 'Take It Easy' on the Hull House kitchen radio. Jill kneads the dough and silently reminisces about her times with Sonya.

Shu walks into the kitchen hoping to cure his hangover from last night's full moon party.

He loudly proposes. "Anyone want Bloody Marys?"

Jane laughs. "Sure, let's start the day with vodka cocktails."

Chuck is exercising on the third floor when he looks out his bedroom window and sees a Lincoln Continental limousine stop in front of Hull House. The driver opens the passenger door and a couple dressed in the latest European fashion steps out.

The Coast Guardsman yells. "Check the limo out front. Looks like we've got visitors."

I put on my blue jeans and go downstairs to meet the new arrivals. I open the front door to see Mike dressed in a black Johnny Cash style suit, with a large gold chain around his neck. Debbie looks like Audrey Hepburn wearing an elegant Givenchy design and a stylish Halston hat.

Mike shakes my hand as I give his girl a welcome hug. "You guys look great."

Debbie embraces Jill, while handing her a small wrapped package. "This is a graduation gift from me and Mike."

Jill opens the gift. Her eyes light up, with a broad smile as she hugs her girlfriend. "A diamond and opal necklace. It's beautiful, but it costs too much"

Debbie chuckles and flashes a flawless five carat diamond on her finger. "Don't worry. Mike can afford it. Look at the ring he bought me."

Jill leads her guest into the kitchen. "That's the biggest diamond I've ever seen. Let's talk over a cup of tea?"

Debbie nods her head and follows her friend. "Sure, I want to tell you a secret, but you must promise never to tell anyone."

Jill sees the look of urgency in her friend's face. "I won't tell a soul."

A big smile comes to Debbie's face. "I'm pregnant. No one knows, except Mike and my mother. I don't want Johnny to find out, until we get married next month."

Jill hugs her friend, while thinking to herself…'What would Jack do if I got pregnant? Would he marry me and have a family?'

"Debbie, I'm so happy for you."

At the same time, I'm on the front porch with Mike and three large hardside Samsonite suitcases. "Jack, let's take the bags to your bedroom and set up the triple beam scale."

I lead Mike to the second floor. The big Floridian unlocks a suitcase and reveals ten kilos of cocaine with coiled snake logos. He pulls out a Buck knife and cuts open a package, pouring pearl white rock cocaine onto the dressing table.

"I brought you another ten 'uncut' kilos. You'll be a millionaire by Christmas."

He chops the cocaine rock into long lines of crystalline powder and hands me a rolled hundred dollar bill. "Jerry ran off with a million in cash and I owe Little Ray three million. I need you to take twenty kilos to Maui and pick up a million from J.R.. You get a hundred grand and travel expenses for flying the coke to Hawaii and returning to Florida with my cash."

I snort a line of near pure cocaine and shake my head. "Rudy's five kilo deal is happening this weekend and Joey should be settling his bill tonight. Jill and I are planning to retire somewhere in the Caribbean. Why don't you send one of your cousins?"

The big Floridian frowns. "Scott and Shaun are already collecting money and Corby is on parole. I'm dead if I don't get Little Ray's money. Jack, we've been 'back to back' for years. You've got to help me."

I'm wondering what I'm getting into, when I answer. "Sure, I've got your back'."

Mike sets up another round of cocaine while we listen to Jimi Hendrix play 'All Along the Watchtower'. The big Floridian inhales a long blast of coke and hands me the rolled Ben Franklin with a wide grin. "You can live like a king anywhere in the world after this deal."

Mike removes a small black leather case from his luggage and opens it as I inhale another line. He pulls out a loaded Smith & Wesson .357 revolver. "Use this to cover your ass."

I frown while reluctantly accepting the weapon. "Man, I'm counting on stealth and evasion, not firepower."

Mike shakes his head. "Good karma never stopped a bullet."

The bedroom radio plays 'The CBS Midday News with Douglas Edwards'. "The White House declared Timothy Leary and Daniel Ellsberg the 'Most dangerous men in America', while Reverend Billy Graham discusses the Watergate hearings with President Nixon at Camp David this weekend."

***

Later that night, the moon is high in the sky above Hull House when Joey and Teresa Palermo arrive in his Porsche 911 Carrera RS. Joey's masculine bravado is missing when he walks up the front steps carrying a brown grocery bag.

My intuition senses something's wrong when Joey hands me the paper bag. "Jack, I only have two hundred large. I'll get the rest by next week. Rudy's buyer put off his deal until tomorrow tonight."

I give Mike the bag of money. "Joey, this is my Florida partner."

***

Late the following night, John Lennon sings 'Instant Karma' on the radio. "Ring." "Ring."

I pick up the telephone. "Hello."

Joey's distressed voice answers. "Rudy got busted with five kilos. He's in Charles Street Jail and the cops will be all over us in twenty four hours. I don't think Rudy will rat on us, but jail could turn him inside-out. I'll have Teresa check with Mo about bail and lawyers. You and your friend should get out of town tonight."

I'm speechless while Joey continues. "Man, we'll stay in touch through Chuck. Get lost for now and hope for the best."

Joey's voice disappears into a dial tone.

Uncontrolled fear fills my mind as I think...'We're screwed!'

I'm dazed and confused as I slowly walk back to the kitchen and pull Mike aside. "Rudy was busted with five kilos and Joey says we better leave town today. It doesn't look good for collecting any more money and I've only got eighty thousand in the house."

Mike stares at me in disbelief, then quickly composes himself. "We have to hit the road. You and Jill take two cases to Maui and collect my million. I'll cut you both in for ten percent each way if you guys cover travel expenses. That's two hundred large. Debbie and I'll take the other suitcase on Amtrak to New York. We'll leave it with Johnny's nephew in New Jersey, then fly to Florida empty handed."

Jane and Susie agree to watch Lucille until our return from Hawaii. Jill gives her friends tearful hugs and twenty thousand dollars to hold in case we need bail money. I hand Chuck twenty big ones for the same reason.

Jill and I divide the rest of the cash while listening to Mike's instructions. "Seal everything airtight in the locked Samsonite cases and fly first class to Honolulu."

At dawn, Chuck's Cadillac arrives at the Boston ferry dock. We quickly unload our luggage listening to Janis Joplin sing on the car radio.

"Freedom's just another word for nothin' left to lose...".

I give Chuck the .357 revolver and shake his hand. "Keep this until I get back. I'll call Blackie's Mattapan Deli next weekend and leave a payphone number where you can call me. Thanks, brother."

The commuter boat leaves the dock on time and turns west towards Boston as a pale yellow sun rises in the east. Mike pulls me close. "Go to Lahaina, Maui and check into the Pioneer Inn. J.R. eats dinner at Longhi's restaurant every night at nine. He said you should meet him there."

Mike hands me a piece of paper. "If you need to talk with me, call this number from a pay phone and ask for 'Miami Mike'. Leave a number and a time for me to call you back. I'll figure out the time zone from the area code."

My Army buddy gives me a desperate look. "I'm counting on you. Get back to Florida as soon as you can. The cops are watching the Marina Bay, so go to Pier 66 instead. The staff will let me know you checked in and I'll pick you up."

The ferry arrives at the Boston dock fifteen minutes later and the girls lead the way into South Station. Signs indicate Amtrak trains are south, while Logan Airport is north. Debbie and Jill linger in a tight embrace with tears in their eyes."

Jill hugs Mike. "You take care of this beautiful girl."

I hug Debbie and give Mike a firm handshake. "See you in Florida."

Jill and I take the MBTA subway to Logan Airport and run through the terminal to a United Airlines ticket counter where I ask a young male agent. "We want two one way first class tickets to Maui?"

He smiles and searches the computer database. "We have a twelve o'clock to LAX, but the next Honolulu flight I can get you on is three o'clock tomorrow afternoon. I can't sell Honolulu to Maui tickets, but I can reserve seats on Hawaiian Air flights to Kahului tomorrow."

The young agent points to a row of telephones on a nearby wall. "You'll need to call a 800 # and reserve a hotel room near LAX."

He retrieves the tickets from the printer. "That will be one thousand two hundred ninety nine dollars. Please put your luggage on the scale."

Jill gives me an anxious look when I put the heavy Samsonite suitcases on the scale and count out thirteen, one hundred dollar bills. The agent hands me tickets and bag claims. "Your luggage is checked through to Honolulu. The flight boards in two hours from gate eleven. Have a wonderful trip. Aloha."

I turn to Jill as we walk towards the gate. "I can't believe Rudy's in jail and we're flying twenty kilos of coke to Hawaii. I need a stiff drink."

I order Bloody Mary's while watching the NBC Today Show on airport bar television as Barbara Waters announces the news. "Delaware Senator Joseph Biden will join the Senate Judiciary committee investigating the Watergate burglary. U.S. Marshals regained control of Wounded Knee after the American Indian Movement abandoned the village. In sports news, Bobby Riggs continues to challenge Billie Jean King as he prepares to play Margaret Court in a tennis 'Battle of the Sexes'."

Jill and I board a giant Boeing 747 after drinking Bloody Mary's. I follow her into the first class section. We buckle up and order champagne while the ninety ton jet roars down the runway and rises above Boston Harbor heading west towards California.

A pretty blond stewardess announces. "Dinner will be served with a movie. Today's film features Sean Connery as James Bond in Ian Fleming's 'Diamonds are Forever'."

I press a plastic baggie into Jill's hand. "Look what I found hidden in my jacket? Why don't you powder your nose."

Jill excitedly smiles at me when she rises from her seat. I hope to join the 'Mile High Club' as I swallow a Quaalude with my champagne. I pick up a Vanity Fair magazine and listen to Foghat play 'I Just Want to Make Love to You' in my earphones.

The first magazine story discusses how President Nixon's Justice Department harassed John Lennon and why Lennon's song 'Imagine' expresses hope for an earthly utopia.'

Jill suddenly drops into her seat and angrily throws an empty plastic baggie onto my magazine. She gives me a frozen stare and pushes me.

"You bastard! I found black hair in the bag and dumped it in the toilet. I bet it's a pubic hair from that whore in the Registrar's office."

I shake my head while thinking... 'Damn, that was three grams of top quality coke. Charlene did go wild, after a couple of toots. We ended up screwing in the office storage closet on her lunch break.' "Jill, I don't know where that hair came from."

My buddy's stare penetrates deep into my stoned psyche. "Jack, you've become a different person since you started dealing coke. You were going through the motions the last time we made love.

I don't feel we're together anymore and our lives are headed in different directions."

She pulls a blanket over her head and turns away from me as the Quaaludes and alcohol take hold of my thoughts... 'I hope Jill feels differently when we get to California.'

The sun is high in the sky upon our arrival at the LAX Hilton Hotel. We quickly register and order room service, two steak dinners with local red wine. The two of us swallow Quaaludes with glasses of California Pinot Noir and fall asleep fully clothed on the king size bed.

———•———

"Ring, ring." "Ring, ring."

I open my eyes slowly to an empty wine bottle and a tray of leftover food as I answer the telephone. We must have passed out last night. "Hello."

The hotel operator's voice sounds irritated. "Sir, it's one o'clock checkout time. Please settle your bill at the front desk."

I can't believe we slept nearly twenty four hours. We have to catch our flight to Hawaii. "No problem, we'll be right down to pay the bill."

Jill looks up with tired bloodshot eyes. "What's going on?"

I get out bed. "Our plane leaves in two hours. We have to pick up our bags in Honolulu."

Jill quickly walks into the bathroom. "I'll clean up."

Today's desk clerk is a gray haired older woman whose Hollywood dreams were forgotten long ago. She lights a Virginia Slims cigarette and puts it in an ashtray. "Your bill is ninety six dollars, with tax. Minus your fifty dollar deposit, you owe forty six dollars."

Jill gives the clerk a hundred dollar bill and collects her change as we quickly exit the hotel.

When the hotel shuttle delivers us to the terminal we hear an announcement. "United Airlines flight seven to Honolulu is boarding first class passengers at gate eleven."

Minutes later, we take our seats as the Captain announces. "Buckle your seatbelts and prepare for take off."

The first class stewardess serves champagne cocktails in crystal glasses with purple orchids when the Boeing 747 takes to the air as I search for empathy in Jill's blue eyes.

"Buddy, we've got to stick together. Everything is riding on it."

Jill gives me an earnest look. "You're right. We have to pick up the bags in Honolulu and get them to Maui. But, that doesn't change how I feel about your betrayal. I don't want to argue. I just want to get this over as fast as possible."

She turns away from me and pulls a blanket over her head. I close my eyes and enter into a restless dream…

…A heavy set female US Customs agent frowns at me. "Do you know the penalties for smuggling narcotics?" A raven cries 'Nevermore-Nevermore' as a tall man dressed in black hands Johnny Lionetti a shining sword under a bright full moon…

———◆———

I wake in a daze when the stewardess announces. "Sir. Miss. Buckle up and raise your seat back for landing in Honolulu."

Jill's eyes open as the stewardess continues her announcement. "It's five o'clock in Honolulu, Hawaiian Standard Time. All luggage will be available at carousel thirteen."

Suddenly, a chill runs through me... 'What if our luggage didn't make it?'

As we approach the bag claim minutes later, I notice uniformed Hawaii Agriculture officers walking Beagle dogs and think to myself... 'Can those little dogs bust me?'

Jill gives me a distressed look when the baggage carousel stops and our bags aren't there. "Jack, do you think they found the coke?"

A large tanned Hawaiian man dressed in a United Airlines uniform suddenly appears with a friendly smile. "You never get bags. No problem, they come early."

He points down the corridor. "Lost bag office over there."

We cautiously enter the office. I hold my breath while giving the baggage checks to the clerk. She glances at the tickets and leaves the room. A portable television on the counter has Jack Lord in a 'Hawaii Five-0' re-run. "Book'em, Danno."

A minute later, the smiling clerk reappears carrying two Samsonite suitcases.

"Lucky day. I find your bags."

I'm relieved to see the locked suitcases. We have to hurry to the Hawaiian Airlines terminal, if we're going to catch a Maui flight tonight. I offer the clerk a twenty dollar tip. "Thanks so much for your help."

She smiles beautifully and dismissively waves her hand at the cash. "No problem, Bra."

Jill and I dash to the outer-island terminal and buy tickets on the last 'Valley Isle' flight. We check our bags and join passengers boarding a Hawaiian Air DC-9 bound for Kahului.

Jill sits and turns to me. "I'm so nervous, we have to get rid of this luggage tonight."

I smile and signal the flight attendant. "Stewardess, two double vodka tonics please."

We arrive on Maui while a waning full moon rises in the evening sky over Haleakala mountain. The Kahului Airport baggage area is small and our suitcases are the first to come out. I grab them both and lead Jill to the Hertz rental car stall near the terminal.

The clerk is adamant. "If you don't have a major credit card, you must leave a thousand dollar deposit to rent a car."

I reluctantly count out ten one hundred dollar bills. "OK, I need a car with a large trunk for our bags."

The attendant hands me the keys to a new Plymouth Satellite. Ten minutes later, I'm driving the rental car towards Lahaina through sugar cane fields under a cream white moon following road signs to the Pioneer Inn.

I ask the young Hawaiian clerk, after we check into the quaint plantation style hotel. "We're meeting friends for dinner at a new restaurant called Longhi's. Can you give us directions?"

He smiles and points to the west. "No problem, Bra. Longhi's at the end of Front Street."

Lahaina is filled with tourist families strolling along the waterfront during the early evening. At the edge of town, a restaurant sign appears 'Longhi's'. It's after ten o'clock when I park under a street light in front of the restaurant and lock the car.

A barefoot Einstein look-alike, approaches us and introduces himself.

"I'm Bob Longhi. Welcome to my restaurant."

Jill smiles. "We're here for dinner with our friend J.R."

Our host escorts us into the restaurant. "Follow me. We have champagne on ice and a top shelf bar if you prefer a cocktail. An exceptional dining experience awaits you. The waiter will explain today's menu choices."

Bob Longhi leads us to a table in the back of the restaurant. J.R. stands out in the crowded restaurant wearing a cowboy hat. He's eating dinner and drinking champagne with a pretty curly haired blonde. Jill approaches the table and gives the tan teenage girl a hug. "Michelle, I'm so glad to see you again. This is my friend Jack."

Michelle warmly smiles at me. "Nice to meet you Jack. This is J.R."

The California cowboy appears elated that his cocaine shipment has arrived. He hugs Jill and offers me a limp handshake. "Have some Dom Perignon. We just finished dinner."

Michelle places her hand on my thigh when I take a seat next to her. "We're glad you're here."

J.R. smiles at Jill. "Are you hungry?."

I'm on a different page than my host. "We ate on the plane. Let's take care of business."

J.R. smirks. "OK, we'll go to my place on the hill. I'll drive Jill and you take Michelle, so you don't get lost in the cane fields."

The California cowboy takes Jill's arm and leads her towards the exit, leaving me to pay his two hundred dollar dinner tab with tip.

Fifteen minutes later, we arrive at a bougainvillea shrouded plantation house overlooking Lahaina with a beautiful view of the nearby island of Lanai. Night blooming jasmine and gardenia flowers scent the evening air as we exit our vehicles.

The yard is filled with cars and motorcycles painted in many shades of brown. A muscular black and tan Doberman Pinscher stands guard next to a 1963 'split window' Corvette coupe.

When we enter his home, J.R. directs our attention to photos of naked girls covering the hallway walls. He points and begins to describe past romances. "These are my Hawaii ladies."

I'm getting impatient. "Glad you're having fun in the sun, but Mike sent us to deliver product and pick up cash. We've got twenty untouched kilos in the car trunk and you're supposed to give us a million in large bills. We've got a job to do."

J.R. shakes his head from side to side. "Here's the problem, my cash is on the streets in L.A. and I have to fly there. You guys can easily turn these suitcases into ten million, if we parlay the profits in Vegas."

I've got issues with this latest plan. "I can't front these suitcases. Mike needs cash now."

The California cowboy grins. "OK, we'll do business tomorrow. Let's play in the Jacuzzi tonight."

Michelle removes her t-shirt and exposes her voluptuous bronze breasts.

"Let's party."

Both girls strip away their clothes and jump into the steaming hot tub. J.R. goes into his bedroom and returns with a cocaine covered mirror. "Hollywood is hot for this stuff. Jack, pass the coke around while I open a bottle of Dom Perignon."

Minutes later, we're all naked in the hot tub drinking champagne and snorting cocaine. Michelle is surprisingly at ease with J.R. charming Jill with Hollywood stories. The pretty Maui girl's olivine eyes sparkle when she passes me a fat joint.

J.R. stands and takes Jill's hand. "You have a perfect body to sculpt. Michelle, entertain Jack, while I show this pretty lady my artwork."

Inside a cluttered sculpture filled room, J.R. hands Jill a Quaalude and fills her champagne glass. He gently presses his body close to her. "You and I should fly to L.A. We'll have a lot of fun in Hollywood and you could meet Steve McQueen or Warren Beatty."

Jill swallows the pill with champagne. "I want to party in Hollywood, but I have to talk to Jack first."

Meanwhile in the hot tub, Michelle's soft breasts gently caress my chest while she shotguns cannabis smoke into my lungs. I close my eyes and seconds later open them to see Jill standing over me. "Ugh!"

Jill grabs a beach towel and strides towards our rental car.

"Jack, we have to talk now!"

Michelle slides off me, with an impish smile. "Baby, I like what I feel."

I jump out of the warm water, exposing my naked body to the cool night air and pull on my jeans. I follow my buddy in the moonlight towards the rental car.

Jill Jensen coldly stares at me, with seething anger. "Jack, we're not together anymore. This deal is 'fifty/fifty' and I don't expect anything good for us back in Boston. We have two suitcases full of cocaine and nearly forty thousand dollars. Flying with J.R. to

L.A. works for me, so I'll take ten kilos and the cash in my purse. You can do what you want."

I'm thinking to myself... 'This deal doesn't smell right and I have to speak with Mike.'

Jill puts her hands on her hips, with an exasperated look.

"We're free agents and I want my half now."

The argument is lost and I passively surrender. I open the car trunk and pull out a Samsonite suitcase. Jill takes the case and keys. She shoulders her small clothing bag and drags the hard suitcase towards J.R.s' house.

I lock the trunk and walk up the moonlit path back onto the deck. Michelle is smoking a joint in the bubbling Jacuzzi and the large Doberman guards J.R.s' bedroom door.

Michelle grins when she sees me. "Jill is with J.R. and his dog 'Bogart' won't let you in there. All of us were supposed to fly to California tomorrow, but it looks like J.R. is taking your girl and leaving us behind."

My relationship with Jill is ending and I don't trust J.R. All I know is, I can't fly back to Florida with no cash and ten unsold kilos of cocaine.

Michelle's alluring smile shines in the moonlight. "Come in, the water's hot."

I pull off my blue jeans and join her in the steaming Jacuzzi. The radio plays Bob Dylan singing 'I'll Be Your Baby Tonight' when Michelle passes me a joint.

I draw in a deep toke. "This weed is sweet. Where's it grown?"

The enticing island girl smiles. "It's Maui pakalolo, grown on Haleakala."

She smiles seductively as she slides across the candle lit hot tub and retrieves a baggie from beside the Jacuzzi. "I've got Quaaludes."

We both 'toot' lines of cocaine while swallowing 'ludes' with gulps of champagne. Michelle's green eyes sparkle when we passionately kiss and caress each other.

A half hour later, we're totally exhausted in a loving afterglow.

My lover impishly smiles at me. "Jack, it's only midnight. The Pioneer Inn bar is open and the piano man plays until four. Let's go dancing."

I chuckle. "OK, we'll party in Lahaina Town."

<hr>

Bright midday sunlight interrupts my peaceful sleep. Michelle is nestled next to me with my face buried in her blond curls. We closed the Pioneer Inn bar last night and made love in my hotel room until sunrise.

Michelle is a wild party girl, but what am I going to do now that Jill is with J.R. and Mike's deal is a bust? The cops could be after me and I have to speak with Mike.

My lover opens her eyes, with a cheerful smile. "I know where you can sell your coke. My husband Jim buys Thai Stick from the Honolulu 'Brotherhood'."

I'm stunned. "You're married?"

The pretty Maui girl smirks. "Don't worry, we're separated and I do what I want. He loves me and doesn't want a divorce."

Fifteen minutes later, I'm counting my remaining cash while thinking to myself... 'Last night's dinner and bar tabs were serious, but I'll have eighteen thousand after I get the rental car deposit back. I hope I can trust Michelle. She's my only hope of getting Mike's cash.'

Michelle searches for pot 'roaches' in the ashtray and shrugs her shoulders. "J.R. will take Jill and the coke to Vegas like he did with me and I'm sure he'll lose everything betting heavy on Blackjack."

She gently kisses my cheek. "Baby, we can fly to Honolulu and stay on Natalie's boat for a night or two. She's my mom and has to take me in. Besides, she loves young studs and I'll have to protect you from her."

I chuckle knowing my options are limited and Mike needs cash now. Michelle's plan is the only one I've got.

"OK, I'll buy airline tickets. Call your husband and we'll stay with your mother."

BROTHERHOOD
OF THE MOON

Michelle sits beside me enticingly dressed in a nearly transparent lavender sarong on a late afternoon Hawaiian Air flight from Maui to Honolulu. I'm preoccupied with a cocaine-filled suitcase in the plane cargo hold, that could put me in prison for twenty years.

A smiling flight stewardess asks. "Would you like something to drink?"

I return her smile. "The lady and I'll have a couple of Mai Tai's. Thanks."

The tanned stewardess chuckles. "The Hawaiian word for thank you is 'Mahalo'."

A Quaalude and my first drink disappear in a gulp. I signal for a second round while Michelle tells her story. "Natalie hasn't been much of a mother. She and her boyfriend live on her sailboat in Ala Wai Harbor."

Michelle finishes her first drink. "Dad was a Marine Captain in Vietnam, when Natalie ran off with the base golf pro. Teddy is much younger and the three of us sailed to Honolulu two years ago on the boat she got in the divorce."

Immediate worries slowly dissipate after a second Quaalude and drink. My companion surprises me when she whispers in my ear. "Teddy tried to fuck me when I was sixteen. He and Natalie had a fight in a bar and she left with a sailor. Teddy came back to the boat alone and when I woke up he was on top of me. I told my mother, but he denied it and she believed him."

Michelle smirks. "My life changed the day 'Super Lock' fixed the locks on Natalie's boat. Jim Donnell took me to dinner at Chuck's Steakhouse and we got married the next week. Aliya was born nine months later."

I gasp. "You have a kid?"

She looks at my troubled face with a childlike smile and nestles closer to me. "Don't worry, Jim's mother takes good care of Aliya in Honolulu."

<hr>

Mike Casey drives a rented Lincoln Town Car on Interstate 95 towards Jacksonville this dark night. He and Uncle Pat are taking Corby to Ma Casey's farm on the Florida-Georgia border. Nauseating dioxin fumes from nearby paper mills engulf the Lincoln sedan racing northwest into the Okefenokee swamp.

Mike turns to his uncle. "It's Memorial Day and Jerry is still missing with my money. Jack hasn't come back from Maui and I'm paying Little Ray ten percent monthly 'vig'."

Uncle Pat swallows a gulp of whiskey and passes a half full pint of Jack Daniel's to his son. "I guess Jerry got more than his share this time."

Corby grabs the liquor bottle and swallows a double shot with two Quaaludes. His tattooed muscular arms flex as he clenches his fists in anger and returns the bottle to the front seat. "I told you Siegel is no good."

The eldest Casey cousin continues his rant. "Mike, I never blamed you when Jerry left me to do two years in Raiford. I'm owed a piece of that punk before Little Ray feeds him to the sharks."

Mike knows he must control his cousin's thirst for revenge as he hands him a burning ganja joint and a small envelope. "Corby, we have other problems. Johnny's lawyer got you unsupervised parole and your job is to guard the farm. Here's a couple thousand. Stay out of sight and leave Jerry to Little Ray and the sharks."

———◆———

Back in Lighthouse Point, Debbie walks into her mother's kitchen the next morning. Mary Lionetti is serving breakfast to her husband and smiles at her daughter. "Good morning dear. I hope you're enjoying living next door to us."

Johnny Lionetti looks up from the New York Times. "Debbie, you didn't tell us about your trip to Boston. My family in New Jersey told me you were wearing a large diamond ring when you visited them. Are you and Mike engaged?"

Debbie blushes and rushes into her stepfather's strong arms. "Mike asked me to marry him, but Jerry stole a million dollars and Mike has to pay Little Ray soon. Thank God, cousin Louie helped us out."

Johnny is startled. He shakes his head and gives his wife a worried look as he stands. "I have to take care of business. Mary, I'll call you later."

'Don' Lionetti hastily leaves the room as Mary affectionately hugs her daughter. "Johnny and I want to help take care of your baby."

Debbie's chestnut eyes widen with anxiety as her mother smiles.

"Sweetheart, I told him the good news. He's so happy. We're planning a private wedding for you in June and an Italian honeymoon before your pregnancy shows."

Later at the Mai Kai Restaurant, the Tiki Bar torches burn brightly and the floor show is about to begin. US Attorney Tom Stack hopes his date will let her hair down as a waitress in a Polynesian costume serves the bar's signature 'Mystery Drink' with two straws.

Mary Ellen O'Connell sits next to the US Attorney while swaying to hula music. "Tom, I fly to Washington in the morning. Let's take care of business before we drink. This is classified from Director Helms' office. The White House plans to fight narcotics trafficking by creating the Drug Enforcement Administration to work with the State Department. Your Florida drug interdiction team will be expanded, but your jurisdiction is still confined to U.S. borders. State will call the shots offshore."

Tom Stack smiles when his date releases her long strawberry blond hair from a work day bun. Mary Ellen's emerald green eyes sparkle as she picks up her 'Mystery Drink' straw. "I'm sure you'll have plenty of fish to fry in Florida. Now, let's have some fun."

At the same time across town, Lieutenant Dan Brady and Sergeant Dick Guerrette are on a stakeout at the Marina Bay Hotel. The two policemen sit in an unmarked Ford Galaxie surveying the hotel parking lot, while eating McDonalds cheeseburgers. Dan finishes his second burger with a handful of fries and a swig of Coca Cola. "The 'Fed's' have new wiretap 'intel' on suspicious boat traffic at a New River address."

Sergeant Guerrette chokes on a mouthful of beef and nervously gulps 7-Up. "What's the address?"

The lieutenant shakes his head. "That intel hasn't been passed down the food chain."

Nearby at Little Ray's New River houseboat, 'Don' Lionetti lights a Montecristo cigar and swallows his single malt Scotch. Little Ray frowns and pours his boss another drink. "I knew something was wrong when the Casey kid asked to pay vig on his bill. My people will hunt Siegel down and he'll be shark chum after I get my money."

Johnny Lionetti turns to Jimmy the Jockey. "I need to move a thousand kilos of gold to the Bahamas for shipment to Italy. My Vatican banker will meet you in Nassau and arrange the transfer."

Jimmy frowns. "Boss, the boat is still waiting on engine parts."

'Don' Lionetti angrily shakes his head. "Get the repairs done now. No more excuses."

———————

A Colombian flagged coastal freighter docks at a Montego Bay commercial wharf on the last night in May. Anthony Ascot and Francisco Diego Valencia sit in a black Rolls-Royce Corniche parked near the ship on this moonless night. Francisco uses a flashlight to signal the ship captain and two Leyland Comet trucks waiting in the shadows. Instantly, a half dozen men dressed in black jumpsuits begin unloading cargo crates in the darkness.

Francisco turns to Tony with a cunning grin. "Anthony, our friends at the C.I.A. have supplied us with M16 rifles and ammunition. Start recruiting our 'Freedom Militia'. Tons of my product will be shipped to your warehouses in the coming months."

———————

Ten days earlier, Michelle and I arrived in Honolulu on a sunset flight from Maui. My cocaine-filled Samsonite suitcase appeared first on the baggage carousel and I let the hard case circle twice while checking to see if anyone else was watching it. A white

GMC van with a 'Super Lock' logo stops at the terminal entrance when I pick up the case.

The tanned driver wearing a NAPA hat over a sandy brown ponytail steps from the vehicle and shouts. "How's it, 'Scooch'?"

Michelle smiles and waves. "Jim, where's Aliya?"

The van driver answers while nonchalantly extending his hand to me.

"She's with my mother. How's it? Jim Donnell here."

I shake the locksmith's sturdy hand. "Jack Collins. Nice to meet you"

Jim Donnell puts my suitcase in the back of the van. "Scooch, I've found a room you might want to rent. My history professor owns a place near the U. H. Manoa campus on Tantalus Drive."

I take the passenger seat and Michelle sits on my lap. Jim smirks. "Scooch, do you want to smoke some 'Kona Gold'?"

Michelle perks up, with a broad smile. "Is the Pope Catholic?"

Jim passes her a fat joint and a BIC lighter. We drive in a 'purple haze' to Honolulu's famed Ala Wai Harbor filled with sailing vessels from around the world.

The van stops in front of a forty four foot John Alden 'Cutter' named 'Take a Chance' docked next to the Hawaii Yacht Club. Tempting BBQ beef aromas permeate the evening air when I step on the dock.

A tall tan blond man, dressed in a Speedo swimsuit and Hawaiian floral print shirt cooks meat on a charcoal grill. He recognizes Michelle and Jim with a nod.

He then turns to me as I remove my suitcase from the van. "How's it? I'm Teddy. I'll lock your luggage in the dock storage locker. Anyone want a beer? We've got Coors on ice."

An older Michelle look-alike with frosted blonde hair steps up from the galley. Teddy turns to the shapely beauty coming on deck. "Honey, get some beers. I have to stay close to the grill."

I carefully observe Teddy lock my suitcase in the dock locker as Michelle introduces me. "Jack Collins, this is Natalie. Watch out, she's a 'Maneater'."

Natalie smirks while opening the cooler. She hands me a beer with an alluring smile and turns to her daughter. "Nice to meet you, Jack. My dearest child, it is so nice of you to visit."

Michelle smirks and takes her mother's arm. "What's in the blender?"

Mother and daughter go below deck. 'Let It Be' plays on a nearby radio as Teddy sips his beer and flips grilled meat. "Jack, do you play golf? I work at the Waialae Country Club and can get you cheap greens fees. I'm a nine handicap and Jim's a twelve."

Jim taps Teddy's beer can with his and turns to me. "My handicap with women is worse. Jack, do you surf? This island has some of the best waves in the world."

I chuckle when I think of my East coast surfing and mini-golf experience on Cape Cod. "I'm no golfer and the surf in the Atlantic isn't like the Pacific."

Michelle returns topside. "Pina coladas for everyone."

The cabin light reveals Michelle's buxom silhouette through her thin sarong as she fills mugs with the blended rum concoction. Teddy winks. "That's my girl."

Michelle stops pouring cocktails and frowns. "Teddy better not get another 'woody' for this girl."

Jim takes a piece of BBQ beef from the grill. "On that note, 'I'll exit stage left.' Scooch, see you tomorrow morning and we'll go see Aliya at my mother's place. Later in the afternoon, you and Jack can check out that room for rent."

Jim gently kisses Michelle's cheek and waves to his hosts while walking towards his van. "Mahalo, Teddy and Natalie. Nice meeting you, Jack."

The pony tailed locksmith disappears into the night shadows as Michelle hands me a plate of BBQ beef, rice and potato salad with a cold Coors beer. I smile and raise my beer to Natalie and Teddy. "Mahalo for your hospitality."

A short time later, Natalie softly kisses my cheek and winks at her daughter. "Jack, you're sweet. Michelle knows the cleanup drill. Teddy and I are hitting the sack. You guys sleep in the aft berth. See you in the morning."

Michelle leads me into the sleeping berth after we finish cleaning the ship galley. 'Witchy Woman' plays on the radio while she slowly removes her sarong and string bikini thong. I'm aroused as I pull off my t-shirt and Levi's.

Michelle whispers. "Babe, break out some coke. I want to make you a 'snow cone'."

I shake my head. "I can't open the package, until we get a place."

My lover mounts me and kisses my nipples while gently massaging my crotch. "OK, I'll give you a 'snow cone' tomorrow."

Bill Withers sings 'Use Me' as we climax together in the moonlight.

———◆———

Cooing doves and ship rigging rattling in Pacific Ocean breezes wake me the next morning. Warm soft hands gently fondle my morning 'Johnson' as I open my eyes to see Michelle's mother slide on top of me. Minutes later, she quivers with orgasmic pleasure and collapses in my arms.

We lie entwined together in a loving afterglow gently caressing each other. "Jack, I'm glad Teddy went surfing and Michelle is with Jim. Now, I've got you to myself this morning."

Natalie rests her head on my shoulder as I examine my predicament... 'Damn, what am I doing screwing Michelle's mother? I'm a fugitive six thousand miles from home with a suitcase full of cocaine.'

The high pitch squeal of an overweight vehicle's worn brakes shatters the midday calm. Michelle and Jim can be heard in vigorous discussion as van doors close. Natalie looks up and instantly rolls off me. She grabs her panties and bra while retreating into the bathroom while I quickly pull on my jeans. Michelle boards 'Take a Chance' and shouts. "Jack, are you up?"

I'm pulling a t-shirt over my shoulders when I go on deck to see Jim Donnell removing my suitcase from the dock storage locker. Michelle hurries over and gives me a tight hug. "Jim wants to take us to check out his professor's house in Manoa."

Michelle smiles at her mother when she appears on deck. "Mahalo for your kokua."

I hand Natalie a Ben Franklin. She puts the bill in her bikini top and gives me a lingering hug. "Come back soon. We'll have a real party next time."

The afternoon sun shines brightly on multi-colored flowering trees lining Manoa Valley streets. Jim's heavy GMC van slowly rolls up Mount Tantalus overlooking Honolulu.

Jim passes me a burning joint. "Professor Lee teaches at U.H. and runs the Waianae Legal Aid office. He owns Manoa House and rents rooms to students. The estate has a greenhouse and two acres of tropical gardens along with the main house and garage."

I'm preoccupied thinking to myself... 'I've got to call Chuck in Boston to find out what's going on with Rudy. I can't call Mike until I know what's happening.' "Jim, how soon can we hook up with your friends?"

Sensing my desperation, Jim gives me a reassuring smile. "I left word with the 'Brotherhood' and they'll get back to me in a couple of days. These islanders do things at their own pace."

Michelle slyly smiles, gently squeezes my thigh and seductively whispers in my ear. "Baby, break out your stash. I want to give you a 'snow cone' party."

I know better, but I relent to her gentle touch. "OK, if we rent this room."

Jim steers his van into a gated entrance and past an empty guard house. Sweet ginger and plumeria blooms scent the tropical air as we drive through mango and avocado tree orchards.

A three story coral stone mansion, surrounded by multi-colored hibiscus plants is at the center of the estate overlooking Honolulu. Stepping stones lead up a steep slope onto a screened front porch. I easily envision F. Scott Fitzgerald's 'The Great Gatsby' crowd dancing in this elegant building.

A square jawed Teddy Roosevelt look-alike stands at the front door. His eye glasses and teeth shine in the setting sunlight when he greets us with a wide smile. "How's it? You must be the couple who wants to join us. Robert E. Lee here. No relation to our great Virginian general."

Jim shakes his professor's hand. "This is Jack Collins and my wife Michelle, the mother of my daughter."

Michelle gives Jim a 'love tap'. "You didn't have to say that."

Professor Lee firmly shakes my hand. "Call me Bob. I hear you're from Boston. I went to Boston University. I can't believe the Celtics and Bruins lost in the playoffs this year. Do you think the Red Sox can win the Pennant?"

I chuckle. "This might be the year they break the 'Bambino Curse'. Bob, you've got a great place here."

The professor smiles. "My grandfather built Manoa House fifty years ago, during the 'Roaring Twenties'. I inherited it, along with the property taxes and maintenance."

Bob opens the front door. "Come inside and I'll show you the second floor suite. It has a separate bath and there's a futon bed already set up. Manoa House is a drug free co-op, but smoking is permitted in the greenhouse and gardens. We allow wine and beer at our daily sunset meal. All expenses and chores are shared equally. The rent for this room, with utilities and house expenses for two residents is three hundred dollars a month."

Our host leads us up the stairs to the second floor. He opens the door into a large bedroom, with panoramic Honolulu city views. Michelle squeals with delight. "I want to sleep here."

Bob Lee smiles at me. "Two months rent and a three hundred dollar security deposit is required. Also, both landlord and tenant agree to a thirty day notice clause."

I remove nine hundred dollar bills from my wallet. "No problem, we'll take it."

We follow the professor downstairs into the kitchen. The back door opens and a wide eyed Asian girl appears. Bob's smiles.

285

"This is Rona Chong, Legal Aid's newest paralegal. Rona, this is Jack and Michelle. They rented the second floor suite and are joining us for dinner."

A second tanned island girl enters through the back door. Her flowing sienna hair and golden eyes shine in the kitchen light. Bob gives her an affectionate hug. "Malia meet our new roommates, Jack and Michelle. Malia Spencer is my girlfriend's sister."

Rona prepares fried rice and vegetables, while Malia chops fresh vegetables into a salad as Bob walks towards the front door.

"I'm going to the store for beer and wine."

I hand our new landlord a twenty. "Get a couple of six packs of Miller High Life and whatever wine you like."

Ten minutes later, another Asian girl enters the room. Professor Lee follows her, carrying two grocery bags. He hands me change and a beer while introducing the almond eyed beauty. "Michelle and Jack, this is Akiko Kawamoto. She's one of my brightest students at U. H."

After a short prayer, we begin the evening meal. Professor Lee turns to me. "Jack, what's your degree in?"

I smile. "It'll be American History, when I finish my senior thesis."

Bob smiles. "I majored in American History too. The title of my senior thesis was 'Innocence Lost, November 22, 1963'. America was optimistic after World War II during the 50's. JFK's assassination and the Vietnam War have ended that optimism."

Akiko interrupts in a soft, but forceful voice. "Professor, I would question your premise of American optimism and innocence in the 40's and 50's. Many American citizens were disenfranchised and denied their Constitutional rights. 'Jim Crow' laws ruled the 'Old South', unjustly incarcerating African Americans and Japanese American citizens were imprisoned in alien internment camps during the war."

Professor Lee nods his head. "Akiko, you're right. I was naive back then. If I were writing today, I'd write about American individualism and community responsibility."

Akiko thoughtfully smiles as the professor continues. "Individualism captivates Americans to the point of narcissistic self absorption. An individual's freedom must coexist within a communal social contract."

Later, the kitchen radio broadcasts CBS 'The World Tonight' with Douglas Edwards as the dinner clean up begins. "Senate Watergate hearings will be televised live nationwide this week. The United States Supreme Court reaffirmed Roe vs. Wade legalizing abortion. Kentucky Derby and Preakness winner Secretariat is heavily favored to win the Triple Crown at Belmont Park next month."

Jim walks into the kitchen and gives me two joints as I finish washing the pots. "Jack, here's some 'pakalolo'. We'll have lunch at the Kuhio Bar & Grill tomorrow."

I take my gift, with a grateful smile. "Thanks for the stash. I need to make some long distance calls tomorrow morning. Where's the nearest pay phone?"

Jim turns for the door. "The closest one is at the corner 7-11."

A short time later, Michelle and I enter our bedroom with bright Honolulu city lights shining through the bay window. A jasmine scented candle lights the room with a queen size Futon in the middle. A bottle of 'Dr. Bronner's Castile' soap, folded bath towels and a note rest on top of the made up bed.

Bob Dylan sings 'Just Like a Woman' on a nearby radio as I read the note with a smile. "Akiko and Malia welcome us to the household."

I put my suitcase in the closet while Michelle strips off her clothes. "Jim makes me wear a bra at his mother's place and I can never find a comfortable one."

My lover slides next to me on the futon. Her soft breasts glide across my chest. "Baby wants a 'snow cone' tonight."

I shake my head. "Not tonight. I can't open the suitcase until I get a buyer."

Michelle frowns and pulls away from me. She jumps up and struts into the bathroom. "I'm taking a shower."

My excitement turns to frustration. "I guess I'm Charlie Brown and you're Lucy pulling the football away as I'm about to kick it. What am I supposed to do with my stiff one?"

The question remains unanswered as the bathroom door closes. I chuckle to myself... 'Every guy knows how to spank the monkey.'

Water flows in the shower as I enter the steamy bathroom. Michelle smiles when I open the shower curtain to see her soap covered bronze physique. "Does 'Baby' want her 'Daddy'?"

<hr />

I'm awakened by warm sunlight with Michelle sleeping next to me the following day. Morning sex entices me, but I have to get to a payphone ASAP and call Chuck. I'll need a serious hideout, if the cops are on my trail.

An hour later, my Boston phone call continues to depress me. Rudy is charged with felony narcotics distribution and I told Chuck to give Maureen ten thousand for a bail bondsman.

The 'Super Lock' van horn sounds outside in the driveway. I grab my wallet and wake Michelle. "Babe, get dressed. Jim and I have to take care of business."

Jim passes me a 'wake and bake' joint when Michelle and I get in the van. "We have to get over to my mother's house before Aliya takes her nap."

He looks at Michelle's buxom body in her near transparent sarong and shakes his head. "Scooch, this isn't a date. Why aren't you wearing panties and a bra? We're going to see my sixty year old mother."

Michelle whines and pulls on a pink bikini thong. "I didn't have time to get ready."

Jim smirks. "Scooch, put a bikini top on too. My mother doesn't want to see your 'Tits', unless you're breastfeeding Aliya."

The Super Lock van cruises through city traffic onto Kaimuki heights above Diamond Head. Jim stops in front of a small one story plantation bungalow. A gray haired woman sits in the shade on the porch, while rocking a tiny baby in her arms.

Jim waves to his mother as Michelle puts on a pink bikini top and pulls her sarong tight. She jumps from the vehicle with a disgruntled look as Jim pats her butt. "See you in a couple of hours, Scooch."

Michelle pouts. "Come back soon. I don't want to stay too long."

The overloaded GMC van drives towards Diamond Head. Colorful rainbows above Manoa Valley mesmerize me as Jim parks the van in the shade of a huge Banyan tree.

The Kuhio Bar & Grill is busy with conversation and laughter when we enter. Tiny raven haired Asian waitresses hustle drinks from the bar, with hot and cold appetizer plates. Jim takes a seat in one of the wood paneled booths and pulls out a twenty dollar bill. "Put a 'Jackson' on the table in front of you, then the waitress knows you're ready to spend money like a drunk sailor."

A petite, almond eyed girl takes our order. Jim smiles. "We'll have two large Kirin beers, two hot sake and 'da kine pupu's'."

Our waitress notices the cash on the table and smiles. She returns, carrying 22 oz. bottles of Japan's finest beer with frozen mugs.

Jim looks at me intensely. "I have to find out what you have to sell? I'll need a taste of your product for the brothers."

He swallows some beer. "Let me update you on the 'Chamorro Brotherhood' and their leader, Manuel Guerrero. Manny is 'Chamorro Royalty'. I met him as a Peace Corps volunteer in the Mariana Islands when his father was Governor of Guam. He ran into me again at the Outrigger Canoe Club a couple years ago. Manny lives in Honolulu with his smuggling partners, Eddie and Rocky Flores."

I interrupt my host when our waitress delivers porcelain bottles of steaming sake. "What's up with you and Michelle? Are you OK with me and her being together?"

Jim pours hot Japanese rice wine into matching porcelain cups. "I'm in love with Michelle and she's the mother of my daughter. We'll get back together and raise our child when she gets over her wild streak. Now, let's talk business."

The locksmith looks into the jukebox selection. "Do you like Bob Dylan?"

I don't hesitate. "He's the poet of our generation."

Jim drops quarters into the music machine and leans closer to me as 'Rainy Day Women #12 & 35' fills the booth with sound. "Manny knows the right people to move your product anywhere in the world. His father got Mayor Fasi to hire him as a Honolulu international trade consultant."

I nod my head. "Sounds good, but I need to meet him soon."

The locksmith smirks and chugs his beer. "Let me tell you a parable Manny told me after J.R. ripped me off.

'... A monk approaches a stream and notices a snake on the shore. The reptile asks for a ride and the monk hesitates. "You're a snake and you'll bite me."

The serpent answers. "I promise not to bite you, if you help me cross this stream." The monk assists the snake and when they finish the crossing, the viper sinks his fangs into his benefactor's arm causing him to scream, "Why did you bite me?" The reptile's reply. "What do you expect? I'm a snake."...'

Jim pauses and smiles. "Manny is always on the lookout for snakes."

I finish my beer just as a pretty waitress delivers thinly sliced raw tuna, with hot wasabi and soy sauce. Jim begins to assemble the unique Asian eating utensil called chopsticks. "Fresh Ahi sashimi, fit for a king. Order another round of drinks and I'll show you how to use the 'sticks'."

Plates of teriyaki steak, corn on the cob and Korean kimchi are served with another round of Kirin and hot sake. Jim's attention returns to business. "We'll know if Manny wants to meet you, after he tries your product. Michelle loves cocaine and she said the 'blow' you have is the best she's ever had."

The Jukebox plays 'I Walk the Line' when we finish the last of the sake and I throw another Andy Jackson on the table. "Let's go to my place and get a taste for the brothers. I need to hook up ASAP."

Jim's smile widens. "OK, we'll pick up Scooch on the way."

Later, afternoon rain showers create rainbows as a red orange sun sets over the Waianae Mountains while I unlock my suitcase at Manoa House.

Michelle smiles with anticipation as she watches me cut open a kilo and fill two Ziploc baggies with cocaine rocks. I hand one baggie to Jim and tightly reseal the open kilo as he stares at the remaining unopened kilos. I close and lock the suitcase. "Tell your man, I have ten kilos for a half million cash."

Michelle says, "I was miserable listening to Jim's mother complain about me."

Jim laughs. "What do you expect? Mom is 'old school' and you're no school."

I intervene. "Babe, do you want a line?"

Scooch gives me a hug and squeals with delight. "Daddy makes 'Baby' happy."

Jim gives me an appreciative nod of his head. "See you guys tomorrow." He walks out the door as Junior Walker plays 'Shotgun' on the radio.

Later, bright Honolulu city lights dominate the view from the bedroom bay window. Michelle's olivine green eyes twinkle in the candlelight as we 'toot' pure cocaine lines. Led Zeppelin's 'Whole Lotta Love' plays on the radio when I stretch out on the futon.

Michelle unzips my blue jeans and quickly coats my hard-on with cocaine crystals. "Baby wants to lick 'Daddy's snow cone'."

It seems like an eternity later, when I euphorically climax and drift into a dream...

...Father Joe Mullen S.J. stands over me as I lie naked in the full moon light. "The sins of the flesh will send your soul to Hell"...

I wake when Michelle gently kisses my neck and whispers in my ear. "Baby wants another snow cone."

I shake my head and pull two Quaaludes from a plastic baggie and swallow one. "Babe, you're insatiable. Take a 'lude' and get some sleep."

Michelle swallows the pill and gently strokes my chest. "Baby wants a snow cone."

I shake my head again. "Scooch, take a break from the coke."

In the background a radio D.J. announces. "Da Island weather today on Oahu. Plenty of sunshine with 'mauka' showers. Light three foot surf swells from the south and west. Now, let's listen to The Rolling Stones, 'You Can't Always Get What You Want'."

I fall back into a Quaalude induced dream...

...Screeching black ravens circle above as Jill drags a heavy suitcase into a blood red sunset. Auntie Claire holds a silver cross high and declares. "The Devil is everywhere. Resist temptation and seek the love of your savior, Jesus."...

———◆———

The next morning, a door slams and sunlight fills the room. I groan and shield my eyes. "Damn, my head hurts."

Jim Donnell stands in the bedroom doorway. "Jack, are you going to sleep another day?"

I'm startled. "How long have I been out?"

Jim laughs. "Way too long. Michelle got up earlier and I took her to see Aliya. I've got news from the brothers."

I stand and walk to the bathroom. "I need a Bloody Mary and a joint. What's the news?"

———◆———

The Florida hurricane season begins the first day of June. Mike Casey and Johnny Lionetti smoke Montecristo cigars with 'Jimmy the Jockey' in Johnny's Pompano Park harness race track office. The jockey lights his cigar. "Secretariat will win the Triple Crown and become the greatest thoroughbred in history."

'Don' Lionetti sips Glenfiddich single malt Scotch and gives Jimmy a frustrated look. "I'm tired of waiting for engine parts. I don't care what it costs. Get my boat ready to move the Bahamian gold shipment."

Johnny seems to have the world on his shoulders when he turns to Mike. "The Colombian wants his money."

Mike turns to his mentor. "What are my options? I'm paying ten thousand 'vig' a day."

Johnny shakes his head. "Get cash now, even if you discount your price. Ray will take care of Siegel and I'll cover your 'vig'."

———◆———

Later that same night, Uncle Pat smokes a Lucky Strike while blending his favorite tequila concoction at the New River compound on this moonless night. Suddenly, his dog growls and runs towards the front door. The old sailor turns out the lights and chambers a round in his Colt .45.

Uncle Pat drops on the floor and low crawls to the kitchen window. He peers into the dark courtyard to see two black Cadillac sedans enter the compound, followed by four gray Chevy Panel trucks. The six vehicles park next to Little Ray's house boat.

The old sailor recognizes the tall Colombian getting out of the first Cadillac, surrounded by four armed bodyguards. Eight muscular men in green uniforms step from the panel trucks as Little Ray appears and shakes Francisco's hand.

Little Ray unlocks his concrete storage bunker and the men dressed in green quickly transfer dozens of plastic wrapped bales into the panel trucks. The bunker is closed and locked as the Cadillac sedans follow the Panel trucks into the darkness.

Uncle Pat returns to the kitchen and turns on the light. He puts his weapon on the table and lights a cigarette while reactivating the blender. One hour later, the old sailor passes out on his bed oblivious to the world around him.

———◆———

A near full moon shines brightly over Ocho Rios this night in June. Anthony Ascot and Francisco Diego Valencia stand on the Jamaican north shore bauxite shipping pier. "Anthony, I'll control the cocaine trade like John D. Rockefeller controlled the world oil market. American 'free trade' allows me to ship my products everywhere. A small assembly factory will be added to your warehouse and my freighters will deliver cocaine filled aluminum 'ingots' to Europe from this pier. Have you recruited our 'Freedom Militia'?"

Tony scowls and shakes his head. "I've had some success in West Kingston, but Michael Manley's popularity with the poor has been a problem."

Nearby, Auntie Claire approaches Joy Brown sitting under a flowering mango tree in the Arawak Hotel courtyard. Auntie attempts to hand Joy a leather bound King James Bible. "Miss Brown, change your ways. My nephew has chosen a path of evil. Save yourself."

Joy violently shakes her head and quickly retreats into Tony's apartment.

———————◆———————

Back in Florida at the New River compound, Mike sits with Uncle Pat in the main house kitchen. The formica table is covered with empty beer cans and whiskey bottles. The old Navy sailor shakes his head.

"My bet on Secretariat winning the Triple Crown didn't pay much."

Mike swallows another Jack Daniel's shot, followed by a Budweiser chaser. "My luck isn't any good either. Jerry is still missing with a million dollars and J.R. isn't paying his bill. Scott and Shaun are behind on their collections and I can only hope Jack finds a buyer for the ten kilos in Hawaii."

Uncle Pat swallows a shot of 'Old No. 7'. "Mike, did you stash cash on the farm?"

Mike frowns. "Not enough. I'm counting on Johnny controlling Little Ray."

———————◆———————

The Jacksonville Beach 'Foxy Lady' strip club is busy tonight. Federal Narcotics Agents Dobbs and Thorsen are on assignment, trailing Corby Casey. Dobbs drinks a club soda and watches naked girls entertain sailors on shore leave.

Agent Thorsen stares at a beautiful blond pixie strutting to T-Rex's 'Get It On'. "Damn, she's gorgeous. I wish the government would let us expense cash tips."

The pretty dancer leaves the stage and sits next to the narcotics agent's tattooed quarry. Agent Thorsen shakes his head with extreme disappointment. "I can't believe she hangs out with a freak like Corby Casey."

<hr>

The next day, dark rain clouds conceal the June full moon over the New River houseboat. Little Ray pours Courvoisier V.S.O.P. into Jimmy the Jockey's glass.

Jimmy shakes his head in a confused alcohol stupor. He chugs his cognac and cries out. "Why did my little granddaughter have to die? Tell me why?"

Little Ray refills the jockey's glass and apathetically stares into Jimmy's bloodshot eyes. "It's time you stop being a sucker and make real money."

The diminutive jockey nods his head. "Yeah, I got peanuts, while Johnny made millions."

Little Ray snorts a huge cocaine line and grins. "Jimmy, you'll make a hundred grand if 'American Dreams' stays dry docked another two weeks."

<hr>

On the other side of the country, a cream white June full moon shines brightly over Diamond Head as the Super Lock van slowly drives up Round Top Drive. I finally got invited to meet the 'Brotherhood'.

Jim passes me a burning joint as we approach a wooden plantation house overlooking the city. "Jack, don't go 'East Coast' on these guys. Manny and the Flores brothers are professionals and Asian people have to save face, so be cool. Also, Christine Holt lives with Manny. She's Hawaiian surfer royalty and isn't in the smuggling business."

The van parks in front of the house. I close the van door and follow Jim onto the porch. Normally I wouldn't bring the suitcase to a deal, but my options were limited and the 'Brothers' want to see the whole package.

Jim rings the front door chime. A smiling Pacific Islander unlocks and opens the door. "How's it, Jim?" "How's it, Eddie?"

Super Lock turns around and hands me his business card. "Call my answering service when you need to be picked up. Good luck."

I'm apprehensive as the ponytailed locksmith walks towards the van. The smiling doorman identifies himself. "I'm Eddie. You like one San Miguel beer? 'Da Boss' be back soon."

I pick up the suitcase and follow my host into a windowless air conditioned room at the center of the house. A black leather sofa and chairs surround a round Koa wood table with a glass bong and ashtray on top. Sheets of thick plastic cover the floor. The ponytailed islander points to a chair and continues walking into the kitchen. "Bra, I get beers."

My host passes me a cold San Miguel and fires up the bong as I take a seat in a comfortable La-Z-Boy chair with my suitcase next to me. Eddie releases a cloud of sweet blue gray smoke when he hands me the bong.

I inhale a toke. "This weed tastes like Thai smoke"

A relaxed feeling comes over me as I finish my second beer. A side door opens and a Bruce Lee look-alike dressed in a red kimono appears. I stand to greet the newcomer and notice his eyes stare behind me.

A cold chill comes over me and my stomach tightens when I turn to see Eddie standing six feet away, pointing a Winchester twelve gauge shotgun at my face.

Eddie grins at me. "Bra, meet 'Da Boss'."

I turn back to the man dressed in a red kimono slyly smiling at me.

"Jack, my name is Manny. I can tell you're new to the smuggling game. Eddie could shoot you in this sound proof room and no one would know."

I take a deep breath trying to stay cool. Manny grins at me. "I have a better idea. Bring your suitcase and join me in the next room. We have business to discuss."

I'm led into an adjoining bedroom. A triple beam scale sits on a glass coffee table next to a king size bed. A huge 'Fist of Fury' movie poster of Bruce Lee in a fighting stance hangs on the wall above the bed.

Manny turns to me. "If the product in your suitcase is as good as the taste you gave Jim, my buyers will purchase what you have. Show me what you've got."

I'm still recovering from staring down a loaded shotgun, but I've got to keep cool and get down to business. I unlock the suitcase and reveal the contents. "I have ten kilos minus my stash. Check any package. I guarantee quality."

Manny pulls out a Buck knife, stabs a middle kilo and removes a piece of rock. He places a small taste on his tongue and rubs it against the roof of his mouth. His eyes sparkle and a broad smile comes to his face.

"Tastes good. I'm getting a rush already."

The 'Brotherhood' leader thoughtfully looks at me. "Jim said you want a half million for the suitcase. I'll take it, but you have to 'front' me for a month. Do we have a deal?"

I extend my hand with a tentative smile and think to myself… 'This suitcase could put me in prison for life and my only chance to get Mike's cash is with the 'Brotherhood'.'

A half hour later, I'm drinking beer and smoking bong hits with Manny and the Flores brothers when the Super Lock van horn sounds. Manny hands me a Ziploc baggie filled Thai weed and gives me a firm handshake.

"I'll get in touch when your money comes in."

I walk out the door and can't believe my eyes. Jill sits in the van passenger seat with her long blonde hair curled into a full 'Afro'.

Jim smiles at my reaction. "Look who called my answering service."

'Stairway to Heaven' plays on the van radio as Jill and I lovingly embrace. "Buddy, are you alright? How did you find me in Honolulu?"

Jill bursts into tears. "I didn't know you were here. J.R. stole my suitcase and dumped me at LAX. He told me to look up 'Super Lock' in the Honolulu 'Yellow Pages'."

Tears continue to run down Jill's face when we arrive at Manoa House. I lead her into the kitchen where Malia and Akiko are drinking tea. They immediately stand and comfort my buddy. "Come have a cup of 'Constant Comment' tea with us."

I leave Jill to Malia's and Akiko's kindness. I'm glad she isn't hurt, but I don't have Mike's money and I've traded a cocaine-filled suitcase for a bag of weed.

———————◆———————

Late the next afternoon, the sun sets over Manoa House while Gabby Pahinui plays slack-key guitar on the radio. I'm smoking

Thai weed and drinking Jack Daniel's whiskey under a Banyan tree in the garden. Michelle took my cocaine stash and left town when she heard Jill was in Hawaii.

My phone calls to Boston and Florida were depressing. Joey isn't talking and Mo needs more money for Rudy's lawyer. Mike is desperate and he gave me a Jacksonville pay phone number to call 'Miami Mike' once I get his cash.

I drift into a deep sleep, listening to Carlos Santana's 'Black Magic Woman'...

...Siddhartha and I sit in Manoa House garden watching Kamala dance in the moonlight as Hermann Hesse's words from 'Damian' resonate in the darkness. 'We stood before it, berated it, made love to it, prayed to it: We called it mother, called it whore and slut, called it our beloved, called it Abraxas'...

I wake to Jim nudging my shoulder. He hands me a folded piece of paper. "Jack, here's a note from Jill. Rona's husband beat her up and the police said they can't do anything, so Bob Lee arranged a safe house on the Big Island. Jill took Rona, Akiko and Malia to Hilo today. They plan to hide Rona at a Mauna Kea ashram."

B.B. King sings 'The Thrill is Gone' on the radio as I unfold the piece of paper and walk into the greenhouse. I swallow my last Quaalude with a gulp of Jack Daniel's whiskey and turn on a light to read the note.

'Jack,

You're very dear to me, but we're no longer together. I feel good about helping Rona escape her abusive husband. We'll be at Guru Zerkel's Ashram for the next month. After that, I'll probably go back to Vermont. You keep the money we left with Chuck. I'll do the same with the cash Susie and Jane have. You know J.R.

ripped me off and I'm sure you'll let Mike know what happened and I'll write to Debbie.

Stay well and good luck, your buddy Jill'

———◆———

The following night, I'm blurry eyed drunk in the greenhouse listening to 'Have You Ever Seen the Rain'. Unexpectedly, a smiling Eddie Flores enters the room followed by a petite blonde dressed in a pink t-shirt and red mini skirt.

I'm fixated on the blue eyed doll in high heels approaching me. Eddie hands me a San Miguel. "Da Boss wants me to make sure you OK."

I smile. "Thanks, I'm cool. Please introduce your friend."

Eddie replies. "Jack meet Jolene. She's my new girlfriend."

MILE HIGH CLUB

Johnny Lionetti and Mike Casey smoke Cuban cigars in Johnny's red Cadillac convertible as the sun sets above Ft. Lauderdale. "Kid, collect your money and get it to Ray this weekend. The Colombians expect to be paid next week."

Mike frowns. "My money is all over the country. It's impossible to collect everything by this weekend."

'Don' Lionetti pats his future son in law on the shoulder. "Go to the Ft. Lauderdale Executive Airport corporate jet hangar. My mortgage company rented a Learjet to help you make collections. You and your crew become a rock band on a promotional tour. Put the heavy artillary in instrument cases and bring extra luggage for the cash. Give the pilot twenty large with your itinerary. Get this done quickly, you and Debbie have a wedding in Captiva next week."

The sun is high in the sky over Honolulu when I wake up at Manoa House two weeks after my meeting with Manuel Guerrero and the Flores brothers. I passed out in the greenhouse again last night. Jill called from the Big Island yesterday. She's glad to be out of the smuggling business and living in Hawaii. Guru Zerkel is helping resolve her emotional conflicts through yoga and meditation. I'm happy for my buddy, but I'm up 'shit creek, without a paddle'.

My recent phone calls to Boston didn't have good news. Chuck Lievi said Rudy Losordo started 'shooting' heroin when he got out on bail and a 'Grand Jury' is investigating Joey Palermo for interstate narcotics trafficking.

Chuck agreed to drive Jill's and my stuff to Vermont in Donna Dodge. He'll settle any outstanding Hull House debts with the cash I left him and give the rest to Maureen Fitzpatrick for Rudy's lawyer.

Manny picked me up yesterday in a new metallic blue Datsun 240Z. He says my cocaine suitcase is in nightclubs from Honolulu to Bangkok and I'll get six figure money this week. I left a message for 'Miami Mike' to call the 7-11 payphone this afternoon at 3 p.m. Hawaiian time.

Dark clouds and rain showers fill the afternoon sky over the 7-11 store when I answer the pay telephone. Mike Casey's voice sounds distressed. "Jack, I can't talk. Get all the cash you can and catch the United Airlines 'red-eye' flight to Chicago. Go to the O'Hare executive jetport. I've rented a Learjet and I'll meet you tomorrow morning. Watch out for 'Feds' profiling couriers at the airport."

I'm speechless, thinking to myself... 'Mike is desperate and I've got nothing for him.' "Ok, I'll get what I can and see you in Chicago."

An hour later, I'm sitting on the black leather sofa in Brotherhood House waiting to see Manny. Jolene strides into the room wearing a transparent pink negligee and no panties. The hallway light reveals her hourglass figure. She smiles and struts past me into the kitchen. "Jack, I'm having a beer and a bong toke. You want a cold one?"

This girl excites me as I return her smile. "Sure, I'll have a beer. Where's Eddie?"

Jolene opens the refrigerator and grabs two San Miguel beers. "Manny sent him on a North Shore delivery. Let's fire up the bong."

I've got a good buzz after a beer and a couple of bong hits when Manny appears and signals Jolene to leave the room. I try to disguise my desperation with a smile. "My Florida partner needs cash and I'm flying the Chicago red-eye tonight. What can you get me in the next couple hours?"

Manny pours Jack Daniel's whiskey into two shot glasses and puts a small brown ball of 'opium gum' in the bong. We tap our glasses and drink the whiskey shots. Manny fires the pipe and passes it to me. "Jack, I have a very profitable business proposal for you if you join the 'Chamorro Brotherhood'. We're all for one, one for all. A brother's request is another brother's command. Once you join, you're in for life."

The Chamorro leader's chestnut eyes stare into mine. "Are you in?"

I nod my head, knowing I'm 'between a rock and a hard place'. "I'm in. Tell me what to do."

Manny's left hand instantly pulls a Buck knife from his belt. He draws the razor sharp blade across his right palm creating a thin streak of scarlet red blood. Next, he does the same to me.

His dark eyes continue to stare into my eyes when our bloody palms clasp together. "When you think you've met a fellow brother. Shake his hand and put your left hand over your heart. A true brother will do the same. Ask him, 'Is the moon full?'. He'll answer, 'The full moon always shines bright'."

Manny hands me a towel and opens a cabinet. He pulls out a .38 Smith & Wesson snub nose pistol in a brown leather shoulder holster. "This is my gift to you. Now wash up and let's discuss business in the kitchen. Rocky prepared a Chamorro delicacy for supper and you're our special guest."

We walk into the kitchen where Rocky Flores stands over a steaming five gallon pot on a gas stove. He smiles at me and slowly lifts the lid, exposing a furry head with nut brown eyes cooking in bubbling liquid.

Manny laughs at my surprised look. "Fruit bat with garlic and chili peppers in coconut milk. As our new brother, the first eye is yours."

My thumb digs a bat eyeball from its socket. I'm attempting to save face by swallowing the optic orb with a shot of Jack Daniel's, when Jolene enters the kitchen wearing blue jeans and leather boots. Her enticingly firm breasts protrude through a lime green t-shirt.

The Chamorro leader eats the second bat eyeball and turns to me. "Jo is wearing a plastic bustier/bra under her t-shirt that allows her to carry a kilo of product."

Jolene adds a taupe blouse over her t-shirt, followed by a suede jacket. Manny hands her a tan leather shoulder bag. "Now, she looks like a professional woman on a business trip and no one will suspect she's a smuggler."

Manny signals Jolene to leave the room and stares at me intensely. "Jack, I've collected three hundred seventy five thousand of the half million I owe you. My business proposal is simple. You have South American cocaine and I have Asian heroin. I'll trade one of mine for two of yours. This is a good deal for both of us."

He removes a cardboard box and two shopping bags from a closet. Rubber band wrapped cash bundles tumble onto the kitchen counter. "We've got some counting to do. You'll take your partner three hundred fifty thousand with a pound of my product to start our new venture. Jo agreed to carry the package for a thousand dollars. Bring me a cocaine suitcase from Miami like the last one and I'll have the rest of your cash when you return."

Manny reaches into a closet and removes a large black leather briefcase with a combination lock. "This is my money travel case. The lock code is seven eleven. Seal the cash in plastic and put it with the .38 at the bottom under your clothes. I've arranged for a brother to get you past the airport Agriculture Inspection and metal detectors."

Manny shakes my hand. "It's safer to fly first class. You and Jo better get going."

Minutes later, I walk into the living room. Jolene's pale blue eyes look up from a Cosmopolitan magazine she's reading. I smile. "Jo, are you ready to fly to Chicago?"

She grins. "I'll go anywhere with you, baby."

Two hours later, the United Airlines Boeing 747 flying nonstop to Chicago's O'Hare Airport has finished boarding. Derek and the Dominos play 'Bell Bottom Blues' in my ear phones as a first class lounge stewardess pours champagne into crystal glasses. I mailed Jill a letter letting her know Chuck is driving our stuff to Vermont in Donna Dodge. I hope my buddy finds happiness in her life.

Jolene cuddles me. "The only other time I've been on a plane was when my agent flew me to Honolulu to work at the 'Lollipop'. He promised me thousands of dollars, but the bastard stole everything."

My glass of champagne disappears in a gulp and I quickly signal the stewardess. "Two Smirnoff martinis with olives and a screwdriver for the lady."

Jolene reaches into her shoulder bag and hands me a pill with a kiss on my cheek. "No one ever called me a lady before. Here's one of my Demerol 'period meds'."

307

I swallow the pill with a gulp of vodka and listen to my travel companion. "Jack, I wish my mother could see me flying first class. Mom was sixteen when I was born and didn't know who my father was. I was two when she married my step-dad and we moved onto his Montana ranch."

Jo pulls me closer and whispers. "I grew up with four step brothers. Everything was cool until they gang raped me last Christmas. I showed my mother the bruises and she blamed me. I was lucky to get an abortion at the women's clinic and the lady doctor helped me move to Nevada."

She sips her drink. "I was topless dancing in Reno when my so-called manager talked me into going to Honolulu because the 'Lollipop' club's customers prefer blondes."

Jo squirms in her seat. "I have to adjust my brace in the girl's room."

I smirk. "I still have a gram of coke. Let's powder our noses and join the 'Mile High Club'."

We hurry to the toilet. I open the door with a wide smile. "After you, my lady."

Just as I attempt to enter the toilet cubicle, a stewardess intercepts me. Her hand grasps the door tightly. "Sir, you cannot go in there with your girlfriend."

I stare at the frowning stewardess while reluctantly returning to my seat and passing into a dark nightmare...

...I'm naked on my knees at the edge of a lake. A black robed Ninja approaches me. His Samurai sword glints in the moonlight as ravens cry warnings in the darkness...

Three hours later, Jolene and I enjoy fresh snapper entrees with a California Chardonnay, flying seven miles above the Pacific Ocean on this moonless night. The stewardess announces. "Tonight's movie is 'Friends of Eddie Coyle', starring Robert Mitchum and Peter Boyle."

I recognize the film title and chuckle out loud. "This movie was made near my college. I wish we could smoke a joint on this plane."

A cheerful Asian stewardess offers us dessert menus. "Would you like after dinner cocktails?"

I respond, "Can we have a couple of cognacs and a Cuban cigar?"

The stewardess feigns a smile, shrugs her shoulders and rolls her eyes as she retrieves the cocktails. Minutes later, Jolene dozes in my arms as I fall asleep listening to Savoy Brown playing 'Needle and Spoon' in my ear phones.

—————◆—————

I awaken to a stewardess's announcement. "The seat belt sign has been turned on. We land at Chicago O'Hare airport in thirty minutes. All passengers take your seats and prepare for landing."

The huge jet touches down in the 'Windy City' early Sunday morning the first day in July. I hurriedly retrieve my locked briefcase from the overhead storage. Jolene and I rush past strolling passengers into the terminal. "We've got to find the private jet airport."

My tropical Hawaiian attire draws stares from the fellow travelers hustling through bustling O'Hare Airport. A smiling baggage porter directs us to the executive airport shuttle. Minutes later, I see Mike and his cousins standing on the runway tarmac when we approach the terminal.

They look like a 'Band on the Run', wearing blue jeans and matching black leather jackets. Mike spots me and gives a thumbs up. "Jack's here."

The big Floridian shakes my hand. "How much did you bring me?"

I shrug my shoulders. "Three fifty large and a 'Golden Triangle' package."

Mike gives me a disappointed look. "I was hoping for more cash."

I shake my head. "If Little Ray wants his money, he'll have to track down J.R. in Nevada."

A cool Lake Michigan breeze chills the air as we follow Mike and his cousins to a nearby Learjet. A uniformed pilot smiles while helping Jolene mount the steps into the jet plane. "Buckle your seat belts and no smoking the wacky weed. I don't fly stoned."

Powerful General Electric engines push the Learjet 25C down the runway. Mike reaches into his backpack. "We can't smoke ganja, but we have coke and Quaaludes with a top shelf bar to get sky high on."

Mike turns to his cousin. "Scott, I hope the New Orleans bikers come through."

The big Floridian crushes a cocaine rock on Jolene's makeup mirror and looks at me. "Little Ray's men tracked Jerry to Reno."

Corby grins and opens his guitar case, revealing a Smith & Wesson M76 submachine gun. "I got this for Jerry Siegel and J.R."

Mike inhales a line of coke and passes the mirror to me. Jolene removes her bustier to 'Living Loving Maid'. She hands it to me when I pass her the cocaine covered mirror as Shaun pours vodka martinis for everyone.

Jolene frowns. "Jack, I hate wearing this brace."

Mike hands out Quaaludes and turns to me. "Little Ray is going to kill people, if he doesn't get paid soon. I need Johnny to get me more time to pick up the money."

The big Floridian looks at the plastic bustier and toots another line.

"What did you bring me from Asia?"

I hand him one of the eight plastic wrapped packs in the brace. "This is two ounces of pure heroin. I brought a pound and my contacts want to trade one for two of coke."

Mike nods his head. "Maybe we can do a deal in the future. Right now, I need cash."

The whine of General Electric CJ610 engines indicate the plane is decelerating into the New Orleans airport flight path. Jolene begins cleaning up the drug paraphernalia.

Mike puts the heroin in his backpack and gives his cousins marching orders.

"Scott, you and Shaun pick up the seven hundred large they owe me. Get back here ASAP. Corby, hang here in case there's trouble."

The Learjet comes to a stop at the airport terminal and the captain opens the cockpit door. "You can smoke cigarettes in the lobby. We're going for lunch."

Scott turns to Mike after the pilot and copilot walk into the terminal. "Let's give the bikers a taste of the 'junk'. I bet they'll pay top dollar for it."

Mike cuts open a package with his Buck knife. He fills a small plastic baggie with white powder and passes it to his younger cousin.

The two Casey cousins return to the terminal an hour and a half later. Scott's perplexed expression foreshadows disappointment when he enters the jet cabin. "I only got a quarter million. They said everything's on the street and we'll get the rest in a few days. The bikers really liked the 'H' and they want to buy everything you got."

Mike shrugs his shoulders. "I'll sell them a pound after they pay their bill. Scott, stay here and call Ma when you get my cash. I've got to fly to Florida."

The pilots return from the terminal. Scott exits the plane as the Captain enters the cockpit. "Is everyone on board?"

Mike answers. "Yeah, he's staying here and we're good to travel."

The flight tower gives the Learjet the go ahead to fly across the Gulf of Mexico into Florida. A somber mood grips the plane's occupants when the executive jet lifts off into the afternoon sky. Mike has a desperate look as he gulps Jose Cuervo tequila from the bottle. "Let's get hammered."

Jolene smiles and winks at me. She tugs on my arm and pulls me into the tiny toilet in the back of the plane. I close the door and the two of us somehow fit into the cramped space. We both drop our blue jeans. Jo pulls off her T-shirt and sits on the sink. She contorts her flexible torso and arches her back against the faucets with her legs held high. "Do me, Jack."

I'm kissing Jolene's firm pearl white breasts as we harmoniously orgasm together. Suddenly she screams. "My back's on fire!"

I pull her away from the hot water faucet and force open the lavatory door. We tumble from the toilet into the passenger cabin attached at the hip. The Casey cousins burst into laughter as we roll on the floor.

The laughter stops at the sight of Jolene's beet-red lower back. Mike reaches for the ice. "Man, that looks like a bad burn."

He hands me the ice bucket. "Cool her burns fast."

Jolene moans as I apply freezing ice to her skin. Mike hands me a cocaine filled baggie. "Coke will dull the pain. I use it for toothaches."

I sprinkle white crystals over Jo's red backside turning it into a powdered sugar donut. "The ice should prevent second degree burns."

Jolene inhales two long lines of cocaine, then swallows a Demerol with a double shot of Jack Daniel's whiskey. I pull on my blue jeans and cautiously help her dress. "Thanks Jack, I'm feeling better already."

The powerful Learjet engines begin to decelerate again when the Captain announces, "We're approaching Jacksonville. Prepare for landing."

Lightning filled storm clouds dominate the sky this Sunday afternoon. Turbulence shakes the executive jet as the pilot struggles to land on the wet tarmac. We exit into the rain and walk towards two black Ford 150 pickup trucks parked in the airport parking lot.

The local news plays on the radio as the trucks exit the airport... "White House Counsel John Dean's Senate testimony is expected to implicate John Mitchell and President Nixon in the Watergate cover up. In local news, a tropical depression could bring heavy rain and gale force wind gusts to South Florida tonight."

<hr />

Two Ford pickups arrive at a Jacksonville Beach housing complex a half hour later. Everyone follows Mike into a second floor apartment. I join the Caseys in the living room, while Jolene goes to the bathroom to check her burns.

Mike locks the front door and closes the curtains. "Jack, Corby knows Asian 'junk'."

The big Floridian pulls the open two ounce package of heroin from his backpack and hands it to his older cousin. "This is the same shit that put you in a Navy brig."

The former Navy medic's jaded face comes to life when he examines the crystalline powder and places a taste on his tongue. "Mike, this is good dope. You can step on it and have customers begging for more. Let's toot the 'King' and 'Queen' together."

Jolene returns from the bathroom. "My back feels better. Who's the king and queen?"

Corby chuckles. "King Heroin and Queen Cocaine. I'm the 'Doctor' and I'll prepare your 'Highway to Heaven' anyway you like."

Mike hands his older cousin the remaining heroin packages. "Beat this back to a pound and I'll sell it to Scott's bikers. Don't take too much for yourself."

I hear a key open the front door and to my surprise, Kim Terry enters followed by her sister, Karol. The twins are dressed in matching peach miniskirts and carrying bags of groceries. Karol gives Shaun a kiss, when he takes a bag from her.

Kim hugs Mike. "I'm glad you're home."

She smiles at me. "Jack, how've you been? Introduce your girlfriend."

Jo pulls me closer as I return Kim's beautiful smile. "Jolene, this is Kim."

I'm wondering about Mike and Kim's relationship when Corby returns to the living room with eight two ounce heroin packages. He hands them to Mike in return for a cash-filled lunch bag. "Corby, I'm flying to Lauderdale in an hour. Take this fifty thousand to Ma at the farm and don't go too crazy on the 'junk'. Let me know when Scott gets my money and Jack will fly the pound of 'H' to New Orleans."

Mike turns to his youngest cousin. "Shaun, drive your truck to Daytona Beach. Mo owes me two hundred fifty large. Collect what you can and get down to Lauderdale tonight."

<hr />

At the same time on Sunday afternoon in Lighthouse Point, Mary Lionetti watches Debbie try on a chosen pearl white silk wedding gown for her impending nuptials. Gowns and bridal catalogs are piled high throughout the room.

The young bride looks at herself in the mirror with satisfaction. "My pregnancy won't show in this dress."

Debbie turns to her mother with a sigh, after reading a recent letter.

"Jill and Jack split up. I hope she finds the right man some day like I did."

<hr />

Later at sunset, dark clouds fill the sky above the New River compound. Uncle Pat is disappointed when he sees Mike drive a rented Lincoln Town Car into the courtyard without Scott and Shaun. The old sailor takes a gulp of Jack Daniel's as his nephew enters the main house. "Debbie is with Mary in Lighthouse Point."

Mike dials the Lionetti home telephone number and is relieved to hear his fiancee answer. "Babe, I just got back in town. I need to speak with Johnny. Is he around?"

Debbie sighs. "He went to Miami Beach. He's meeting some important people today. Baby, I miss you. When are you coming home?"

Mike struggles to reconcile his passion for Kim Terry, while knowing it could destroy his relationship with Debbie and her stepfather. "I have to talk to Johnny ASAP. I'll be home after I count Little Ray's cash. Stay with Mary until I get there. I love you."

Debbie kisses the telephone. "I love you too."

The big Floridian puts the phone down and turns to me. "Put the cash in the kitchen. We have to count a million in tens and twenties. Did you bring the .357 I gave you?"

I shake my head. "No, I left it in Boston. I've got a loaded .38 in my briefcase."

Uncle Pat removes a Remington 1100 twelve gauge shotgun from the closet as the big Floridian hands me the elastic brace and heroin. "I'll need you and your girl to fly this to New Orleans. I'm going to talk with Johnny tomorrow. He's the only guy who can control Little Ray."

I dump the contents of my briefcase on the kitchen table and strap on my .38. I repack the case with the heroin bustier under my clothes as Mike picks up the plastic wrapped cash. "Take a taxi to the South Beach Clevelander Hotel and stay there until I call you. Put your pistol in your check in luggage when you fly to New Orleans."

I give my Army buddy a concerned look. "What's going on between you and Kim?"

316

Mike nods with a pensive smile. "We got hot and heavy after you last saw her. Debbie and I are getting married next week and I can't stop seeing Kim, so I moved the twins to Jacksonville Beach."

Suddenly, Moonshine barks. Instinctively, all of us reach for our guns as Uncle Pat looks out the window. "Mike, you won't believe what I'm seeing. Jerry Siegel is walking in here."

BLOODY SUNDAY

Michael Casey assesses his dire circumstances as dark storm clouds obscure a blood red sun setting over Ft. Lauderdale... 'Johnny Lionetti is meeting important people in Miami Beach tonight and I can't talk with him until tomorrow. Johnny has to stop Little Ray before he kills someone.'

Mike and Uncle Pat observe Jerry Siegel cautiously enter the New River compound and approach the main house front entrance. The old sailor opens the door as his nephew chambers a round in his Colt .45 and aims the handgun at his childhood friend's face. "Where's my money?"

Jerry instinctively raises his hands and quickly argues his defense. "J.R. took the cocaine and said he'd fly two million to you. I was in Reno trying to double my Christmas ganja money when Little Ray's killers show'd up. Luckily my girlfriend works at Harrah's Casino and she warned me."

Mike lowers his .45. "You wouldn't be here, if you stole the cash. Where's J.R.?"

Jerry shakes his head. "Last I heard, he's shacked up in Lake Tahoe with that Maui girl. Mike, you got to square this with Johnny. I've got nowhere else to go."

Earlier, Don Lionetti eats breakfast with Jimmy the Jockey in Lester's Diner this same Sunday. "Santo called a 'meet' with Johnny Roselli and Frank Ragano in Miami Beach. I want you and Ray to move my gold to the Bahamas today. No more excuses."

Jimmy nods his head as Johnny swallows a gulp of coffee. "I'm sending Mary and Debbie to Italy this week."

———⬥———

Later that morning at the New River boathouse, Little Ray Jackson cleans and loads his weapons while watching Jimmy the Jockey nervously pace the floor. Little Ray has Humphrey Bogart's fevered look in 'The Treasure of the Sierra Madre' as he locks a 9mm clip in a Uzi submachine gun. "Let's have a drink before we take off for Nassau."

Jimmy goes to the bar and puts ice in glasses. "I'm having a cognac. What about you?"

The disfigured gangster nods his head. "Double Jack Daniel's."

The jockey pours Courvoisier XO cognac and Jack Daniel's whiskey into the ice filled glasses, while Little Ray bends over a cocaine covered table mirror and inhales two huge lines of pure cocaine.

Little Ray has a demonic grin when he hands Jimmy the Jockey a rolled Ben Franklin. "Let's get going. We've got to move Johnny's gold before the storm gets here."

———⬥———

Meanwhile in Lighthouse Point, Johnny Lionetti hurriedly returns home in response to his wife's frantic phone calls. He charges into the kitchen to find Mary and Debbie in tears.

Mary tosses a cocaine filled plastic baggie onto the kitchen table and screams.

"Our daughter must stop taking this poison for our grandchild's sake."

Debbie howls. "I don't do a lot. Just enough to get through the day."

Mary shakes her head. "Think of your baby. Stop drinking and smoking."

Johnny shakes his head and removes a large manila envelope from his sport coat. "I have two first class tickets to Italy with twenty thousand cash in this envelope."

The Miami 'Don' gently takes hold of his stepdaughter. "Debbie, listen to your mother. We want your happiness. Go to Lake Como and stay at the villa I rented for your honeymoon. You can get married in Venice after Mike and I take care of business."

Debbie gives her stepfather a terrified look. "I won't go to Italy without my Mike. We planned to get married on Captiva."

Mary pulls her daughter close. "Listen to us. We only want what's best for you."

<hr />

Ominous storm clouds fill the sky above Ft Lauderdale. Lieutenant Brady and Sergeant Guerrette drink hot coffee and tea in a gray unmarked Ford Galaxie sedan parked near the New River as palm trees sway in gusting winds.

The sergeant lights a Marlboro Light cigarette. "Dan, nothing is happening in this weather. Let's go home before the storm gets worse."

Thirty miles south at the Miami Federal Building, U.S. Attorney Tom Stack has been called to an emergency meeting with State Department liaison Ms. O'Connell. It has been weeks since he saw Mary Ellen and he hopes to renew their relationship outside the workplace.

Ms. O'Connell smiles when the U.S. Attorney enters the room. "Tom, I just returned from D.C. and I have an update from Langley for your ears only. President Nixon plans to announce the formation of the Drug Enforcement Agency this month."

Mary Ellen pauses. "On a personal note, the job doesn't allow for what happened at the Mai Kai. I had a great time, but my work is my life."

Tom Stack's poker face attempts to hide his disappointment. "I understand."

<hr />

'Hey Jude' plays on the radio as a red sun sets over the Terry twins apartment. Karol Terry watches Corby Casey methodically prepare a syringe filled with the 'King' and 'Queen'. Karol is on a 'speed ball' run with Corby tonight.

Nearby, newly appointed D.E.A. Agents Dobbs and Thorsen monitor the 'Foxy Lady' strip club telephone lines from a windowless Ford cargo van on a side street behind the club.

Navy Corpsman Casey's short lived medical experience taught him how to tie off a bicep and force a syringe needle into a forearm vein. The former medic slowly draws crimson red blood into the syringe chamber and releases the tourniquet. He pushes the plunger forward and drives the potent cocaine heroin concoction into Karol's bloodstream.

She closes her eyes with a contented smile. "Baby, I'm coming."

<hr />

Back in Ft. Lauderdale, Mike Casey weighs plastic garbage bags filled with twenty dollar bills as the night sky fills with menacing storm clouds.

"Jack, the count is short. I'm desperate. Call Boston and see if Joey can help me out."

I dial Joey Palermo's home number and patiently let the telephone ring. Finally, a woman's voice answers. "Hello."

"Teresa, it's Jack. How's everything going?"

Teresa responds. "I can't believe you called. The coke you sold Joey put him in Bridgewater mental hospital and no one here wants to talk with you."

The phone line goes to dial tone.

Suddenly at the front entrance. "Bang!" "Bang!"

Uncle Pat opens the solid mahogany door to see the barrel of Little Ray's ivory handled .357 pointed at his face. "Where's my money?"

The old sailor's eyes widen as the powerful handgun is pressed against his nose. "Ray, we've been collecting your money all week."

Little Ray violently waves his pistol in the air when he notices Mike and Jerry in the kitchen as he walks into the living room and dumps pearl cocaine rocks on a Formica table.

The wild eyed gangster crushes the rocks into crystalline white powder with the butt of his revolver. He then fills his nose with cocaine and scowls while surveying the room. "You're all shark chum, if I don't get my money!"

Mike points to four large paper shopping bags and a cardboard box filled with cash. "There's a million five hundred here and I'm expecting another million in a couple days."

The mobster glares and points his pistol at Mike.

"Motherfucker, I want all my money."

Little Ray puts the shopping bags in the box. He takes the cash and struts past Uncle Pat through the front door into the storm. "Drunk, get the fuck out of my way!"

Uncle Pat slams the door and raises his middle finger. "Fuck that punk."

Adrenaline pumping, Mike commands his uncle. "Call to battlestations! Chief Petty Officer Casey, you and Jerry guard the main house."

The big Floridian turns to me. "Jack, get over to the Clevelander on South Beach and I'll call you tomorrow."

Ten minutes later, a taxi cab pulls into the New River compound. Jolene trembles in my arms as I tell the driver our destination. "The Miami Beach Clevelander Hotel."

We arrive at the hotel after a seemingly endless drive in pouring rain. I pull out my cash roll and hand the taxi driver a Ben Franklin. He gives me a stunned look. "Your fare is only twenty four dollars. Don't you have anything smaller?"

Jo gives the driver two twenty's from her purse. "Keep the change."

Powerful easterly winds blow in from the ocean as Creedence Clearwater Revival plays 'Bad Moon Rising' on the radio. I point at the turbulent seas. "The weather is getting worse. Let's order Joe's Stone Crab fried chicken dinners."

———◆———

Earlier on Sunday afternoon off the east coast of Florida, Little Ray is at the helm of 'American Dreams' as the Hatteras Sportfish powers towards the Bahamas through rising Gulf Stream swells.

Jimmy the Jockey removes Penn Rod & Reels from the stern as lightning filled storm clouds fill the western sky above Florida.

Unexpectedly, Little Ray's ivory handle pistol presses against the back of Jimmy's head.

"Bam!"

A .357 caliber bullet cuts through Jimmy the Jockey's spinal cord. Brain tissue and blood scatter in the wind as the jockey's body collapses off the boat stern into the rolling seas. Little Ray quickly wipes the bloody murder weapon with bleach and returns to the bridge.

Jimmy's body floats on the ocean surface in a pool of crimson red. Little Ray reverses the powerful diesel engines and sharp steel propellers chop the corpse into fish chum. "You dirty rat son of a bitch, you're shark bait."

A short time later, Little Ray runs full throttle towards the Hillsboro Lighthouse.

———————◆———————

At the same time at the Arawak Hotel in Jamaica, Anthony Ascot and Joy Brown smoke cocaine while drinking Clicquot champagne on their canopy bed. Tony assumes Francisco's plan to collect overdue debts in Florida will be successful tonight.

Tony fires the last freebase rock with his blue flame torch as a crimson red sun sets. He inhales cocaine vapors into his lungs, then slowly releases the sickly smoke into the air.

Joy desperately looks for more cocaine freebase. She frowns and shoves Tony's shoulder. "You smoked it all. Give me another hit."

Without hesitation, the back of Tony's hand crashes into Joy's face. Blood spurts from her nose as she howls in pain and runs for the bathroom.

Tony screams. "You want another hit?"

———◆———

Late Sunday night in Florida, 'Don' Lionetti drives through pouring rain on Federal Highway towards Lighthouse Point. Johnny wonders why no one showed up at the Fontainebleau meeting and Mary didn't answer his phone calls.

The car radio announces an urgent weather bulletin. "An early season tropical depression has come ashore in South Florida. Up to six inches of rain and fifty mile an hour wind gusts are expected for the next twelve hours."

Johnny steers his red convertible east on Sample Road and races across the Lake Placid bridge. His apprehension intensifies when he drives the Cadillac into the driveway courtyard. "Where are Ray's men? They're supposed to be on guard."

Heavy rain soaks his clothes when Johnny runs towards his home. An eerie silence heightens his suspicions as he cautiously approaches the front entrance and tries the house key in the door lock. "God damn it. The lock is jammed."

'Don' Lionetti reaches into his pocket and pulls the hammer back on his Smith & Wesson .38 'Special'. He runs to the back entrance and charges into the house. "Mary! Debbie!"

Johnny can't believe his eyes. A terrible pain grabs his heart as he falls to his knees. "I'll kill the bastards who did this!"

Heavy tropical rains inundate the New River compound as midnight approaches. Uncle Pat understands his duty and hopes black coffee will sober him up.

Suddenly, Moonshine barks at a vehicle entering the compound.

'Riders on the Storm' plays on the radio in the Ford pickup entering the New River compound. An exhilarated Shaun Casey smiles upon arriving at his final destination.

"I made it. Mike needs the hundred thousand behind my seat."

The youngest Casey cousin parks the black truck next to the main house and chambers a round in his 9mm Beretta. He runs through the rain and pounds on the locked front door. "Open up."

Moonshine barks when the deadbolt clicks and the heavy mahogany door opens. Uncle Pat greets his nephew with a big smile. "I'm glad you're here. Mike's in the guest house." Moonshine charges up, welcoming Shaun with a wet dog lick.

Shaun asks his uncle. "Why is the gate open?"

Uncle Pat looks confused. "Little Ray controls the gate."

"Bam!" "Bam!" "Bam!" "Bam!"

Bullets suddenly tear into Shaun and Moonshine. The black Labrador painfully howls and drops to the ground with blood gushing from her wounds. Shaun attempts to duck through the front door as AK-47 rounds rip into his head and neck.

Crimson red brain matter covers Uncle Pat's face. He screams into the storm as his nephew dies in his arms. "God Damn you, Little Ray!"

The old sailor struggles to lock the front door while firing his Colt .45 at shadows moving in the courtyard. The acrid smell of gunpowder fills the night air as steel jacketed bullets tear into the house walls.

Jerry draws his Browning .40, but drops the loaded handgun when he stumbles. "Bam!"

A bullet rips into his left leg and he falls to the floor screaming in pain. "I'm hit!"

Uncle Pat retreats into the kitchen and turns over a heavy oak table. He leans it against the window and fires his last .45 caliber rounds. Blood flows from Jerry's leg wound as he hyperventilates and screams. "God help me."

The old sailor picks up the Remington twelve gauge shotgun and fires into the darkness. Bullets coming from all directions pin him down in the cinder block building.

Mike Casey grabs his Colt .45 when he hears rifle shots and runs to the guest house side door. He sees gun flashes exploding throughout the New River compound and quickly drops into the mud. He slowly crawls towards the main house.

"WHAM!!!"

The main house propane gas tank explodes in a massive red-orange fireball.

Seconds later, the guest house tank erupts into another fiery blaze.

"WHAM!!!"

Flaming red orange mushroom clouds engulf both buildings as the big Floridian opens a Ford pickup door. Mike pulls himself onto the front seat while frantically searching for keys under the floor mat. His cold wet hands fumble the keys as he hurriedly starts the engine and races towards the compound exit with his 'Foot to the floor'.

Suddenly, a gunman steps out of the night shadows and fires a Kalashnikov rifle at the escaping pickup truck.

"Bam!" "Bam!"

———◆———

At the same time in Lighthouse Point, Tears stream down Johnny Lionetti's tormented face as he kneels in his family's blood while Ralph Renick concludes the WTVJ late night newscast on the living room television.

"John Dean testified during last week's Senate Watergate hearings that he was fired after he told President Nixon of a 'cancer in the White House'. Meteorologist Bob Weaver's stormy weather forecast is coming up next."

The stunned Lionetti patriarch glares at Mary's and Debbie's severed heads resting on the kitchen table in a pool of crimson red plasma. Their lifeless terror filled eyes stare blankly into space as a dark shadow fills the room.

Without warning, the razor sharp edge of a Samurai sword decapitates the Mafia leader's head from his body with one bloody stroke.

———◆———

Storm clouds fill the sky above the Miami Beach Clevelander Hotel the following morning. I'm rubbing aloe salve on Jolene's back while drinking a breakfast Bloody Mary and thinking to myself... 'I'm glad Jo's burns are healing nicely. I hope Mike calls soon, so we can fly back to Hawaii.'

Jolene turns on 'The Jack Lalanne Show' as I walk into the shower. I'm wondering if Mike spoke to Johnny about Little Ray, when a news bulletin interrupts the television program.

"The Broward Sheriff's Office reported a New River boat compound burned to the ground early Monday morning. Four people are confirmed dead and two were hospitalized with severe burns. A similar fire destroyed the Lighthouse Point home of mobster John Lionetti. Both incidents are believed to be gang related. A black Ford pickup, with Georgia license plates was seen leaving the New River fire and driving north on I-95. Please call the Broward Sheriff's Office at 305-443-5800, with information. All calls are confidential."

'Stomach acid rises in my throat when Jolene begins to cry. I'm feeling sick and dizzy while wondering if Mike Casey was driving the black pick-up. Damn, I have to hide the heroin and gun!'

I dry myself and pull on my jeans. I notice an air conditioner vent when I exit the bathroom and think to myself... 'Maybe the dope and pistol can be hidden in there.' "Jo, get dressed. We're outta here."

The vent cover is easily removed with a dime coin from my pocket. Luckily, the dope filled bustier and holstered .38 pistol fit inside.

Fifteen minutes later, Jolene wipes tears from her eyes as we rush out of the Clevelander Hotel into a waiting taxi. I hand the driver a Ben Franklin. "Get us to Miami Airport fast."

At the airport terminal, we jump from the taxi and run to the United Airlines ticket counter. "Two one-way economy tickets to L.A. and Honolulu."

The ticket agent smiles. "The flight to Los Angeles is leaving in thirty minutes. If you don't have luggage, you can connect to Honolulu today."

I quickly hand over the cash. He gives me two tickets. "The flight is boarding, go directly to gate seven now."

Jolene and I run hand in hand towards the gate. She charges through the metal detector without a sound and I hurriedly follow her.

Suddenly, a badge is thrust against my face. I'm stopped in my tracks by a huge man wearing a black suit and dark sunglasses.

He starts to frisk me. "Federal Narcotics Agents. We're checking for illegal narcotics."

I'm temporarily stunned and hastily give up my contraband. "I only have two joints."

The narcotics agent growls. "Don't be a smart ass punk. I'll flush that shit down the toilet. We want the dope in your carry-on baggage."

The older, bald agent takes Jolene's shoulder bag while I unlock my black case and hand it to the oversized agent blocking me. The bald agent pulls a vial of pills from Jolene's bag. "What are these?"

Jolene coolly answers. "My doctor prescribed Demerol for my period."

The agents are distracted by my lover's taut breasts protruding from her tight t-shirt while they search our meager belongings. I ask the older agent. "Sir, we only have two joints and we need to catch this flight to make our connection in Los Angeles."

The senior Federal agent shakes his head in frustration. "OK, you can go this time, but we're watching your kind these days."

The airport public address system announces. "Final boarding flight 711 to Los Angeles. All passengers should be on board. Gate seven is closing in five minutes."

Jolene and I grab our carry-on bags and run for the plane. A United Airlines agent is locking the door when we arrive at the gate and I yell. "Wait! We've got tickets to L.A."

The agent smiles and reopens the gate. I hand her the tickets and follow Jo running down the ramp. We rush onto the plane and buckle up in our seats as the stewardess closes the plane door.

I plug my earphones in to hear The Beatles playing 'The Long and Winding Road'. Jolene sighs with relief when I say, "Honolulu here we come."

<hr>

Previously on Sunday night at the Arawak Hotel in Jamaica:

Anthony Ascot continues smoking cocaine in the darkness while Joy Brown wipes blood from her nose as she escapes from his apartment. In her panic, the entry door is left unlocked.

Minutes later, Auntie Claire opens the door to see her nephew re-lighting his glass pipe. She enters the room with her Bible in hand. "Anthony, I must exorcize the Devil from my family."

At the sight of his aunt, Tony releases a cloud of blue gray smoke. He drops his cocaine pipe and quickly runs through the open door. Suddenly without warning, a sharp steel blade cuts into his chest. Crimson blood flows from his left lung.

Tony sees his teenage lover holding a bloodstained knife and painfully screams. "Woman, you stabbed me!"

The same dark night in Lighthouse Point, Florida:

Francisco Diego Valencia wipes his 'Muramasa Katana' Samurai sword clean and sheds his blood spattered Ninja suit as he steps over 'Don Lionetti's severed head on the kitchen floor.

The Colombian walks out of the house and boards 'American Dreams'. Seconds later a massive fiery explosion engulfs the Lionetti home as Little Ray steers the seventy foot Hatteras Sportfish into the boat canal.

'Sympathy for the Devil' plays on the ship stereo...

"...If you meet me, have some courtesy, have some sympathy and some taste, use all your well-learned politeness or I'll lay your soul to waste..."

EPILOGUE

On July 1, 1973, the White House formally announced President Nixon's authorization of the Drug Enforcement Administration. "This federal law enforcement agency will be the 'tip of the spear' in America's 'War on Drugs'."

That same day in Boston's 'South End'...

A white male, with long blond curls is found dead in an alley. The police suspect a heroin overdose. The only clue to the individual's identity is a tattoo ('Rudy', with a pair of drumsticks) on the right bicep of the deceased.

———◆◆◆———

'I'm a world of power and all know it's true...
Use me once and you'll know it too...
I can make a mere schoolboy forget his books...
I can make a world class beauty neglect her looks...
I can make a good man forsake his wife...
Send a greedy man to prison for the rest of his life...
I can make a man forsake his country and flag...
Make a girl sell her body for a five dollar bag...
Some think my adventures are a joy and a thrill...
But, I'll put a gun in your hand and make you kill...'
'King Heroin', James Brown

Printed in the United States
by Baker & Taylor Publisher Services